THE
QUEEN'S SPADE

THE
QUEEN'S
SPADE

SARAH RAUGHLEY

HARPER
An Imprint of HarperCollinsPublishers

Library of Congress Control Number: 2024946950
ISBN 978-0-06-334438-9
Designed by Corina Lupp
24 25 26 27 28 LBC 5 4 3 2 1
First Edition

To the children who don't fit.

And don't want to.

PART ONE

LADYLIKE IN THE EXTREME

For her age, supposed to be eight years, she is a perfect genius; she now speaks English well, and has a great talent for music. She has won the affections, with but few exceptions, of all those who have known her, by her docile and amiable conduct, which nothing can exceed. She is far in advance of any white child of her age, in aptness of learning, and strength of mind and affection; and with her, being an excellent specimen of the negro race, might be tested the capability of the intellect of the Black . . .

—*Captain Frederick Edwyn Forbes, 1850*

ONE

Rochester, England – June 27, 1862

A YOUNG LADY can take only so many injuries before humiliation and insult forge a vow of revenge.

The story I'm about to tell you may make you uncomfortable. Greater still the shock may be for those of you bound by quaint rules of morality. I won't judge you. In fact, I give you permission to hate me.

I'm no heroine. I feel no inner struggle over any supposed codes of ethics, nor have I lost sleep over the "wrongness" of my decisions.

You'll understand why soon.

Or maybe you won't.

You've been warned.

Revenge takes time, you see. And I have been patient. Today, on June 27, 1862, in Rochester, England, Mr. Bellamy, the former editor of the *Illustrated London News*, danced like the famous drunkard he was in his foyer while his wife was with family in Yorkshire. Tripping over the expensive Turkish rug, he took another swig of whiskey through his thin lips and held out one chubby white hand for me to take. I did, with a smile, and we danced together. I suspected it was what he'd been waiting for all these years. For me to finally cast off the costume of civil British society and become the wild "animal" he thought I truly was.

"Dance, Sally, dance, my dear!" The slobbering Mr. Bellamy demanded it of me even as the scowling portrait of his wife glared down on us from the floral-patterned wallpaper.

His breath was as foul as rotted eggs. Just as I expected, the balding man was still prone to the wiles of "exotic" young girls. "Dance now, Sally!"

I obliged. My legs were trained in many genres. They could perform a waltz to perfection. Ten years ago, when I was presented to him in that wretched woman's cold drawing room, he couldn't stop looking at those legs with his lecherous eyes. If only he'd realized then why they were shaking. If only he'd realized that they were the quivering limbs of a frightened child newly stolen from Africa.

"Queen Victoria's goddaughter," Bellamy said as he intertwined his fingers with mine. "The enslaved African princess given sanctuary by the Queen. How I've wanted you for so long . . ."

My stomach churned as I thought of his sickening looks and not-so-subtle advances, never returned for a decade until now.

"Why, Mr. Bellamy!" In the editor's foyer, I jumped a little and bit back my anger when the stupid drunkard's free hand reached lower than the crease of my back. His pants tightened as he stared at the teasing glimpse of my breasts tightly bound in a laced off-white corset. Now that I was freshly eighteen, there was no reason for him to hide his carnal desires.

Yanking his hands off me, I grabbed the whiskey and poured it down his throat, making sure he downed this bottle, the third he'd managed in my presence due to my insistence. "Tell me again what it was like to climb the Duke of York's tower with the famous Antoine Claudet."

My voice was pleasing to the ear, melodic like music. I'd learned how to make it this way. It was how I survived. I rubbed the bald spot on his head because I knew British men like him loved to be flattered like children.

"Or better yet," I added with a wink, "perhaps you can tell me in your bedchambers?"

There was a term used among the British men who expressed their deepest fears and most hypocritical, insatiable desires concerning girls like me, the reason why so many of their wives feared when their husbands would travel overseas to lands unknown: "going native." It was as if there was something all too alluring about the possibility of breaking every fetter of Victorian codes of conduct and plunging deep into the dark bosom of devilry. For Bellamy, I had been too carefully watched by Queen Victoria and her royal lot for him to make a move. But now his wife was away. I was here. A secret meeting. No one would ever know. The history books would certainly never tell the tale.

Mr. Bellamy's unfocused eyes rolled to the back of his head and his laughter echoed across the flower-patterned wallpaper as he let me take his hand and lead him up the winding staircase. He was already hastily unfastening the buttons on his breeches with the other.

I stifled an irritated sigh. Not everyone on my list would be this easy, but I'd studied them well.

Everyone had a weak point.

Once Mr. Bellamy reached the top of the stairs, I made sure the sweep of my foot was quick and quiet.

And then he tumbled down the stairs.

With his scream stuck in his throat, his soft flesh silently collided with the wood with dull thumps, except when his elbows knocked against the walls. I looked away. Bellamy died when his neck twisted with a crunch on the floor.

As saliva trickled from his open mouth, I stayed my trembling hand against my heaving chest. The memories of his advances throughout the years calmed my breaths. I shut my eyes and forced myself to think of them: the way he'd grab my flesh after licking his fingers. The sickening words he'd whisper in my ear at social events when he thought no one was watching. He wanted to defile my body and so now his lay crumpled upon the wretched ground.

The police would rule this a foolish accident. A former editor fired from his newspaper for his boozing ways. Wife away. Empty bottles of alcohol strewn about. The story wrote itself.

Mr. Bellamy's head bled across the smooth wooden floor.

Don't dare judge me. I was a princess before I was a slave. Rulers have done worse for lesser injustices. And to a royal, insult is the greatest injustice of all.

Make no mistake about my intentions. Bellamy's death at my hands wasn't the end but the means to it. Indeed, death wouldn't be nearly satisfying enough of a goal. Sometimes I wondered if the British even feared it. Those "civilized" people seemed to have an oddly ghoulish fascination with *la mort* if their rituals and superstitions were anything to go by. Mrs. Bellamy would soon be covering her mirrors to make sure her husband's spirit wouldn't become trapped inside them, lusting after younger women for all eternity.

No, Bellamy's death was not the goal. There was one fate the British elite feared more than they ever could the afterlife.

From behind a tree just outside the compound, I watched a carriage slow to a stop outside Bellamy's open gate.

Right on time. Punctuality was such an admirable trait.

A young man stepped out of the carriage first. "Mr. Reynolds, the gate's open, just like the letter told us it'd be." It swung wide with a creak at his touch. "Blimey. The door's probably unlocked too."

Another man followed him out of the carriage. It was George Reynolds, editor of the *Reynolds Weekly Newspaper*, who held the anonymous letter I'd sent him, taking it out of the breast pocket of his tan overcoat. After checking the contents again, he waved his assistant over, and together they entered the house. And I knew once they found Bellamy dead on the ground, surrounded by bottles of booze with his pants down, they'd leave with the story of the year.

The Illustrated London News had many rivals. What better than a salacious story with accompanying pictures, not-so-tastefully drawn, to raise the sales of a competing paper lagging in profit? And if the printed story would bloody the nose of their advisory, all the better. Two birds. One stone. George Reynolds knew this as well as I knew of his lack of scruples.

A destroyed reputation. A rotted legacy. Humiliation and ruin. This is what the elite feared more than death. And this was precisely the fate I aimed to unleash upon them.

Useful, how everyone seemed comfortable underestimating me.

On the carriage ride back to my home on the outskirts of London, I stared at the card between my two fingers: the Queen of Spades. I'd considered leaving it at the crime scene. But I'd only begun. I didn't want to be caught just yet.

I'd once read somewhere that a wrong is unredressed when the avenger fails to make herself felt as such to him who has done the wrong.

I wouldn't make that mistake.

TWO

I MET MY enemies on a chilly autumn night. November 8, 1850. I would
never forget it.

"What a pretty little thing." The noblewoman refreshed herself in the
humid air with an antique French hand fan. Even to my young eyes, she
was clearly showing it off.

This was her drawing room and she seemed proud of its decorations—
carefully curated French décor from the Napoleonic era. She was the only
woman of the group, and clearly obsessed with her own wealth. Traveling
across shores to an unfamiliar country stretches one's sense of self into a
million distinct pieces, all of which mock you with their grotesqueness.
Yet nothing was more grotesque than this room: the ugly mismatched
colors of the walls, the gaudy chandelier hanging too low from above our
heads. Two couches the color of blood and a rickety wooden sitting chair
enclosed the confined space, each piece of furniture blocking the open-
door exits, and thus my escape.

I knew then it was too late for that anyway.

It was my first night in England. At seven years old, I stood alone
among strangers, barefoot on a scratchy carpet painted in frightening
patterns. I was supposed to be asleep in preparation for my first meeting

with Queen Victoria. But too many had wanted to see me before I was officially presented to the royals.

I counted six frightening creatures in those couches and chairs, their hollow eyes gobbling me up with at an excruciatingly slow pace, as if these predators didn't have the decency to finish me off in one go. They looked like monsters to me. These must be the *eseku* my late mother warned me about when she told me tales at night. Of course, they had to be—they were too hairy and too ready to abduct me. They had to be evil spirits. That's what my mind decided.

Their figures loomed close, watching, observing, dissecting every inch of me with grins as hot and seething as coals. I could see my impending death and a part of me welcomed it.

"You don't see any of those jarring features you often find in females of the African race," came the raspy voice of the man seated in the chair directly across from me. "You know, the ones that make them look so *ferocious*." The vile words had come from Captain Frederick Forbes of the British Royal Navy. My captor and self-proclaimed savior. Lieutenant and commander of the HMS *Bonetta*.

He was in awe of me. So too was his brother and accomplice, Captain George Forbes. Like Frederick, George was a noble descendant of the Pitsligo and Culquhonny branch of the House of Forbes. He'd helped retrieve me from the Dahomey Kingdom.

On the other end of the circle, the woman tilted her head and tapped her stupid French fan against her hawklike nose.

"Oh yes, I know," she said. A lie. As blatant as all her other lies would be. She hadn't noticed. She was too preoccupied with studying me. "My husband's father once saw the Hottentot Venus in Piccadilly," she said, and I couldn't understand then why some of the adults rolled their eyes at the mention of her husband. They knew then what I knew now:

this woman's obsession with the Phipps family pedigree was as embarrassing as the funnel shape of the brown hair atop her head. "The Colonel Phipps found that African thing such a horrendous sight. But this girl is almost . . . *ladylike*."

She said the word *ladylike* as if it were a wholly foreign concept for one who looked such as me, with my low brow, flat brown nose, and large red lips. I should have been enraged, but though I could understand English, her words came out a jumbled mess to my ears. Hottentot? Piccadilly? Were these foods? Creatures of some sort?

But the words, strange as they were, carried an unmistakable venom in them that crossed the boundaries of language. My little body shook. I knew I would die that day. I could feel it.

Ladylike. To say I now understand the word would be an understatement. Its meaning, its idiosyncrasies and patterns, have been engraved without my approval into my very flesh, my very bones. The word is a weapon, a sword meant to cut flesh. And ever since I understood that, I began to wonder: Was that what had made me so different from Ade? Did it come down to simple features, the reason why they let me alone live?

In the drawing room, on one of the blood couches, the lone Scotsman of the bunch glanced at me with his sunken eyes, a scarecrow in a kilt. And at the end of their circle, the photographer in their midst laughed. "Thank goodness her buttocks isn't nearly as large. I won't have to feel so disgusted capturing her likeness."

There was a hum of agreement among the group. My gaze shifted across each of them. And in my terror, the piercing image of them, of that moment, was etched into my memory: the hawklike woman, sneering beside the photographer. The Scotsman and George, both scheming and churlish. Captain Fredrick Forbes. And next to him, equally as taken, was Mr. Bellamy.

Six fiends in all.

They spoke of my cranium. The vagabond races, you see, according to these ilk, were less intelligent, and this was biologically evident by the size and shapes of their heads. Not the gentle oval patterns of the settler, no, but the protruding face bones of the vagabond. They needed to be sure. The photographer had brought into the room a tool that could measure the size and width of an animal's skull, and the brothers used it to measure mine. The sharp, curved tongs pinched my skin, drawing blood from my temples and tears from my eyes. What were they doing? Why wouldn't they stop? They didn't even notice my whimpers. They *had* to be demons.

Of course, demons come in all forms. Everyone had their obsession. The obsession Mr. Bellamy had frightened me. Even as a child, I sensed it, tightening my whole body whenever our eyes would meet. Once the brothers were done confirming that I did, in fact, have the kind of oval-shaped head characteristic of civilized men, Mr. Bellamy fidgeted in his seat near the Scot. Something illicit slithered behind his gaze like minnows. I could see it in those hungry eyes.

"Her buttocks are quite shapely . . . ," he whispered, though he quieted himself quickly.

"I'm not surprised she seems exceptional from the rest of her tribe. The girl is a genius," Frederick Forbes added, perched on his couch. "I didn't know what to expect of her intellect after I saved her from that barbarian King Ghezo. But she learned English in a year and is already on her way to mastering French."

He said this with pride, as if he hadn't slapped me every time I recited the words incorrectly. I could still feel the hot sting on my right cheek.

"Never did I expect your diplomatic voyage to the Dahomey Kingdom would yield such an unexpected result." The Scotsman's unkempt red beard made him look like a man born of the woods despite his proud and pompous attire, courtesy of his gains as a merchant. "Saving a slave girl from human sacrifice and convincing Ghezo to give her as a gift to the Crown—how did you put it?" He tapped his wrinkled forehead. "'From the King of the Blacks to the Queen of the Whites.'"

"Perhaps we simply couldn't resist those docile eyes." George Forbes swirled a glass of brandy in one hand. And when his eyes met mine, I shivered. "McCoskry, you should understand better than anyone the allure of saving such children from the evils of slavery."

McCoskry, the Scotsman as I now knew him as, remained silent. I didn't realize it then, but the man would soon be on his way to my continent. There, he would become the Acting Consul of Lagos—a rather forgiving way of framing his rule over the Yoruba people.

"You did well in bringing this child to England." The hawklike woman nodded to Captain Frederick Forbes, who beamed with pride. "Queen Victoria will certainly accept her tomorrow."

And then, with a cavalier grin, Bellamy asked me to dance for them. "Yes, little Sally. Dance for us! The dance you Africans do!"

My heart refused. *I am a princess*, I wanted to tell them, but my blood pumped with fear. The eseku were wily creatures. I could grab a knife and try to stab one. It was what my instincts told me to do. Defend myself and escape. But cutting the eseku would only make them multiply. Could there be more of these beasts?

"Dance for us!" The Scotsman began clapping. The woman joined in, though the crack of her palm was muted by her fan.

I was sure they would kill me if I didn't. But I wouldn't let myself. Not at first.

I am a princess! I wanted to *scream* at them as my little languid body eventually succumbed and began to obey their command, twitching with sheepish movements.

"Have her take off her clothes too," the woman said with a flippant wave of her finger, crossing her legs shrewdly. "I'd like to see how different she is from the Hottentot. I will not have you send an unshapely girl to Her Majesty."

My name is Omoba Ina, princess of the Yoruba tribe's Egbado Clan! How dare you demand this of me, this insult? Biting back my tears, I stripped off my clothes with shaky hands and danced indeed, for this was to be my new life in England.

Like the Hottentot Venus, I was in a cage surrounded by them.

I learned very quickly. They were not eseku. They were British—demons, perhaps, of a different sort. This land, England, was a liminal space between heaven and hell where all sorts of monsters roamed. The Queen of this monstrous empire at least should have had the humility to acknowledge her *own* monstrosity. But that was the great irony, wasn't it? The truly monstrous never recognized themselves as such.

The next morning, on a cold day, I was presented to the Queen. Inside the stateroom of Windsor Castle, a frigid, haughty chill pricked my skin and knocked my bones as if to tell me to stand up straight. It was the grand meeting of two queens, leaders of mighty nations . . . but I quickly realized only one of us thought of it that way. Queen Victoria saw it quite differently. There, in the vast marble hall decorated in velvet and gold, in front of a crowd of waiting staff, servants, secretaries, and other persons of interest, she looked down piteously at me. It made me quake with anger, but I kept still. I knew the price of showing my true emotions.

"What a curious gift the Captain has given you from the jungles of the dark continent," said Mrs. Phipps, that frumpy, dreary-haired brunette with her French antique fan flitting away, and she was not alone in the illustrious marble halls. Bambridge, the ghastly photographer, was with her. And so too was Bellamy, McCoskry, and both Forbes—Frederick and George.

"A curious gift," George Forbes said, "but an amiable, suitable one."

And I can dance too, I thought bitterly.

Curious. Yes, I was a "curiosity." Those six villains made sure I knew it too as they debased me the night before. The memory of writhing naked in front of them would not be so easily erased.

But no moment was more debasing than this.

Queen Victoria rubbed her filthy hand across my shaved head, just beginning to prickle with woolen black hair, and laughed as my stomach churned. She delighted in her gift.

"Tell me, what is this child's name?" she asked Captain Forbes.

I opened my mouth to speak for myself. But the words *Omoba Ina* never had the chance to slip through my lips.

Forbes answered for me. "Sarah Forbes Bonetta," he told her proudly, the name he'd dreamed up to foist upon me without my consent. Three words that sounded like whimsical rubbish, but Queen Victoria sparkled at the sound of it.

"Amiable and moldable," the Queen said, approaching me slowly, like a leopard stalking its prey. She soaked in the sight of my modest white dress and perfectly learned courtesy. "So very clearly *moldable*."

The gears were turning in her head; I could see it then. Despite the softness of her small features, Queen Victoria had always held her back pin straight: a young mother not only of her children but of an empire with an appetite insatiable enough to devour the world. I could see that appetite in the sinister flicker of her lips, the glint of those piercing blue eyes.

I knew it then. She was the seventh villain. The most dangerous of them all, for she had the most power.

Without wasting a minute, she turned to one of her ceremonial officers. "Send word to all the newspapers: Britain's African Princess. And my new goddaughter." She lifted her pale hands as if she could see the headlines materialize in the air before her very eyes. "Britannia under Queen Victoria has indeed become the most developed country in the world. We are mankind's very moral fabric with the Crown standing upright as the head. We have shown countless pieces of proof of this over the years." She bent down until we were at eye level. "But perhaps none sweeter than this poor little Negro child. She is *exemplary* amongst them."

Our eyes were locked. I remembered then the steely determination of my parents. Their gazes that didn't waver even as they were cut down by the Dahomey. I felt that same fire in me as I aimed my glare to set fire to this rival queen.

"Don't worry, Your Majesty," said Captain Frederick Forbes with a quick nod, giving me a too-hard slap on the back. "I've already ensured Mr. Bellamy will keep up a steady stream of stories. The other editors will follow suit in no time at all."

"Very good." And shamelessly, *infuriatingly*, she rubbed my chin with her finger as if I were a dog. "Even a slave can be transformed into a lady through Britain's compassion."

A child tabula rasa. England's great civilizing project. I'd been reduced to propaganda. My body went stiff from the cruelty of it all. I could tell that she wanted to "save me." How else to prove Britain's superiority? The name they gave me was proof of it. Abram and his wife had been given new names too after being saved by divinity.

I suspected the Queen thought herself a god too. With a stretch of her hand, she'd saved a little African princess from death. The Queen of the Whites, others called her, and she relished it. The Savior of Barbarians around the Globe.

No one had wanted to save Ade. Not when the seas dragged his wretched body down to the depths of the Atlantic. No one cared, because he wasn't *exemplary* in their eyes.

Ade was Yoruba, like me, and of the same Egbado Clan. But unlike me: sickly. Slow of intellect—or so they accused him. He just didn't pick up English as quickly as I did. And he was malnourished. No matter what they gave him, his body remained deteriorated. He wasn't a "handsome Negro." He was not "sweet" or "good-natured" like I was seen to be. He didn't smile when told to; in fact, he was rather partial to a nasty scowl whenever strangers spoke to him. He wasn't suitable at all as a present for the Queen. Deadweight. Nobody would miss him.

That's what the Forbes brothers decided before they tossed him overboard. Ade. Another freed slave of the Dahomey Kingdom. My confidant. My only friend.

None of that mattered to *them*.

After witnessing Ade's murder, I'd curled up in the dusty sack they'd given me to sleep on the ship floorboards and held my breath for as long as I could before passing out, thinking of his last words to me.

Their "love" for you is conditional, Ina.

And when I thought of that very dark truth, as Queen Victoria stretched out her hand to welcome me into her royal family, I suddenly wanted to *destroy* her.

Their "love" for you is conditional, Ina. Never forget that.

Ade's ghost would never let me forget it.

THREE

Chatham, England – June 30, 1862

MAMA TUGGED AT my bonnet. She wouldn't stop fussing with my white shawl either, not until I finally pushed her wrinkled brown hand away with a playful bat.

This far-too-spacious, luxurious carriage that seated a family of four had more than enough room to accommodate the blue billows of my dress. It was sent by the Queen herself. A novel sight here on Canterbury Street. Of course, I was already a novel sight to the white women of the genteel neighborhood, their children always turning to them and hungrily gripping at their aprons whenever I walked out of the house. A carriage, though? Some of them stuck up their noses and burned with jealousy.

But why wouldn't Queen Victoria send me such things? I was her most intriguing colonial jewel. From the time I was presented to her, I was the favorite story she loved to tell: the orphaned African princess saved by the honorable Captain Frederick Edwyn Forbes. The Crown reveled in recounting my narrow escape from death by human sacrifice at the hands of that barbarous tribal "brute," King Ghezo. The people reveled in it too, at all levels of society it seemed, gossiping about their monarch's mercy from their pubs to their country clubs. I would know. I'd been in both.

I was the Queen's favorite card to play.

"I'm off!" I told Mama with a bright smile as the carriage came to a stop just in front of the gates. I fluttered my fingers at the blonde young woman glaring at me by the streetlamp, her basket of bread trembling on the crook of her reddening arm. Really, envy was so uncouth.

The East Cowes seafront on the Isle of Wight always sparkled seductively underneath the stars at night, but that still didn't make the long journey from Chatham worth it. Stopping by London on the way would only add more hours to an already-tiring journey. I had to get a move on. A lady's work is never done.

The chill, unusual for summer, nipped at my dark skin. Mama was dabbing her eyes with a blue silk handkerchief as if I were the one getting married. But why wouldn't she be in tears? The charge of Mrs. Elizabeth Schoen, the wife of a reverend—both *Africans*—had been invited to a *royal wedding*: the wedding of Princess Alice, Queen Victoria's third child and second daughter, to Prince Louis of Hesse. To Mama, it was the greatest honor she'd ever been given. Well, aside from when the Queen herself had personally chosen Mama's family to house me in Palm Cottage upon my return from Sierra Leone. In merry old England, social climbing was the pastime of the white elite as much as it was the dream of the "civilized" Black hopeful.

Mama waved at me as if seeing a sailor out to sea. "Goodbye, Sally! Have fun!"

She had no idea of what raged inside me. Three nights ago, she hadn't noticed me leaving the house, nor climbing back up the stairs and entering my room late at night. I suppose with Reverend Schoen away to the countryside for work, she was taking advantage of the newfound extra time for sleep she had on her hands.

"But not *too* much fun, of course, Mama." I winked, wondering with a sigh if Harriet had gotten the opium den ready for the after-party. The door closed and I was off.

Their "love" for you is conditional, Ina.

Tugging my shawl over my knees, I leaned over in my seat. "Driver. Can we stop by St. Giles in London?" Could he hear me over the squeaky wheels rumbling over stone?

Silence. My throat tightened, and I fixed my face into an amicable smile. "Driver! St. Giles? London!"

"London?" he repeated over the horses' clomping. "Why there?"

I lay back against the leather passenger seat. "To see a friend," I told him.

I had my *own* cards to play.

Sibyl Vale lived close to Covent Garden. Outside the rickety front door-steps of her crumbling apartment, her doe eyes widened at the sight of my carriage stopping and my little brown head peeking through the window.

"Come in, Sibyl! Quickly! Hurry now!" I added when she hesitated a little too long. I needed her tonight; my plan depended on it.

Her long blonde hair had been washed and combed into submission. She'd truly prepared for this wedding. The lavender travel dress I'd sent fit her impeccably and she'd done her best to scrub off the smell of the slums. The apricot perfume was the pièce de résistance: a faint waft of it to dull anyone's senses. It was Uncle George's favorite, or so she'd told me.

"Sibyl, you look wonderful!" She looked modestly acceptable. I took in the sight of her and forced a smile. "How have you been? I hope you haven't been nervous these past few days. Did your brother help you prepare?"

"My brother?" She snorted. "Don't make me laugh. If I told him I was trying to meet Captain Forbes again, he'd go positively rabid. He nearly murdered him the last time he stood me up." She shuddered. "Believe me, Sally, you haven't seen him when he's angry."

If only she knew. "Well, that's why we won't tell him." I put a teasing finger to my lips.

"Oh, Sally, do you really think George will be happy to see me?" Sibyl's green eyes were wet with desperation. "When we parted ways over a month ago, I thought that was my last shot to . . . to . . ."

To marry him and play out her Cinderella fantasies. Uncle George wasn't ready for commitment and the Forbes family wouldn't have him marry someone of "low birth," especially after the untimely death of his brother Frederick, taken by malaria. Strange how they were fine with being associated with me, a strange African girl. But then, that very association had given them access to the royal palace and a kind of fame few Brits had.

"He loves you, Sibyl, trust me! You just have to convince him." The very idea of romantic love playing any part in these marriage matches from hell made me sick. I'd seen enough sad housewives to know love was bait to trick a woman into a lifelong prison. And I'd seen enough of Uncle George to know that he'd cheat on any woman he married given the sliver of a chance. It was all so ridiculously insulting to one's intelligence. "He loves you," I repeated anyway. "And this venue will be the perfect venue. What's more romantic than a wedding?"

I put my hand on hers. Even after everything I'd given her—the clothes, the shoes, the perfume, the wedding invitation—she still hesitated to let me touch her, as if the long white glove wasn't enough of a barrier between us. Insult upon insult. She'd been like that the first time she met me in Uncle George's London home too.

"She's not only my niece—she's Queen Victoria's goddaughter," Uncle George had told her with a hint of pride and a little smile at the improbability of it all.

The slick of disdain turned into forced acceptance, like a young boy shoving vegetables down his throat lest his mother scold him.

"He'll be traveling back to London immediately after the wedding. You *must* make sure he meets you tonight," I told her as the carriage clattered through the busy streets toward the chapel. "It's nonnegotiable. You *did* receive the undergarments I sent you?"

I never could figure out why the British acted so scandalized by the very mention of sex when there had to have been tens of thousands of prostitutes in London alone. The amount of pornography you'd find in one household.

I nudged her in the arm. "This is important, Sibyl. The way to a man's heart is through his groin, you should be old enough to know that by now. You want Uncle George, you must seduce him."

I touched my gloved hands to my lips and sat back in my seat. Perhaps that was a little too much for her.

Sibyl shifted uncomfortably. "You seem a little too comfortable talking about your own uncle in such a manner."

Uncle in name only, clearly, if our differing complexions didn't give that away. "I'm just looking out for you," I said with a shrug. "If you don't use what you have to bring him back to you, another woman will."

That got her. Her jaw tightened for a moment. Then Sibyl hung her head. "You're right. It's now or never. It's either George and I meet after the wedding at Regent's Park and all my dreams come true . . . or I spend the night with my brother at that bloody pub he's so fond of."

The Lamb & Flag, which he frequented every weeknight after his work at the mills.

"Sibyl, if Uncle George loves you—if he truly loves you—he'll do it. And trust me, Ms. Vale, he *loves* you."

Whether he did or not didn't actually matter to me. What mattered was that he *desired* her in the way men want things when they want them.

More than a little disturbing, of course, because she was barely older than me. Such matches weren't uncommon in Britain—the ones with age gaps in the double digits, I mean. How many politicians flaunted their schoolgirl wives without an ounce of shame? It never seemed to matter to certain Brits, particularly those looking to climb the social ladder. And for an older man with lurid appetites like his—well, surely a pretty young lady like Sibyl fawning over him at his age was like a twisted fantasy made real?

But Uncle George had his responsibilities. He had to uphold his family's honor, now more than ever after his brother and my "savior" Frederick died tragically. That was what kept him and Sibyl Vale apart. But for Sibyl . . . well, a secret nighttime rendezvous and a race against the clock for true love was the pinnacle of romantic. It had worked for one Cinderella. As long as Sibyl believed she was next, my plan wouldn't fail.

Harriet had just better do her job.

In East Cowes, Sibyl and I spent the night at a friend's villa before waking up in the early hours of the morning to dress for the wedding. The simple gray dress I'd sent fit her impeccably. And the perfume would lure Uncle George like a siren.

"Why wear such a drab color to a wedding?" Sibyl asked, and I thought it'd be better to let her see for herself. This wasn't going to be a . . . *usual* royal event.

Our carriage came to a halt inside the vast complex of the Osborne House, the summer home of Queen Victoria and Prince Albert, God rest his soul, or whatever they say. Arched windows climbed up spiraling Italian bell towers that glistened the color of the sunset. Sibyl's gasp reminded me that not everyone was used to such royal opulence. Looking up at the estate, I wondered if it was any bigger than the Chapel Royal of St. James's Palace, where Princess Victoria had been married, or even

Buckingham Palace. So many wings fanned out across the grounds. Though my shoes touched the cobbled stone, off the path was a sprawling garden, expertly cut and designed as if the greenery were meant to be a painting in and of itself.

Dozens of carriages had already begun to gather. July 1, 1862, would forever go down in history as the wedding day of nineteen-year-old Princess Alice, Queen Victoria's third child, and Prince Louis IV of Germany, the future Grand Duke of Hesse. Under the cloudy skies, the commotion of men and women of the highest standing clustered together sent a tickle of electricity up my spine.

It wasn't the first high-society event I'd attended. That didn't matter. Even for the most powerful and well-connected of patrons, each social event was a test in which at any moment one wrong move could set off a cataclysm that would signal one's fall from grace. For the elite, social disposal was an ignominy akin to being cast out of the heavens.

But I was already in hell.

Trumpets. They were about to announce me.

Stand up straight, Ina. Remember to smile. You must always smile while in their presence. Look pleased. Look grateful.

I'd gotten used to many mantras. This was just one of them.

"Presenting Miss Sarah Forbes Bonetta."

Named after a murderer and a ship. They'd called it my "christening." I could spit.

I gave a demure nod instead as I stepped out of the carriage as carefully as I could. Winds from the English Channel buffeted me from all sides, but I kept my chin high. As Sibyl scurried mouselike behind me, I strode through the throng outside and entered the house, which had been transformed into a temporary chapel for the sake of the wedding.

Well, it was a wedding.

It was also a funeral.

"Sally, what is this?" Sibyl recoiled at the sight before her. Straight faces. People weeping. Red eyes behind wet handkerchiefs. The shadow of death hovered over the dining room where Princess Alice was to be married. "Why is everyone—?"

"Just act natural," I told her, standing up straight. "Remember, you're at a royal gathering."

Sibyl nodded. Though they'd long buried him, the royal family carried on as if still freshly mourning Prince Albert's death of typhoid fever last year. But for those struggling in the London slums, the death of a man barely known to them would mean less than where their next meal was coming from. I didn't blame Sibyl for being unaware of the context. Perhaps I should've warned her that this wouldn't be a normal wedding.

Those who weren't used to me were either offended by or scared of my presence, but by now, most of royal London in 1862 were at least aware of Queen Victoria's young African ward.

Four years ago, during the wedding ceremony of Queen Victoria's first daughter, Princess Victoria, and Frederick III of Prussia, every woman had been decked out in their finest attire inside the Chapel Royal, blue and pink and lavender dresses adorned with flowers. Now everyone, even the bride, wore a simple white dress and hid their faces.

But it was still a wedding nonetheless. The upper class had to show their superiority *somehow*. And so military men still flashed every badge they'd earned by razing a tribe or slaughtering a regiment. Top hats and bonnets, black suits and sashes, bald heads and jelly-slick teeth, all as if to say, *We're still nobles, just very sad ones at the moment.*

Letting myself behave a little giddily as a "friend" would in this situation, I gave Sibyl a playful nudge. "Don't let the mood get you down. Most of the guests will go back to their balls and parlor games once they get back to London. Remember why you're here. Uncle George is sure to be around. Go find your prince," I told her.

Her gaze darted from the royal velvet drapes to the dangling chandelier, like she didn't know which she coveted more. But with a nod, she scurried off to find her military catch.

Just before the ceremony started I could see the two of them chatting, Captain George Forbes in his black suit, fidgeting like a toddler who'd had his secret found out. He must have been wondering how in the world a lowborn woman could have found herself at a royal wedding. But he wasn't moving away. He flinched but didn't run when she touched him. That was a good sign, but not a surprise. I studied my targets well. Everyone had a weak point.

The ceremony was as dreary as the weather. From the back of the crowd, I couldn't see the Queen herself, but I could just pick out Princess Alice in bridal white and a wreath of orange blossom and myrtle, flanked at each side by her sisters as bridesmaids. Her fair-skinned handmaidens carried her long train pooling on the green rug as she knelt in front of the archbishop. "Little Alice" and I were almost the same age. We were both princesses, but how very different our lives had turned out.

She was a quiet enough girl. I'd played with her when we were children. It was when we were in the garden of Windsor Castle that she lost my affections. What had she been thinking when she put her hands, dirty with licked honey, into my carefully coiffed hair? Hair that, mind you, had taken two painful hours to wash and comb so I could make myself *presentable* enough to be in their *illustrious* royal presence.

"African hair is so angry," she'd told me back then, feeling my hair, rubbing it down to the scalp with her sticky, cold fingers. "Not silky and sweet like ours."

Ah yes, perhaps—if "silky and sweet" was British slang for "limp and prone to graying and disappearing by one's thirties." The number of bald spots I'd seen in Windsor Castle alone on even the youngest of men always made me want to laugh out loud. But I couldn't.

23

I couldn't say anything out loud.

"Well, it's certainly *sweet* now!" Prince Albert, otherwise known as "Bertie" had piped up, and followed through by picking up the honey jar and dumping more on my head. Bertie, the boy who would be king, was often punished for his bad behavior. But this time, throwing his mother's African ward into distress was met with pleasant laughter before the toothless scolding came.

"Were you *really* a princess?" he'd asked. "You people don't have *real* princes and princesses like we do. No way!"

My proud father and beautiful mother, murdered by the war-hungry Dahomey King Ghezo, flashed before my young eyes, along with myself in those old days, with my shaven head and my happiness. That is, before Captain Frederick Forbes put me in an English girl's clothes. Then they called me *civilized*.

Bertie and Alice laughed and laughed as my honeyed hair caught bugs like a flytrap.

Smile. Laugh along with them, Ina, I'd told myself. And as my eyes burned, I made a note to write wonderful letters to Queen Victoria about how kind Alice was and what a gentlemanly little fellow Bertie had become. Smile and laugh until your body breaks into pieces from the humiliation because their love is conditional and the alternative is not to be desired.

At least King Ghezo made it clear who his captives were.

The royals cried throughout the wedding, but while I fixed my face into something akin to sympathy, all I felt inside was a cold emptiness. Where was this outpouring of grief for me throughout my life, me an orphan who could still remember every brutal strike of the blade that dismembered my family? How was I to measure their empathy whenever they saw me and said "poor Sally" before snickering behind their hands at a joke just told? It was only fair I give them the same energy they'd always given me. It had taken time, but finally, I was prepared.

The wedding ended, leaving the attendees to either continue weeping or at least attempt to mingle. Ah, and there came the next name on my list: Uncle George. Strangely, he had been adamant about my calling him "uncle" from the days he brought me over to England on the HMS *Bonetta*. Not even his brother Frederick was so stubborn about it. Perhaps it was some kind of compensation. Frederick had been given the credit for saving me, with his brother simply along for the ride, as usual. Of course, he wanted to world to know he was the little Negro's hero too. Close enough to be family.

"Sally, you're looking well." Sticking his arms behind his back, Uncle George gave a gentlemanly bow. It was what a middle-aged captain was expected to do, even toward an eighteen-year-old African girl. "Frederick would be so pleased to see you're growing up so beautifully."

Indeed, over the years, many had become quite jealous of my glamorous beauty, which I maintained meticulously just to spite them, though I don't think any of them would admit it.

"I see you were talking to quite a lovely woman," I said in a teasing voice.

"Yes." Uncle George's breath hitched. "Yes, well, she's an old acquaintance of mine. An old friend—" He paused. "Uh, no, well . . ."

Your greatest love, you mean. I grinned because my research was never wrong. "I hope things are going well between you."

"Yes, well." He lifted his chin almost in defiance of his embarrassing display. "I've known her for some time," he said with a new tone of put-on authority. "Kind girl, very kind girl. A rather unrelentingly protective brother, though."

His face paled and I could tell he was thinking of that brash, trigger-happy man, James Vale. I'd spied on him weeks ago, my face covered in a black shawl at a tavern. He had a great right hook, and no beer bottle seemed capable of surviving his swing when he aimed it at someone's skull. He was indeed a volatile, protective brother.

A brother who'd lose his mind if ever his darling sister's honor were to be torn asunder.

Uncle George shook his head. "But never mind that. Come, Sally. Shall I introduce you to some of my friends?"

He offered the crook of his arm to me. I stared at it for a little too long.

Holding my breath, I took his arm and let him escort me through the crowd.

How long had Ade been able to hold *his* breath before the waves entered his lungs?

As obnoxious wedding music filled the hall, I shuddered. I didn't want to hold George's arm any longer than I had to; feeling his pudgy arm reminded me of Ade, poor Ade. And remembering Ade dimmed my vision and made my teeth grit so hard they'd break unless they could sink their points into the juicy vein in someone's neck.

I greeted the other attendees. Princess Alice had been instructed to trade in her white wedding dress for black mourning clothes. On her wedding day. Whether she wanted to or not didn't matter. When the Queen orders, you follow.

Speak of the devil.

"Oh, there you are, Sally." Queen Victoria herself, dressed in funeral black, though in a dress still fit for a monarch, waved me over like she would her child. She looked around and made sure everyone saw her do it too. "You intelligent little thing. Come and greet us properly."

Look overjoyed, Ina. Look grateful.

Or they might get rid of you before you can get rid of them.

"Oi, Sally!" Prince Albert, named after his father, was next to his mother with his gold-brown hair slicked back. The Queen started calling me "Sally" for short. Then everyone else did too. He always insisted that we called him "Bertie"—his inner circle, as well as his prostitutes. The ones he held dear to his heart. He gave me a slight bow; his buffoonish grin ruined his otherwise handsome face. "Good of you to come. None of my mates at Cambridge believed me when I told them I was close with a pretty little African princess."

"Oh? You've managed to keep from getting kicked out of school, then?" I muttered under my breath.

His grin widened, but in confusion this time. He tilted his head. "What was that?"

I covered my lips with a gloved hand and coughed daintily before turning away.

What a joke. He'd been crying throughout the wedding, shielding his mother from view along with his little brother Alfred, who by now had escaped the gloomy scene. I could still see the tint of red in his eyes. Perhaps this was his way of trying to shift the mood, but it was clumsy at best. And if he was going to lighten up the atmosphere, he could do it without using *me*, but what else could I expect from him?

He winked at me, but I paid him no mind. As his smile drooped, I smirked behind my gloved hand. It satisfied me to no end seeing his childish pout every time I ignored him.

But then Queen Victoria herself stretched out her hand to me. "Come, Sally!"

Now, this was a command I couldn't ignore.

At the Queen's beckoning, I gathered with the other ladies, many of them shifting uncomfortably at the sight of me but nodding their heads nonetheless because I was, of course, Queen Victoria's famous god-daughter. Her favorite story to tell. Proof of her endless charity, wisdom, and compassion. And because to them I seemed to be grateful for it all, there was no reason for them to turn on me. Yet.

"Captain George," she greeted him, and Uncle George looked as if he'd ascended to heaven.

"My Queen." His bow was deep. He'd have never shown my parents the same respect had they lived. "I'm so very sorry. I mean, congratulations—well . . ." He paused. He wasn't sure which was appropriate.

The Queen had loved her husband. She hadn't been the same since he'd died. To others, it was a tragedy. But to me, it spelled opportunity. With her defenses down, it was now or never.

"My Sally, you are so very beautiful." She clasped my chin with both hands. "Poor thing. I know this weather isn't very well-suited to your kind."

Like Bertie, she was using me to lift the mood. To make herself feel better.

Play your role, Ina. I curtsied. "I'm quite *moldable* to any weather, Your Majesty." I kept my eyes low because if I raised them and saw that exaggerated piteous gaze, I'd want to strike at her immediately. She was the one with the dead husband. How dare she look at *me* with pity as if my existence itself was enough reason?

She rubbed the side of my cheek. The lace of my bonnet rubbed against my skin. "I've heard so many strange things have been happening lately. People dying of strange accidents. People I used to know quite well. Like Mr. Bellamy from the *London News*."

I froze.

"Bellamy was a dirty old man and a drunkard." Bertie laughed. "They found him with his pants down surrounded by bottles of alcohol. You should see what they're saying about him in the press. The pictures alone. How shameful."

Bertie was one to talk. Booze and women weren't the vices of old men only. As he shook his head, I stared at the floor, my heart giving a painful thud against my chest. And when I slowly lifted my gaze, Queen Victoria's shocking blue eyes arrested me.

"It reminds me of the odd circumstances of our dear Captain Frederick Forbes's death."

My mouth ran dry. And because I'd trained myself not to remember, I shoved his dead eyes out of my mind. "Yes, it was an awful shame. Some kind of sickness, I believe. Malaria."

"So the letter said. But we never found his body." Something darker crept up into her warm expression, a flicker of her eyelashes that told me she was studying me. "It's strange, Sally. I think it's strange, at least."

She narrowed her eyes curiously because I didn't answer right away. I couldn't, not with these wild thoughts suddenly racing through my mind. Did she know? But how could she? How could such a thing be possible . . . unless she was having me followed? Was she spying on me?

A battle of wills between two queens. Except only one of us thought of it that way.

"Maybe it was the Mannings!" Prince Bertie's oafish yell broke through the silence that stretched between the two of us royals. "Maybe they buried him under the kitchen floor and stole his money like that other bloke."

Another ill-timed joke. Smatterings of skittish laughter peppered the room because the prince had told a joke, so laughing was in order, but the Queen was in mourning, so was laughing *really* okay? The crowd was split and nervous.

The Queen gave Bertie a look that could have withered the garden plants outside. That was his cue to shut his mouth. Bertie obliged, his cheeks flushing red, his bottom lip curled. Before his father's untimely death, I didn't think their relationship could get any worse. Oh well. He'd surely find solace tonight between the legs of one of the chambermaids, as usual.

As if her face had never so much as crinkled, Queen Victoria gave me a warm, motherly smile. "I'm sorry, Sally. Perhaps, I'm just a little sensitive these days. It's good to see you're well despite all these things. Don't pay attention to the gossip and focus on your studies."

"Yes, Your Majesty."

If, for one second, I let my smile slip. If I made the white men feel attacked or threatened or, goodness forbid, uncomfortable. If I became any less than the grateful, "good" child whose existence proved their superiority? In that one second, it would be over for Sarah Forbes Bonetta.

Queen Victoria dismissed me. Then I gave my congratulations to Alice in black and her uncomfortable German husband.

At all times, I was standing underneath the point of a knife.

I pushed myself through the crowd of sycophants anxious to greet and console the new royal couple as Harriet, who'd changed quickly into a black dress, slipped up to my side, her bonnet obscuring her rigid chestnut hair, parted down the center like her frumpy mother's. As expected of a future confidential attendant to the Queen.

"Everything's ready back in London," she whispered, and I could smell apricot fumes curling off her words. Standing by the billowing red curtains draped along the ancient chapel walls, the one or two reporters allowed into the room were busy writing. They'd come to me for a comment soon enough.

The thought of Mr. Bellamy dead in his London home gave me a quick chill. But it was short-lived.

I already knew this would be messy when I started.

"Where?" I asked over my shoulder while keeping my affable grin steady for the reporters I graciously waved to. Certain places were a no-go. Ah Sing's, for example. It was too famous among the elite. Most of the men at this wedding would find their way there after nightfall. And certain dens were on the docks. Too many sailors.

"Rui's den over on the East End," she answered dutifully. "He's made his preparations."

I grinned. It was newly established, one where the lower classes languished. Royals and noblemen wouldn't frequent it and it was nowhere near the ships at sea. Uncle George would feel safe there. Anonymous. Good. I knew Rui was ready. "And the card?"

"Slipped into his jacket without him ever noticing me, as you instructed."

Harriet sounded proud of herself. Strangled by her parents' royal expectations and with no resources to act out alone, she was the perfect choice for my accomplice. And, I knew, their relationship was so strained that Harriet wouldn't have even cared if I decided to one day tell her that her mother was on my list. I knew why Queen Victoria had chosen her as an attendant-in-training. Leaders preferred the loyalty of the broken and weak. But by giving her power, she was forever loyal to me.

"Good. Just make sure you get to the Lamb & Flag in time."

His greatest love or his greatest vice. I already knew which one Uncle George would choose.

I nudged Harriet in the ribs and, for just one second, let my real smile show. This was not the gracious grin of English upper-class society beaten into me by the missionary schooling they'd forced on me in Freetown. This was my, *Ina's*, true grin. The one I gained after Ade died and I realized that false masks were perfect veils for those who dreamed of revenge.

Who said I was anyone's good child?

"Get my carriage ready. I have to get back to London by nightfall."

FOUR

THE COBBLED STREETS were clouded in fog. Very few "respectable" people would find themselves out here so late at night, or so they insisted, except I always somehow found them stumbling around inebriated from drugs and alcohol, or descending the steps of brothels, laughing gaudily with two women on each arm as they indulged the pleasures of the East End.

This particular den was rather small and in a part of the neighborhood that made it much easier for the lower classes to frequent. There were more famous and prestigious opium dens for the rich to waste away in. But then there were the most morally hypocritical among the wealthy—a special breed whose uprightness formed the core of their very family name. Their fond taste for the powder would bring them *anywhere* so long as there was no one around to see their image crumble.

The Forbeses were respectable people, you see. All of Britain knew that they'd bravely saved an African child from slavery and death at the hands of an evil tribal king. They were practically heroes of the abolition movement. And the young boy they'd drowned? Well, no one knew about him, so what did it matter?

A boy who had lived and died with no one to mourn him but me.

In the dead of night, one of Rui's men stopped me outside the dingy den. He had a strange scar in the shape of an X etched over his left eye and carried with him the mask I'd asked for, but— What was this? Why was it black and beaked like a crow?

As I took the mask from him, the man slunk away, his cap down. Then I realized.

"The mask of a plague doctor." I rolled my eyes. I had asked Rui for something that would cover my nose and keep out the smells from the den lest they make me weak-minded and addicted like the rest. Our taste for humor didn't match at all.

The mask covered my whole head. Once on, a mixture of smells overtook me: cinnamon, myrrh, and even honey. Wrapping my dark hooded cloak around me I entered the den.

The narrow corridor opened up into one, simple, dilapidated room. People lay on wooden bunks and slouched by the fire. They made their pipes of old penny ink bottles and glittering thimbles. Smoke nearly obscured their languid bodies from sight. Normally, I would have stayed clear of this place, but there was a man I was looking for.

"Dear . . . oh, my little deary!"

I jumped. Near the painted wall, a man grabbed my right wrist.

"The devil's finally come to take me away . . . ," he said, staring into my crow mask. I didn't know whether to feel sorry or disgusted. The Egbado had more self-control. The sweet plantains, swaying palm trees, and fresh breeze against my skin. I'd trade it in for this any day.

"Sorry, friend, but this one's *my* little deary."

Wrenching my arm out of the man's grip, Rui turned his chiseled face toward me. "Come with me, little princess," he said with a delectable wink, and began leading me through the den. "Enjoying the mask? I had it made especially for you. The fifty-five herbs inside the beak are keeping you from inhaling the smoke. And other compounds."

It was how plague doctors used to work centuries ago, constantly surrounded by poisoned air. I knew Rui must have had something in his tall nose to keep him from succumbing to his exposure to opium. I hated to admit it, but I was rather thankful he had no mask covering the thick curtain of lashes covering his expressive brown eyes or the crooked tilt of his dimple-edged grin. Nineteen and too handsome for his own good, he was filled with tricks as much as charm.

One of those tricks was his very name. It wasn't his. But then, "Sally" wasn't mine. Aliases were quite fine to use between coconspirators.

Another one of his tricks was a trapdoor that led to a rather well-ventilated basement. He was about to pull me through when I stopped.

"Wait," I said, and looked around because I thought I saw him. Out of the corner of my eye, I was sure I saw him—

In my search, my gaze landed on a crook of the room even dingier than the others. There, a man sat curled up in the corner with a pipe and a dirty blanket covering his head as if it would take away his shame.

I was right. And though I knew I would be, it was a pathetic, *infuriating* sight indeed. He looked disease-ridden, like he existed to be covered in filth. The veins bulged out of his dilated pupils. *This* was the man who purported to be of a higher class of human than Ade and I. The man who slapped Ade when he couldn't form his English words quickly enough despite haphazard attempts at teaching him.

This was the man who'd made me *dance*.

Biting my lip, I bristled with the anger that I'd learned by now to keep burning under lock and key lest it leak out at the wrong moments. Captain George Forbes. I knew he couldn't pass up the invitation. A Queen of Spades card had been slipped into his pocket. On the back of it: the address of a yet-undiscovered den, along with the promise of free drugs and perfect anonymity.

During the year I'd spent on the HMS *Bonetta*, George had spent many a night with his favorite pastime, even after once being beaten senseless by his brother Frederick. "An embarrassment to the family," I once heard him say once I knew enough English words.

Poor Sibyl, but it was a good lesson for her. There were no true princes in this country.

The crow's beak hid my evil grin as Rui tugged me through the trapdoor. On the way down the narrow staircase, he took off my mask and gently pushed me against the wall. Without the smoke, I could see his figure, slim but firm. He wore a red corset over a golden-brown shirt and tight pants made of leather. I couldn't say I didn't like it. I couldn't say I didn't like it when he pressed his body against me either.

It was always when we were so close that my body warmed and my legs itched to be around his waist. He was a tease, criminally. Been so since the day we met and formed our illicit partnership in the dark of night. Running his hands through his short black hair, he took in the sight of me before reaching into my cloak. The caress of his hand against my collarbone made my heart flutter and my back arch almost instinctively. He leaned in, his lips lightly touching my ear.

I caught his wrist just as he slipped it out of my dress. My calling card.

"You're still obsessed with this, I see." He waved the Queen of Spades in front of my face. "Makes playing cards with you dreadfully boring."

I snatched it out of his grasp. The haughty look of the black queen arrested me.

"I take it you have everything in place for Captain George Forbes's complete and utter disgrace." Rui brushed my cheek with the back of a finger. "Though from the sounds of your plans, should we make one mistake, you'll end up with another dead body on your hands."

"Oh, I don't want Forbes to die." I tilted my head to the side as I reminded him. "What I want is a scandal. What I want is his family in shambles."

"So you told me the first time we met." Rui smirked and turned his

35

eyes upward as if he were remembering that night in the East End. "Scandal and ruin for those in the Queen's orbit. And if murder should come into the equation—"

"Then it is only because it was part of their path to ruin," I finished. "Trust me. Uncle George deserves death for what he's done. But not yet. Just stick to what we agreed to. James Vale will be difficult to control. His fists are his weapon of choice. Are you ready for that?"

"With the body count I've accrued in my time in Limestone, I think you can trust my ability to take on one drunken brute. But that's beside the point."

Rui leaned in smooth, the little hairs on his cheek brushing against my skin as he whispered in my ear, "This is a very dangerous game you're playing."

A game that required me to seek help from the most unlikely of partners. My skin buzzed at his touch, but I hid it well. "It's not a game I expect to finish alive. That makes things a lot easier."

"I wonder." Rui took my chin in his hand and lifted it until our eyes locked. "Even a prideful princess has her flaws, as we all do. And when one's cracks start to show, well, you never know when unexpected fun will happen."

"You little bastard—you *are* here!" The roar of a furious man shook the floorboards. "You chose *this* over my sister?"

The fish was hooked. Harriet had done her job. I slid on my mask. "It's showtime."

Just as I turned to leave, Rui grabbed my arm. "And what kind of show are you hoping to see?" The tinge of uncontrolled excitement in his voice seemed somewhat out of character for a young drug lord who had himself completely under control at all times.

I was almost annoyed that he couldn't see me sneering. "The kind that ends in vindication."

"Even if it also ends in blood?"

My little hands clenched into fists. Both orphans in a strange land, from the day Rui and I met, we'd birthed a unique kind of rapport. He'd worked hard climbing through the ranks of the underworld, while I had done my best climbing to the upper echelons of the British elite. Both feats required grit. One couldn't gain without getting her hands dirty.

"What's it to you?" I snapped back as the commotion upstairs grew louder.

Rui gave me a sidelong look, his expression almost mischievous as he soaked in my anger. "It's just fascinating, I suppose. Seeing a princess fall."

"I've already fallen. *They* made me fall."

They made me fall when they killed my friend and took me to be a *gift* for another ruler when I would have rather died with pride as a ruler myself.

"How much farther is there to go, I wonder?" Rui said no more as he let go of me and, with his hands up in surrender, backed away.

Trembling a little, I ran up the stairs and through the trapdoor.

There was James Vale, with his closely shaven blond hair, baring his teeth at Uncle George in his corner, his blanket pooled upon the floor, his back flat against the wall. Vale must have come straight from the tavern. He was tipsy and red-faced, just as I'd predicted.

But when I looked at Vale more closely, my hands numbed.

A gun. A little pistol cocked and pointed at Uncle George's forehead. Vale was drunk but his aim seemed sure.

Since when did Vale carry a gun? He was to beat Uncle George senseless for the crime he'd committed against his sister. A gun wasn't part of the plan. How had I missed this?

Some men were yelling or transfixed in shock. Others didn't seem to care as long as they had their pipe. George, though military trained, was by now too feeble-minded to fight back. The moment he tried to move, his feet slid out from under him and he dropped sideways to the floor. With wide eyes, he stared down the barrel to his death.

His death wasn't part of the plan. I wanted his ruin. I wanted Uncle George to live to see his own life crumble before his eyes.

Without thinking, I looked around for Rui. He stood by the trapdoor, silent. Watching. I took a quick step toward him, but he lifted his hand to stay me. What was he waiting for? Did he want to see Vale blow Uncle George's head off?

Did *I*?

What hurt more? Death by a gunshot or death by drowning?

I would never forget Ade's feeble cries as he begged for mercy. Mercy was the one thing they didn't deserve. For what they do to him, me, all of us.

I didn't move. My heart was beating fast, though with curious skips. Each haggard breath electrified my skin.

This is it, Ade. I gripped the card in my hands. *Vengeance.*

Out of the corner of my eye, near the trapdoor, Rui watched me.

How much farther? How much farther . . . ?

My teeth chattered. I remembered Mr. Bellamy's dead eyes and suddenly felt sick. Gripping my head, I tried to catch my breath when a jumble of familiar voices erupted from the den's entrance.

"Captain Forbes?"

The blood in my veins ran cold. Both Vale and I turned, myself in utter disbelief.

"Prince Albert?" I couldn't keep myself from saying it. The prince was coughing, waving the smoke away. I immediately covered my mouth, but it was too late. Bertie was looking at me. Did he recognize my voice? I could see the question in his wide eyes.

Behind him was Harriet, absolutely frantic as she clasped her hands together. "He followed me," she mouthed. Idiot! She wasn't supposed to even *come* here!

"I was wondering what a royal courtier was up to, traveling to the East End at night—and to an opium den no less." Bertie stepped closer and closer to me, entranced. It was like he'd forgotten about Vale and Forbes entirely. "But what's this?" Coughing again, he cocked his head to the side. Closer. "You in the mask." And closer still. "Who . . . who are—?"

I thought quickly, tackling Vale and knocking his gun away. It went off into the air. As the den erupted, as Captain Forbes breathed a whining, relieved moan, Prince Albert ran toward the drunkard, just as I managed to slip past him.

"Wait!" Bertie cried, his hands grazing my cloak as he reached for me, but I eluded him. Out the den's entrance and into the night, I ran without looking back.

FIVE

I SLIPPED INTO the Schoens' little villa just before the break of dawn. I knew the architecture by heart. The winding stairs, the flower-painted wallpaper. The Persian rugs over the concrete floor. Every entrance and every nook. Even with the lights off, my small feet found their way to my room in the corner of the second floor and my head found its way to my pillow—a pillow that I then pressed against my face to stifle a frustrated scream.

I kicked my white bedsheets while flat on my stomach like a petulant child. It was a shameful display. I came up for air, wondering if Mama had heard. Nothing. Well, the woman slept as if her room were a grave, so that wasn't surprising.

Bertie showing up in that opium den. *That* was the surprise.

He'd heard my voice. Damn it, he'd *heard* it, muffled behind a mask though it may have been. It'd been hours since then—did he have me figured out by now? Did he question Harriet? Did she buckle and give me up? Panic had chased me out of London. I could still feel its remnants course in my veins. I should have stayed. I should have followed that pampered ninny of a prince and—

No. I was losing control. Swallowing the lump in my throat, I stood from my bed and carefully removed each item of clothing strangling me.

I left them in a black heap on the floor, soaking in the sensation of the red carpet against the soles of my feet. Its downy contours itched because the carpet was old; it'd started in the drawing room and moved up here only once the Schoens were able to purchase a new one.

The Schoens were not as well-off as one would think. Being on the Queen's radar, enough to become guardians of the Queen's goddaughter, did not afford them any more profit than they made as humble missionaries. Still, the Schoens had made sure that I'd had my necessities and perhaps more: A central table made of mahogany wood. A wardrobe flush against the rightmost wall. A small bookcase filled with books I was forced to read while in Freetown. More recent fiction, like the works of the Brontë sisters and Dickens. Older classics like *Paradise Lost* and *Gulliver's Travels*. Voltaire and Shakespeare. Of course, various editions of the Bible. It would have been odd to the Schoens to leave any of these out. Otherwise, they might have questioned the veracity of my "proper" upbringing.

There were other books that I was able to secure through the British and Foreign Anti-Slavery Society. Particularly moving were the memoirs of slaves in the Americas and the West Indies. Mary Prince, John Brown. More, still more. Across the ocean, the no-longer-united States had just begun a war over the right to continue their owning and bartering of Africans like chattel. Here, in my room, I read about the cruelty of slavery with mixed emotions. I myself was once a slave, a victim of the Europeans' murderous trade in which even the Dahomey king sought his fortune. My rescue by Captain Forbes and my subsequent adoption into Queen Victoria's family as her goddaughter were meant to symbolize a victory of British abolitionism. Queen Victoria made sure it did.

No longer a human sacrifice and living in Britain, I wasn't like the slaves fighting for their lives in other places of the world. I had so many things, even just in this room. These books. The washstand. The chest of drawers in the corner. A tall mirror next to my bed. My little hands cupped my heart-shaped, hollowed-out face as I looked into it. How dare I complain? That's what they would say in the Anti-Slavery Society if I ever told them how Ade's death had left me a body without a soul. How my identity had been stripped from me, like carving skin with a knife, layer by layer. And then the flesh down to the bone.

I didn't like to, but if I stared hard enough at my hands, I'd surely be able to see the deep purple scars made from strokes of a strap courtesy of the illustrious educational system of the Female Institution in Freetown. The strokes on my back were more noticeable. Superintendent Sass wasn't one to go easy on even a child's flesh.

To make a puppet, one must kill a live thing first. Children then played with the little wooden doll not knowing or caring about its former life as a magnificent tree.

Perhaps that was the most frustrating of all. Puppets were not allowed to give voice to their frustrations. They, like me, were not allowed the grace of that ever-elusive soul.

I slipped a picture of myself I'd sketched out from underneath my pillow. With each stroke of the quill, I'd reproduced as well as I could the portrait William Bambridge had taken of me when I was thirteen, five years after I was first brought to England. The Queen had beamed with such pride after it'd been completed; she must not have noticed the emptiness in the eyes. Since the portrait technically belonged to Queen Victoria and Prince Albert's private collection, I couldn't take it with me. I sketched it from memory on my own and left the eyes blank so that I wouldn't forget that this hollow creature was what they truly thought of me.

"Mr. Bellamy. Mr. Bambridge. Uncle George. McCoskry. Phipps . . ." I chanted my list as I stared at my marionette other in ink.

Several breaths more grounded me. After slipping on a straight white chemise, I pressed the backs of my legs against the wooden frame of my bed before letting myself fall onto the mattress. The high collar of my nightgown felt tighter than usual. Like a noose.

I didn't care if all this were to be taken away from me. But I had plans. I wouldn't be carted off before I finished them. An uphill battle against a ubiquitous enemy with unlimited power. Among the slave narratives I'd read, that was one theme I could relate to.

One cannot defeat the enemy without cleverness and clear thinking.

I shut my eyes and considered my predicament. Bertie might only still have suspicions as to who was under the mask that night. The opium and the distortion of my voice behind the plague doctor's beak left room for reasonable doubt. As for Harriet, the girl joined my scheme only thinking I'd cause scandal and embarrassment for her mother's friends. After seeing Vale with a gun and Captain Forbes seconds away from his head being blown off, her rebellion could waver. She had no idea I was behind Mr. Bellamy's death.

But how many hours had already passed since then? If Harriet had betrayed me, if Bertie was sure of my presence, I would have gotten a visit by now from a man summoning me to Windsor Castle—or the police station. No, there was no need to panic yet.

Besides, even in the event of a disaster, I still had cards to play. A prince and a courtier together in an opium den on the East End. Well, that offered several possibilities.

I grinned.

Tomorrow, I would have to find a way to ferret them both out.

"Oh no you don't!" Mrs. Schoen came barreling down the creaky wooden stairs just as my hand touched the knob of the front door. "No more socializing for you, Sally, until you help out around here."

Blood rushed to my face as I let my arm drop to my side.

"Yes, Mama," I said dutifully as she passed me and strode into the kitchen, cursing under my breath when she was out of earshot. Lazy mornings by the riverside in North Kent were still meant for chores, according to Mama. More so with her husband, Reverend Schoen, out evangelizing somewhere in England miles away and their daughter, Anne, teaching somewhere out in the countryside. I sensed that was partly the reason for Mama's frustration as she beat the carpets into submission on clothing wires behind the house.

"I wasn't trying to do anything terribly 'social,' you know," I told her while we washed dishes in a basin. Mama poured water from the teakettle delicately so as to not burn my hands while I scrubbed.

"What?"

"Earlier, you said 'no more socializing.'" The clean metal bucket was for rinsing but the water was far too cold. I flinched with annoyance when my hands cut through the surface. And I was already annoyed today. "I was just going for a walk. That's all. It's not like I spend my days mindlessly flittering about looking for a good time."

"Did I say you were?" Mama sounded exasperated. Like I was a child. I hated it.

I bit my lip, my cheeks red. Normally, whenever I was irritated with Mama, I was much better at hiding it. But every once a while, it slipped out. "It sounded like it."

Mama wiped her brow with a soapy hand. "Trust me, child, I know you're far more responsible than other young girls your age."

Other girls—like the elites she desperately wanted me to emulate. Otherwise why did she spend so much of our savings on the latest dresses and hats?

"But responsibility *is key* for any woman," Mama continued. "When you wake up in the morning, it's not to go for walks, it's to keep your house. That's how you'll win a good man."

My hands felt colder than the water. A good man. Like the reverend, whose evangelical mission always conveniently kept him far away from home and his lonely wife? And when he was home he wanted his food and a good rest. All the while Mrs. Schoen was withering away. I shuddered to think what would happen if I weren't here. What depths of sadness she would fall into. But that was "marriage": the life I was supposedly aiming for.

I bristled and turned from her to hide my grimace. The only men I was concerned with were the ones I was trying to destroy. And at the moment, Bertie topped that list. While I was here washing dishes, he could be telling the Queen everything. The thought made my spine snap like I'd been hit by one of Superintendent Sass's straps. Trapping that little git before he could expose me was my top priority.

But first: sweeping the house. I banged my head against the broomstick after Mama shoved it into my hands.

Well, these weren't nearly as bad as the grueling tasks I was given at the Female Institution. Not more than a year after I landed in England, the Queen had sent me to Sierra Leone to receive what she considered a "proper" education. An all-girl missionary school just filled to the brim with little Africans ripe for rearing. And what did they have us children do? Plant crops, plow fields, not to mention the domestic work we performed at the homes of the missionaries—all without pay, of course.

Remembering that hellhole made me quiver with rage, but it wouldn't be sated just yet, not until I could escape the house. After cleaning up, Mama sat at the table in the drawing room nearly slumped and sent me to make some tea. Her full cheeks were reddened from fatigue, her large eyes sunken.

"You look tired, Mama." I approached her with a steaming cup and, after she accepted, brought some butter and bread for good measure. "Eat up, and then go take a good rest."

"Thank you, darling." She held my head with both hands, rough from years from domestic work, and gave me a soft kiss on the forehead. "But I'm fine."

"Oh . . ." I swallowed the lump in my throat.

She blew on the surface of her tea, and sipped. "Come sit, Sally. What's better than tea and bread in the afternoon? You need to eat to keep up your strength. I don't like how gaunt you've been looking these days."

I smiled weakly. It was true: revenge hadn't had the best effect on my appetite. Mama was probably the only one who would notice the slightest change in my pallor.

What had begun as a pastime for Queen Victoria and her ladies had quickly set the upper classes aflame across England. Teatime: what a splendid way to fill that void between lunch and dinner. I'd seen the ritual while visiting Windsor Castle; the ladies-in-waiting would make sure to have their finest on outside in the gardens under the afternoon sun. But Mrs. Schoen and I were no ladies-in-waiting. We were actors, mimicking those wealthy white women as we'd been taught.

Was Bertie having tea with his mother now, telling her all about Uncle George in the opium den?

I did as I was instructed anyway, pulling out a chair and sitting across from Mama.

"Sally, your hair has become a bit rough since the wedding," Mama told me, buttering her bread. "Appearances are everything, you know. We live in a superficial world."

"I know, I know," I said, drinking my tea, flustered. Mama was always fretting about how I looked. Clearly, being judged by these people every day had done a number on her psyche. She did her best to transform into them, but she *wasn't* them. Trying to get as close as possible was a survival technique she aimed to pass on to me.

"You're getting to that age," she ranted on. "It's an important time for you. There are so many good men out there looking for a partner and . . ."

Whenever she started this kind of talk, I drowned her out almost by instinct. I didn't need to work that hard anyway. My mind was already half-distracted with the various Prince Albert scenarios. How likely was it that he would admit to his mother that he went anywhere near an opium den? But then, if he really did see me that night . . .

". . . And you know, finding the right partner for a woman is of the utmost importance," Mama finished.

"Really?" I dropped my teacup on the table with a rather loud clunk, determined to shift the direction of the conversation now that the topic of marriage and men had finally come to an end. "Shall I break a vase and heat it in the fireplace, then?" I rubbed the black curls lining my fore-head.

Mama scrunched up her nose in disgust. "Oh, heavens no. You'd better not touch a single one of my vases, child." And with a huff, she added, "Where did you even learn such a thing?"

From home. When I was little, whenever we needed to comb our hair, we'd use pieces of a broken pot and heat it over a hasty fire. The heated concavity of the vase helped straighten out the thick curls when we rubbed the broken clay on our heads. It wasn't to achieve straight hair; it was to make the curls a little easier to comb through. I quite liked shaving my hair entirely. My head was cleanly shaven when the Dahomey killed my parents and enslaved me.

A shaven head wouldn't do here. Not if Mrs. Schoen could help it. It wasn't "proper." Mama herself had a full head of hair, which she tamed down to two braids down the back of her skull. With her high black collar, she indeed looked suitably Protestant.

Light knocking on the door drew my attention from my tea. Mrs. Schoen went to answer it and returned with a letter.

I knew that red seal.

"My Sally, it's a letter for you from Prince Albert!" She handed it to me, beaming with excitement.

My whole body went rigid. So Little Bertie had made his move.

I had to calm down.

"Why, aren't you popular?" Mama said, giggling behind a hand. "Are you sure something interesting didn't happen at the wedding that I should know about?"

Sometimes, that petulant, childlike side of me had half a mind to tell her that I was being pursued by one of the Queen's sons just to see her head explode with panic. Imagining things was all fun and games, but one mustn't fly too close to the sun. Especially women like the two of us. She almost certainly would have told me this.

I unfolded the letter.

"What does it say?" Mama asked, tilting her head to the side.

It took a special skill to read Bertie's crass handwriting. He didn't mince words. There was only one line written here:

Be at Hill House today at four o'clock in the afternoon so we can speak face-to-face.

And his royal seal at the bottom. He certainly wasn't a poet.

Damn it. I folded it up quickly. "Just thanking me for being present at his sister's wedding."

"Three days late? Well, I believe it's better late than never." Mama folded her arms.

It was bound to happen sooner or later. I was a girl with a plan to get things done. Not to be taken lightly. If this was to be a battle between minds, it went without saying that I had the upper hand.

Hill House, then.

I could see the Royal Navy Dockyard from outside Hill House. The place had housed senior naval officers and several royals over the many centuries, so why not an irritating prince?

I arrived promptly. The royal naval coat of arms hung on the chestnut walls of Hill House. The short man who opened the door almost shooed me away the moment he saw me. I was used to it. I always carried an old newspaper with my photograph with me so they could confirm my identity.

"Sarah Forbes Bonetta—oh, you're *her*?" He looked me up and down. My attire matched the name of Queen Victoria's famous goddaughter: an eggshell-white pinafore, a billowing green dress, and a bonnet covering my hair. But for men like him, something about a Black woman dressed in the elaborate clothes of the upper class inspired suspicion regardless of the evidence presented. He brought out a monocle from his jacket pocket and began examining the newspaper. I tried very hard not to roll my eyes.

"Humph." Finally, he relented, straightening up. "I was told to expect a woman like you."

Which meant this inspection was entirely unnecessary. The greasy oaf. Plastering a smile on my face, I gave him a ladylike nod and showed him the letter.

Be at Hill House today at three o'clock in the afternoon so we can speak face-to-face.

And his royal seal at the bottom.

The doorman gave the letter a sidelong look. "Three o'clock? I thought the prince was expecting you later?"

"I did only as the letter instructed me to do." I absently tugged at my long white gloves. "It's almost three now." At least according to the grandfather clock in the corner of the foyer. I folded up the letter and slipped it into my pinafore. "It's not proper to be late for a meeting, especially with a royal. If you would please?"

"Uh, b-but—" The man's thin lips pursed in indignation, and a quick flash of worry in his eyes was enough of a clue that my suspicions were true. After a pause, he relented and showed me to the staircase that would take me to the second floor of the south wing, where Bertie was staying.

Bertie should have locked his door. I made sure the hallway was empty before I opened it to the sound of frenzied panting—both his and that of the woman he was crushing against the bed frame.

The prince's time in the military, however controlled, was certainly serving him well. Now that his clothes were strewn about the floor, I could see he'd gained weight; his back muscles were more defined, his arms thicker and hairier than the scrawny sticks I was used to. I wondered how long they'd carry on before they realized I'd already shut the door behind me.

I leaned back against the door with a casual yawn. That seemed to do the trick. The blonde woman, whose languid head had been rolling from side to side against the wall, gasped and immediately pushed the prince away from her. It took a few awkward tries to get Bertie to stop; he yelled when he glanced behind him and practically threw the poor naked girl off the bed.

"S-Sally!" he sputtered, and immediately searched for something to cover him, except his clothes were all on the ground.

I could barely hide my giggles as I watched him wrap a white bedsheet around his pelvis while his paramour du jour scoured the floor for something to cover herself.

"Sally, what on earth are you doing here?"

"Goodness, but didn't you summon me?"

Always catch your enemy off guard. Then *you* have the upper hand.

The letter I'd forged had done the trick—each word the same, except for the meeting time. Trips to Windsor Castle had provided me plenty of opportunity to nick his royal seal. It wasn't as difficult as one would think. Boy Jones managed to pilfer from Buckingham for years before they shipped him off to Australia. When his seal went missing, Bertie didn't tell his mother. He just did as always: got another one. Replacing items like he replaced women.

"You're early." With a scowl, Bertie slipped off the bed. After yanking the nameless woman off her feet, he began pushing her toward the door with nothing on but the skin she was born in. He shoved the rest of her clothes into her arms before shoving her out of the room.

"How cruel," I remarked, watching him adjust the bedsheet around himself. "There's quite a draft out there."

"She'll be fine."

I walked by the arched windows, the velvet curtains predictably drawn. If I were any other lady, this would be scandal. But Bertie and I had grown up together, and he knew telling the Queen what I'd seen would be bad for both of us.

The room had its typical royal indulgences. At the center of the room was a four-poster bed with golden tassels hanging from the green drapery. The floral wallpaper depicted red parrots perched on trees. In nearly every corner were grand leather couches, and above me a crystal chandelier hung from the ceiling, illuminating the perfectly clean red-and-green rug. The room had golden-framed mirrors stuck on the walls—everywhere. I wondered if Bertie much liked looking at himself when he was with women. A shuddering thought.

"Why on earth did that bloody doorman let you in early?" Bertie muttered.

Sitting down on one of the couches, I crossed my legs and gave him a sidelong look. "Well then, Bertie, why did you ask me to see you? Surely it wasn't to give me a front-row seat to . . ." I hesitated and stared down his sweaty body, from his chest to the bedsheet he was dragging around. "Whatever this was."

His face was still boiling red. I wouldn't look away even if he told me to. Instead of facing me outright, he positioned himself strategically halfway behind the green drapes of his bed. It was as good a shield as any.

"I wanted to ask you something."

"Certainly not my permission. You're old enough now to engage in a number of activities, though I don't think your fiancée would approve of this one." *Satisfying* wasn't a strong enough word to describe how it felt to see Bertie stiffen up. "Alexandra, I believe her name was? The Princess of Denmark."

Bertie cleared his throat to buy himself some time. He was hedging his bets. Finally, he opened his mouth again. "There are some establishments in London that a lady should never go near. Especially over on the East End."

"Do you mean a lady like the one who just left here with nary an undergarment on?" I pointed to the door.

Flustered, Bertie made sure the drapes properly covered him.

"Sally, I want to know where you went after my sister's wedding."

"Oh, that dreadful affair." I tugged at my gloves again. "Of course, congratulations to your sister, but goodness, there were times during the ceremony I felt as if I were attending a funeral. Needless to say, I went home to Mama as soon as I could."

"Well, my father casts as large a shadow in death as he did in life." And those shadows passed over Bertie's face as his expression wilted. His father had never approved of his gallivanting ways, and his tragic illness and death did nothing to sway his son, much to the Queen's sorrow. Was it rebellion or compulsion that kept a girl in his bed?

"I'm sure if your father could see you now—"

"That's not important." Bertie waved me off and turned his head from me, though not quickly enough to hide his shame. "Are you sure you went home after Alice's wedding?"

"Of course. Do you have any reason to believe I didn't?"

Bertie stepped out from behind the green drapes to reach inside the dresser drawer next to his bed. And in his hand . . .

"It looks like a playing card," I said, my tone neutral. "The Queen of Spades."

The one Harriet had slipped into Uncle George's pocket. Bertie was watching my expression very closely. I frowned and blinked as if endlessly curious.

"I found this in an opium den on East End. Aren't you always fiddling with this one?"

Rui was right. It was a bad habit I had to get rid of.

"It's a playing card." I scoffed as if he was a fool. Well, he was. A suspecting fool.

"I followed Harriet there. She told me it was *yours*."

I didn't so much as flinch because I knew it was a lie. His tell was a slight tremble in his bottom lip. "She did not." I said it confidently, confidently enough to shake his resolve. "And I can barely believe Harriet would find herself in such a place of ill repute."

"She was." The lift of his chin told me he was finally telling the truth. "I saw her with my own eyes."

"Then I guess the better question is, what in the world were you doing in an opium den in London after your own sister's wedding while your family is still in mourning?"

A direct hit.

"I—I told you," Bertie stuttered, his jaw locked. "I followed Harriet to the East End and—"

"And did she go inside the opium den like you did? And why follow the young lady Harriet in the first place? I'm well aware of your appetite for women, but surely you're not in the habit of stalking courtiers in the dead of night, are you?"

For several moments, Bertie didn't know what to do. I took advantage of the silence. Rising to my feet, I picked his trousers off the floor and handed them to him.

"Bertie, what in the world is going on with you?" I made sure to add a soft tone to my voice. "Opium dens and women? Really, what would your mother think if she knew about all this?"

"That's not—" Bertie started as I shook my head and turned away from him. "You've got me all wrong."

"And now you're accusing me of terrible things. How *heartless*." Sniffling, I walked toward the window, placing a hand on the curtain as if threatening to open it and expose his secrets for the docks to see.

Bertie wasn't a tough nut to crack. A mixture of embarrassment, shame, and confusion was enough to make him relent. "Harriet was there, but she said nothing about you. Nothing at all. I—I lied," he confessed.

I showed Bertie my most heartbroken expression. "Oh, Bertie . . ."

"Harriet said she was there following Captain George Forbes. She found him by accident on his way to the den and had to verify with her own eyes."

"What did you say?" I frowned in disbelief. "Harriet followed *Captain Forbes*?"

"I believe he's your uncle, correct?"

I covered my mouth with a dainty hand. "Uncle George? At an opium den. That can't be true! If the Forbes family ever found out . . ."

I knew seeing me in distress would make him believe he now had the upper hand. He puffed out his chest accordingly. Everything about him was so predictable.

"Don't worry, Sally," he said. "No one has to know about that night.

Not about your uncle George and not about me either. Let's just the both of us drop it."

If you catch my drift.

I nodded. "You're right. Let's just drop it."

And drop it we did. I left him to dress, my eyes lingering on the Queen of Spades for just a second before shutting the door behind me. Bertie was out of my way for now.

As for Captain Forbes, well, Bertie was more than a little mistaken. The Forbes family would know soon enough about his disgrace in the opium den. As a matter of fact, in a few days, they'd have a hearty helping of disgrace to deal with.

I'd make sure of it.

SIX

BEFORE I COULD take down Uncle George, I needed to see where I stood. I needed Harriet.

"James Vale has been arrested? Already?" I kept my voice low and calm because there were ears everywhere inside Windsor Castle. I made my trip the very next day. An excuse to see the nervous courtier. Funny, when I told Mama I had a present for the Queen, she was suddenly all too delighted at my socializing. I guess as long as the chores are done.

Outside in the gardens, shadowed by the crown of ancient turrets, Harriet and I stayed close to the stone balcony, our dull gray outfits darkening the carefully hewn evergreen hedges behind us. I stuck out a gloved hand expectantly. Shifting sheepishly on her feet, Harriet handed me a pair of brass binoculars.

Through them, I could see Queen Victoria sitting at a round mahogany table, covered by the sun underneath a canopy as black as her clothes. Her women puppets kept her company, including Harriet's mother, Mrs. Phipps, who had a Napoleonic ruby around her finger. Like that blasted fan she cooled herself with the day I met her. As long as it was French and inspired jealousy in the hearts of her friends, she'd obtain it somehow.

The women drank only the finest tea in the palace, but even from up where I stood, I could see they were doing most of the talking. The Queen's colorless lips barely touched her pristine porcelain cup. A dreary black veil covered half her face. Her apathetic expression was not the one of a mother who'd just married off her second daughter but that of a wife in mourning. Everyone knew why the Queen had become so mirthless and depressing. But nobody would dare bring it up.

Next to me, Harriet fidgeted with her fingers. "I'm so sorry. I didn't know Bertie would follow me—and that Vale would bring a gun! I mean—a *gun*." She repeated the last word in a breathless hush, peering down below because there were red-clothed soldiers guarding the Queen everywhere. Although I'd reminded her again and again that acting natural was paramount for this plan to go off without a hitch, Harriet Phipps had a tendency to melt down when things didn't quite go according to plan. And Vale being locked up mere moments after his attempted murder of Uncle George was not according to plan.

"I saw the whole thing outside from where I was hiding," Harriet explained. "Bertie had someone call the police to the den before running off."

"Of course because he didn't want to be caught there himself." I lowered the binoculars. I could use some tea myself. Or coffee. As much as I hated the stuff, it had a strange calming effect on me, sharpening my thoughts. "I suspect you followed up on Sibyl's furious, protective older brother?"

"I met with Sibyl this morning. She's already gone to visit her brother in custody. The poor girl's heartbroken, but she has no idea Forbes was ever in the opium den."

"Which means Vale has already been silenced. The Forbes family moves quickly." I'd already calculated the Forbeses' ability to pull some strings with the police to keep their son's shame away from the gossip pages. If things had gone to plan, Vale would have beaten the tar out of

Uncle George with Rui controlling the situation, ensuring Uncle George stayed in the den and Vale went free to spread the word of his sister's lover's debauchery. After word had spread, the Forbeses's plans to keep the matter silent would have come to nothing. Of course, things didn't go so perfectly. They rarely did.

It was a good thing thinking quickly was a particularly salient talent of mine.

"Uncle George is probably sobering up at home thanks to his overprotective parents. We'll have to draw him out again. As to how?" I tapped my fingers across the rock ledge. "Well. Let's just say I'll have to ensure Rui makes good on his promises."

I remembered to spread my lips into an amiable smile because Harriet scared easily. Showing my true face would only keep her jittering in her petticoat.

Harriet leaned in conspiratorially. "And then what?"

"Ladies."

Thankfully, Lord Ponsonby wasn't exactly stealthy. I could hear the dowdy man coming from a mile away; his breathing was always so loud. He wore a similarly uninspiring gray outfit to match ours, his black tie tucked underneath a sullen coat. "Sullen" was the dress code whenever Queen Victoria was near. Everyone at Windsor Castle knew to conduct themselves accordingly. As one of the Queen's main court officials, Ponsonby would never betray her whims. Then again, some court visitors, like Mrs. Phipps, slipped in a lavish item here and there.

Ponsonby stroked his white beard as Harriet and I both curtsied to him. "Her Majesty is going for a pleasant walk through the gardens and has requested your presence."

I peered down into courtyard at the little woman the nation had turned into their own private demigod.

I bowed my head, Harriet following my lead. "Of course, my lord."

I never did answer the girl's question: What happens after I draw Uncle George out of hiding?

I make him meet a fate far worse than Vale.

That the palace guards couldn't sense my bloodlust made me question their professionalism. They didn't even flinch as I passed by them, my shrewd eyes on the humped figure of the aging monarch. Like a floating ghost in a graveyard, Queen Victoria led her procession into a secluded part of the garden. We ladies marched behind her down an avenue of tall trees clipped of all their branches lest one catch and tear the sleeve of their monarch, or the train of her dress, God forbid.

"A pleasant walk," Ponsonby had promised us. This was more of a death march. The Queen's ladies were graveyard silent, each turning to each other, egging one another on to be the first to break the silence. I could see them fretting from where I stood—behind them, of course. Always behind them.

"Look how far you've come in just a few short years," Anne Schoen once told me, before her profession as an educator took her into the English countryside. "All because of Queen Victoria's kindly interest in you. How many days have you spent at Windsor or Osborne to stay with one of the officers in Her Majesty's household? How many times has the Queen sent for you herself?"

Anne was like her mother. She knew the works of Ottobah Cugoano and Mary Prince, but could not understand their anger because "times are different now." We're accepted now—the very point of abolitionism, according to some. We're *accepted*.

As the trees towered over me, casting shadows in the cloudy gray morning, I wondered if Queen Victoria would ask me to sing for them like when she'd fetched for me at Christmas. I was very bright and clever, and had a talent for music. It was what she told her guests whenever she made me sing. What was it last time? Something from *I Puritani*, that blasted opera. I ground my teeth but kept my gait perfectly measured in the presence of the other women. Measured. Ladylike.

Mrs. Phipps turned back and glared at her daughter next to me, giving the poor girl a start. There was no way any words could form under the stifling shadow of her mother's crippling expectations. Pressing her lips together, she played with her fingers instead, her eyes downturned. But what was a failed test for Harriet was for me an opportunity.

I cleared my throat rather loudly, because one didn't speak to the Queen until spoken to. It was just one of her rules. But the rules didn't say you couldn't snake her attention first.

"Dear Sally, you're not developing a cold again, are you?"

When Queen Victoria stopped we all did. When she spoke, we all grinned and found her words the most interesting ever spoken.

I shook my head. "Oh, no, Your Majesty. I've been of the best health for quite some time now."

The ladies nodded in approval—all except Mrs. Phipps, of course, who bristled and snuck her daughter another disapproving look, as if to say, *Why couldn't you have gotten the Queen's attention?* Just the usual overbearing, doddering nonsense from her.

"You're so far away. Come, walk near me."

The matter-of-fact tone in her voice wasn't any different from usual. Despite this, her words had a chilling effect.

The Queen had ordered it. I had no choice but to oblige. Mrs. Phipps's scowl deepened as I passed and soon she was squawking, now that the Queen had allowed the ice to be broken.

"That's good to hear, Sally. You always had such a weak constitution. I remember you developed a cold as a child no more than a few weeks after you first arrived to England."

After she made me dance. My fingers clenched into fists, but I kept my breaths measured despite the rising temperature.

"Why, even my dear husband was worried, as busy as he was."

I rolled my eyes, and I was sure Harriet's toes were curling with embarrassment. The other ladies smirked. They knew how hard the woman had worked to marry into the Phipps dynasty as well as anyone else.

"You were of weak constitution, you poor thing," Queen Victoria said.

No, I wasn't. Shortly after I'd arrived in England, I had one coughing fit. One. The air was colder and drier than what I was used to. And because of that the Queen had decided that England's environment would surely kill me. That's when she sent me to Freetown, Sierra Leone. To the Female Institution, under the direction of Miss Sass, the superintendent, leaving me to the mercy of her myriad corporal punishments. If an African like me was to gain a proper British education, then I would need to do so in an institution situated in my "native" land. That's what Queen Victoria had said.

But I knew the truth. I remembered all too well the first time I attended an official event at Windsor Castle. The irritated violinists at the front of the Audience Chamber had to play louder to cover up my coughing, but the gossip from the ladies and members of Parliament couldn't be so easily erased. The Queen was particularly irate that night.

I was sent to Freetown not even a week later.

"I hear that the Anti-Slavery Society has been asking you to make speeches at events, Your Majesty," I said to her, repressing the sudden whispers of anger within me. "Like the public event they're hosting next month hence. But you've been turning them down?"

"I'm not my husband," she said quickly, making the other women wince. True, abolitionism was more of an interest of Prince Albert's. At school, I was forced to memorize the speech he gave at Exeter Hall twenty years ago. Funny, he never seemed taken with me whenever I showed up to court.

"Besides," the Queen continued, "I have no desire for public engagements at this time."

I had a feeling, but I wanted to be sure. Knowing that there were limitations on the Queen's movements would be useful for whatever schemes I planned in the future. But there was more I needed to be sure of.

"And what of your children, Your Majesty? Are they well? Everyone was so down at the wedding."

Maybe I could find out what the Queen really knew.

"Princess Alice's wedding dress was beautiful," Mrs. Phipps piped up as if she was competing with me. Who was I kidding, she was clearly competing with me.

"Yes, it was indeed," added Mrs. Mallet, a close associate of the court, her raven hair always done to mimic the latest styles of women half her age. "A wreath of myrtle . . . and that orange blossom—"

"Oh, stop." The Queen waved her hand dismissively. "Anyone with a working head on their shoulders could tell she was miserable. They were all miserable. Sally is quite right."

I hid a smirk behind my hands as the Queen's ladies recoiled.

"They've all gone off now, out doing their business. They couldn't get away from me fast enough."

"Surely, Bertie sticks around," I said, and watched her expression closely.

It hardened. Sharper than the edge of a stone.

"Where that boy goes and what he does, I no longer have any desire to find out." The venom in the Queen's tone could have melted the bordering trees.

Well, that was good to know. The Queen's hatred for her son meant even if he did have a change of heart or found out something he shouldn't, he wasn't going to go running off to Mummy anytime soon. I had the upper hand there, then.

The pebbles of the smoothened dirt walkway crackled beneath my boots. I didn't realize I was smiling openly until I felt the Queen's eagle eyes on me. The moment I turned, her blue pupils contracted and she faced ahead, expressionless.

"As you know, I have three children myself," said Mrs. Phipps, turning the Napoleonic ruby around her finger. "My youngest, Albert Augustus, stopped sending me letters the moment he joined the King's Royal Rifle Corps at the top of his class." The other ladies looked like they wanted to groan. "Oh, how they can be so wicked to their mothers."

I didn't need to turn around. I knew Harriet's shoulders were slumping. Her mother prattled on about the children she was actually proud of until the Queen cleared her throat and the party fell silent with the caw of a crow.

"Indeed, children ofttimes forget their parents when they've gone away to school. You didn't write much either, Sally, when you were in Freetown. At the Female Institution, that is."

I physically recoiled hearing her speak the name. My muscles spasmed down to my toes. Though I covered it well, clasping my fingers together, I wasn't foolish enough to think the Queen hadn't noticed.

"The Female Institution has been rebuilt," the Queen said. "Did you know that, Sally?"

My heart stopped. The single crow soared above us and disappeared into the graying clouds. I couldn't answer right away.

"The Female Institution?" Mrs. Mallet turned to another woman.

"In Freetown," the woman whispered back. "Sierra Leone."

"Yes, in Sierra Leone." The Queen straightened her shoulders. "It's been years since that dreadful event happened. Eventually, the Church Missionary Society decided to build it back up again. They recently sent me word about it—and that the school has a new head: Miss Sass."

The blood rushed from my head, weighing down my entire body. My arms felt heavy enough to drop to the ground. The sound of that name from anyone's mouth—suddenly my hands stung, as if they were being strapped again. One whack. Another

And the Queen—she was watching me. She was watching me as intently as I ever watched her. Before I could compose myself, she cleared her throat. "Julia Sass."

"What?" I blurted out rather impolitely, if the reactions from the ladies were anything to go by. "I'm sorry," I muttered quickly.

The Queen held up a steady black-gloved hand. "It's quite all right. I assumed such a thing would shock you."

Yes, indeed she did. Which was why she said it—in front of everyone. Several pairs of eyes were now on me. The Queen had called me to her side for a reason. Furious with myself, I swallowed my anger and clasped my hands together.

"And Julia Sass is—"

"A family member of the *old* superintendent, Emma Sass," the Queen answered. "A cousin, perhaps. I don't know much about Emma's family and I never did ask, especially after that woman was fired. The Church Missionary Society is even thinking of renaming the school. I wonder how you feel about that, Sally?"

"Isn't that the missionary school Sally attended when she was young?" Mrs. Phipps chimed in unhelpfully. "The school that burned to the ground?"

All eyes were now on me. And perhaps it's precisely what the Queen wanted.

If guilt was what she was searching for now as we walked nearly side by side, she wouldn't find it. The squeeze of my throat and heat flooding my face were but a by-product of fury—the fury nurtured in that bottomless hell of an educational facility.

64

Those among the Queen's congregation smart enough to pick up the tension between us would surely spread the gossip around the elite circles. The Queen wouldn't want that, not when it came to me, her favorite card to play, proof of her everlasting mercy and philanthropy.

It was a dangerous game we were both playing.

"I'm so glad," I told her, and made sure I sounded it. "I'm sure the new school will be open for decades to come. Although I'm surprised you'd keep up with its news. It's only one school in Africa, after all. Unless you're keeping close track of me." I laughed. "But that would be a little smothering, wouldn't it?"

Some more light laughter to break the tension. Apparently, it wasn't entirely effective.

"The Queen adores you," Mrs. Phipps said with a cluck of her tongue as if she wanted to add *I can't fathom why.* "There's nothing sinister about it, silly girl."

"A silly girl she is not," Queen Victoria said quietly, and with a little smile added, "Though sinister? Perhaps only in your sense of humor, child."

A dangerous game. I returned the smile in kind. "I learned from the best."

SEVEN

THE FEMALE INSTITUTION was a proper educational institution that contributed greatly to my rearing. There, I learned how to hate. How to be cruel. How to kill. And all with a smile.

Sierra Leone. 1855.

"Sally. You haven't answered my question."

A year of awakening.

That year, on a particularly hot day, I stood in the superintendent's office, back straight with my arms out as she had ordered me to, but even before being summoned to this godforsaken room, I'd promised myself that this time, it would be the only order of hers I'd follow.

"Nor do I intend to, Miss Sass."

I knew the whack on my hands was coming. Emma Sass's cane bit into my skin, unforgiving as usual.

I knew what Sass wanted and I wouldn't give it to her.

I was twelve years old, student number twenty-four of the Female Institution in Freetown, Sierra Leone. A particularly revelatory place for me.

The superintendent's room seemed like a repudiation of everything she considered to be too African. It was a room of suffocating order and a deep hatred for color. Drab gray curtains covered the windows, with only a sliver of space to let the sunlight inside. The wooden planks for floors reminded me of the ships that carried me to England, and then to Freetown once the Queen had banished me here.

I'd spent four terrible years in the Female Institution, a school sponsored by the Church Missionary Society. Every day, the other girls and I would sit respectfully in the school chapel and listen to the preaching of a holy white man of God. God's plan, you see, was for all the savages of the world to achieve enlightenment. If all Africans would only learn from Britain's example, there would be fewer tribal wars, fewer enslaved, and fewer events of chaos that ripped parents from children, or even murdered the children themselves. We learned the Bible. We learned housework and sang music from a robust repertoire of the European classics. We learned how to be human. And when we rebelled, we learned just how intimately Britain's Christian education embraced corporal punishment.

Miss Sass set her cane down on her desk and picked up my copy of the Bible, which one of the teachers had shown to her in distress. Holding it out in front of me, she flipped through the pages she'd bookmarked, each defaced with a single sentence.

Their "love" for you is conditional.

"For years, the teachers warned me that your apathy had devolved into something quite alarming," Sass said. "Devilish, even. At first, I thought you were simply slow to adjust to environments, but this." She flipped to another defaced page. The same words in ink tore through the page, defiling the beatitudes. "Do you have no respect for the word of God?"

Sass said this with the fury of a British missionary staring down at the empty eyes of a child who should have been more *moldable* than this.

"*Their 'love' for you is conditional.* What does this mean?" Sass slammed my Bible onto her desk next to her cane, which clattered expectantly. Waiting. "Shall I tell the Queen that her goddaughter has been spending her days in school mocking the Church?"

"Tell the Queen?" My smirk was chilling, though I wasn't sure when it had become so. "I see teaching the Queen's African goddaughter for a few years has given you delusions of your importance. That you think the Queen would even bother to read the letters of a bottom-feeder schoolmarm like you—"

And as I devolved into laughter I felt the hot sting of a second whack. A third. A fourth. I clenched my teeth and squeezed my eyes shut, but the fifth ripped my lips apart as I gasped for air. I wasn't allowed to wipe the tears of pain dripping down my cheek. But I wouldn't do it anyway. I'd promised Ade that I wouldn't give anything of myself, least of all my heart. They didn't deserve it.

Their "love" for you is conditional.

Ade's last words were all I had left of him now. They were true then and even truer now. Miss Sass's cane caught me around my neck and lashed me around the eye. The other teachers would explain it away like they did all the other bruises. Each wound was a lesson, Sass had told me once. Another brick laid for the foundation of my rearing into the good God-fearing woman and wife I was destined to be.

I spent the rest of the morning in my dorm, lying on the floor bloodied while the other students were in their lessons listening to Bach. For a moment, my heart convulsed and I thought it would stop. I held my breath and felt it thump wildly against my chest.

I thought of Ade, too sick to fight his way to the ocean's surface. How terrified he must have been when he felt the beating of his heart grow more frantic, knowing there was no air to calm it. Knowing that the pain wouldn't end until he was dead.

I held my breath so I could understand his suffering, and not for the first time. I kept my lips pressed shut so I could feel his fear as acutely as if it were my own. I held it until I passed out. Until my body couldn't take it.

There were only a couple of dozen students being educated at the Female Institution. It wasn't difficult to devise a plan to get them out of the dorms.

"Samuel Crowther is here preaching in Freetown! Yes, *that* Samuel Crowther! Miss Sass has given us the day off. Let's show initiative by attending his sermon!" I shouted to them.

Most of them had been terrorized into asking no questions.

I waited until the school was empty. All the teachers had gone home to their children.

That night, the Female Institution burned down.

One of Sass's cigars had done the trick. As a missionary and especially as a woman, she would never admit publicly to using one. Well, she would have to now. Especially when she'd have to explain to her superiors at the Church Missionary Society why she'd left a cigar lit upon one of her students' open Bibles. How sickening, how very despicable that her carelessness had caused such an exorbitant loss of property and money.

Nobody had died in the fire. I wasn't a killer. Not yet.

All the lessons I had learned from the Bible had told me that I should have been wracked with guilt. Every novel I read had morals in it. The heroes and heroines always learned something. And if they did something bad, they would be struggling with their demons, unable to hide from what they'd done. My brain whispered to me in English: this should and would become my lifelong trauma. But that's not what I felt in that moment.

The relief that washed over me as I saw the building burn from afar made me feel as if Ade was thanking me in a way. The flames represented a rage I could no longer express to the outside world behind the cold mask they had beaten into me.

Sass's life was ruined. She was stripped of her title as super-intendent. Kicked out of the missionary fold. Her reputation in tatters.

A few days later, I wrote a letter to Queen Victoria telling her that I was unhappy in Freetown and wished to return home to her, and the Crown granted my wish.

That was truly the beginning. I embraced the pain—realized it needn't be my enemy, but my guide.

If Queen Victoria was curious to know the truth about what had happened to the school, she'd learn soon enough—the truth I'd learned while educated by the missionaries: that cruelty was the point and the method. And I would need to be even crueler if I was going to send my uncle George to hell.

EIGHT

DAMN RUI FOR making me search for him—*wait* for him. As if he was the one in control.

"I need to see your *master*," I told a redheaded boy I knew was one of his in the alleyway by the den. I'd already been here looking for Rui throughout the day. It was out of desperation that I circled back.

"Ain't here, miss" was all he said with a tart tongue. "Piss off."

I gave him the worst grimace I could muster, making him jump, and stomped away.

It was the kind of rudeness I expected in London. They were more open about their disdain for me here, which I found odd, since street markets were home to a far greater variety of people, all in close proximity. After I left the boy in the alley, I found them all here amongst the street folk: the Irish fishmongers and Italian fruit sellers. Dutch girls selling brooms and Indian chimney sweeps. Oftentimes I could tell them by their accents—like the German shoving clothes into my hands, hoping I'd buy.

"I'm sorry," I told him as politely as I could, and when I rejected him, he muttered a rather rude swear in his native language. I only understood it because I'd made it a point to learn all the iterations of "that word" in every language the moment I realized just how frequently it popped up around me in these lands.

People tended to divide themselves into castes even here. Mama and Reverend Schoen tried very hard to keep me from these parts and the working classes, who she considered to be the stewards of intellectual degradation and moral vice. And yet even here the English costermongers proudly separated themselves from the Jewish vendors selling the very same nuts in great barrows—and they didn't associate with those only who sold tea and coffee in fixed stalls. How dubious the reasons humans found to separate themselves from those they deemed different. It didn't matter that so many similarly struggled to fill their children's stomachs.

I saw them all here in this crowded street, shouting, trying to get the attention of passersby, all the while being distrustful of one another—distrustful of me.

It really didn't matter where I was in this land. I didn't fit.

But neither did Rui. Rui was a denizen of the darkness. He'd said so himself—that it'd taken him years to turn himself into such to accrue power and men willing to do his bidding. Perhaps that was why we never seemed to meet when the sun was up.

He made himself furiously difficult to track down. There wasn't any way to contact Rui unless he wanted to be contacted. So, after a stroke of genius, I took matters into my own hands. The sun was already setting by the time I made my way to West India Dock Road and stood in front of the expansive building, longer than it was tall: the Strangers' Home for Asiatics, Africans and South Sea Islanders.

Its two stories of windows glinted in the light of the dying sun as I walked up the front steps and into the center. Yes, it was a center, run by missionaries to house soldiers returning home, or waiting to be recruited by the East India Company to head out eastbound. I wasn't there when Queen Victoria's husband, Prince Albert, laid the foundational stone six years ago. I wasn't there when the first lascar was lured in by the

Christian missionaries who ran the establishment, concerned about their terrible treatment and lack of payment. I was here now to search the laundry rooms and dining halls—the bathrooms and libraries filled with Bibles translated into different Asian and African languages.

It had been two days since my verbal joust with the Queen and my wits were still alight with cunning. I was here because Rui was here. I knew he was. I'd followed him enough times to learn he came every second Friday.

I knew the area. My reconnaissance skills were second to none. The immigrants in the surrounding area were welcoming, but busy, too busy to notice someone like me stomping the ground, though this was one of those special areas in England an African girl wouldn't stand out so much anyway, princess or not.

That's why he didn't see me coming.

"Found you," I said, the moment I spied his figure on the second step of the wooden staircase leading up to the dormitories.

At the sight of me, Rui's eyes widened. It gave me a little devilish thrill knowing that just the glimpse of me could spark a reaction in him.

"Didn't think I had it in me, did you?" I winked.

His fingers immediately clasped around a brass pocket watch in his palm, but it was too late—I'd already seen it. He stuffed it hastily inside the pocket of his gray pants, but the silver chain still jutted out a bit.

He looked so . . . respectable in his white-and-black-striped vest pocket, his black hair combed down, his back straight as if he were a student at Eton College. This wasn't the Rui I was used to. He'd been engrossed in conversation with a bright-eyed man in a turban, speaking with a polite but stern tone in a language I didn't recognize. It was an important conversation about an important topic. I could tell that much. But I only managed to catch two words coming from Rui's mouth: *mērē pitā*. What did it mean?

I didn't have time to ask. Rui barreled down the steps and, without so much as a greeting, dragged me out of the building by the crook of my arm.

"W-Wait!" I stuttered, stumbling down the steps as Rui yanked me around like a child does a doll until the West India Dock Road was long behind me. "Unhand me, you pillock!"

He did, but only once he found an alleyway to throw me into.

We were on Commercial Street. I made note of the signpost because I'd long learned that being aware of one's surroundings was crucial to survival. I slapped Rui, but his jaw was set so tight, his high cheekbones could have cut my palm.

"How dare you drag me across the streets as if you were sweeping them with me," I whispered though we were alone in the dank alley.

"How dare 'I'?" Rui hissed, taking a furious step forward. He angrily combed his fingers through his hair, throwing it into disarray. "How dare '*I*'?"

I was loath to admit that I found the slightly venomous glint of danger in his dark brown eyes to be slightly exhilarating. I knew he wouldn't do anything, not to me. It was all bluster. But then, he truly was irritated. Squeezing his hands into fists, he turned away from me, calming himself down. Then he turned back, his black bangs ruffling in the slight breeze as he tilted his head.

"How did you know about Strangers' Home?"

"You mean how did I know your connection to it?" I folded my arms and for the first time realized the slight chill in the air had my hair standing on end. "I have my ways, as you have yours. I suppose I know more about you than you realize."

With a spiteful grin, Rui swaggered toward me, forcing me back until my shoulder blades could feel the rough brick of the shop behind me. He placed his hand against the wall just above my shoulder and shook his head. "You know *nothing* about me, little princess."

74

It was I who drew my face close to his, letting my cheeky smile nearly brush his lips. "We'll see how long that lasts."

A test of wills. I wondered how badly Rui could see in my eyes that I wanted to know more about him. How he'd attained such a crooked life, how he'd come to command his men with a powerful grip as surely as a captain did his army. It was Rui who relented, finally, with a sigh.

"Tell me what you want from me first," he said with a calm but still menacing tone. "Then we can have a debate about who violated who."

I scoffed. Violation? All I did was track him to some missionary halfway house. But now wasn't the time to argue. "I have something in mind for Captain George Forbes, but it will take men and resources—both of which you can provide."

"For a fee, of course." Rui lowered his head so that he was at my eye level. It took me a beat to realize my shoulders had flown up to my ears.

"Of course," I answered, exhaling, my flushed face defiant.

His eyes glittered. "*My* fee."

My heart thumped against my chest. "I wouldn't have it any other way."

Intrigued, Rui raised an eyebrow. "Oh? And your plan?"

Explaining my schemes always gave me a thrill, perhaps because of how clever it all sounded to me. The promise of mischief. Of mayhem.

"I will tell you," I said. "But first—do I have your word you'll follow through with your part?" I lifted up my hand for him to shake. "Without complaint and with complete and utter loyalty to me? Even if it kills the both of us?"

At first Rui was stunned into silence. Before long, his laughter echoed in the night sky. "You truly are twisted." But despite the condemnation in his words, Rui bent down on one knee, took my hand, and kissed it. My breath hitched.

"Luckily," Rui said, his tender lips still close to my skin, "there do exist causes in this world that I would gladly die for, princess. No—*Ina*."

Ade's words echoed in my mind.

Their "love" for you is conditional, Ina.

"Stop," I said quickly, pulling my hand out of his grip and turning my face from him. My body stiffened. "Don't call me that name." Why? Why did my body flush with discomfort?

It was my name, after all. My name slipping through someone else's lips.

It'd been a decade. The last time I'd heard that name, someone died.

"Forgive me. 'Princess,' then." And Rui stood and bowed.

It wasn't the mocking bow of a man who considered me his lesser. I should know—I'd seen enough of that in my lifetime. It was gentlemanly. Respectful.

I held my breath and thought back to the sellers in the London streets and their cruel sneers as I passed by. The ladies who glared at me while I walked near Queen Victoria at her behest. Queen Victoria herself . . . all those midsummers she had me sing for her guests.

Could this man be different? The possibility of it sent a pleasant but fearful shiver down my spine.

"I told you there was still yet further for you to fall. But I wonder if you're ready."

"Concerned?" I asked, remembering his warning in the opium den. But it hadn't been concern in his voice back then. That day, there'd been a hush of hunger in his expression as he waited for mayhem to unfold. I knew that hunger. I knew what happened when I let it grow out of control. And I knew the ecstasy that came with sating it.

Like, say, when a building burned down.

"The world says there are rules to follow, you know." He tilted his head. "There are many in *civil* society who would find you unseemly for bearing such ghastly thoughts."

"Damn the rules."

Rui came close to me and cupped my chin. His hands were large but careful. They were the kind that could strangle a man to death, yet be so gentle as to not leave a mark. Just as he'd done to the lustful nobleman who attacked me on the West India Docks the night we first met. That disgusting blue-eyed devil who ripped my dress and tried to taste my chest with his nasty, foul-smelling tongue. After months of following my sources to find and enlist the criminal prince, he'd revealed himself in a way he knew I'd never forget.

"I heard you've been looking for me," he'd said with a frightening grin after ordering his men to dump my attacker's body in the Thames. A frightening grin. An exhilarating grin. "Which means you may be as dangerous as I am."

How far would I fall? How far was the limit for a girl who'd lost everything that mattered to her? I couldn't say. All I knew was that seeing Rui murder a man in front of me that day was more bewitching than it was unnerving. It had made me wonder and dream things I didn't dare speak out loud, not even to myself. Perhaps that was my answer.

I drew his hands away from my face. "Make sure you're ready for tomorrow. Uncle George won't escape retribution this time."

Rui held his hands up in defeat, backing away from me with a crooked grin. "May God have mercy on his poor soul," he said with a little laugh.

"Please. That old man has never prayed a day in his life." I brushed off my sleeve and left the alleyway.

NINE

"OH, UNCLE GEORGE, this is awful! Bend your knees at least . . . ," I ordered him with kindness and concern as I dragged his sluggish flesh into the carriage with me. Uncle George moaned, his mind addled with drugs. Of course, he'd gone back to the same den, just as I'd predicted. Vale's arrest had only validated every lesson his privileged life had taught him—that no matter what wrong he committed, he'd never have to face consequences as long as his powerful family protected him—and they would always protect him.

I was counting on that.

Rui stuffed the rest of him into the seat next to me. Our eyes met, but he said nothing. There was nothing left to say. We both already knew the plan.

I let that lunk of an "uncle" tumble sideways onto my legs while Rui shut the carriage door and hit it twice, signaling the driver. The horses began clopping down the street.

"Ugh . . ." Uncle George rubbed his sweaty forehead, not even having the decency to keep his hands off my arm afterward as he tried to right himself. With his head on my lap, he peered up at me and squinted as if seeing me for the first time. "Miss Scarlet?"

My blood ran cold.

"Miss Scarlet, that you?" His lips drooped into a randy, lopsided grin. "Never thought you'd make it to merry old England . . . Come just for me, did you?"

Miss Scarlet was a name I remembered from my days on the HMS *Bonetta*. As the Forbes brothers used to play cards with their crew above the deck, they'd talk about their sexual exploits—the native women they'd conquered. From the sounds of the story George told that cold night, whatever Miss Scarlet gave to him, it wasn't given willingly. And he seemed quite proud of it. I doubted he'd even bothered to learn her true name.

It's what explorers of "high standing and breeding" did on their travels across Africa, India, and beyond, quiet as it was kept in the tales they told when they returned home to their families. But I was not Miss Scarlet. The sunken eyes in his pale, dirty face were playing tricks on him. Good.

I was counting on that too.

"Uncle George," I said as he began clumsily writhing his body like a peacock preparing to plume. "It's me, Sally. It's Sally," I repeated before he could grab my arms again.

He paused, his eyes wide. Then he grabbed my cheeks with his sallow hands.

"Sally? Sally?"

"I've come to help you, dear uncle."

He gave a relieved sigh. "Oh, I see." And when I pushed into his hands a folded piece of paper with white powder inside, he dropped back against my lap with a languid smile.

"You won't tell Mum and Dad about this, will you? I know I can count on you. Good girl, Sally, good girl. You've always been such a good girl."

His little triumphant chuckles were as addled as his mind as he sniffed the opiate.

I'd seen quite a few drug users in my time devising my plans and I'd come to learn something. In this rotten world, there were too many reasons to numb one's pain and too many options to numb it. If not opium, then alcohol. If not alcohol, then sex.

Did Uncle George have pain to numb? If so, what was it? The loss of his love, Sibyl, too young for his advances anyway? Or the death of the brother he would never measure up to? That I didn't know. I didn't ask. There was no need to. It was the British Empire that illegally shipped opium to begin with, smuggling thousands of tons of drugs into China to fatten their pockets despite the destruction and misery it wrought upon another country's people. The wars Britain fought and won to keep their illegal drug trafficking alive, to keep money and control flowing into British hands. How many lives did it ruin?

Was Uncle George high the day he killed Ade?

I'd learned once from my parents that one's ancestors would always demand generational blood for wrongs committed. This was recompense.

I must admit, I didn't believe Rui when he told me he owned properties across London—including three here in Whitechapel. But according to his men, he had deeds under a variety of false names. Well, if some could use crime to gain money and power, why not him?

The carriage came to a halt in the top end of the street. We'd walk from here.

"Sally." Uncle George resisted as the horse clopped off back around where they'd come because this particular street was too narrow for the size of the carriage. "Sally, what are we doing here." Uncle George could barely find his feet. But I could tell he was uncomfortable for another reason.

"Uncle, we're here for our appointment. Don't tell me you've forgotten already."

"Appointment?" He looked around. "Here . . . ?"

Whitechapel in particular had a bad reputation. I knew many of the stories I'd been told were embellishments of the elite who held prejudice toward its residents—the poor, the immigrant. I felt no safer in West-minster, Marylebone, and the other "posh" areas of London's West End than I did here in the East End.

The streets were, as expected, overcrowded. Adults and children, chickens, horses and cattle—they all seemed to have somewhere and nowhere to go at the same time, packed into a labyrinth of narrow roads and alleyways with barely any streetlamps to light the way through the foggy night.

This was the result of the grand industrial revolution, the grand lie the British told themselves about their civilization, a lie that could only live on ignoring the vast difference between the rich and the poor. With all their factories and machines ever encroaching into cities too small to house them, with the residents here being worked to death, barely able to scrape together food for the night. What was the point of so much ill-gotten wealth when the cost was too high?

If I were alone, I probably could have slipped by here unnoticed. I wore a dark shirtwaist and skirt that swept the filthy streets where sewage waste carried unspeakable scents into the air. It was nothing to me walking these dangerous streets at night. But what must it have looked to Uncle George, whose sunken, bloodshot eyes took in too many sights and too many smells? Uncle George, the captain who shiv-ered like a frightened rabbit when he bumped into a particularly burly costermonger?

"Oh, Uncle George, how has your mother been doing? Is she over her coughing fits?"

Idle chitchat was the best way to gauge someone's mental state. Uncle George, with his teeth chattering and his eyes darting around, clearly wasn't doing too well.

"Wh-What? Sally, what was that?"

Uncle George nearly tripped over his own feet. I pulled him back up again and began patting his frock coat when the man muffled his scream. I turned to where he was staring and could see what he did.

The lanky little boy with a black mask on his face. Harlequin, in the tradition of the Italian carnival. Rui certainly did have a flair for the dramatic and the money to pull it off.

I turned to Uncle George with a concerned look. "Dear Uncle, what's wrong?"

"D-Did you see that?" He pointed in the boy's direction, but the boy had disappeared into the crowd.

I shook my head. "See what? Uncle George, are you quite all right?"

He searched around for a minute longer before giving up, but the fright the child had given him had sunk deep into his bones. He would not so easily be rid of it.

"Come now, uncle," I said, and began dragging him again. The street hadn't stopped its rhythm. The specter was only George Forbes's to see. And that fact alone seemed to make him paranoid. He looked around him, his shoulders raised to his ears, like a man lost in a dream.

"Sally, what . . . what was our appointment again?"

"Uncle, this was your idea." I squeezed his wrist.

Smoke from men cooking raw meat on the street rose in wafts around our faces.

"It was?" He rubbed his nose. I could tell he wanted more of the very drug that made his mind slower to reason. "Was it . . . ?"

I found Rui's man in the middle of the street, his white face blackened by soot, sitting on a cage of chicks in a cluster, eating a morsel of bread, paying no mind to the chirps. There was one way to tell whose men were Rui's: the tattoos over their left eyes that cut into their eyebrows for those who still had them. Some might mistake the crossing lines for an *X*. The men themselves probably didn't know the curving lines stood for *chi*: the twenty-second letter of the Greek alphabet. Rui had probably meant for it to have double meaning. "Chi" had connections to his heritage. In China, it was linked to traditional medicine. But it also symbolized to Plato the existence of the soul, a force that connected all living beings. Proof that we were all connected. Through love.

Through hate.

"Let's wait inside here," I said, and pulled Uncle George inside a dirty red building Rui's man gestured toward with a flick of his head:

MR. POTTER
TAXIDERMIST

Painted in silver on a blue-painted sign.

"Sally!" Uncle George suddenly screamed because there the child was again, beyond the cages of chickens, hiding behind a vending both selling packets of tea. This child was wet. Water dripped from his hands and mask. The crowds were too busy to notice, too enraptured in their own affairs to notice the child pointing at him with a gloved hand.

It was then that when I looked into Uncle George's disoriented eyes, I saw that a memory was forming behind them. A memory of a ghost.

The rise and fall of Uncle George's chest quickened as the man stared at the goat's head mounted on the brick entrance.

"You know I never liked these places," Uncle George hissed as we walked inside.

"Did I?" I whispered, and closed the creaky door behind us. I certainly didn't remember the story his mother loved to tell of her little Georgie running from a social gathering in tears because of the bear's head exposing its teeth in the family's parlor.

The tight room was filled with tools for gutting, skinning, cleaning, and mounting animals, and each of them looked like rusted instruments of torture. Body parts lay on the shelves next to drugs and liquids. Cleaned skins lay on the front table, on display like loaves of bread at a bakery. The lone lamp in the corner cast shadows across empty eye sockets.

Uncle George didn't know where to look. He searched for some reprieve from the macabre nightmare, finding a little cellar door in the leftmost corner. But in a place of death like this, where could that door lead? Only deeper into hell. He stayed close to me.

"Sally," Uncle George said in barely a whisper, his hands trembling. "Do you have any more of the . . . the—"

Drug. He was too ashamed to speak it, but the twitch of his body and the way he batted at his ears erratically said enough. When I didn't answer he looked around.

"Where is the shopkeep?" he asked.

Gone. And paid handsomely for his troubles.

I made my way through the rusted steel instruments and animal bones to the lamp, pinching out the flame of the candle while Uncle George was preoccupied with the skulls that reminded one of the heads of demons. Casting us both into darkness.

"The light has faded," I said.

Uncle George whipped around. "Sally?"

"Wait here."

I hurried out of the shop. And while Rui's man blocked the door so Uncle George couldn't escape, I slipped around the back so I could watch the show from the little window by the display of bird skeletons.

The doorknob began rattling. Uncle George was trying to get out. That's why he didn't hear them coming up the stairs.

Five skinny boys in devil's masks and black gloves, soaked from head to toe. Water tracked from their wet shoes and their mouths, which gargled nonsense words. Five boys who chanted a name he must have thought he'd never hear again.

"Ade . . ."

They wore the wet, ragged clothes of street orphans. The same clothes the Forbeses had given to Ade when taking him aboard the HMS *Bonetta*. The same clothes he died in as he drowned in the ocean. Their shoes slurped and squished with each step they took toward him.

"I'm seeing things." Uncle George sluggishly rubbed his eyes. "This isn't real."

"You're a murderer, George," said one boy, tilting his head.

"You killed me."

"How could you kill a child?"

"Stop it!" He pressed his back against the floor, but the drugs in his system left him bare of his usual motor skills. Trying to reach for the doorknob, he fumbled and slipped to the floor instead. And beyond the devil boys he would have seen them—the dead animals strewn across the room. The horned skulls staring at him judgment.

"Child murderer."

"Monster."

"No!" Uncle George pushed through the boys and ran toward the desk, squealing with fright as he bumped into sharp instruments hanging from the low ceiling. "No!" His hands slipped upon a carcass in his bid to find a weapon to fend them off. As his knees knocked, finally, he picked up an abandoned candlewick and began swinging it wildly at them as if it were a weapon. "Stay away from me!" he cried, and swung so wildly he lost his balance and dropped to the floor. "I'm a hero of the Crimean." His red eyes were bulging. "You can't do this to me!"

A pause. The boys raised their right arms at the same time, each accusing finger pointed at him.

"You will not see heaven." I whispered it at the same time as they did.

Screaming, Uncle George ran to the cellar door in the corner and stumbled downstairs.

It was there, in that dark den of dead rats, that I locked him for the next twenty-four hours.

Some may understand me. Others won't. Sometimes, I wondered if I understood myself.

I certainly didn't understand the world of the British elite. Their skewed and cruel notions of what can cause shame and humiliation. The way they had turned hiding from view what they considered to be "shameful" into entire institutions. The way they had criminalized sickness.

I didn't understand the world of the British elite, but I knew how to turn their grotesque preoccupations into weapons to use against them.

Rui's man released the old navy man only once his senses had completely gone. Uncle George was shoved into the streets, his drug withdrawal in full swing, and by the time members of high society found him, he was wandering Trafalgar mumbling about dead boys.

"No, don't leave me alone, Mummy." He clutched at his mother's pearls as the doctors tried to restrain him in his bed. He'd already attacked her once inside, which prompted the old woman to call for more security. The private hospital inside Queen Street, Edinburgh, certainly could provide it. But the drugs he pleaded for they could not provide.

"Do what the doctors say, Georgie," ordered Lady Forbes sternly, dressed in her full attire because even in this utterly humiliating moment she needed to show off her wealth and prestige.

"How long am I to stay here?"

And when Lady Forbes refused to answer, Uncle George let out an anguished wail.

I stood at the door, as still as Ade's specter as Lady Forbes cried into a handkerchief. Uncle George had committed many crimes. I didn't consider becoming addicted to drugs one of them. But his family did. The shame of it all for Lady Forbes—shame that had been on full display on the city streets before she and her husband had had a chance to hide it from their friends. Rumors were already running rampant. First the indignity of the Vales and now this. How was she to hold her head up at tea parties?

You see, that's all these people cared about. Not life or death. Humiliation. Lady Forbes didn't ask about her son's health. Only that the doctors kept what they did to him in the confines of the hospital a secret.

Disgusting. But what else could I expect from Queen Victoria's kingdom? An unequal, unjust society filled with absurd ideologies.

Perhaps delivering Uncle George to this place made me just as unjust, but I didn't let myself indulge in anything akin to guilt. All I could see was Ade in my mind's eye, smiling at me. Telling me to embrace the moral gray.

Even if it meant I would one day be hated.

"Sally." Uncle George, now completely wild from his drug withdrawal, finally noticed me in the room after his mother had left.

"I'm sorry, Uncle George," I said, clasping my hands against my chest, faint from the horror of it all. "I had to tell your mother about everything. I had to help you."

By now his mind was still playing tricks and his memory was faulty. He wouldn't have been able to put the pieces together even if they'd fallen into his lap.

He struggled against the doctor's hands. "Tell them, Sally. You were there. You were on the ship—a good little girl. Tell them, I didn't kill anyone."

I stared at him, a child murderer in denial, more desperate for a fix of drugs and validation than justice for the life he'd stolen so callously.

"But I was there, Uncle George." I bent down and whispered in his ear out of everyone's earshot, "I was there when you murdered that little boy . . . when you drowned him in this ocean. When I learned that there was no such thing as a 'savior' in this world. Do you deny this?"

He breathed in. He breathed out. His eyes glazed over and in that moment I knew he could see the shadow of that boy's face. His expression as his body sank below the ripples of the waves. But he shut his eyes again and shook his head, more forcefully this time. He shut himself to the truth. He showed no mercy. And so neither did I.

Cruelty was the point.

I parted my lips. "*Ibi redibis non, morieris in bella peribis.*" I didn't translate it. If he knew his Latin, then he already knew what I'd said.

Here you will never return. You will die in this war.

He was screaming my name even as I left the room. Screaming, cursing, and begging for a fix. The doctors had their hands busy. Neither they nor Uncle George noticed the card slipping from my hands and onto the floor. The Queen of Spades.

"You were ruthless, as expected," Rui told me that night when I met him at the West India Docks. We watched the steam rising from the ships, the sea breeze ruffling clothes.

I smirked. "And your boys did their part."

"They were only too happy to oblige—with a bit of payment, of course."

They made more that night than they would have pilfering pockets, that was for sure.

"And now it's time for you to do something for me." Rui reached into his black jacket and pulled out a small piece of paper. Squeezing it between two fingers, he handed it to me.

I looked at it suspiciously.

"You remember the deal we struck," Rui said, putting his hands into his pants pocket. "Remember, this isn't a one-way street. I help you. But I require something in return."

"I'm well aware of that," I said, snatching the paper from his fingers. Only a name was written there in messy cursive.

John Brown

"Who's this?" I looked up at him, an eyebrow raised, but Rui didn't answer. "Not the abolitionist John Brown?"

"No. This John Brown is an old servant of the late Prince Albert. Use your connections to get him to London by any means necessary. Into the Queen's court." Rui's black hair fluttered against his forehead. "Once I've confirmed he's arrived, I'll continue bankrolling your reign of terror."

"Terror." I laughed a little when I said the word. But then Rui grabbed my hand and pulled me toward him. He raised my fingers to his lips, kissing them lightly before looking up into my startled eyes.

"But isn't that precisely what you want, little princess?" He slipped his arm around my waist, pressing the small of my back with his hand. Forcing me to him.

Yes. I wanted terror. Chaos. And maybe a little more than that. My body flushed as Rui's mouth brushed my neck.

"Get him here within one week." His breath prickled my ears. "You can do that for me at least."

"That's a tight timeline. Is he another man of yours in secret?" I asked, annoyed at myself for how breathless I sounded. I couldn't catch my breath. Not with his body against mine.

"That's for me to know." He pulled away from me, rubbing my cheek with a finger before stepping away. "I'll be waiting."

Rui was right. This really was a dangerous game.

An excited inhale passed through my lips as I smiled.

TEN

A DEAL WAS a deal. As much as Rui helped me with my schemes, I had to help Rui with his. I didn't mind giving him a hand with whatever gambit he was planning—as long as the price wasn't too high.

Bring this John Brown into the Queen's circle. Should be easy enough.

Bertie's attendants had a habit of reading all letters sent to him before giving them to their prince. This request has to be on the quiet. It would work out for both of us that way.

I was Mrs. Schoen's obedient little doll for the next few days, studying and doing my chores in Chatham. One day, when I was helping Mama plant roses in the front yard, I was greeted by this jewel of a conversation.

"People everywhere are talking about what happened to Captain George Forbes. Even out here." Mama wiped the sweat forming round her neck under the hot afternoon sun and gave a paranoid glare at our neighbors down the street. A few of them had taken to gossiping about us, but that was a normal occurrence here when you were the only Black family in the area.

Kneeling in front of the dirt next to our front porch, I ran my fingers along a rose petal. "Gossip tends to spread very quickly." I said it without emotion.

"Yes, and that's what's so awful about it!" Mama shook her head and bent down next to me. "Oh, the poor Queen! The other day at the coffee shop, I heard Mrs. Wilkinson cluck about the Queen's poor company."

I stooped over because pretending to smell the rose helped hide my grin. All of it would lead back to the Queen. And soon there'd be more to damage her reputation.

Mama sighed. "I just hope Her Majesty is okay."

My grin turned into an irritated scowl. There she went again. "You know, Mama, sometimes, to me, it seems very much like you would rather be the Queen's adopted goddaughter in my place." I snorted. Or maybe she was just bored because her husband was never around.

Mama gave me a soft knock on the side of my head with her knuckle. I pursed my mouth closed as she continued gardening and tittering on about the Queen. I didn't know what it was about Mrs. Elizabeth Schoen that made me act like such a brat. She wasn't my mother. My mother had been brutally murdered years ago.

But although I couldn't admit it to Mrs. Schoen, my heart shook whenever this woman bought me clothes or coaxed me into drinking my favorite tea. I complied whenever I remembered she did all this while her husband was away. And he was always away. Or maybe they just looked alike. Something about the smoothness of her round nose and the delicate curve of tiny ears that reminded me of my real mother, long dead.

I shook my head. This was all just sentimental nonsense. I had to get back to my real work.

Once the chores were done, I was off to London. Pall Mall.

I'd always felt Pall Mall was an interesting contradiction. Separated by garden and fence from the squalid pandemonium of the London roads, Pall Mall held a kind of tranquility—at least from the outside. It was a street that housed some of London's most magnificent buildings, where only men of standing could frequent their classical architecture.

But what did those rusticated stone blocks hide from the public? Gentlemen's clubs. Of every kind. The chaste and the debauched. Pall Mall was the beating heart of a wealthy man's social life. Marlborough House, which was to be the Prince of Wales's main residence once he was officially married to Alexandra of Denmark, was hidden from civilian sight, tucked away in the corner between St. James's Palace and Green Park.

Perfect for the so-called Prince of Pleasure.

"Miss Sarah Forbes Bonetta," the doorman introduced me as I entered the corridor. As if anyone was listening.

I smirked as I floated elegantly through another set of double doors, into the main hall. What a nice gathering Bertie had managed to put together underneath the two-tiered chandelier hanging from the vaulted ceiling. Nearly all were young people who'd already debuted into society. Hoop skirts of every bright color took up space on the marble floor, false curled hair under silk bonnets. Young men's lounge jackets were strewn to the side, bow ties just a little unkempt, enough to tantalize. While some violinist played music in the corner, many of the young guests paired up, holding gloved hands, chatting, touching, and downing whatever wine was passed to them by discreet servants—discreet, because the servants knew as well as the youths that whatever drugs they passed between them had to be kept quiet from their parents.

"Sally! Sally, is that you?"

I instantly recognized the woman, though she was half blindfolded in silk. Giggling, she slipped a young man's hands off her waist as the loose blindfold finished tumbling down her brown neck. There were nail marks on his. I didn't want to know whatever game she was playing. The young man didn't seem to want to stop groping her. She had to elbow him in the gut before he got the message.

"Lady Gowramma!" Waving my silk hand fan, I moved to greet her only to have her grab my hand and pull my arm to the side. She looked me up and down, as she usually did whenever we crossed paths at functions. "I dressed especially well for you, for I suspected you'd be here," I added with a little chuckle.

The devil's red from head to toe. The pleated silk neckline of my dress hung off my sharp shoulders. Gowramma touched her bottom lip, appreciating the sight of my slender bare arms flowing out from underneath the short sleeves.

"You look delectable as usual." She took my hand and spun me around as if leading me in a dance. "You know I've always been strict about how you present yourself, for good reason. The most important reason being that it drives the little rich white girls here crazy when you look unspeakably gorgeous."

She poked me in the ribs and flicked her head to the side. Sure enough, there was a pack of them sneering at us from the other side of the room.

"I've been in this country longer than you," said Gowramma. "I know how things work in English high society."

"If I recall, you were presented to the Queen the same year I was."

"But then you went off to boarding school in Africa. It's the time spent that counts, you know."

We'd had this debate before: who had spent more days in English captivity, though for Gowramma it was always in jest. I doubted she saw living here as captivity at all. Despite the British ruining her father, the ruler of Coorg, he had apparently always been grateful to the British who helped him retake his kingdom from Tippu Sultan. Alliances bred strange bedfellows.

Sometimes, Gowramma would tell me stories of her past—the English manners of her numerous siblings, her father's habit of dressing her in the European style. From those tales, it was clear to me that

Anglophilia was something of a norm among the Coorg elite. These days, from what I could see, she rather liked her new life in England with her wrinkled white husband thirty years her senior—John Campbell, a military man.

"How is your senile better half?" I asked as she patted down her long brown hair from the center part. "I take it the Lieutenant Colonel doesn't know you're here?"

She waved her hand dismissively. "Oh, he's at home with Edith. I told him I was having theater night with the girls."

"And if Edith needs anything?"

"The nannies will handle it, I'm sure." She exchanged a lustful glance with a young man whose face was half-obscured with a feathered masquerade mask.

Rather flippant way to treat her daughter, but I wasn't one to judge. The idea of having a child sent chills down my spine worse than the thought of being a kept woman. Gowramma and I were peers in too many ways and yet so different at the same time. Like me, she was a former princess, born to the last ruler of the Coorg kingdom in India. Like me, she was taken by the British military and presented like a trophy to the Queen. But she didn't seem to mind it at all. Only two years older than I, she was already a mother. And while Queen Victoria had wanted her to marry a fellow Hindoostani, she had her sights set on the good old-fashioned wealth of a European nobleman. Her daughter, Edith, was a product of her persistence, though of course the child was nowhere to be seen here.

I liked Gowramma. Her innate ability to defy the odds for the sake of whatever fun she could still have as a married woman was commendable. But sometimes my fellow princess reminded me of who I could have been had I been a little more compliant—even *grateful* toward the Queen. And that led to visions of a nightmarish future should I fail to hold on to the rage that glued me together.

"I'm looking for the Crown Prince of England." I peered through the thick crowd. "You haven't seen him here, have you? Although I wouldn't be surprised if you haven't." I tugged the blindfold off her neck. "Seems like you've been a little busy."

Gowramma snatched back the blindfold, smiling secretively at the servant who passed by, averting his eyes. "Oh, I'm sure Bertie's around here somewhere, buried in women." She paused and gave me a sidelong look. "But whatever could *you* want with him?"

"That's my business." I folded my arms. "Feel free to carry on with yours, dear."

Before I could leave, the Indian princess gripped my wrist and pulled me close. I could feel her tongue close to my ear. "Aim high, dear Sally, but not too high. You know the rules."

Rules. Yes, that was the nightmarish future she reminded of. One filled with their rules.

"Your conception of what and who are considered 'high' needs some adjustment." She gave these people far too much credit. I rolled my eyes and continued through the hall.

Some gentlemen stretched out their hands and offered me a dance as I passed as if it was some prize for me. As if I should have been grateful to dance with such louts. Still others looked on and whispered behind their hands:

"Is that the fabled African princess?"

"Queen Victoria's ward?"

The hairs on my arms stood on end. I clenched my teeth and hid my scowl behind a silk fan, wishing I could use it as a weapon. The sharp tips would be put to good use.

"Imagine getting to have a dance with her—I can't imagine a better parlor story."

I heard every word. Which is why when the young man looking for a tale to tell approached me for a dance, I very stealthily and quite by accident stomped my heel into his foot.

"Please excuse me." I bowed my head as tears of pain dripped from his eyes.

It was an odd sensation, existing in this liminal space, belonging nowhere, and yet so hypervisible I couldn't escape them. Even if they hated me, they wouldn't let me be. Ironic. As if my very existence was necessary for the forging of their own identities, they kept me locked by their gazes, burdening me with the responsibility of their contradictions. Their eyes hungered with both disgust and obsession, longing and fear—opposites that laid the bedrock of their imperial design. The rules of British society never made any sense. Why live by them?

I looked for Bertie, but he was not among the bouquets of flowers by the walls or the tall candelabras a safe distance from the red velvet curtains. I knew he'd be where the true action was, so I continued to push past perfumed bodies until I reached the front of the hall, monitored by the golden-framed portrait of Queen Anne, more than a century dead.

"May I have this dance, my lady?" Another offer.

"Maybe next time. Forgive me." I didn't even turn. I'd already spied cigar smoke seeping out of the door in the corner. The true action . . .

"Surely just one?"

I felt his hand gripping my shoulder, and it wasn't some light touch. His fingers pinched my bare flesh as if he meant to tear off an arm. Shocked, I whipped around, fighting the impulse to swing at him.

"Didn't I tell you—?"

The young man nearly yanked off my hand, pulling me into a dance I didn't want—this boy with cheeks so sunken and lips so parched it looked as if he hadn't had a meal in days. His long face stretched into a grin as he spun me around, satisfied with the attention we were getting from the others, who watched us in awe and amusement. Despite my seething glare, his green eyes sparkled with victory. They were hungry. But not the kind of hunger I'd seen in any of the bored young men and women looking for a bit of a thrill. It wasn't lust either. I was old enough to recognize the musty smell of a man in heat. This wasn't that.

He was like a hunter who'd captured his prey. That was it. It was as if he'd been waiting for a deer with a crossbow in hand. An unnerving shadow passed over his expression.

Familiar. Something about him felt familiar. Was it his sharp facial features? The aura of hateful arrogance?

"Student number twenty-four, correct?"

I flinched, shocked. That was my number in the Institution.

I pursed my lips together for a moment. Just that act alone made his crooked smile wider, his back straighter. Despite years of training my face to do as I pleased, I was giving far too much away, but I couldn't help it. I hated being surprised.

He was tall and lanky, but as he danced, he didn't seem to care about maintaining a dignified posture—imposing was what he aimed for. His hands held mine just a pinch too tightly. But even that pinch felt calculated.

"I'd heard rumors you'd returned to England." His curly mop of light brown hair covered part of his fan-shaped ears. "Good to see the weather suits you here. I can't say I'm used to it quite yet. I don't think my mother told me enough about England to prepare me for it."

"And what do you mean by that? Who are you? Are you from Free-town?"

Now that I thought of it, his accent wasn't the same as all the other English here. Part of it sounded familiar. English-speaking Brits who grew up in Western Africa all had this obnoxious quality to their voices. Even back when I was a child living with my clan, I saw enough of them to parse out the differences. It wasn't like us speaking English. Maybe because there wasn't really anything at stake for them. Rather, their accents always reminded me of the careful, strategic overconfidence of the short, stumpy men I'd seen working as colonial administrators and pastors. They struck each syllable with a kind of clumsy presumptuousness that you weren't allowed to laugh at despite having every reason to. Of course, even before I was torn from my parents, I knew I'd be thrown in jail if I ever actually laughed at one of them.

There were plenty of them in Freetown too.

"I asked you several questions." My whisper was menacing, perhaps more so because of how I managed my expression into a polite smile.

And he matched them both. "Oh, trust me, I heard them."

He didn't seem to mind that I ripped my hands from his grip. In fact, he was amused.

"Let's do this again sometime, student number twenty-four. I have no doubt we will."

Why did that amicable smile hit me like Miss Sass's cane across my hands? I bit the inside of my cheek, my body flinching instinctively as he bowed his head and walked off.

ELEVEN

THAT BOY WAS from Freetown. And he knew something. He left dread in his wake as he disappeared into the crowd. Who was he? What did he know about the Institution?

What did he know about *me* at the Institution?

It couldn't have been nothing. It's not like my schooling was a secret. I was the Queen's goddaughter. Very little about me was secret unless I strove to make it so. Was I projecting my own sadism onto that irritating little grin of his?

My mind started racing before I realized I'd stood in the same spot for too long. The spectacle of the dancing African princess was over. The guests had already gone back to the drugs and drinks. I had to get back to my business too. Unearthing the boy's secrets was just another item on my list, to be crossed off in the near future.

I turned once again to the door no one seemed courageous enough to enter, the one with cigar smoke seeping out of the corners. Making sure no one was watching, I entered.

Now, how had Bertie snuck in cabaret dancers? I shook my head in disbelief. In the center of the small drawing room, Bertie enjoyed them well enough, lounging with a cigar in his mouth and his legs spread in a caveman V on a love seat across from the door. The love seat, a few paces in front of the door, was just big enough to fit the three women who clinked wineglasses and whispered seductively in his ear. It wasn't enough space for Bertie's smoking gentleman friends from the army, though. But they didn't seem to mind. Instead, they slumped behind the couch when the cabaret dancers lifted up their frilled skirts on their makeshift stage—not too much, of course. Just enough to show their long white stockings and a hint of white thigh. The boys went crazy, hollering like the hooligans they swore they weren't.

Right when the show became a little too hot, I slipped in front of him.

"Your Highness! We meet again!"

Bertie's jaw dropped as I stepped on his vest, which had been abandoned on the carpeted floor. He pulled his hand out of his pants and a pillow out from behind him to immediately cover his lap. For what reason I, in all my girlish innocence, couldn't fathom.

"S-Sally," he bumbled, his face flushed. "Wh-What are you doing here?"

"You'll forgive the intrusion. I know you're incredibly busy with these—actresses, I presume?" I tilted my head and pointed to the girls now standing up pin straight, furious, on the love seat. He has certainly had a weakness for actresses. "Nonetheless, I have something of grave importance to discuss with you, Your Illustrious Highness."

I bowed deeply. His red ears told me he didn't expect me to catch him twice in one week. "I wasn't expecting to see you. I don't recall inviting you—"

"Nonsense. I'm always invited." I took a step closer to him. Our knees nearly touched. "Besides, this really is a matter of grave importance. It's about your grieving mother, you see—"

"Sally, love!" Bertie jumped out of his chair, leaving the women frustrated, and grabbed me around the crook of my arm. "Why don't we talk somewhere more private, eh?"

Too bad. I wasn't quite finished killing the mood. But he pulled me into an empty adjacent room regardless, away from the bustle of the party. The air was musty and the room was somehow still dark despite the oil lamps gathered around the pristine pool table. Yet another room meant for only a chosen few. He shut the door in a huff.

"What is it, then?" he said, loosening the scarf around his turned-up collar. "Mother found out I was here and sent you to throw something at my head? A bust of my father's?"

His face was flushed. I knew the mention of the Queen would disturb him. I turned from him, staying near the dark mahogany walls. "Now, why would you think she'd send me to do something like that?"

"Telling me off is all she does these days, when she's even in the mood to see me." Bertie strode over to the pool table and gripped its wooden ledge. "Ever since Father . . ."

He fell silent. I could see his knuckles paling from how tightly he gripped the table. He didn't need to continue. Everyone in the Queen's inner circle knew what had happened in the days leading to his father's death. That whole affair with Nellie Clifton, his father's fear that he could have impregnated her, the scandal that would rip through England if an actress gave birth to the young Crown Prince's illegitimate child. Was it a coincidence that his father fell ill so soon afterward? Queen Victoria didn't think so.

I had to approach the matter delicately. "I know full well what has happened to the royal household after the Prince Consort's death." I tugged the dark red drapes with a tender touch. "The sorrow. The strange rituals as if to make His Majesty's memory real."

Like how the Queen would wear nothing but black; even at her own child's wedding, she flitted around like a wraith. I'd seen, once, at Osborne House, Prince Albert's portraits draped in black cloth as is to keep his spirit from crossing over to the other side. I heard from the servants inside that they'd been ordered to keep his private rooms pristine—as if the Queen's husband would return to them one day.

It wasn't love. I didn't buy that it was. For had the Queen truly understood love, then she couldn't have so hastily torn me from my people. It felt something more akin to obsession and dependence. I saw it in too many couples, brought together by duty and compulsory procreation. How quickly their minds became feeble as they went through the insipid rhythm of marriage and the doldrums of the everyday.

I'd seen my parents butchered, my friend drowned, and my clan torn asunder. But over one dead husband, the Queen had vowed never again to be seen in public until her own dying day. And how many families had the Crown decimated? How many nations had the British Empire brought to ruin? She was acting like a child.

"It's why you can't stand to be around her, isn't it, Bertie?"

When I said his name, Bertie looked at me, hesitantly at first, before letting go of the pool table to face me. He wasn't an ugly child at least. I could see why those women were drawn to his long, handsome face, light eyes, and sculpted chin. They didn't see what I did: the contemptibility born of birthright and privilege. He was at once angry at me for being right and yet still looked to me for guidance. I wasn't surprised when he grumbled childishly in the affirmative.

"She's miserable," he told me, biting his thin pink bottom lip. "She's making us all miserable. The whole household."

"But Bertie: she is a woman without her husband. Without her greatest love. She just needs support, that's all." I moved close, my dress sweeping across my ankles.

Bertie flashed a bitter smirk. "She doesn't want my support."

"It doesn't have to be yours. There is a man that I believe could carry the burden. Mr. John Brown from Balmoral. I was told of him by some of the courtiers."

Harriet. She was good on these occasions too. John Brown was Prince Albert's outdoor servant, devoted to his last day. The Queen knew of him. Remarked upon him fondly. Well, she loved her Highlanders. I wonder how much of this Rui already knew.

"Yes, I know of him. My father trusted him and held him in high esteem." Bertie stroked his chin with a finger. "He's a strong-willed Scot. A man's man, loyal to the Crown."

"John Brown is the man to draw Her Majesty out of her morbid state, I just know it."

I took a chance and touched his arm, just beneath his elbow. It surprised him. Anything gentler than my usual annoyance and disdain for the childish prince would shock anyone. His clear blue eyes dilated as he sucked in a breath and pursed his lips.

He was looking at me. At my soft nose and large eyes. At my mouth. At my beauty.

"Are you sure he could help my mother if he was at her side?"

I nodded. "If you run the idea by Lord Ponsonby, I'm sure he would agree too. It would show your leadership. Show that you're taking charge in these matters, like a Crown Prince should. You are Prince Albert's eldest son. I'm sure the entire nation would appreciate it."

He swallowed, his Adam's apple bobbing against the tight skin of his neck. And as he silently nodded, I breathed a sigh of relief.

Snapping out of his thoughts, Bertie cleared his throat and straightened his back, as if remembering a royal was supposed to look the part. He smoothened out his golden hair. "I am intrigued by your suggestion and will take it into my consideration."

In other words, he would do exactly as I said and present the solution to Lord Ponsonby as if it were his idea all along.

I gave him a little thankful smile and bowed my head as he walked toward the door. Soon this John Brown would be on a boat to England.

Whatever it was that Rui wanted from him, this at least meant our partnership and my plans could continue.

Bertie's hand lingered on the knob for a fleeting moment before he turned back around. "Oh, this conversation does remind me," he said. "Sally, make sure you go to Windsor Castle before the night ends. I heard that my mother's been asking for you of late."

Windsor Castle again? I narrowed my eyes. "Pardon?"

"Sorry, I might have forgotten to tell you. I was so wrapped up in the—" He gestured toward the door, the debauchery outside, before shrugging affably. "But it's not a problem, is it? Just pop over there now while you're in the city. You don't mind, do you?"

He didn't wait for my answer. With a sheepish smile and a wink, before I could prod him any further, he left me in the smoky room.

"God, this place really has become a casket, hasn't it?" I whispered to Harriet as she showed me through the silent hallways of the castle. It never ceased to amaze me every time I entered the castle. Nobody spoke. Even the footmen were dressed in mourning black. The female courtiers were given more choice and kept their show of suffering to a despondent gray. But if they were suffering in truth, they certainly didn't show it:

"You've heard what happened to Captain George Forbes," I heard one whisper as I passed, her eyes following me. "He was close to Her Majesty, wasn't he?"

Another courtier nodded. "More than one of Her Majesty's close friends has met a horrible end. My sister says they've been cursed."

I stifled a grin. In a way they were right. But soon my flesh crawled from a sudden chill as Harriet ushered me inside the Queen's sitting room.

Queen Victoria, the head mourner in a never-ending funeral, sat at her desk, the layers of her black silk taffeta dress spilling onto the floor. Her poor young ladies-in-waiting stood behind her dutifully but stiffly as she wrote one of her letters with black ink and quill.

"Your Majesty, Sarah Forbes Bonetta," Harriet announced me, and I raised an eyebrow in her direction. She sounded so different here. So solemn and formal—not the usual bumbling ninny shadowing me, begging for orders. Her hands were shaking as she clasped them together, waiting for the Queen's response.

None came. The Queen continued to write her letter. Always with her letters. But somehow that was a response in and of itself. Harriet bowed and, after giving me a furtive *good luck* glance, left the room.

Portraits of Prince Albert were everywhere, as were the black veils meant to signify the Queen's sorrow. Only a woman so self-involved could turn her home, her child's wedding, into a reflection of her own grief. Wind whistled eerily through the arched window, slightly ajar. I was to stand here in silence until the Queen was finished with her letter.

Finally, the paper was folded. The quill in its well. She handed the letter to one of her ladies behind her, who hurried out the door to deliver it. And when she finally looked up at me, I bowed accordingly.

"Sally."

"Your Majesty."

Silence. The Queen sounded as if she had not slept. Her eyes were steely and the sharpness in her voice put me on edge.

"I heard of your uncle's unfortunate case." She spoke without patience or kindness.

"Yes, ma'am."

"Lady Forbes is beside herself. We all wish him well."

Did she? I remembered full well all she had to say about the "mad" Lord Adolphus Vane-Tempest after one of the many times he was sent to an infirmary to recover from one of his fits. The way she tittered and mocked the man's abused wife, a bridesmaid in her own daughter's wedding, was appalling. Needless to say, I doubted her capacity for sympathy toward the struggles of others.

If anything, her shortness with me had more to do with the palace gossip: another of the Queen's friends had met his demise, and surely it had something to do with the Queen's recent, jarringly sudden transformation into a caricature of a despondent witch. Those courtiers seemed to believe it. Perhaps all in her circle were cursed by association.

Queen Victoria closed her eyes and clasped her hands together, the black sleeve of her mourning crepe draped across the desk.

"One of my ladies saw Captain Forbes wandering Trafalgar Square. He spoke of ghosts and ghouls and other frightful things. But he also said something strange."

The way the Queen stared into my eyes felt as if she held a dagger to my throat. The woman could be a ghoul herself when she wanted. My heartbeat sped up. I had to remember to breathe. In and out. I relaxed my shoulders when I noticed them inching closer to my ears.

"What, Your Majesty?"

Queen Victoria didn't blink. "That he was with you the night he saw them: the ghosts and the ghouls and the other frightful things."

Unlike during our walk in the garden, I didn't miss a beat. "Your Majesty, you know as well as I do he isn't well. You also must know of his . . . dependency on certain substances."

"Indeed I do. Which is why it was especially curious that, allegedly, when he asked for his opium, he said you would give it to him. That you had done so before. His good little girl."

Remembering Uncle George's languid head lolling around on my lap, I suppressed a shudder. "Me? Your Majesty?" I clutched my chest. "Why would I do such a horrid thing? Uncle George's habits are the deepest source of shame for the Forbes family."

"The ramblings of a madman are not usually so specific."

If she wanted to accuse me of something, the morbid cow should have just come out and said it. Though I wanted to goad her into it, I couldn't let the mask fall, but my irritation was surely starting to show by now, flickering like fire in my eyes to match the ice in hers.

Out of a red box placed upon the corner of a desk, the Queen brought out another letter. "His misfortune reminds me too gravely of his other brother's misfortune. For the Forbes family to suffer the loss of two sons. *Those* sons. It is, at the very least, unsettling."

Or perhaps it was I who was unsettling. Years of wearing a mask after my own tragedy had sometimes made it difficult to discern just what a "normal" reaction to tragedy was.

It was then I realized, with my hands clasped together, that my reaction was exactly what the Queen had been monitoring.

"Too many strange happenings follow you, Sally. Doesn't it bother you?"

"Well, I didn't come to England under the best circumstances, Your Majesty. If my life is an odd one, then perhaps it's my fate."

"Was Miss Sass committing suicide her fate?"

My heart stopped as she peered into my eyes. "What?"

"Was it, at the very least, odd?"

My whole body flushed. I could feel moisture gathering beneath my hairline. Sass committed suicide?

"Something else the Church Missionary Society told me. The superintendent took her own life almost two years after the Institution burned down."

The flush had turned into a sudden chill. Too many thoughts raced through my mind. Miss Sass . . . dead.

I had to keep calm. But memories of that woman's face flooded into me. I'd made sure nobody had died in that fire. If lives were ruined and jobs lost, that was but a small price to pay for my misery. I didn't think anyone would die.

I thought of Mr. Bellamy and the broken neck of his corpse at the foot of the stairwell. My breaths quickened. The Queen could surely see the rise and fall of my chest.

I wrung my palms, trying to keep my emotions, my guilt, from spiraling any further, and my hands began to ache. I looked down at the brown skin. Yes, if I concentrated hard enough I could see them—the scars from the Sass's lashings. Suddenly, I could feel it too: her cane tearing apart my flesh.

My expression turned cold again. "How terrible. I didn't know." I tried my best to fake sincerity. I had to. Someone had written to Queen Victoria of things better left forgotten. There was no telling what this witch really knew. "But I was a child in those days. How could I know?"

I had to convince her.

The weight of the conversation sucked all the air out of the room. The ladies-in-waiting behind the Queen shivered slightly, as if moving their bodies any further would make them bloodied victims of this knife-like tension.

"I'm not blaming you. But things don't happen by accident. Our past can affect our present. The dead can affect the living. Sometimes even our own emotional states can affect the world around us."

I didn't blame the ladies-in-waiting for exchanging confused glances. Victorian spiritualism wasn't for everyone, though Queen Victoria seemed to like it enough to transform her palace into a morbid shrine to her dead husband. How ironic, considering how desperate they were to teach us Christianity.

"Unfortunately, I can't say I've brushed up on my esoteric theory," I said, trying to keep my annoyance to a minimum. "But are you saying, Your Majesty, that I'm somehow manifesting these evil things?"

Perish the thought. Wishing was for the weak. You wring blood with your own hands.

"I've seen people say similarly frightening things about Uncle George—and about Your Majesty as well." With all the modesty I could muster, I gestured to the darkened windows. "They're saying terrible things befall the company you keep. The people who *love* you. For my sake, I hope such superstitious nonsense isn't true."

The Queen fell silent. I was too good of an actress. She wasn't sure what to think. She wasn't sure what was happening, except that it was happening and it filled her with dread.

"Yes," she whispered. "The people are talking." Taking her quill and dipping it into its inkwell, she began writing once again. "Mrs. Schoen has mentioned to me that you have been quite busy these days. Out and about, especially in London."

I clenched my jaw. Was Schoen my guardian or the Queen's little spy? "I do fancy myself a stroll or two during the day. I'm a young lady, Your Majesty."

"Precisely. And a young lady such as yourself would benefit from taking on the duties all young ladies must bear once they come of age." She looked at me. "You are a very smart girl, Sally. And all very smart girls need discipline and restriction."

The specter of Sass and the burning Institution haunted my thoughts as Queen Victoria continued writing.

"And what do you have in mind?" I asked quietly. I wish I hadn't.

The answer hit me like a blow to the head.

"Marriage. Promptly and without delay."

I couldn't feel my arms. I thought of Gowramma, her screaming baby and her wrinkled husband, and *couldn't feel my arms*.

"What?" My mouth had dried. I wasn't even sure the word had come out clearly.

"I've already procured your prospect. He's been exchanging letters with me for some time over this issue and I've decided to grant him permission to take you back to his homeland."

"*Take* me?"

The ladies-in-waiting looked scandalized behind the Queen, for surely they'd heard the indignation, the naked anger in my voice. Take. Take me? Was I something to be taken?

But of course I was. It was why I was in the forsaken country in the first place.

A possession to be given and to give in return. Like a child's toy passed around from one hand to the next. I thought of the hollow eyes of the self-portraits I drew of myself and shuddered down to my bones. The Queen was nonplussed. Absorbed in her letter, it made no difference to her how I felt or what I thought on the matter. Her word was law.

"And who is this man you've been conspiring with behind my back?" I hissed, my fingers clenched. "Without even asking my opinion?"

"Captain Davies. A wealthy gentleman from Lagos, one of my colonies. By my decree, you are to marry him before the end of next month. August fourteenth is the tentative date. I suggest you prepare yourself before then."

If I were a doll, then I was one made of cracked glass shattering to pieces with each cruel word of indifference spoken from the Queen's mouth. One month. Marriage to some man I didn't even know. One month. One *month*? But what of my plans? What of my revenge?

Mr. Bellamy. Mr. Bambridge. Uncle George. McCoskry. Phipps . . .

My list. I wasn't finished. *Take* me? He'd been given permission by the Queen of England to take me in one month? Was I hostage? Was I to be a captive all my life?

And that's when I realized in a fit of chilling despair . . .

She'd checkmated me.

So swiftly and without delay.

Power. Power was devastating. With power you didn't need intellect to move your pawns in a game of chess. Speak a word and at will they will move where you desire with the outcome of your choice. The power to mold bodies, bring them together and move them to different parts of the world like chess pieces on a board. That was a monarch's power.

This was why I hated Queen Victoria above all the others. This was why she was my most dangerous foe. There is no power more devastating than that bestowed by divine right. It was a tantalizing power and I could only counter it with my carefully curated rage. And where would that rage go once I was locked inside my gilded cage? Where would I go?

Would such an "I" even still exist?

"Your Majesty—"

"The matter has been settled, Sally. *I've* settled it. The letter is being sent to Captain Davies as we speak. He's only too happy to bring you back to West Africa with him."

Ah. So that was the letter she'd been writing. I wished I'd snatched it out of her wrinkled hands and stuffed it down her throat. *The matter is settled.* We'll see about that.

"You will meet him once he arrives in London and learn to obey him as his wife."

Discipline and restriction. Well, that was one way to cut a problem off at the knees.

"Sally, poor child," the Queen said, now suddenly donning the expression of a kind matriarch. It infuriated me. "This is a rite of passage that all women must pass through. But once you do, you'll feel it: the peace you'll find once you've settled down. I was once against marriage myself when I first became queen. But being with my Albert and experiencing his love was the greatest gift anyone could have given me."

The greatest gift indeed—besides me, that is.

How ghoulish. She spoke of love, but only to *move* me—both my heart and my body. Control. She was lovingly handing me over to another master. And I was to lovingly accept. That's what love meant to a British queen.

I couldn't stand it. I wouldn't stand this any longer. She hadn't beaten me. The pieces were still in play.

I refused to lose.

Mr. Bellamy. Mr. Bambridge. Uncle George. McCoskry. Phipps.

Queen Victoria.

There would be no peace for me until I had completely destroyed her.

"Yes, Your Majesty." I bowed and left her room.

PART TWO

AN INTELLIGENT LITTLE THING

Others would say "He is a good man and though you don't care about him now, will soon learn to love him." That, I believe, I never could do. I know that the generality of people would say he is rich and your marrying him would at once make you independent, and I say, "Am I to barter my peace of mind for money?" No—never!

—*Omoba Ina, aka Sarah Forbes Bonetta, 1862*

TWELVE

Sierra Leone, 1854

I GREW ANGRIER with each deliberate strike of my white chalk stick against the black tablet. It didn't matter that I was just one of three girls at this desk that was too small for us, like each of the wooden tables in the Institution's forsaken claustrophobic classrooms. It didn't matter that the other girls were eyeing me nervously, begging me silently to calm down, for if Miss Sass, at the other side of the room, saw how I was man-handling the chalk to the point of breaking it, she'd surely give me the cane—again.

But why did I have to continuously inscribe and re-inscribe the writings of this man, this Samuel Crowther, a slave-turned-bishop from Yorubaland? Why was his certainty of Africa's "regeneration" through the Queen of England's help so important for me to learn that I had to write it again and again until I could feel his teachings in my bones?

Miss Sass flew to me from the other side of the room, grabbed me by the ear, and lifted me up. Hot pain sizzled through my little body. The other girls held their breath as she plunked a book in my hands.

"Show me that you can read this passage," she demanded.

I winced, wanting badly to rub my ear, but if I did, it would earn me a whack. Squeezing my eyes shut and opening them again, I peered down at the passages Sass pointed at. I'd read this one before. Crowther's writing on his most recent expedition.

I sucked in a breath and read. *"I asked whether the inhabitants of the Go—"* I paused, gulped as Sass raised an eyebrow, and tried again. *"Gomkoi were Pagans and Mohammedans; and was informed that they were all Pagans; that the males wore some sort of cloth around their loins, but the females only a few green leaves. On asking whether they were cannibals, I was answered in the negative."*

Miss Sass looked disappointed I'd read it so well. There was nothing to criticize. "Now, children, what do you think Samuel Crowther meant when—"

"But why does it matter of these people are pagan?" I said, closing the book with a snap. The girls all stared at me, terrified. A plume of smoke curled up to my nose. I sniffled a little, but continued. "Why is their nakedness worth mentioning? Why would either of these things suggest that they are *cannibals*? I don't understand it."

I didn't dare look up to see the grimace I could feel bearing down on me from the superintendent. And when Sass got a belt out of her desk and began beating my hands, I cursed my loose tongue as tears pooled in the corner of my eyes.

But I couldn't help it. It wasn't Crowther but Miss Sass's intentions I didn't trust. The lesson hidden in this rote memorization didn't feel right. It felt insidious. All of us little African girls in our white bonnets and black Evangelical dresses down to our ankles reading about cannibals and pagans. There was something in this lesson that didn't sit right with me even if I couldn't articulate why at the tender age of eleven.

Three strikes. My hands burned and my back quivered in pain. One of the girls rubbed my knee to calm my distress. Miss Sass had just put her belt away when a gentle knock came from the door.

"Ah! He's arrived!" Suddenly brighter, Miss Sass walked through the lifeless classroom with only two windows and opened the door to reveal a tall man. "Our guest. A distinguished gentleman, by any measure."

Whether she was attracted to him or not, I couldn't tell. She drank up his dark brown skin, full lips, and sharp brows. His black hair had been shaved down to nearly to the scalp, a thin carpet. I could tell he was military. It was that stern expression that wouldn't soften despite how hard he tried in the presence of us children.

But he wasn't unkind. No, I could tell that too. He looked at each of us with the dignity we were never given by our teachers—certainly not by Miss Sass. There was no reprimand when I locked eyes with him. He didn't force me to lower my head in penance. After Miss Sass barked at us to stand, he greeted me with a nod the way he would any other equal. I appreciated that at least.

The man went to stand at the front of the classroom by the fireplace. We were made to curtsy to him. I noticed, however, that the teachers did not.

"Girls, we are joined today by a most esteemed guest I am hoping you will learn from." Miss Sass stood beside the pulpit and ushered the man to it. "His name is Captain James Pinson Davies, and at the age of twenty-six, he has already served with the British Royal Navy—of course, in the West Africa Squadron. Everyone, quickly say hello."

Like drones we answered in unison. We were tired, of course, as we always were past noon after the punishments and the embroidering. But Miss Sass must have thought it was some kind of once-in-a-generation anomaly to see an accomplished African man, and that the mere sight of one should stir us into a frenzy. It didn't. It was quite mundane actually, especially for someone whose father was a king, but I was somewhat interested in learning about this Captain Davies anyway.

"Hello, girls. It's good to see you children working hard on your studies."

He was dignified, proud, and wanted everyone to know it. I understood the impulse and wholly believed it was something that could only be learned in the most brutal circumstances. No one could ever convince me otherwise.

"I studied in a school like this too: the Church Missionary Society Grammar School in this very Freetown."

Another victim. I wanted to shout it, but could already feel the sashes against my back.

"Mathematics and geography, Greek, English, Latin. I've learned it all and I'm sure in time you will too. I don't believe I'm being too bold in saying this, but you youths should count yourselves lucky; it's in institutions like these that you'll separate yourselves from your peers as the elite of our future African society."

Did he mean from the naked, pagan cannibals? But his bright eyes shone with genuine earnestness. He truly believed what he was saying. He was excited for us, for our futures—the ones only a chosen few like him were lucky enough to have.

In his twenty-six years of life, Captain James Pinson Davies had been a teacher, an officer, and a merchant. He was off to Lagos soon to grow his business.

"I have a penchant for industry. But one cannot just take from the world. You have to give something back. That's why I'll be focusing on philanthropic work along the way. Only then can you consider yourselves truly rich."

He was a veritable saint. Truly a perfect example of what was possible for people like us. Miss Sass's lesson here was now crystal clear.

"If any of you children have any questions for Captain Davies, ask them now," said Miss Sass. "And I will accept no slouching or bending of the head as you speak."

Ironic given the punishment she doled out when we did venture looking her in the eye as we spoke. Many of the tired girls asked the simple questions that led to simple answers. He was born in 1828. Yes, he had been to Abeokuta and he planned on going to Lagos soon. No, he had no children, as he was not yet married. He was also interested in cocoa farming.

And through it all, Miss Sass made her way around the tables, slowly ghost-gliding on the hardwood floor. She only stopped at my table. I didn't look up at her. I knew she saw my tablet—that Crowther's words, which were supposed to be re-created faithfully in chalk, had devolved into the word *CANNIBAL?* in capital letters followed by a stream of *HAHAHA*s that was only paused when Captain Davies walked in.

Miss Sass's fury could always be felt through our thick dresses. My body would soon burn with pain again. I knew it all too well. So I turned and raised my hand.

"Yes, child," said Captain Davies.

"Miss Sass has always taught us that the Bible bids us to return good for evil," I said, lowering my hand, feeling a keen sense of satisfaction when I heard Miss Sass's breath hitch in her wrinkled old throat. "I read it once in a book too. Do you believe this to be true?"

"Yes." Captain Davies answered so quickly, he looked surprised at himself. He pressed his lips together tightly, his chest lifted, but stuck there as if he were holding in a breath. And something about it all made me feel upset for him. Upset for myself. Upset for us all. Looking at him, I didn't know whether to feel proud or furious, indignant, hopeful, even sad. I just didn't know. I knew what I was supposed to feel. What they wanted me to feel—us to feel.

Relaxing his shoulders, he answered again, more calmly. "Yes, I believe this to be true."

His answer continued to haunt me for a long time.

Windsor Castle, England – July 9, 1862

"I refuse, Mama!"

"You terrible girl! You will get out of this carriage, walk through those gates, and meet your husband!"

I gripped the leather armrest. "No! I said no!"

The coach driver could probably hear us. The horse had long come to a stop, but I didn't care. I wasn't getting out. I would have stripped right there if I could. Mrs. Schoen, ever the Queen's pawn, was only invited to this lunch to make sure I couldn't escape. The Queen surely knew Mrs. Schoen enjoyed living vicariously through the adopted African princess. She surely knew all mothers seemed to turn into ghouls when their wills were defied.

Mrs. Schoen grabbed both my shoulders roughly. "The Queen herself arranged a marriage. A marriage for *you*. To a wealthy businessman of your race. Do you have any idea how—how few people will ever be able to say that in their lives? How privileged you are?"

"Privileged? To be stuck in a gilded cage? To have my independence stolen from me?"

"*Independence?*" Mrs. Schoen said the word as if I had suddenly lost my mind. She swirled it around on her tongue with such disdain, I could feel the last bit of my carefully crafted self-control slipping away. "A girl of eighteen—what kind of independence do you need, exactly? Are there more parties you wish to attend? Or do you—" She clutched her frilly white blouse, one of the fancy ones for the occasion. "Do you already have a man? Have you already given yourself? My good Lord, have you already *dirtied* yourself—"

My heart skipped a beat as I thought of Rui's breath on my neck. Then when I finally noticed the warmth between my legs had swelled in the presence of my *guardian*, I felt suddenly sick as much as I did violated. I could barely stutter out a "N-No!" with a clumsiness that made me realize she was winning. She was winning with her raving, socially climbing insecurity alone.

Was there something about mothers? Did they have some sort of preternatural ability to get under your skin so thoroughly you wanted to scream and tear your hair out at the same time?

"No, Mama, I am a virgin." I gritted my teeth from the indignity of even having to admit it. "Though if I were to lose my purity, you would not be the first person I informed. Nor the second. Nor the third—"

"The devil has gotten into you, Sally." She shook her head with the sense of urgency of a priest at an exorcism. Funny, because like most in the Queen's circle, she hated Catholics. "How can you speak to me like that? Your guardian. Your mama? How can you be so hurtful? So insensitive to me? You have no idea how much I've sacrificed to raise you up since you came back to England from Sierra Leone. I treated you like my own daughter."

"Yes, you have a daughter, Anne. Why don't you go bother her about *her* virtue?"

"Anne is *married*, as she should be." Mrs. Schoen's fingers dug into my flesh. She wasn't just furious. She was terrified—terrified of the possibility that my obedience was somehow perhaps not unconditional. "And if you end up becoming an unmarried spinster, the shame I'll have to suffer will be something you could never know anything about—"

"Oh yes, because how could a former slave who saw her whole family die ever understand suffering like societal gossip."

"Stop talking about the past and look towards the future. *Our* future." Her desperate dark eyes hadn't softened even as she held my chin with both hands. "*Our* future is at stake here. Sally, this is a world where appearance is everything. You must look the part, speak the part, play the part, or you will be judged. By *everyone*. You will be ridiculed."

The carriage driver knocked on my door. I ignored him. "And will you die because of that, Mama? Is there some secret poison hidden within ridicule that I just don't know about?"

Mrs. Elizabeth Schoen, the unhappy wife of a minister who seemed perpetually elsewhere, closed her eyes, sucked in a deep breath, calmed herself, then gave me a piercing look.

"You're making me the villain, Sally. How is that fair? It's not. It's not fair at all! You know I would rather die than hurt you. You know I would rather put a knife to my own throat and slit it than hurt you. None of this is to make you sad. I'm doing this *for* you."

Some kind of trickery was happening here, a manipulative sleight of hand, and I wasn't even sure Mrs. Schoen realized it herself. My face screwed up. "And you should just listen to me. That is the right thing to do. I quarreled with my own mother. I didn't know I'd lose her so soon. I wish I could have more time with her. I wish I could have listened to her wisdom when I had the chance. I won't be here forever."

"Your mother . . ." My cheeks flushed as I tried to imagine her, but her brown face was featureless in my mind's eye. I guess I was rather uncreative when it came to some things.

"She was free here, even before slavery ended. A lucky woman in that sense. But seeing others, she knew all too well the precious gift of being able to keep one's child. The preciousness of that bond between parent and child." She cupped my face with a hand, a tear forming in the corner of her eye. "If I were to die, then you'd really see. And by then it'll be too late. Do you want that, Sally?"

Be wholly obedient to me now or you'll hate yourself when I die. Oh yes. A manipulative sleight of hand indeed. And it was heinous because of how effective it was. The idea of her sudden death began taunting me. I imagined Mrs. Schoen, a little girl quarreling with her mother. Then I remembered quarreling with my own, when we were eating bean soup with my father and she made me sit with my legs closed like a "woman of the Egbado."

Mothers were always the same. But, as I bit the inside of my cheek hard and pursed my lips together to keep from bursting into tears, I realized that I feared losing another.

Look at me. During the span of one conversation, I'd become an emotional murderer, a hateful ward, a potential whore, and a spinster. The actual subject at hand—my arranged marriage—was long buried underneath the parade of guilt-inducing indictments Mrs. Schoen launched at me with terrifying precision.

I looked in her eyes and realized what I knew all along. My marriage to a man I didn't know wasn't about me at all. My future wasn't mine. It was never supposed to be.

Was there anything in my life that was supposed to be mine?

This time the driver knocked on Mrs. Schoen's door and, without wasting a moment, she jumped out of the carriage. Together the two opened my door. I tried and failed to keep it shut, but they managed to drag me out onto the street.

Well, now that I was here, I couldn't very well act out, could I? There were too many people watching.

Mama counted on me thinking this. She knew I wouldn't act out, not here at the gates of Windsor Castle, with the servants ready to usher us into the palace. I saw her little satisfied smile and, for one half second, lost my mind. I wanted to throw off my coat and my knickers and run naked through the streets wearing leaves on my groin like those pagan "cannibal" fellows Crowther wrote about years ago. I wanted to climb the gates and pee on the lawn.

It wasn't ladylike. I didn't want to be ladylike.

I had to be ladylike.

It was at once my weapon and my noose.

You have one month to find a way out of this, Ina, I told myself as Mama and I were led to the dining hall. Pageboys were already running around coordinating between the chefs and the ushers bringing the guests in for lunch. *One month. Use that head of yours and get out of this.*

We guests were to stand by our chairs. I counted at least forty, of which I was in the middle. The long egg-white table could handle at least that much.

As Mama preened next to me, I peered around. Bertie stood almost directly opposite me on the other side of the table. He caught my eye and winked at me. I ignored the idiot entirely.

Elsewhere, Gowramma tapped her foot impatiently with her wrinkled, half-awake husband. A few of Alice's bridesmaids and their husbands.

Marriage threatened to crush me at all sides. I pictured myself a year from now, perpetually pregnant, surrounded by babies in the hell of my living room.

And what of my revenge?

Mr. Bellamy. Mr. Bambridge. Uncle George. McCoskry. Phipps . . .

I spied Harriet and her mother, Mrs. Phipps, on the opposite end of the table to my right. I remembered that night as a child in the parlor room and my body shriveled with hatred. The indignity. Her mocking laughter.

126

She was laughing now too. Laughing with a man with hair the precise color of a pumpkin. His beard had grown so long it dipped in the center, reminding me of back home—those soft, overripe plantains too flaccid to keep from collapsing in on themselves. To have such a bizarre tuft of hair growing from his chin . . . any other time it would have made me laugh, but today this was no laughing matter. For the first time in years, I was looking upon William McCoskry. In the years since our encounter, he'd finally become the acting governor of Lagos Colony just last year.

"William, you must tell me all about the colony." I had to strain to hear Mrs. Phipps. "It must have been impossible to deal with all of those runaway slaves."

"I did what I could for them in court." McCoskry's voice sounded like the gravel rolled over by the wheels of a carriage. My body seized. "Of course, very few of them had any real education, so helping them within a *civilized* legal system took some work."

I'd heard. Many fugitive slaves from the Americas and even in the British colonies where slavery had been outlawed had fled to Lagos seeking freedom from their abuse. They were not some topic of chitchat at the dinner table. But Mrs. Phipps and McCoskry carried on as if they were talking about the weather. As if they were comparing the state of their pets . . .

Mr. Bellamy. Mr. Bambridge. Uncle George. McCoskry. Phipps . . .

I was mouthing my list before I could stop myself.

Eventually, I did stop because Harriet was signaling to me awkwardly with her head. Her mother had to slap her back to stop her cranking her neck, but soon I could see who she was gesturing toward.

A familiar face was staring at me. Familiar because I'd seen him just days before.

That unnerving young man. The one with the curly brown mop and the Africanized English accent. The one who promised he'd be meeting me again and soon. He stood several seats down from Bertie, perking up a little when I finally noticed him.

Almost as if to say, *At last, you fool.*

I placed my hands behind my back so he wouldn't see my fingers twitching. I returned his dangerous smile with one of my own. But every cell in my body told me to be on alert.

And then the trumpets sounded. Fanfare. Chin up, spine straight. Hands at your sides.

In walked Queen Victoria, tiny, round, and dour in her black attire, tired despite it only being noonday. Lord Ponsonby, royal court official, kept a slow, accommodating pace as he led her to her seat at the table's head. And he wasn't alone.

In his black frock coat and bow tie, the African man who towered over the Queen carried himself with far more nobility than that witch could ever muster. His hair had receded and his eyes were sunken with age, but Captain Davies was every bit as handsome as when he walked into my classroom all those years ago. Just like then, he smiled timidly with gentle brown eyes. But his broad shoulders and straight back boasted of his pride.

He found me immediately. Our eyes locked and a spark made my spine quiver. The heat rose in my cheeks. I saw the smallest hint of trepidation in his expression that must have mirrored mine.

Mama beamed next to me, rubbing my arm with excitement. Then she blinked. "Wait a moment," she said, touching her lip and tilting her head, "who's that behind the Captain?"

A burly Scottish man in a kilt and royal servant regalia walked two paces behind Captain Davies, Lord Ponsonby, and Queen Victoria—but he was nearest to the Queen, flanking her right side. His downturned eyes and large nose flared with confidence. His dark brown hair framed his face, his beard much more kempt than McCoskry's. He was a hand-some gentleman. Ferocious as if bred in the wilderness. His eyes were only on the Queen.

Bertie was trying to get my attention. And when I finally, much to my chagrin, gave it to him, he leaned in and whispered, "John Brown. It was a good idea."

The man Rui wanted inside the court at all costs. Sweat formed on my palms. There was nothing more exciting than a scheme coming together. But with this sword of Damocles over my head, would I ever know why Rui cared so much to bring this man, this former servant to Prince Albert, by Queen Victoria's side? He hovered over the monarch like a protective shadow as she stumbled to her seat, ready for her soup.

Captain Davies didn't stumble. Several paces behind even Brown, but he kept his head up, dignified. Ah, so the empty seat directly ahead of me, next to Bertie, was for him.

After the Queen sat, we all sat. But before the Queen could begin her assault on her bowl of soup, she stood to make an announcement to the room of guests.

"This is Captain James Pinson Labulo Davies. He is a wealthy businessman in my colony of Lagos and is to wed my ward, Sarah Forbes Bonetta, next month on August fourteenth."

Bertie's jaw dropped. The murmurs from the other guests were short-lived.

"You will congratulate them."

The Queen had given an order. As Mrs. Schoen soaked in the polite and insincere applause, I looked at my fiancé and he looked at me. Nei-ther of us seemed particularly moved. Wrinkles cut paths above his eye-brows. Well, age wasn't one to spare any man. It hadn't battered him too hard, but whereas I'd once seen him as a dignified twenty-six-year-old, he was now, eight years later, a distinguished gentleman. As such, he gave me a bow of the head, with an expression one gives a business associate.

"Wait . . ." In his seat, Bertie looked up from his uneaten soup and turned from side to side. "Sally's getting married? Next month?" He stared at Captain Davies, mouth agape.

Somewhere in the hall, I heard Gowramma snickering.

THIRTEEN

A TROOP OF waiters plonked food down in front of us: consommé à la Doria, topped with white truffles from Piedmont and garnished with game quenelles. No matter the announcement, when the Queen was ready to eat, it was time to eat.

And so the event began in earnest. Chatter erupted. Casual conversation, of the type I was supposed to be having with my soon-to-be husband.

Mrs. Schoen certainly tried. "So, Captain Davies, you were educated in Freetown, just like our Sally."

I was an expert in studying faces. His gave nothing away. "Yes— Mrs. Elizabeth Schoen, is it? The Queen tells me you've been taking care of Miss Bonetta since she returned home to England."

Home. *Home?* The word made my stomach churn. I stared at him, stone-faced.

"Yes, what was it, Sally? The Institution of Good Christian Girls or something of the like?" With a mouth full of soup, Bertie elbowed Davies in the arm. "Though I doubt anyone would call Sally here a 'good' girl. She's rather chilly, this one."

A part of me wanted to see him give the Prince of Wales a withering glower, as the stupid prince deserved, but Davies nodded with a pleasant smile.

"The Church Missionary Society's Female Institution," he corrected the prince, his tone even-keeled. It was as if he were determined not to show an ounce of personality. "And I don't think being 'chilly' is such a bad thing. I much preferred Odile to Odette in my youth."

Bertie swallowed his consommé and subtly looked him up and down. "A fan of ballet, then," he muttered.

Davies gave me another pleasant smile. Dull, so *dull*. My sigh was a little too loud. Mama kicked my shin underneath the table. Not very ladylike.

Mrs. Phipps and McCoskry were carrying on chatting like old friends—like conspirators. Enjoying their soup, were they? I couldn't do anything to them now. The plan I'd already sketched out for their demise would take time—time, I now realized, I didn't have. All because of this arranged marriage, I'd have to rethink and rework *everything*. I gritted my teeth. It took every ounce of willpower not to run over and push their faces in it.

"I recall I might have seen you once at the Institution, Miss Bonetta," Davies continued, interrupting my train of thought. "Many years ago." Irked, I swirled the spoon around in the soup, far too thick to see my own reflection in it. I didn't like soup. It was a good thing I wouldn't have time to eat it.

"Oh, no, please, do call her Sally. It's what we all—Oh my!"

The waiters charged forward as if in a military raid and snatched Mama's soup from her hands. Mama wasn't used to it, but there were rules when one dined with the Queen. When she was finished with a course, we were all finished. Didn't help that she ate particularly quickly.

Mama's shoulders slumped. "I was still eating . . . ," she muttered, confused.

"As were we all, madam." Davies's affable shrug certainly won her over, though that wasn't difficult. She was already fully aboard the

Davies train, and why wouldn't she be with his calm, gentlemanly manners and an elite-level handsomeness that would make any frustrated old lady swoon. Mama did. A few of the patrons were staring at him with a mixture of awe and excitement. Including Mrs. Phipps, who leaned over and whispered something to her daughter. She looked at the two of us and began giggling behind her hand. Wondering if his buttocks were similar to the Hottentot Venus, was she? The witch.

"Côtelettes d'Agneau a la Rossini: lamb cutlets topped with sautéed medallions of foie gras and truffles," announced the waiter.

"Tuck in while you can," laughed Bertie as the waiter clicked his heels and made himself scarce.

"Ah, my favorite! Lamb cutlets." The boy who'd spoken—it was the brown-haired boy from Freetown, sitting just a couple of seats down from the prince. He'd been so quiet, I'd almost forgotten he was there, sitting in his seat with that increasingly snakelike grin. He was the only person here whose name I didn't know. A classic disadvantage. I hated those.

"Did you really meet Sally once at school?" Bertie interrupted my train of thought, pulling my gaze away from the Freetown boy. By now, the Prince of Wales, used to his mother's eating habits, wasn't shy about shoving as much food into his mouth as he could, as quickly as he could. He eyed Davies with a strange sort of suspicion uncharacteristic of him.

"Why, yes, Your Majesty. It was during one of my travels through West Africa. I stopped over at Freetown on the superintendent's urging." He tilted his head, his eyes glazed over with nostalgia. "I'd just turned twenty-six. I'd already made my name in the navy. But I was making my name known in a different way."

"Who *didn't* go to the military?" Bertie muttered, bitterly chugging his goblet of wine.

"You and Sally have so much in common—even similar ancestry, or so I hear!" Mrs. Schoen urged me with that gratingly stiff smile. I poked my truffles.

"So much in common?" Bertie swallowed his wine and looked between the two of them. "Why? Are you a rescued African princess too?"

Once again, nobody laughed at his joke. At the very least, watching the fool deflate gave me some kind of pleasure in this otherwise dreadful luncheon.

"Not a princess, no. Not royalty, but . . ." The warmth in his features was unmistakable as he gazed at me. "I imagine we have more in common than perhaps Miss Bonetta even realizes."

"I wonder how? When we first met, you were twenty-six and on the cusp of greatness. I was eleven, punished for not tying my bonnet correctly," I answered without thinking. But it was satisfying, letting my disdain show just a little. One couldn't wear a mask every second of the day and today, in particular, I didn't quite feel the need to.

Bertie didn't seem to mind. He slithered into the opening I left him. "That's quite a gap in age," he said, and for once I was glad he'd spoken.

I snapped my head up. "And what's the age gap between you and Princess Alexandra, still cooped up in her castle in Denmark?" I was losing patience with his grating voice.

He was still the Prince of Wales. Mrs. Schoen looked as if she were about to faint from my tone. It took Bertie a while to answer.

"About . . . three years . . . I suppose . . ."

"Sounds nice," I answered. "Lucky you."

And he shut up.

We ate our next course in silence. Davies looked incredibly uncomfortable. Good. He should. Who did he think he was, thinking he could swoop in, demand me, and take me without a word of struggle?

"Oh, these roasted potatoes are just lovely! Perfectly spiced, wouldn't you say?"

That boy again. He didn't speak to us, but to the rather taken young woman sitting next to him. A conversationalist and a charmer. Her husband didn't seem to notice. Well, the potatoes were quite good.

Who *was* he?

"Well, if you ask me, something as silly as 'age' has never stood in the way of a good marriage, I'd say." Mrs. Schoen suddenly spoke up on Davies's behalf, her voice more loud and shrewd than she must have anticipated. She glanced quickly at the Queen.

"Don't worry, Mama, she hasn't heard you. You see how she's attacking that lamb."

"*Sally!*" Mrs. Schoen had almost yelled it. And then the thing she feared most happened—a few people, a very small handful amongst the sea of guests, began watching us. She calmed down almost immediately. "I'm sorry, Captain Davies, our Sally hasn't been feeling well for some time."

Yes, she's come down with a case of the "don't give a—"

"But I assure you, she's not usually so *thorny*," Mrs. Schoen continued. Bertie snorted.

"No, no, I understand." Even Davies's laughter was kind, jingling like Christmas bells. I held my fork so tightly, it could have cut off my palm's circulation. "It'll take some adjusting for all of us. For both of us, I mean, Sally."

Both of us? And which one would have more adjusting to do in this situation? The adult man well into this thirties, established with money, wealth, and the benefits and privileges his groin gave him? Or the teenage girl for whom "freedom of choice" might as well have been a poorly written joke in *Punch* magazine, gaudy cartoon included.

"'Sally'?" I drank my wine. "Have we become so close so quickly?"

Though Davies pursed his lips together, his expression felt almost teasing—the kind of teasing an adult gave an unruly child. It made me furious.

"Cailles rôties: roast quails stuffed with foie gras."

I sat back in my chair as the plate came crashing down in front of me. "How much foie gras are we supposed to eat?"

"You know, Sally, don't underestimate the importance of being of the same race and region when it comes to a marriage match." Mrs. Schoen had gathered herself enough to give me a friendly pat on the shoulder instead of the slap I'm sure she wanted to give me. "Queen Victoria conceived of this match herself. I'm sure she had your benefit in mind through it all. It's what she tried to do with the princess Gowramma. Her Majesty had hoped that she would marry that handsome Duleep Singh of the Sikh Empire, and she went and married Campbell instead. Well, you can see the result."

Duleep, another of the Queen's favored godchildren. I sometimes wondered how many of us there were. I peered down the table to find Gowramma glaring at Mama in response to her jab before patting the saliva off of her husband's lips with a napkin. He looked worn. The old man must have stayed up all night gambling again. Or perhaps age made one tired at noonday. If Gowramma really was miserable, she didn't show it. Then again, it was never an easy task, discerning her true feelings about sensitive matters.

"About that." I was talking more than I thought I would during this luncheon, but the words flew from my lips nonetheless. "Gowramma and Duleep felt no love and preferred each other as friends. I suppose they care that one must 'stick to their own race' or that one should do as Her Majesty orders. I wonder, then, why the expectations for me are so different."

"Isn't that clear?" Davies set down his utensils. Something had shifted in his expression. It wasn't stern or hateful. No, he'd put up with my temper well enough. But for the first time, it was almost as if he'd let me see through the cracks in his own mask—*let* me. The furrow in his brow. The concern in his expression. It was almost fatherly. . . .

"The Queen feels differently about you, Miss Bonetta. Given our correspondences, that much is clear."

"Yes, she's Her Majesty's favorite." Mrs. Schoen looked around the hall. "Just look at this luncheon! She loves you so much, Sally. Like one of her own!"

But in the world of the elite, lunches and balls could easily become weapons of war. As I watched the Queen slurp down her food at a maddening pace, I couldn't help but suspect this was nothing more than strategy.

Like one of her own. Something told me Captain Davies wasn't implying what Mama thought he was. "There is something about *you*, Sarah. About you and no one else," he said.

You should be careful. That was what his expression told me. Not of him. Of *her*.

The rest of lunch passed by uneventfully. Davies told us all about his life in Lagos. The celery was baked and the quenelles perfectly fried. The beef was far too rare for my tastes, though Bertie gobbled it down like his ravenous mother. I looked at the halls and saw cages of a prison. I heard Mama's laughter and felt the knife in my back. The only one who looked almost as irritated as me was the prince, though it didn't seem to affect his appetite. He perked right up when dessert appeared. Three rounds of it: savarin cake topped with vanilla cream. Poached apples, creamed rice, and, of course, chocolate profiteroles.

"My favorite," Bertie exclaimed at the same time as the Freetown boy. They caught each other's eyes as the waiter placed down their bowls.

"You too?" said Bertie.

"Well, who doesn't love profiteroles?" The Freetown boy looked as if he'd been waiting for this chance—the chance to exchange words with the prince. Nobody else seemed to notice, because it took a particular kind of personality to enjoy seeing a plan come together.

The hairs on the back of my neck were standing on end again. Something felt wrong.

Bertie frowned and tilted his head. "Have I seen you before?"

How like Bertie to not remember the guests at his own salacious event. Then again, with the amount of alcohol he'd consumed that night . . .

"Nowhere that needs discussing in the palace, I should think." The boy winked; Bertie nodded, cluing in and not so subtly peering at his mother like a boy who didn't want Mum to know he'd just broken the china. That should have been the end of it. I didn't want any more conversation with this boy.

"Your accent sounds rather different than anyone else's here." It was Davies who spoke. Politeness had its limits. I flexed and unflexed my fingers against the tablecloth.

"Oh, I'm from Sierra Leone. Freetown."

"Really?"

"Well, I was born in England, but truth be told, I have few memories of this place. My mother didn't speak much to me about our lives before Africa. She wasn't one to speak much at all . . ."

There was an awkward pause as he trailed off, seemingly losing himself before pulling back into his character. Yes, lest we forget: he was a young gentlemen, sociable and kind to all.

"And you're a friend to the court?" Davies continued. I didn't know if he was curious or suspicious.

"A friend to Lord Ponsonby," said the boy. "He knows some people related to my mother. When I came to England, I went to see him and he was kind enough to allow me to come today. If only he knew what a scoundrel I was, I don't think he would have been so kind!"

Oh please. With his perfectly coiffed hair, freshly shaven face, and harmless expression, he looked as if cherubs could escape from his buttocks at any moment. But he knew that. *I challenge you to think of me as a scoundrel* was what he was really saying.

I cleared my throat. "Captain Davies, won't you eat your dessert? It's quite nice."

Davies was shocked I'd spoken to him with such . . . docility. It was enough to distract him just for a moment.

"I'm not one for sweets." He gave me a timid grin and rubbed the back of his head sheepishly. "But I am curious, lad—" The boy again. I bristled. "Where were you educated?"

"I was schooled at home by tutors. Though I did not want for education. My mother worked with the Church Missionary Society and was a teacher herself. I had all the books I needed, and even if my mother was always so dreadfully busy with her students, my tutors, dare I say, were just as good in the art of instruction as she was."

"I myself went to the Church Missionary Society Grammar School," Davies said, giving him the appreciative nod of an alumnus-adjacent.

"I hope it didn't burn down like Sally's old school," Bertie said before catching himself. I wished he'd choke on his profiterole.

"The Female Institution? God forbid!" said the Freetown boy. "I know all about that terrible tragedy. I couldn't forget it, even though I wish I could."

And the look he gave me just then told me more powerfully than words ever could: he wouldn't let me forget it either. His stare was empty, bottomless as the deepest cavern.

"It took my mother from me," he said without blinking. Not even once. His voice became low in that moment. "It's where she worked, after all."

My body turned cold. It was starting to dawn on me why the boy looked so familiar. Why his presence, since the moment he forced me into a dance, sent my adrenaline pumping slightly faster than it should have. The boy looked straight at me as he spoke. He didn't break contact, even when Mama cooed in sympathy.

"Oh my darling, I'm so sorry. She died in the fire, then?"

"No," he replied. "She died afterwards. By suicide."

So. The ghost of Superintendent Emma Sass had found me at last.

"She left me an incredible inheritance, of course," the boy said. "But still. It was an unforgivable atrocity."

I tried to stay perfectly still, but the sweat on my palms were starting to soak into the tablecloth. And a part of me wanted to laugh at this turn of events because my plot for revenge should have been simpler than this.

In all my years of being in the Female Institution, Miss Sass had never once mentioned having a son. Now he was here, grinning amicably in front of me, and I—

I . . .

"Oh!" Mama covered her mouth with both hands. "How absolutely horrific! I'm so sorry, young man." She shook her head. "Only the devil could allow something so evil to happen."

The boy answered: "Then the devil should be made to pay, shouldn't he?"

A crash. Mama gasped and turned to me. Captain Davies reached across the table in concern.

"Are you okay?" he asked, because I'd knocked over my glass. The little water that was inside now pooled on the tablecloth. All eyes were on me, but his were the only ones I could feel searing into my very flesh.

"I'm okay," I lied, withdrawing my hand so nobody could see it shaking. The waiters came and cleaned up the mess quickly.

Out of the corner of my eye, I could see Queen Victoria watching me. It was just for a moment, before her gaze flickered away. But it was enough. My stomach churned, my throat dry.

I had enemies on all sides, didn't I?

But wasn't this what I asked for when I started on this path for revenge? I desired this chaos in the most silent regions of my heart. This was what chaos looked like.

What it felt like.

My hands trembled on my knees as I thought of Sass. As I pictured her ending her life. I saw bodies piled up upon each other, twisted and screaming.

Guilt. Ah, I felt guilt.

Guilt? Over *her*?

"Sally . . ." Mama hesitated to touch me. "What's so funny?"

Mine was the slightly off-kilter laughter of a girl raised to conduct herself in the most ladylike of ways. A quiet stream that stopped as suddenly as it had begun. I couldn't help it. My lips twisted into the littlest smirk as I considered the sheer nonsense of it all. This was *my* revenge story. How ridiculous. How absolutely *irritating*.

"Forgive me, I should introduce myself." The Freetown boy's graceful bow couldn't hide the secret hate in his eyes. "My name is Dalton Sass: son of the late superintendent. And I'm curious—Miss Forbes Bonetta, did you know my mother?"

I wiped my mouth neatly with a napkin. "It was a long time ago. You must know how quickly memories from childhood fade. Though some memories become seared into one's flesh like the lash of a whip."

"An interesting point. I quite agree." Dalton matched the sharpness of my words with his sinister expression. "I intend to make memories too while I'm here in England." He ran his finger along the blunt edge of his knife. "I shall have to remember to sear them properly so that they'll never be forgotten."

FOURTEEN

"SARAH FORBES BONETTA." McCoskry greeted my mother and me outside the palace, his belly filled with his seven-course meal. "I was overjoyed when the Queen told me about your engagement. Congratulations."

He shook my mother's hand briskly. I thought *I* was the one he was congratulating. Though it was for the better. I could barely stand to look at him. Imagine if he touched me.

"I have to run, but we shall hopefully catch up soon?"

Sooner than he thought.

I didn't close the carriage door quickly enough. I regrettably still heard Dalton's "Congratulations, Miss Forbes! I'll be seeing you" before the slam of wood. My nerves tensed at the sound of his voice. Dalton stood on the street, next to my dapper husband-to-be, his arms behind his back as was the gentlemanly way, while his sharp look promised mayhem. He'd just begun to chitchat with Bertie when the carriage took off down the road back to Chatham.

"That was a success, all things considered. Thank God." Mrs. Schoen adjusted her white shawl over her shoulders. She seemed somehow even more impatient after lunch—probably because she hadn't been allowed to eat her fill. "The Queen has ordered that you begin your preparations for your union in Brighton under the care of Miss Sophia Welsh."

"You can't be serious: marriage training?" I couldn't imagine a more ghastly punishment.

Mama ignored me. "You begin the morning after tomorrow. I knew you'd need time to gather your things and . . . yourself. So I bought you some time."

I hated when Mama was angry with me and I with her. I hated the disapproving perk of her bottom lip and her absolute unrelenting inability to admit that she could ever be wrong about any matter concerning my "rearing." I hated that I knew she did deeply care for me, and that if her perception of the world had not been so deeply twisted by such backward beliefs, we could have gotten along truly, both she and I, without masks and subterfuge. I stopped arguing with her then and there. It wouldn't get me anywhere.

"Miss Welsh is very strict and older than even I, so make sure you respect her. You cannot behave the way you did today. Her Majesty chose Welsh for you herself. You will not give her any problems."

Or Welsh would report me to the Queen. That was the silent warning. And if another building should mysteriously burn down, then what? Well, I suppose Queen Victoria would have her answers about the "strange happenings" that seemed to curiously haunt my every step.

Strange happenings. Like Dalton Sass.

Did he know? I'd left no evidence. How *could* he know? But then again, I was only a child when I destroyed the Institution, and not yet well-versed in the art of retribution. It wasn't out of the realm of possibility that I could have made a mistake—left even the tiniest clue.

Whether Dalton knew or not, I couldn't take the chance. If he had inherited even an ounce of his mother's cruelty, I had to get rid of him and fast.

Bobby Wheeler was a particularly chatty street urchin. After frightening Uncle George into an asylum, he seemed the proudest among the masked boys, excitedly soaking in their victory after they left the taxidermist with their masks off. That job meant fish and chips, some bread, and a sack of coins to take with them to the cellar they lived in, the one underneath an unpopular London tavern where Scotch girls danced and peddlers tried to hawk stale shrimps and pies. The day after the Queen's luncheon, when I finally had a chance to escape back to London, Little Bobby talked about the adventure quite a bit before one of the older boys hushed him.

"Rui told us once a job is done, it's done," said Connor, an abandoned Irish boy who I noticed was trying a little to mask his accent. I hadn't any time to encourage him not to. I doubted he would have listened to me anyway. He glared at me defiantly. "What do you want?"

That childish defiance disappeared the moment they noticed I came with gifts—namely, the engagement gifts I'd been given at the luncheon. Mostly silk and other expensive clothes that would go for a pretty penny in the market. Bobby and his boys were more than happy to give up Rui's location: the Devil's Acre. How apt.

The area was a stone's throw from Westminster Abbey but plagued with poverty. It should have made the Queen ashamed, except she was too busy enjoying her profiteroles as she cried over her dead husband. A selfish wretch, that woman. How dare she call herself a monarch?

I bristled as Bobby rapped his knuckles on the wooden door in the middle of an alleyway. Three times. Pause. Then a fourth. It was some kind of code. The door opened.

"Right this way, miss." Bobby, the little gentleman he was, let me enter first with a sweep of his hand. I descended the rickety steps, the sound of men growling and yelling growing ever louder.

The winding staircase led us to an underground cellar packed to the brim with hollering voyeurs. The entertainment: two half-naked men fighting bare-knuckle, clothed in nothing more than filthy pants stained with blood. I just made out the brawlers from the stairs, but lost sight of them once my shoes met the stone floor. Bookies were taking bets and keeping score in the corner underneath the wooden rafters. Crowds of men growled with delight each time a tooth flew and a spurt of blood washed their faces.

"There you go, miss. Rui should be around here somewhere, I reckon," said Bobby, ducking as a beer bottle flew over his head and crashed against the wall. "I don't think he's been killed yet, at any rate."

I looked down at him, surprised. "Excuse me?"

But Bobby tipped his hat and disappeared back up the stairs just as the rowdy crowd cheered. I'd never seen so many dark bowler hats, cigars, booze bottles, and dirty frock coats in one place at a time that wasn't a dancing room. It was tough to get through all the bodies. The smell of sweat, vomit, and the faintest hint of urine stabbed at my delicate senses. The rectangular pit was made of rapidly peeling clay. It shook with all the hands gripping its ridge and shaking it as they watched the fight below with bloodthirsty shouts. I elbowed my way to the front of the herd, letting out a gasp when I felt a hand pinch my behind.

"Bloody rats," I cursed, turning around to catch the perpetrator, but all I could find were sharp, libidinous grins. This must have been one of those dens of vice Mama had warned me about. And between the gambling and the ceramic jugs of alcohol spilling every which way, I thought Rui had better taste when it came to his dens.

Apparently not. I reached the front of crowd just as Rui jumped into the pit from the other side of the cellar. The crowd went wild.

"Come on, who's bettin'?" The bookie was goading the crowd and they responded.

"Half a crown on the mad lad!" one man cried. "He never loses."

"All right, then, I'll try you a 'gen and a 'rough yenap."

"Right, try your luck! I've got sixpence on the big bloke."

The man Rui was to face was a giant in comparison, with battle scars from previous fights marring his flash from his balding head to jiggling stomach. Rui seemed to enjoy having his ribs punched and his jaw knocked. I didn't hate it either. His tight, lovingly carved muscles, glistening with sweat, contracted with each hit, the blood flying from his Cheshire grin peppering the clay walls of the pit. I didn't hate seeing that crooked smile as he fought back knuckle for knuckle. There was nothing graceful about the way Rui fought. There was no technique—just the pleasure of chaos in landing blow after blow while his baggy brown pants clung to his slender waist with a tightly wrapped belt.

An uppercut to the Goliath's chin had the man stumbling back. The crowd cheered. Rui lifted up his toned arms, soaking it in, turning around to face his audience.

His joy turned to confusion once he saw me at the ledge of the pit. "Sally?"

I didn't have time to answer him before his opponent tackled him from behind. It was a cheap shot. I gripped the ledge, my heart pounding while Goliath pounded his stomach. The idiot was going to get himself killed.

"Rui!" I shouted down into the pit. "You look a bloody mess. Hurry up and get out of there. I need to talk to you!"

"Oh?" On his back, Rui moved his face to avoid Goliath's fist. Knuckles crashed into stone. "It's not terribly important, is it?"

I gritted my teeth. I didn't want to be having this conversation here amongst this rowdy group. "It is. So hurry up with this foolishness and come with me *now*."

Though his opponent straddled him, Rui held his fists back, though it wasn't without effort. Spit launched from his lips. "Since when do you order me around, princess?"

"Since I managed to bring John Brown to England, just as you begged me to."

"What?"

Rui relaxed in that one moment of surprise and got knocked in the across the face for it. I covered my gasp. He really was going to get himself killed if he didn't finish this up quickly.

"Rui!" I yelled, my voice barely discernible from the murderous howls of the audience.

Rui wiped the blood from his mouth. "Well, since you asked nicely—"

He headbutted the man and jumped to his feet while his opponent writhed in pain. Goliath was bigger, but Rui was quicker. He recovered quickly, kneeing him in the gut. A few more punches knocked out two of the man's teeth. I saw them fly into the hungry crowd.

Cringing, I turned away, flinching when a giant thud and a plume of dust made the audience go feral. Rui had just made a few men several pence richer. He lifted his arms in victory before striding toward me and grabbing hold of a man's arm. Together, a few cheering audience members pulled Rui out of the pit and clapped him on the back.

Clapped him perhaps too hard—suddenly, Rui was hovering above me, the smell of his breath, sweat, and blood wafting into my open lips.

"You wanted to talk. Then let's talk." Grabbing my wrist, he pulled me through the throng of spectators, snatching a small sack of coins offered to him from a bookie on the way. He didn't stop dragging me until we'd found a "quiet" spot underneath the stairs. New opponents had taken to the ring, gripping the audience's attention.

Letting out a long, weary sigh, Rui lay back against the cold stone wall and slid down to the floor, wincing with pain but grinning nonetheless. Blood was still oozing from his lips.

"Lady Sarah Forbes Bonetta." He threw up his sack of coins and caught it with one hand. "Now how is it you keep turning up in places I don't expect or particularly want you to?"

With my hands on my hips, I stood over him to make sure my face blotted out the crowd. He smirked. Of course he would. My face was a far more pleasant sight, if I did say so myself. "This isn't a social call. Like I said, I brought John Brown to Windsor Castle. Which means it's your turn. Now you do as I say."

But Rui wasn't paying attention. He lowered his head, staring at the floor. His silence put me on edge. Kneeling down, I took off the white bonnet covering my curly hair and used it to wipe the blood from his lips. His breath reached my fingers, sending a sudden chill through me. And his gaze suddenly soaking me in made me shiver. Though his body soon relaxed, his aura remained intense—almost frightening.

"How did he seem to you, John Brown?" he asked without looking at me, lowering his head. I looked past his chapped fingers to the chain now peeking out of his pants pocket. His watch? He'd had it on his person. . . .

I wrapped my black overcoat more tightly around me. "Hale and hearty. Strongly built from his shoulders to his thick legs. Beard red as flames. If he's your enemy, I don't know, Rui. He may put up a fight."

Rui brought his knee up his chest. "Oh good." His black bangs rippled over his forehead as he lifted his head. "I love a good fight."

His sharp tooth bit the edge of his lip. The sight of it gave me a bit of a thrill. I could imagine the pain this Brown must have wrought him—a pain I knew all too well when I was furiously plotting. The defined muscles of his arms tensed as he flexed his bruised hands into a fist. He was readying himself too. But against what?

Heat rushed to my cheeks. I turned my head away from his body. "Are you going to tell me what you're planning to do to that Scotsman?"

"Are you going to tell me why you tracked me down here while enjoying a perfectly good beating?"

I stared at my now blood-soaked bonnet. "You certainly did get a good beating."

"I did." He paused. "Were you impressed?"

I ignored the flutter in my stomach and let out a cruel laugh. "Hardly," I said. "Just beating each other barefisted. Didn't any of you ever learn about pressure points? Aiming for joints that can be easily broken? You could take apart a man thrice one's size with just a few months' study of anatomy. If you're skilled enough, you could do it without leaving even a trace of murder behind until your enemy was dead and gone—"

I pursed my lips because Rui was staring at me, both eyebrows raised.

"What? I've done some reading in the past." It had become a rather morbid pastime of mine when I returned from Sierra Leone.

He chuckled, shaking his head. "And again, I ask your reason for stalking me."

"I would hardly call it stalking." I thought. "Tracking, maybe—"

"Sally—"

"I'm getting married."

The crowd screamed. Another tooth must have gotten knocked out. But Rui and I only saw each other. He must have seen it—my distress. I suddenly felt nauseous.

As the silence between us continued, I turned away. I couldn't bear to check Rui's expression—which itself, I couldn't bear to admit. And the longer the silence went on the more I fretted like a silly schoolgirl waiting for some handsome lad to talk to her.

Nonsense. I torched my school.

Now, as the silence droned on, the urge to set fire to something else rippled through me until Rui *finally* broke the tension.

With his laughter.

"You're getting married? Well, of course you are! A girl just turned eighteen." Rui slapped his knee and threw his head back. "Oh, you high-society types, you're all so repetitious; it's like you were built from the same factory. One after the other."

Rui's laughter was indistinguishable from the shrieks of the men in the filthy cellar. Now I really wanted to burn something. I clenched my teeth.

"And?" He wiped a tear from his eye. "Who's your husband-to-be?" And he tilted his head. "Is he better-looking than me?"

My heart caught in my throat. Heat rose to my cheeks as I instinctively slid away from him. Few people could be considered, from my perspective, better-looking than Rui. But as far as competitors, objectively speaking, Davies did win handily. "He's a wealthy businessman from Lagos. Incredibly handsome. Polite. He's also fourteen years my senior."

Rui's grin faded, ever so slightly. At least he'd stopped laughing. Rui was quiet for a time. Then he shifted a little to make room for me. I sat down on the floor next to him.

"And when are you to be married?"

"Next month."

"Next *month*?"

Rui seemed genuinely surprised. His jaw hardened. His hands went limp upon his lap. But it was a momentary pause. With one last incredulous chuckle, he ran his fingers through his messy black hair. "Will I get my invitation in the mail? How many of my men can I bring? Plenty to steal at a wedding."

The lopsided smile I used to find so attractive only irritated me now. "Rui. This is serious. I'm getting married. In one month. At which point, my husband will be taking me back with him to Lagos in West Africa. It's all by decree of the Queen."

"So you'll be reunited with the Yoruba people. The Queen must have thought it to be in your best interest."

"How can you say that?" I balled my hands into fists, furious at his indifference. He wasn't even looking at me. He didn't understand. How could he? He seemed perfectly happy here in London getting his face punched in while commanding his army of criminals.

I *did* want to be reunited with my people. I *did* want to go home someday. Being ripped from my homeland was a visceral experience. Flesh split from bone, heart and lungs torn asunder and left as a bloody stain on cold England soil. Maybe once I was home, when the time was right, I would find people to love again. People who would move my battered heart and make it sing once more. A family of *my* choosing.

Ade and I used to boil plantains in a clay pot. We used to eat mangoes together under the fattest palm tree near my home. The other children always envied him—a friend to a princess. My parents inspired fear and awe in our village, yes. But it was simply being important to someone that gave him, a sickly boy nobody would talk to, a sense of a pride.

A family of my choosing. If I could be whole again . . . if this was the way to do it . . .

But it wasn't that simple. Things were different now. *I* was different. I wasn't the Princess Ina they knew—if anyone remembered me at all. I would be an alien returning to them, a foreigner with different manners and behaviors, my accent changed into something gaudy. I sometimes had nightmares of being laughed at by my own people, all of them pointing and jeering at me as I spoke a language I couldn't fully remember because of no fault of my own. The forced separation schemed by the Forbeses had created a chasm between us—and within me. I could admit to *no one* how deep the insecurity was that filled it.

But I did want to go. One day. When my mind and heart were ready. When I'd done all I needed to do here in England to gain closure following the indignities that had plagued my life. On my own terms. On *my own terms*.

That's all any of this was about.

"What about what I want? What about *my* plans?" Sucking in a deep breath, I calmed myself enough to lower my voice. "The Queen suspects me. That is the only reason she's so quickly prepared to ship me out of England."

"If the Queen already suspects you and has so quickly prepared a countermeasure to your schemes, then that only proves you were too sloppy for your mission to ever succeed in the first place." And when I glared at him: "Either that, or you have to accept that Queen Victoria truly has your best interest at heart."

"When it comes to me, the Queen has only ever had her *own* best interest at heart." I remembered seeing the ravenous look in her eye the day I met her as a child. The endless possibilities of what this new toy could bring her. And indeed, toys are meant to be played with—controlled. The Queen's African goddaughter united with a wealthy, British-educated African businessman. A perfect match. Who would disapprove? It was as nature intended, they'd say. It would be remembered forever as yet one more accomplishment of England's civilizing mission with the noble white Queen at the fore. The headlines and history books were writing themselves even now.

I was no one's pawn, least of all the Queen's.

"My, my, Sally, you look so furious." Rui's lacerated hand suddenly enveloped mine, roughly and without apology. It was a little damp with sweat. I had no time to complain, because he yanked me to him, far too close. "But what are you to do? Unless you're confident you can finish your list in one month, it seems the Queen has you beaten."

"That's why I'm here." One thing I hated about being this close to Rui—about the only thing I hated—was that I was sure he could hear feel the rapid beating of my heart through his own chest. "To ask you what I should do."

"Ask me? Advice? *You?*"

"My revenge. My wedding in one month. And there's also this strange man. His name is Dalton Sass. It seems I accidentally killed his mother."

"Well, that's never good."

My stomach was in knots, my heartbeat pounding against my skull as that boy appeared in my mind's eye like a ghost. I thought of his snake-like grin and shivered. He was surely the one who'd written to Queen Victoria about the new "developments" in Freetown. How many secrets of mine did he know? How many had he already told the Queen? Between him and my sudden marriage announcement, I was lost at sea. It felt like my plans were unraveling at a rate too fast for me to even comprehend. "I don't know what to do."

Rui seemed intrigued. But rather than asking more questions, he leaned in close until his lips almost brushed my ears. "Why don't you do what you always do?"

My breath hitched in my throat. "What?" Perhaps it was his hot breath that muddled my thoughts. Not that my thoughts weren't already muddled to begin with.

"Oi, mad lad." A wire-thin man who hid his blond hair beneath a bowler hat kicked Rui's left ankle. With hooded eyelids, Rui looked up. "For a second there, it looked like you were going to throw the fight. Now, you wouldn't ever think of doing something stupid like that, would ya? Because I got a lot of money riding on you these days."

Rui didn't answer, but once Wire Man's gaze slid to mine, a disgusting grin on his face. "What's this, then? Now isn't this a sight. A Negro girl." As my eyebrows furrowed, he laughed. "I love myself a good Negro song as much as I do a flash ditty and a flash song. You sing, little Negro girl?"

I recoiled at the sight of him, standing on my feet, biting the inside of my cheek to keep my rising rage from overflowing. Before he could get any closer, Rui slid between us. It didn't matter that Wire Man was a head taller. Rui's silent but palpable animosity caused the man to stumble back. Wire Man tripped over an empty bottle of beer and fell on his behind.

"On your arse, where you belong." Rui grabbed my hand and turned to me. "Come, Sally."

I didn't argue, though my heart fluttered a little when he stepped on the man's leg for good measure. As we passed through the crowd, I heard myriad conversations, some, as usual, pointed at me: "Not too many of *them* around."

Rui was bloodied and battered—a member of the fold here in the underground fighting ring. But I was in a fine dress and coat suitable for an outing. It confused some. And for others, it was as if my very presence offended them. Well, it wasn't anything I wasn't used to in this country.

Rui led me away from the chaos to the brick wall where only a few men stood a few paces next to us. They looked undoubtedly upper class. Interesting, the places where men of good standing seemed to turn up. One short man dressed like a dandy handed a newspaper over to his much rounder friend. I just spied the cartoon before he folded the page: Queen Victoria in mourning black, her head bigger than her whole body, with gobs of bright blue tears flooding the streets.

"Old girl's gone mad, they say. I know a chap in government from back in Eton. She refuses to see all of them, even the prime minister." The dandy laughed. "Wonder if she's even useful for anything at this point, now that she's in such a state."

"Public opinion is turning against her," Rui said as the men moved away to get a better view of the new fight that'd just started.

Just the thought of it excited me. This was a country of gossip, after all. The very future of the royal family depended on when or if the public would finally realize they never had any need of them in the first place. What I'd done to Uncle George had certainly made the rounds and damaged the Queen's name.

Which might have made her more desperate to get rid of me.

She might have her chance now.

"Sally . . ."

The crowd roared. Another fight was over, almost as soon as it started.

"Why do you fight?" I asked him.

"I've been asked that before." Rui acknowledged an acquaintance with a nod of his head—an older man with scars all over his face and a bald head. Even in his middle age, he was shaped like a brick, and with his shirt off he was ready to fight. "One of the many reasons I've brought shame to my family."

He reached into his pocket. I watched, stiff, as he reached into his pocket and pulled out a silver watch. It was cracked—of course it would be, from the fights. But not broken. He opened it, finally showing me the inside.

The clock didn't work. Both the hour, the minute, and the second hands were stuck at six. The second hand twitched as if trying to escape—a feeble attempt. But it was the black-and-white photo tucked into the clock's cover that caught my eye. In a regular parlor room, a square-jawed man with his hair perfectly combed sat in a wooden chair. Black suit, pants, and a bow tie. Two boys stood next to him, their haircuts revealing their entire forehead. One had soft doe eyes. The other, much shorter, looked uninterested, his expression curved into an uninviting scowl. Their black collars were so high up to their chins it should have choked them. But their father seemed happy. His smile glimmered with kindness.

155

"Your father," I guessed. Rui's eyes hadn't changed. They were still filled with mischief and a little bit of malice. Big and twinkling just like those of the older man.

Rui looked at me, impressed. I couldn't pretend that didn't move me. "A good man," he told me, tilting his hand as he stared at the photo. "Grew up in Xiangshan, Guangdong. Attended the Morrison Education Society School—very prestigious in Hong Kong. Then came to London with my brother and me as a translator. He translated countless Chinese texts into English."

So this was his brother. They looked alike—their heads small, with a sharp tip to their chins, though his brother's face was longer and nose rounder.

"My brother made a respectable life for himself too. He went to Edinburgh and got his PhD in anatomy and pathology. Luk Ham." He laughed, shaking his head. "Such an upright gentleman. He's still in Edinburgh with his wife and two darling daughters. I believe he's involved with the Edinburgh Medical Missionary Society, last I spoke to him."

Luk Ham. The full name of Rui's elder brother. What could Rui's be? Even the tiniest bit of insight into Rui's origins piqued my curiosity. I wanted to know his name, his true name, but a timid part of me pulled me back with a gentle tug. I couldn't ask, not after I refused to let him call me by mine.

Out of the corner of my eye, I saw Wire Man. He didn't approach us—not completely. He stood with his back to the wall a few paces away, his arms folded. He was looking me in particular up and down as he pinched his cigar between his fingers. It was starting to bother me.

"Doesn't seem like you speak to your brother much," I said, shrugging off the growing irritation from that vile, nosy man.

"Well, I don't have too many opportunities to go to Edinburgh, but when I do, his wife, Wai Ming, cooks the loveliest beef dish." And those bright eyes began twinkling again. Even with all the bruising on his face, he seemed to come to life. "His daughters, Yee Yan and Yee Fen, are brilliant, as expected of my father's legacy. Yee Fen in particular seems incredibly gifted in the arts. I'm certain she'll be an actress when she grows up." He closed his pocket watch. Seeing such a gentle smile on Rui's lips made my hands feel warm and my heart feel soft. "Last I saw my brother he didn't even have to tell me. I could see it in his eyes. He is genuinely, extremely happy."

"It is a truly respectable life," I said.

"It is." Rui paused. "And not at all for me."

A vicious cheer erupted from the crowd. Another man had been knocked out cold. His body was sprawled out against the ground, bruised limp.

"Oi, give me my money, Barnes!" cried one man.

"Wait a minute, that bloke cheated. He cheated, I saw him use a knife!"

"What?"

Rui laughed and folded his arms, but this was no laughing matter. The crowd's bickering became more volatile, and I started to feel my heart rate pick up. Soon they'd be out of control. Unconsciously, I grabbed Rui's sleeve, but he didn't move an inch. He was reveling in it—in the mayhem. He drank it in with a shark-toothed grin, and not for the first time I was both exhilarated and terrified.

"My brother believes in playing by the rules. They've served him well. They've given him everything he's always wanted—a loving family, a beautiful home. I say damn the rules." His gaze slid down to me, arresting me to the spot. "Rules are cages designed by those with power to keep us in our places. I enjoy pain and pandemonium far better. I built for myself the life that I wanted. On my own terms. For my own reasons. It wasn't easy. But like I said: I like a good fight."

A fight indeed broke out. This time was barely controlled. Bookies ran out of the way as men piled on top of each other. Panicking, I grabbed Rui's bare shoulders, squeezing myself against him as some men ran for the staircase. One body flew in our direction, hurled by the man Rui had fought, that Goliath. I screamed. Rui wrapped his arm around the small of my back and flipped me around so his body covered mine against the onslaught. The brick scratched my back through the layers of fine clothes, now dirtied and ruined.

"Rui," I said in barely a gasp, seeing a man smash a beer bottle on another's head. "We need to get out of here."

"Do we?"

I looked at him, my mouth dry. "What?"

"Can you fight for the life that you want, little princess, even if it means you break a few rules? Even if it means you get blood on your hands?" He leaned in closer. My grip on his sleeve tightened. "Even if it means you fall?"

I remembered his words in the opium den, remembered him watching me carefully as Vale nearly gunned down Uncle George. As I almost let him.

"Oi." Wire Man took advantage of the mayhem to approach us. Plucking his cigarette out of his mouth, he rounded on the two of us. "You think you can make a fool of me, do you?"

Rui looked around as a dirty shoe flew up into the air. "Who are you again?"

This made the man crazy. He slammed his fist against the wall. "You and your little Negro had better get out of my sight while I'm still behaving myself." He reached out to push me. Rui caught his arm rather easily and shoved him onto the floor. His hat flew off his head, revealing a shocking bald spot in the center of a blond rug. He didn't much appreciate this. But just when I thought Rui would step in to defend me, he backed off.

"Rui?" I said, my breath quickening as I looked between Rui's retreating figure and Wire Man floundering on the floor like a rhinoceros getting ready to charge.

"If you want to take the life that you desire," Rui said to me, "the life you deserve, you have to fight for it. And perhaps, little princess, you'll have to get your hands dirty. So? What will you do? What are you willing to do to get everything you want in life?"

The man began hurling horrendous racial, sexual epithets my way and my mind turned blank. I suddenly remembered dancing naked in the parlor filled with jeering adults. The tears in my eyes with each of Miss Sass's strikes of her canes. The searing indignity of William Bambridge, royal photographer, ripping my Egbado tribe beads from my neck as he took my first portrait for the Queen.

I remembered Ade, drowning in the Atlantic Ocean.

I clutched my chest, my fingers curled around the peach lace fabric. I felt suddenly dizzy, suddenly feral. Suddenly bloodthirsty.

"Oi!" And he called me that word again just before charging at me.

I took off my shoe and slammed the sharp heel into his temple. I kept hitting him until he hit the ground. Arranged journeys. Arranged photos. Arranged luncheons. Arranged marriages. Arranged murders. Everything in my life since meeting Queen Victoria had been, in a word, *arranged*. A strategic, slow death of my identity until I was nothing more than an empty doll whimsically named after a slave ship. No more. No more conditional love.

No more.

I used my other foot and stomped on the man's face until he wasn't moving anymore.

"I will take the life that I want with my own hands," I whispered, wiping the blood off my shoe. The red smeared the brown of my skin. "No matter who has to die to make it happen."

Rui stared at the bloody mess of the man on the ground. Not even he expected this amount of rage. But it was time he saw it. It was time they all witnessed me peel off the straitjacket of polite society. My viciousness made Rui's eyes glaze and his chest still. He bit his lip as if trying his best to tamp down something dangerously carnal rising up inside him.

Then he smiled. "That's my girl. . . ."

FIFTEEN

"SALLY, THERE'S SOMETHING I've found out," Harriet whispered underneath the sprightly key of Felix Mendelssohn's Rondo Capriccioso, Op. 14. I put a finger to my lips, silently telling her to wait. Queen Victoria sat in the front row, listening to the pianist who played her favorite musician's piece in the center of the Audience Chamber. A miserable Bertie sat next to her, and yet mother and son seemed a world apart. The Queen wouldn't look at him.

The sunset-colored room boasted some of the most beautiful paintings—portraits of royals from the past—all underneath a choir of angels painted on the sky-blue ceiling. On both sides of a long red carpet were three rows of oak chairs, the carpet stopping at the foot of the grand piano and the performer's bench.

I was tired of having to come up with reasons to come to Windsor Castle. This time it was to thank her for my engagement luncheon. The Queen had already given my gift—a brooch stolen for me courtesy of Rui's men—to one of her ladies-in-waiting, who spirited it away to parts of the castle unknown. The Queen would never wear it—she much preferred more "exotic" pieces—something like the Koh-i-Noor, stolen by Britain from the Taj Mahal and given to her as a present by her late husband.

The piece had finished. After our modest applause, I leaned over to Harriet. "We're going," I said, and stood up to leave, terrifying the poor girl—nobody could leave before the Queen did. Those were the rules.

"Sally?" The Queen looked perplexed, but still eagle-eyed as she turned to face me. "Is there something wrong?"

I met the guests' disapproving stares with a modest grin. Mrs. Phipps looked particularly venomous, sitting in front of us with her friend and friend-to-the-court Mrs. Mallet. Though it irritated me to no end, I was always ready for their judgment. It was uncomfortable for some just to see me here despite my years coming in and out of the royal circle. For them, the least I could do was stay quiet and complacent so they could forget my presence.

Not this time.

Clutching my stomach, I bowed my head. "Your Majesty, please forgive me. I seem to be feeling unwell."

"Perhaps some medicine will help," said Harriet quickly, following my lead. She was clearly trying to avoid the cluck of her mother's tongue and her quiet but heavy disappointed sigh. "I know where to find some."

The Queen hesitated.

"Oh, come on, Mummy, don't torture the girl any longer," said Bertie before adding under his breath, "like the rest of us."

The Queen clearly pretended she hadn't heard him. She didn't respond, but with a wave of her hand, she let us go.

"We won't disturb you any longer," Harriet promised.

The Queen's eyes followed me as Harriet led me out of the room.

The moment the guards had closed the giant wooden double doors behind us, I shook off Harriet and began striding down the halls. To business.

"What information have you collected on Miss Welsh?"

At this, Harriet puffed out her chest with pride. "I've collected every bit of news I could on the woman—her list of associates, dead and alive. Just as you asked."

I'd already been trained in domestic norms through brutal education, all to make me a future "angel of the house." I didn't need "marriage preparations." But the pointlessness of these wife lessons was exactly the point. They were a distraction that would keep me in Brighton for far longer than I could afford. The Queen knew that. I needed Welsh out of the way.

Harriet led me to an empty servant's quarters. Inside the tiny, musty room, the bed frame pushed against the brown wood walls looked barely big enough to fit an adult. She reached into her blouse and pulled a folded piece of paper out from her chest. And when I read it, I recognized a name on that very list.

"Inspector Charles Wilkes . . ." I narrowed my eyes. "I've heard this name before. . . ."

I searched my memories. Yes, the name had come up . . . when I was learning everything there was to know about the Photographic Society of London. The Photographic Society was of peak interest to me, not only because it was under the royal patronage of Queen Victoria and Prince Albert, who'd taken a keen interest in photographic technology, but also because the society had many illustrious members—including one William Bambridge.

Charles Wilkes had no connection to Bambridge, though he'd worked with the society before to capture an art thief. Still, as I stared at the name written in ink on Harriet's parchment, the beginnings of an evil plot began to hatch in my mind.

Wilkes was not only my connection to Welsh. He could be my key to taking down Bambridge too.

My blood began to boil over in excitement.

Mr. Bellamy. Mr. Bambridge. Uncle George. McCoskry. Phipps . . .

Queen Victoria.

The gears in my head were turning, churning out frightful ideas that I could barely keep up with. But what with this talk of photographers . . .

"Come with me." I pulled Harriet out of the servants' quarters before she could protest. The red-suited guards of the palace didn't flinch even as we flew past them in the winding halls. Harriet was tripping over her feet as I dragged her by the wrist, but I was too delirious with opportunity to slow down.

"Photography was one of the Queen's favorite pastimes, especially when Prince Albert was alive," I told Harriet as we rounded a corner.

"Of course." Harriet tried to catch up with me. "Still is. What does that matter?"

"Haven't you heard the rumors?" The click of my heels echoed from the high ceiling. "Apparently Queen Victoria's interest in photography goes beyond the confines of so-called civil society."

Queen Victoria's perpetual black attire wasn't the only reason some ladies of the court had secretly taken to accusing her of being deep in the occult.

We had just rounded another corner when I heard a shout from the end of the hall.

"You devil!" A man's voice. Lord Ponsonby.

I pushed Harriet behind the corner, put my finger to my lips, and poked my head back around.

The sweat on Lord Ponsonby's bald spot gleamed clearly from the glare of the lamps. The Queen's secretary was shaking all because of the man showing him a letter pinched between his two fingers.

My stomach felt like ice. It was Dalton Sass. And judging from his taunting expression, he clearly had the upper hand in whatever situation this was. My heart beat faster. I could feel my blood flooding my palms as I rested a hand against the cold marble wall. Leaning in, careful not to reveal myself, I listened intently.

"I don't want too many things in life, my good lord Ponsonby. I haven't had much in my life either. My mother wasn't a particularly kind one. But I've always loved piano. The Queen and her guests are listening to a wonderful pianist at this very moment, aren't they? I would love to be one of those guests." He took a step closer to Ponsonby, who stumbled back on his shaking legs. "That's all. And then nobody would have to know."

And then nobody would have to know *what*? What weapon was Dalton holding to Ponsonby's throat?

That letter. I frowned. It was smaller than your usual commercial notepaper. And from here, it almost looked dyed; its faint yellow hue felt oddly familiar. Even without being able to see a single word, I knew its contents were as venomous as his grin. I felt it in my bones.

"What's going on?" Harriet asked, but I shushed her immediately. I had to hear everything.

"I'll go to Her Majesty," Ponsonby hissed. "Once she knows what you have in your possession—"

"She'll blame you for so flippantly bringing me into her circle in the first place. You were the one who invited me to Miss Bonetta's engagement luncheon." Dalton checked his nails. "You're the Queen's secretary. Aren't you supposed to be more careful? And yet you let something like this happen. How irresponsible of you."

From the fear in Ponsonby's eyes, it was clear one could kill with words as good as any other tool of destruction. Was it blackmail? What else would scare the old man so?

"A-All right . . ." Lord Ponsonby visibly deflated as he acquiesced. "But—!" He squared his shoulders and tried very hard to look taller. Like a little boy standing up to a bully. "Don't you go near the Queen with any of this."

The Queen? I frowned, my left ear pressed against the corner of the marble wall I clutched. Just what were they talking about?

"Sally? Whatever are you doing?"

Harriet and I jumped and turned behind us. It was Mrs. Mallet with her arms crossed and a thick lock of her raven hair falling down the side of her head in ringlets.

I pursed my lips. It was by either convenience or design that she found me here. Mrs. Mallet craved the Queen's attention as much as her other stooges. I had to be careful around her.

We straightened our backs and dusted off our dresses as if nothing at all had happened.

"I've given her the medicine," Harriet said quickly, nudging me in the ribs with her rather sharp elbow.

"I'm well again. It's a miracle."

We scurried off past Mrs. Mallet, but I didn't forget. Inspector Charles Wilkes. Miss Welsh. Bambridge. Victoria. Mallet. Dalton. Pieces on the board. Too many to count, but not impossible to play.

I just needed my battle strategy.

First: "Harriet," I said when we were out of earshot of Mrs. Mallet, "find out where Inspector Charles Wilkes lives, will you?"

He was about to become a very useful piece on this chessboard. But he wouldn't know until it was too late.

SIXTEEN

WHEN I WAS young, whenever the Queen would invite me to Windsor, whether on Christmas or midsummer, Mrs. Mallet would meet me at the station, sometimes with her daughter Eva. She was a good friend of Mrs. Phipps and friend to the royal household. I wasn't surprised Queen Victoria used her to spy on me.

That was very clearly what this was. As if her bumping into me in the middle of Windsor Castle wasn't obvious enough. Why else would the Queen suddenly insist that she take me to my "wife education session"?

Several days after my last visit to Windsor Castle, we were on our way to London, where we would catch a train to Miss Welsh in Brighton. Little Eva had come with her mother. Eva, now seven years old, laid her head on her mother's lap in the roomy carriage. Though Eva loved rides, she could never quite seem to keep her eyes open whenever in a locomotive in motion.

"Mrs. Mallet, would you be very upset if we stopped for some coffee in London?" The carriage wheels hit a rock that nearly shook the silly hat off Mallet's raven head. I helped adjust it for her. Little Eva didn't seem roused from her rest in the slightest. "I'm just so nervous about meeting Miss Welsh. I'm worried she'll be a little too strict with me."

Surprised, Mrs. Mallet patted Eva's head absently, looking around the carriage with a nervous grin before nodding. "Of course, Sally, why-ever not?"

I knew why she was nervous. In the royal household, I was the Queen's adopted goddaughter, proof of her miracle hand that extended across the globe. But in public, I was simply a Black woman in a rather nice dress. The public would surely ask if they saw us: *What are you doing with someone like that?*

It was what she was thinking. Her eyes gave it away the moment the carriage dropped us off on a busy street. Mrs. Mallet was checking for reactions.

Under the furious morning sun, a bright-red-and-yellow carriage clopped past the white commerce tents where gentlemen and women bartered for posh items that would give their homes the adequate wealthy façade they so desired.

I sat, with my terrible cup of coffee, at an open café on the other side of street. Across from me on the other end of the small white table, Mrs. Mallet fidgeted in her seat. Eva sat between us, eating her cake like the happy child she was.

"This is quite a lovely spot, isn't it?" I kept my voice low and calm as I was served some rather foul-tasting coffee.

"Yes," she said, her bottom lip curled. "Lovely."

She needn't have worried. There was a reason I didn't object to Mrs. Mallet bringing Eva along like she always did. A middle-aged white woman, her angelic child, and an African girl. I knew how any passersby would interpret the three of us. The young woman who served us coffee didn't even flinch. What would she care about a woman with her daughter's nanny?

An irritating misconception, to be sure, but in this case, at this café, I wanted to be invisible. Mrs. Mallet's gaze was stuck on a group of gentle-men laughing and patting each other on the back at the table a few paces down from us.

So was mine.

"Wilkes, good man, you have done it again!" said a large-nosed man in a bowler hat. "Your promotion is well-deserved."

The large-nosed man clapped the back of his friend, whose mustache drooped and fluttered about like the leaf of a palm tree. Charles Wilkes's cheeks were redder and puffier than usual. It must have been the booze he snuck into his tea. The chatter at the coffee shop was that he always asked the waitresses here to give him a little spike before he went to work.

It had been a few days since I'd read his name on Harriet's list of Miss Welsh's associates. Of course, I wasted no time stalking him. By now, I didn't know *all* this coffeehouse's gossip. What I did know, how-ever, was that his favorite waitress wasn't here.

An interesting absence.

"Excuse me," I said to a waitress who weaved around one of the white tables. "I've been here before and Andrea Bradley used to brew the most wonderful spot of tea. I'd love to have it again. Do you know where she is?"

Mentioning the name Andrea Bradley had affected the waitress the way I'd expected it to. She looked as uncomfortable as Mrs. Mallet did now.

"Andrea hasn't been here since—" She shut her lips quickly. Of course she did. In this wretchedly patriarchal society, Andrea, in her state, would bring too much negative attention to the coffee shop. She likely decided to leave before Wilkes was any the wiser.

"Are you close with her?" I asked. "Do you know where she lives?"

The waitresses folded her arms, closing herself off to me. I thought quickly. "It's really for my mistress." I gestured toward a confused Mrs. Mallet. "Her dreadful cold is interfering with her ability to converse with others. So wished for me to implore you on her behalf."

The wrinkles on Mrs. Mallet's face creased as she narrowed her eyes. I reacted quickly. The moment she pried open her lips to protest, I placed my heel on her foot under the table. A little threatening pressure caused her to hush.

"Would you tell us?" I continued meekly to the waitress. "I'd love to have a chat with her when I get the chance." I put a few shillings in her white apron pocket.

The waitress felt around her pocket and pursed her lips, blushing. "She's in Bethnal Green. Old Nichol Street. Everyone there knows her. Just ask around and you'll find her quick."

"Good." Taking the heel of my shoe off Mrs. Mallet's foot, I sipped my coffee as the waitress scurried away.

Wilkes took a shot out of his alcohol-spiked coffee, laughing with his chaps. He wasn't a target of my revenge. I didn't even know the man. Nevertheless, some sacrifices were necessary in a war.

"Sally, why did you—what on *earth* are you doing?" Frowning, Mrs. Mallet rubbed Eva's little raven head as the girl gulped down her pastry.

"Just small talk. I have a question for you too, Mrs. Mallet—interestingly enough, *about* talk." I took the first of the crumpets I'd ordered for myself and gave it to Eva. The child liked her sweets. "Some at Windsor Castle have some rather disquieting things to say about the Queen's current mood. They act as if the Queen of England is dabbling in the dark arts. Then again, when I spoke to the Queen personally some days ago, it did seem as if she'd been rather taken with spiritualism as of late. Is that true? Surely, you would know."

Mrs. Mallet shifted uncomfortably in her seat. It's not something that she would talk about freely, but given her connections, and the twitching of her fingers, it was clear she knew something of a scandalous nature as I figured she would.

"I'm not sure what you mean?" the woman lied.

What a waste of time. I tilted my head. "You mean she hasn't been engaging in any strange photography sessions lately?"

Mrs. Mallet's eyebrows flew up to her hairline. That's how I knew it was true. Still, Harriet couldn't get her hands on concrete evidence— only gossip. I needed Mallet for the physical element of this scheme.

"Sally, you shouldn't ask such things!" Mrs. Mallet folded her arms in disapproval. "What if the Queen knew you were asking such rude questions?"

"And if the Queen didn't know, you would tell her, wouldn't you?" I sipped my coffee. "It's why she ordered you to accompany me to and from Brighton?"

Mrs. Mallet unfolded her arm and let her hands rest on the table. Her fingers gripped the white tablecloth. "Sally . . ."

I swirled my cup. "First of all, you certainly won't be following me anywhere. You'll continue to *pretend* to do as you're told, but in actuality, I'll go to Brighton—and everywhere else—on my own." I said all this without looking at her. "You will also not tell anyone of our discussions from now on. But you will tell me all you know about the Queen's strange behaviors."

Mrs. Mallet's hands clenched into fists. "*Sally—*"

"You'll do so promptly and without delay so that I won't tell others that you had to steal money from your mother-in-law to pay for little Eva's governess." I patted Eva's head, but she didn't respond. She never responded to much when cream filling was in her mouth.

Mrs. Mallet's face turned pale. "What . . . what did you just say?"

I shrugged. "You've done a good job so far covering up your husband's gambling problems. Nobody knows—*yet*. But I didn't think you'd steal from your own illustrious in-laws."

"That isn't true!" Mrs. Mallet said in a hushed whisper, her wild gaze flying about the open café.

With a sigh, I offered Eva the last of my uneaten crumpets. But before I gave it to her: "Eva, you're always with your mother. Does she have the tendency to take things that aren't hers from time to time?"

"You mean nick things?" Eva swallowed her food. "Oh, all the time."

I gave her the crumpet.

Betrayed by her little angel. The Queen's unsuccessful spy deflated.

"Your thread work is impeccable, Miss Bonetta. But you'll need a more tender touch if you're to one day knit dresses for your infants."

I tried not to scowl at Miss Welsh. The idea of having children near me sucked the life from me. Sewing was Wife Lesson Number One. Welsh wasted no time shoving a white sheet of cotton into my hands, expecting me to transform it into a baby's cap.

There were no children here in Welsh's tiny, stuffy sitting room, where the floral pattern walls were mismatched with the red carpet and green velvet couch, and red, orange, and brown chairs. Chairs that in particular were very uncomfortable. Welsh, with her scarecrow figure, sat pin straight in one and expected me to do the same.

Not true for the woman who sat near the fireplace in the violet rocking chair. She was even older, so she could sit however she liked. In her rumpled dark blue dress, she hunched over with her beaklike nose and glared at me through her glasses as she knitted a scarf. Who was she again? Miss Welsh's older sister? Cousin? Mother? Hard to know: the woman wouldn't say a word to me, though her eyes never seemed to leave me.

Age was starting to hollow out Miss Welsh's oval face. With a crooked finger, she pointed at the cap-to-be in my hands. "Concentration and focus, Miss Bonetta. Concentration and focus are the key to perfection."

Oh, I knew that all too well. The connections I'd made in the past few days were evidence of that: Inspector Charles Wilkes, Miss Welsh, William Bambridge, and—if I moved my pieces just right—Queen Victoria. What a tangled web of deceit and vice the elites of society lived in.

I would destroy all of them in one fell swoop. And I knew just how to do it: with concentration and focus.

"Being a wife is about delicacy and self-sacrifice," Miss Welsh said, her white hair held up in a tight bun that tugged her eyebrows up, causing her to look eternally surprised. "You must embody that concept in your very flesh—in how you speak to your husband, behave around him—"

"Pleasure him." The older woman's voice was rough as bark, but I understood her perfectly. I stared at her in shock while Miss Welsh clutched the collar of her white blouse.

"No, Mother!" Ah, so it was her mother. Welsh's pale cheeks finally got some color in them. "That's—"

"I am curious about that." I put down my sewing needles and white cotton. "How exactly am I meant to pleasure my husband if I am to be delicate and modest at all times? It feels somehow like a contradiction," I asked very seriously.

I could tell by the sputtering of Miss Welsh's lips that she didn't have an answer. She was too busy being scandalized. "That is—"

While she flailed, I gazed upward at the gaudy chandelier, thought about it, and shrugged. "Well, I suppose if I cannot pleasure my husband, then he can always go to the whorehouse."

"Miss Bonetta!"

"Speaking of improving oneself," I interrupted quickly. "I was told by one of the associates that an upstanding friend of her father's is about to be promoted. I believe you know him: Inspector Charles Wilkes—well, soon-to-be chief inspector now."

Miss Welsh seemed pleased at the sound of his name.

"Yes, Wilkes is a family friend! A very close family friend." She nodded at her mother, who had, unfortunately, after her momentary and delightful outburst, gone back to glaring at me. "His promotion at Scotland Yard has been years coming."

"I heard he worked with that Jack Whicher on that dreadful Constance Kent murder case a few years ago. For him to be promoted before Whicher is quite the feat. I'm sure the papers can't get enough of him. How amazing that you're so close."

Flattery, even of the smallest kind, went very far with these types. Miss Welsh preened like a peacock. "Well, that's the result of good breeding."

Right. I tried not to roll my eyes while on the job. "Good breeding indeed. Why, you should throw him some kind of party to celebrate! A garden party perhaps? Here in Brighton. It would be so lovely."

Miss Welsh mulled it over quite shamelessly. What was the point of having connections if one couldn't flaunt it? Clearing her throat, she pointed again at my unfinished infant's cap.

"Concentration and focus, Miss Bonetta," she reminded me.

"Yes, yes, but isn't this also part of my training? Married ladies are expected to chitchat as we do our duties. Else why even have a sitting room?"

I got her there. Gossip was the number one currency here for a reason.

"At least think about it. It would be a wonderful opportunity for the chief inspector and such a lovely surprise for his wife. You'll be the talk of Brighton for days. Maybe even weeks."

I waited patiently for Welsh to relent. That didn't take long.

"I'll think about it," she said, straightening out her shoulders.

The party was set for Thursday, promptly at five. That, at least, gave me a chance to reach out to a very special guest in London—Bethnal Green, to be precise. Old Nichol Street. This was an invitation I knew wouldn't be declined.

Focus and concentration were indeed a woman of society's greatest weapon, especially when a party was involved. Welsh put hers together with lightning speed. By Thursday her efforts had come to fruition. Little white round tables filled her backyard garden, decorated with flowers and the best of the plates in her cupboard. Of course, the old men here didn't care and their wives still had things to complain about—the teacups, bowls, and saucers, though made of expensive porcelain, were old in design and simply out of fashion. There was only one maid to spare between them. Still, the fruit was fresh and the bread and cakes freshly baked.

And, of course, the tea.

"Is this Darjeeling tea?" One old man with a tuft of black hair sniffed his steaming cup with approval. "Miss Welsh, why, I don't say. I haven't had this since I worked overseas in the East India Company. What wonderful nostalgia to go with these lovely biscuits."

I'm sure the folk working their fingers to the bone in the Queen's Indian plantations didn't quite share the same lovely nostalgic feeling when thinking about the tea they gathered. I plastered on my smile and offered him a cucumber sandwich. I wasn't officially a maid, but Welsh only had the one. She was reluctant to go ahead with the celebration until I offered my services. Unsurprisingly, something about me serving her friends scones and tarts didn't feel strange to the old woman and her mother. I didn't even have to insist.

On the other side of the crowd was Harriet, offering her mother some sherry. Miss Phipps was a busybody. I'd need her mouth running for this little scheme to succeed.

There he was at the head table decorated with white and purple geraniums: Inspector Charles Wilkes of Scotland Yard, newly promoted, with a long, drooping brown mustache, an anchovy finger sandwich halfway down his throat and his faithful, snooty wife by his side. They crushed daisies beneath their feet as they went from friend to friend shaking hands and accepting congrats without an ounce of modesty between them.

"Miss Bonetta. I believe there are more tea cakes in the kitchen," Miss Welsh said, ordering me around like her personal servant as she sat down and talked with a friend.

"Of course, Miss Welsh." I bowed graciously.

"Oh." She waved me over and leaned in to whisper so her friend couldn't hear. "And my mother alerted me to a recent mouse problem in the living room. Do get the arsenic in the cupboards and lay a trap, will you? I can't be seen to have rodents."

I thought I noticed bite marks on the door frames. "Of course, Miss Welsh," I said again before giving Harriet, eyes ever on me, a rough nod.

As Miss Welsh prattled on—"Isn't my charge so well-behaved? So different than what you'd expect. The Queen asked for me especially, you know"—Harriet followed me discreetly into the kitchen.

Harriet stumbled into the soup ladles hanging over the softwood table, where the meals were prepared. Surprised at the noise, she grabbed them and held them still, blushing as I stifled a groan. Miss Welsh's plain white kitchen was as modest as most upper-middle-class homes, except all the washing was done in the scullery.

To business. "Did you deliver my message to our special guest as I asked?"

"You know I did, Sally." Harriet, always eager to please. It must have been a lesson bullied into her by her mother. From wherever I was in the garden I could hear her mother nagging her without regard to the other guests. When I noticed the poor girl's hands were shaking as she set the ladles down on the table, I took them in mine.

"Good. So she should be here, then."

Harriet nodded. Her expression softened a little at my touch. "I told her to be here at half past five."

"Before the toast."

"I prepared her transportation and everything."

"Yes, I know, Harriet. You've been amazing so far."

It saddened me a little to see just how far a compliment could go with the mousy brown-haired girl. Her mother was a demon. I knew that much. Even she couldn't hide how happy she was, though she tried, turning to the table, fiddling with the ladles, the plate of tea cakes, and the full pot of spare tea. There were a few unused cups—the ones Miss Welsh didn't think appropriate for the party because her maid couldn't get the stains out of them.

"I'm still not sure how this will help you deal with you-know-who," Harriet said, and I looked around quickly to make sure we were alone. Noticing my expression, she covered her mouth and lowered her voice accordingly. "You know—Bambridge. He's a photographer, after all, and—"

"Yes," I cut her off. That old mother of Welsh's was still in the living room—not that her legs or ears were working at optimal strength, but one could never be too careful. "Well, you'll see once the plan comes together."

"The plan." Harriet smirked, half-sheepish with admiration. "You always seem so sure of yourself. Even despite all you've been through. Your intellect is . . ." Harriet laughed. "Well, far more impressive than mine by any measure."

That was true, but saying that could be considered insensitive by some. Harriet wasn't a bad woman—just an incredibly frustrated one.

"More impressive in *every* measure, really. Smart, beautiful, courageous . . ."

"So you say in one of the many letters you wrote to me earlier this year while you were in Balmoral with the Queen. I received each one—they're in my closet in Chatham."

Harriet's cheeks reddened. I sighed.

"I hope you've stopped that little habit, by the way. Letters can easily turned into physical evidence against you." Or me. I thought of the letter Dalton Sass had shown Ponsonby that day in Windsor Castle and shivered.

"Sorry. I swear I've stopped." Harriet turned her back to me.

"Oh, Harriet. You're capable of much more than you know," I said, giving her the encouragement I knew she needed, and she perked up. I squeezed her shoulder before opening the cupboard.

When I looked back, I saw Harriet's gaze lingering on me. The moment she noticed me watching, she gave me a sad smile. "Mother is just so terrible," she said, pouring herself some tea. "She doesn't see any worth in me. Tells me every day. And yet, she expects me to become Queen Victoria's number one most confidential attendant. How does that make sense? How can I one day be 'The Honorable Harriet Lepel Phipps' if I'm also lazy, stupid, foolish, childish—"

Her nerves got the better of her and she spilled a little on the table. Embarrassed, she grabbed some cloth and began drying it up.

"Don't listen to your mother. She's bored and dead inside." I shuffled around jars of jam. That new book, *Mrs. Beeton's Book of Household*

Management, was tucked away in here too. I doubt Mrs. Beeton would approve of seeing her book in a kitchen cupboard.

"Dead inside? Like I was when they made me junior attendant a few months ago?" Harriet shook her head. "An appointment given to me only because of my father's rank in court."

Sir Charles Phipps was the Queen's private secretary, and Keeper of the Privy Purse, and other nonsense titles I couldn't care to memorize. It was a lot for little Harriet to live up to. No wonder she was rebelling.

"If you don't want to be that woman they'll write about in the history books as her mother and the Queen's good little dog, then create the life you desire. Be who you want to be." My fingers touched a little round bottle. I pulled it out. "Ah, the arsenic."

"Be who I want to be?" Harriet seemed to deflate. "Be who I want to be. Create the life I desire. But what if that's impossible? What if I . . . ?" She paused. "Wait, arsenic?" She blinked when she saw the bottle of poison in my hand. "What's the arsenic for?"

"Yeah, Sally. What's the arsenic for? You planning on killing someone?"

In a flash, Harriet and I turned to the kitchen door. The Prince of Wales had his eyes set on the tea cakes. He let his taunt go unanswered as he sauntered in, but he wasn't alone.

The bottle shook in my hand as I tried to catch my breath. "Captain Davies?"

As usual, his pearly white grin was as perfect as his gentlemanly bow. "We've come to celebrate with you and Welsh. Now don't get mad—" Davies added just as I began to part my lips in protest. "This wasn't our idea."

"'Course not." Bertie already had his mouth full of cake. "We wouldn't even know about that Scotland Yard bloke and his little tea party if it weren't for—"

"Me."

As Bertie began to choke, Dalton Sass slid out from behind Davies's broad frame and went to help him. A few pats on the back and Bertie was back to normal, but I wasn't. I glared at the Freetown boy, Superintendent Sass's son, as he waved to me.

"It was my idea, Sally. I hope you don't mind."

SEVENTEEN

HARRIET THREW ME a not-so-subtle fretful glance, as if to say, *Is this part of the plan too?*

No, it wasn't. Ignoring her, I instead curtsied for our guests. "Dalton Sass, what a wonderful surprise." My voice always became lighter and somewhat airy when I was using politeness to cover up my fury. "I see you've made quick friends with Captain Davies and the prince—such an unlikely pairing, I might add."

"Not so unlikely." Captain Davies was a head taller than Bertie and Dalton but seemed to keep a respectable distance from them at all times. "The prince has been showing me around London. And Dalton here's been stuck to the prince's side."

"I wouldn't say stuck," Bertie mumbled as Dalton helped the last bits of tea cake run smoothly down his throat. "I mean, he hates Mendelssohn as much as I do so he's clearly a good bloke."

Felix Mendelssohn, the Queen's favorite musician. Bertie and his mother had been listening to his composition in the Audience Chamber the last time I visited Windsor Castle. An event at which Dalton was desperate to be a guest . . . desperate enough to terrorize Lord Ponsonby.

All to get to Bertie.

"Oh, how nice, you've made a friend, Mr. Sass. A prince at that."

The slight patronizing drip to my tone was on purpose. Bertie blushed, but Dalton was unmoved. "And how, may I ask, did you find out about Miss Welsh's tea party?"

"Well, Bertie invited me to another lunch the other day and I heard Harriet and Mrs. Phipps discussing it: that the party for the inspector was your idea."

As Dalton ran his long, spindly fingers through his brown curls, I gave a suddenly tense Harriet a sidelong look. Harriet needed to learn to keep her small talk *small*.

"Harriet Phipps and Sarah Forbes Bonetta. It seems you two are close. Closer than I expected." Dalton strode forward, startling Harriet, who dropped her cup of tea on the table and stumbled back so quickly if I hadn't caught her she would have fallen over. "That's interesting. And good to know."

As Dalton's gaze slid to the arsenic in my hand, Bertie bulldozed his way between us. "Where's the party? Outside? That old crone in the sitting room wouldn't tell us anything. I don't think she hears very well." But he must have heard the chitchat outside the back. With a bright, cocky smile, he turned to Davies. "Well, what about it, Captain? Shall we continue our sparring in the garden, then? Unless you're scared to lose to me."

I raised an eyebrow. "Sparring?"

"It seems our prince has taken to competing with Captain Davies on more than one occasion," said Dalton, much to Bertie's chagrin. "I watched a particularly riveting game of pool just the other day."

"I wouldn't call it competing. . . ." Bertie's grumble trailed off.

Davies rubbed the bald part of his head, where his hairline receded. "And what shall we play this time, Your Majesty? I've already beaten you in chess."

Bertie's jaw stiffened. Casting a quick glance to me, he grumbled,

"They must have *something* out there we could do." He strode outside. I could hear the gasps from in the kitchen. The Prince of Wales at a garden party in Brighton. Miss Welsh was probably beside herself.

"Sally—I'm sorry, Miss Bonetta. If I could have a word alone with you?" Davies stretched out a hand. "It would only take a moment."

I looked between Dalton and Harriet. The pair looked like a wolf about to swallow a bunny whole.

"Please?" Davies said when he saw me hesitate.

After a few more moments, I sighed and pushed the bottle of arsenic into Harriet's hands. "It's for the rats, but just hold on to it for me, okay?" I told her. "Hurry back to your mother without a moment's waste. Quickly now. I'll bring the tea cakes when I'm ready."

Get away from him. And don't say a word. I hoped she understood as I followed Davies out of the other end of the kitchen.

Miss Welsh's mother looked utterly disgusted to see the two of us together as we entered the living room. She jiggled around in her seat as if to get away from us. I wasn't sure if her rickety old bones could take even that much movement.

"She's been like that since I got here," Davies said. "I don't suppose it's out of character for her?"

"Sadly, no," I said, looking at the grandfather clock tucked away in the corner. Twenty past five. Ten minutes before my true guest was to arrive.

"Not surprising."

I wasn't used to hearing such judgment and . . . was that disgust? From the upright Captain Davies. He glared back at the old woman, as thoroughly sickened with her as she was with him, and I felt, suddenly, a strange kind of kinship with the man that I hadn't before. It was fleeting, however. His next request was outrageous.

"Let's speak alone in one of the bedrooms."

"Bedroom? Alone? Are you mad?"

"Just for a moment. Please, it won't take ten minutes."

Maybe it was the way Welsh's mother turned from us, thoroughly uncomfortable and disapproving, that spurred me to listen. Whatever wild images were running through the old woman's mind would be worth it if it scandalized her into an early grave.

"Good. Because ten minutes is all I have."

Whatever was going to happen would happen in Miss Welsh's bedroom, which she showed me my first day of sewing here. Why? To show off all of her dresses, of course, handsewn—the same dreary, shapeless dress in different shades of gray filling her closet. Her room wasn't big, but the bed was covered in respectably folded sheets almost fancy enough to pass for expensive, though I'd seen enough in the palace to know the difference.

I sat on the edge, near the window, its dark blue curtains drawn while Davies lingered in front of the dresser next to the wooden rocking chair. Even in the small room it felt like we were as worlds apart as the day I first met him as a child in the Institution. We only had ten minutes. The minute of silence that passed between us was a thorough waste.

"So this is where you're taking your lessons," he said, awkwardly trying to break the ice.

"Yes," I said, amused that he kept his back to me. I could see his broad shoulders and muscular form, outlined by his fitted vest, but not his face. Not his expression—by design, perhaps. "This is where I'm taking lessons on how to be a good wife for you. And do you know what I've learned so far?"

Davies squirmed a little on his feet. Since he wasn't going to ask, I gave the answer without waiting. "Sewing, first. For our children, as I'll be in charge of making the clothes, you see. Cooking will be next, and—I think Welsh mentioned something about pleasuring you."

Captain Davies whipped around, stunned.

"Without enjoying it, of course. How could a woman enjoy sex and still be a good wife?"

He stumbled back until he bumped into the dresser. "Sally!" he exclaimed before clearing his throat. "I—I didn't know you could speak so roughly."

"You don't like it?" I tilted my head, crossing my legs so my yellow sundress fluttered delicately in the still air. "Then how would you like me to speak to you?"

Davies scrunched up his face. I liked that I was making him uncomfortable, upset even. It gave me a devilish kind of pleasure that would have fooled a less intelligent woman into thinking she'd gained control of the situation. But that was the very problem. No matter how intelligent the woman, she never fully had control—not when the differential lines of power were already drawn so thick. And that alone made me want to rush back into that fight club and stomp on someone's face again.

Davies shut his eyes and took in a deep breath. The next time he lifted his head, he showed me a sight I haven't seen of him yet. The captain looked world-weary and serious. Irritated like a father with a child. And absolutely not in the mood for games. "Sally. I'm not your enemy."

"I never said you were."

"You've been treating me as such the moment you laid eyes on me. Maybe even before."

"If you feel that way, then that's your problem."

"No, it's yours." Captain Davies straightened out the lapels of his vest. "Because we are going to be married, Sally. The Queen gave me her permission. Besides, marriage and children are in our culture. If it wasn't me it would have been someone else, but it *is* me. You might as well deal with it now."

Assertiveness. Now this was interesting. I stared at Captain Davies, his stern brows, his set jaw, curious. "You've changed so suddenly, Captain Davies. I feel like I no longer know you."

"You *don't* know me," he countered. "And yet you've judged me. Hardly seems fair."

Where had the always affable, endlessly polite, endlessly smiling gentleman gone? In front of me, here was the stern captain who'd commanded men in battle—a man who would bow to no one. But no, that wasn't entirely true. He did bow to some. But he wouldn't to me.

"I don't know you," I agreed. "And yet I'm forced to marry you because you wish it. Now which of these two situations seems less fair?"

Davies sat in the rocking chair with a weary groan and I wondered if our nights together would be like this. A weary groan and a rocking chair.

"How many marriages do you know have come about through love and courtship, I wonder?" He leaned over, his elbows on his knees, his sparkling coal eyes trained on me. "Did the Prince of Wales court Alexandra of Denmark after falling in love? Did Pastor Schoen know Elizabeth since childhood? Was it a passionate whirlwind of a marriage that brought them together? Love matches. I know of none, except those in fairy tales."

My eyes dropped to the floor. "I never liked fairy tales."

"Neither have I." He clasped his hands together. "The white man's fairy tales tell morals they themselves refuse to live up to. They flounder and make fools of themselves in real life while crafting themselves as heroes in the stories they tell. No, I've never liked fairy tales at all."

I stared at this Captain Davies, fourteen years my senior, and saw a sight I'd never seen before. This man had taken off his own mask, and underneath was weariness—just pure weariness. He'd been wearing his at least fourteen years longer than I, working his way up in the world to the point where he could begin to make requests for women from the

Queen. I wondered what that would do to a person. I turned to face the window.

"But there is one benefit of fairy tales. A lesson I've always taken to heart even in all my travels." Davies stood, placing his hands behind his back.

"And that is?" I waited.

"When a beautiful damsel is in distress, it is up to a handsome, capable man to save her. And that's exactly what I'll do, Sarah Forbes Bonetta."

I whipped around, baffled. "Save me?"

He was dead serious. The mask was fully off. He was a man who saw himself as a gallant knight. And while he had the build, looks, and no doubt skills for it, he was missing just one thing—a woman who actually wanted saving.

"And what exactly are you trying to save me from?" I asked it even though I knew the answer. It was written all over his face.

Captain Davies closed the gap between us. Bending down, he touched my chin gently with his finger. "You are an African princess. Witty and intelligent. Beautiful. You're wasted on them. And if you stay here any longer they will destroy you."

They had already destroyed me. They destroyed me from the moment they took me here, stole my dignity, and killed my friend. Davies seemed to understand that. I looked at the fire in his eyes and remembered Ade, rebellious in front of the Forbes brothers, spitting in their faces with ferocious will despite his weak body.

Their "love" for you is conditional, Ina.

"I know that," I whispered, answering Davies and Ade both. "But I can save myself." I looked up at him, Ade's fire burning in my own eyes. "I will save myself on my own terms."

"You can't."

"I can! This is *my* life! You don't know what I'm capable of."

"I was their slave, Sally. I know what *they're* capable of." He looked suddenly aged there as he spoke, as shadows passed over his face. Captain Davies straightened up. "You're too good to end up being ruined by them. I knew that the first time I laid eyes on you. I'll marry you and take you back to Lagos with me. With me, you'll thrive. With your own kind, you'll thrive, Sally. Just listen to me. You'll see."

I bit my lip, my fingers curled over my knees. "I don't remember giving you permission to call me Sally."

"I'm to be your husband. And you my wife. Shouldn't I be able to call you what your friends do?" He said it with a pleading gentleness that told me he truly meant what he said. And that fact was proof enough that I couldn't marry him. He sounded too much like Forbes as he spoke about "saving" me.

I looked Captain Davies square in his eyes. I needed to know. "Do you love me?"

He cleared his throat. "Of course I fancy you, Sally. You've become a beautiful young woman since last I saw you."

"I asked—do you *love* me?"

He looked away. It was some time before he answered me. "I loved a woman once. And married her. Matilda Bonifacio Serrano."

"Ah. A Spanish woman."

"From Havana."

"I thought such romantic matches don't exist except in fairy tales."

"She died shortly after our wedding. So they don't."

I squeezed my hands together. The clock was ticking. How much time had passed? I'd lost track. I never lose track.

"No, I don't love you, Sally," he answered without any apology in his voice. "But I don't need to love you to see your potential. I need a wife. You need a husband. A real community. A life away from *this*." He gestured around him. The open cupboard of gray dresses. The lifeless furniture. The cold dreariness. "It's my duty as a man and as your kin to give that to you."

"And what is my duty as a woman?"

"To listen to your husband. It is as it has always been. In this part of the world, in every part of the world. It's the *way* of the world. I didn't make it such, but such is the way things are. Please don't make me your enemy because of it."

He was serious as he answered. His voice gentle. The kindness was clear. The belief in what he saw as a simple truth. And there was no wound deeper than that.

Funny. It seemed in this world I could see no one but enemies around me.

"Sally! Sally!"

Harriet's voice came shrieking from below. I stopped the conversation short. I couldn't take much more of it anyway.

"Speech! Speech!"

The guests in the garden egged on the new chief inspector at his head table with their raised glasses of wine. They'd somehow pulled Bertie to the head tea table as well. Nobody seemed to care he had an entire decanter of claret in one hand and was already swaying on in his feet. The Scotland Yard man and his wife was only too happy to accept the congratulations of the future king.

I joined Harriet by one of the empty tables in the back, grimacing when I saw two unexpected guests sitting next to her: Miss Welsh's mother and Dalton Sass. Sass waved at me like a fly that wouldn't stop buzzing in my face.

"You forgot the tea cakes?" he said, sitting back in his chair and folding his arms.

Instinctively, I checked my empty hands. Damn, I had.

"Seems you were busy. Don't worry: Harriet and I took care of it." Dalton gestured around the garden, where guests were helping themselves.

"It's good to see you and Harriet working so well together." I took my seat next to Miss Welsh's mother, who shivered and snorted.

"Somehow I doubt we work together as well as you two do," he replied, his gaze sliding between the two of us.

I gave Harriet a soft smile that made her sit up straight. The panic in her eyes made clear she wanted to explain herself immediately, but I didn't blame her. It didn't take this man long to worm his way into the life of the Prince of Wales. He'd be difficult to shake.

Sass began topping off his tea. "I've poured you some of this excellent tea. By all means, take some. My lovely madam has certainly enjoyed hers."

He reached over and touched Miss Welsh's mother's pale, skeletal hand, and she blushed and cooed, completely taken in by his calculated simpering. She'd already guzzled her tea and, beaming at the insipid young man with a rare toothless smile, was ready for more. But Sass wasn't waiting for her. He was waiting for me.

"The chief inspector is about to make his speech." He gestured toward my teacup. "Drink, Sally."

Harriet was sipping hers delicately, silent but for her anxious expression, which spoke volumes. Now what was wrong with this picture? As if seeing my life play backward, I searched my memories, starting from the time Dalton, Davies, and Bertie waltzed unexpected into the kitchen. I was so flustered. The guest I'd actually invited hadn't shown.

And then there was the letter he wielded like a sword to Lord Ponsonby's throat. Its contents were dangerous. Why else would the secretary nearly wet himself?

Dalton's affable grin hid too many secrets. His mother had never shown me a single smile in all the years I was at the Institution. Seeing her face again, with lips perpetually split from ear to ear, unnerved me.

There was something I was missing. Bertie and Davies had been "sparring." Sparring? Over what? Why in the world would Bertie be so interested in my betrothed husband?

I looked over to the head table, and quite by accident, our eyes locked. For a moment, Bertie's eyes softened before he seemed to panic. With a boorish laugh, he took a swig from his decanter and wrapped an arm around the chief inspector's neck, who took his rough tug in stride because no matter how big his promotion, he could never outrank a prince.

And where was my betrothed? When I left the kitchen to speak with him, I was more focused on making sure Harriet wasn't bamboozled by Sass.

Speaking of Sass. "The tea cakes are lovely, aren't they?" But once again, he gestured toward my tea. "They go great with the tea."

He tipped it toward me with a finger.

Something was indeed wrong with this picture. The fact that I couldn't yet discern Sass's true intentions elevated my sense of danger. I glared at him. He grinned at me.

"Sally!" Harriet dropped her teacup onto the table's white cloth. She looked to the house's entrance. "It's—" Her lips snapped shut and, after a nervous glance toward Sass, she cleared her throat. "It's Captain Davies! What a kind man he is."

I looked to the entrance as well. Indeed, it was Captain Davies, and sure enough, he was as kind as he was noble. For with his strong arms, carefully crafted in the military, he assisted a pregnant woman into the garden. Golden locks poured over her simple blue dress in ringlets.

She's late. "It looks like the Captain needs help." I pushed my teacup toward Miss Welsh's mother, who eyed it hungrily, and stood up. The true show was about to begin.

Before Sass could say another word, I went to the pair, just as Inspector Wilkes cleared his throat, wiped his drooping mustache, and began to speak, much to the applause of the guests.

"First, I want to thank the ever good-hearted and considerate Miss Sophia Welsh, for opening up her home to my wife and me," he said. From her seat, Miss Welsh gushed over being gushed over. I reached Captain Davies as the speech continued.

"Sally?" Davies seemed surprised to see me curtsy, so gracious after the conversation we'd had. He should have known that a curtsy from me was as dangerous an omen as a broken mirror. I took the pregnant woman by her other arm. She was young, perhaps the same age as me, her cheeks rosy and her belly full of life. She had to have been seven months along now.

"Yeah, I know Inspector Wilkes. I knew him, anyway."

That's what Rui's fight-club associate had said when we cornered him the other night after a particularly ferocious battle. James Ratcliff. Bald and full of scars, shaped like a battered brick. He'd come out on top, and when men were victorious they were particularly chatty.

Ratcliff looked me up and down. "Hey, didn't I see you here a few days ago?"

"She's a good friend of mine," Rui had said, exchanging a mischievous glance with me. "And a fan of the sport. She knows all the top players here in Devil's Acre."

"I'm especially curious about you, Ratcliff. Rui tells me you used to work with the Scotland Yard on cases?"

Charles Wilkes was a member of the Scotland Yard himself. He'd joined the original eight of their detective branch and rocketed up their ranks in just a few years.

Luckily, I knew how to control powerful men.

You find their weakness.

"I was local police in Wiltshire," Ratcliff, Rui's old friend, had told us. "Those Scotland Yard bastards, they just come in and take over *our* investigations whether we like it or not. Yeah, I worked with Wilkes once. A damn sodding pompous old man. I wonder how pompous he'd be if his wife found out about his extracurricular activities."

Here, in Welsh's garden, we were about to find out.

"Miss, do you need a seat?" I asked the young pregnant lady, grateful the carriage Harriet had sent had managed to bring her here on time. "Miss—"

"The name's Andrea Bradley." As if I didn't already know. A fun girl. Her rough speech contrasted with what the people here would have considered an "angelic appearance." She stretched out her neck. "God, this baby's killing my back. Hey, where's that Flora Hastings woman? She sent me the invitation to come to this thing—promised a bag of shillings and some good food. So? Where's it? Blast it, food's all gone."

"Flora Hastings?" Captain Davies looked over at me and I shrugged innocently. It was the name I told Harriet to give her. As someone who studied Queen Victoria very carefully, I figured I'd have a bit of fun with this.

Wilkes prattled on about his accomplishments, none the wiser.

"I'm not sure what you mean," I told her, "but I'm sure you need to be off your feet. Here, let me seat you close to the center of the garden. There's still plenty of tea cakes left."

Andrea perked up. "Love me some tea cakes."

A pregnant woman needed to rest her feet and find some food. The chivalrous Davies had no choice but to just go along with it. As we dragged her toward one of the front-most seats, Wilkes's speech, in its final stage, made its expected turn.

"And finally, I want to thank my beautiful wife: Alice."

Alice, done up and soaking in the praise of her fawning friends, covered her lips with her fan. Wilkes, in a display of everlasting love, plucked the fan from her grip and took her hand in his. It was a romantic display of affection that sent the garden tittering.

"Without your constant support, your loyalty, and your faith in me, I wouldn't be where I am today. I'd barely be able to put my shoes on in the morning, I suspect."

The joke was a hit. The garden laughed. Well, Bertie rolled his eyes. But once he saw Davies and me, with our unexpected guest, his eyes were focused.

Wilkes continued. "And if there's anything else I can tell you here, my dear wife, Mrs. Wilkes, it's that—"

"Oi, Sally," Bertie shouted, and, interrupting the mood, waved me over. "Over here. There's a free seat." He pointed at the table nearest the head.

That's when Charles Wilkes saw us. I didn't know a face could pale so fast. Andrea gasped and cursed underneath her breath.

"I-It's t-that . . ." The chief inspector's voice had become so feeble, I could barely hear him. His wife waited for the incoming flattery, but it died on his lips. Nobody else seemed to understand the tension that had suddenly weighed down Miss Sophia Welsh's tea party.

He'd just seen his favorite café waitress.

"You!" Andrea pointed at him with one hand and rubbed her belly with the other. "This party is for *you*? You're shitting me!"

"Charles?" Mrs. Wilkes narrowed her eyes, confused. "Charles, who is this woman?"

But "Charles" was too busy squirming where he stood, his cheeks red. Sweat began pouring down his big ears as he tried to signal to Andrea to be quiet. But once the woman you impregnated crashed your

194

celebration party, it was hard to keep a tight control over things.

"Charles, what is going on?" Andrea and Mrs. Wilkes seemed to scream it at the same time and immediately I saw it—the moment Inspector Charles Wilkes's will broke in two, just enough to make him my malleable puppet.

As chaos erupted in the garden party, I hastily whispered something in Andrea's ear. And, after a moment of considering, she nodded. Charles Wilkes saw this. He saw us chatting and conspiring. The gears in his head were turning. His glassy eyes caught mine, and when I winked at him, he deflated in a sort of confused despair. He didn't know precisely how I'd cobbled together this theatrical event, but as a detective he knew well enough when he'd been defeated by a criminal.

He knew well enough he was mine.

And now that he was, Bambridge and the Queen were next.

I waved to the excited crowd.

"Oh, so sorry for the interruption," I said to the party. "Dear Andrea has told me that her husband sent her here to congratulate Charles Wilkes in person for helping to keep their community safe. Such is the work of a member of Scotland Yard, is it not? They protect everyone, regardless of their status in life. She was just so excited to see him in person."

I sounded gracious enough for the garden party to believe me. Everyone calmed down. Sounds of confusion slowly turned to understanding and fascination. Even Mrs. Wilkes calmed down, breathing a sigh of relief. Of course, her husband knew the truth.

"My husband's even thinking of naming our baby after you: Charles."

Andrea really knew how to drive the knife in. But the deal was done. The inspector was mine for the taking.

"Mother?"

At the back of the garden, Miss Welsh screamed. Harriet held up Miss Welsh's elderly mother, who was holding her withered neck and coughing out blood. The teacup on the table in front of her had toppled over, spilling black fluid everywhere. The same tea I refused to drink.

And Dalton stood over them both, pretending to help the old woman in her hour of need, but clearly annoyed. That was when I remembered.

The bottle of arsenic I gave to Harriet. Looked like she didn't hold on to it as I asked.

EIGHTEEN

ONCE THE PARTY disbanded, Harriet, Andrea, and I cornered Detective Inspector Wilkes in an alleyway not far from there.

"I'll make this quick because your lovely wife is waiting for you a few streets down from here, completely unaware that you got another woman pregnant."

He flinched when I spoke, his thin lips pressed together into a single line.

"You belong to me now. You're going to do exactly as I say until I tell you I no longer require your services," I told him. "If you don't, the whole of England will know who baby Charles's father truly is."

Andrea rubbed her belly, thoroughly pleased, as she'd already gotten her tea cakes and bag of shillings as promised.

Wilkes wiped his sweaty forehead with a handkerchief he pulled out of his breast pocket. "What do you want me to do?"

"In four days, an art gala will be held at the Victoria and Albert Museum. It's a private event, funded by the Photographic Society of London. Many of their members will be there." I'd had it on my social calendar for months, but now it seemed it'd act as the perfect stage for a show. "You are to be there too."

Charles looked at us three women and didn't know who he should fear more.

"She"—I jerked my head toward Harriet—"is part of Queen Victoria's inner circle. Try anything, and you'll have to answer to Her Majesty. You'll see that being a close friend of royalty has its perks."

"And who the hell are *you*?" Wilkes spat. He truly wanted to curse, I could feel it. But his eyes kept darting toward the end of the alley, as if a specter might come upon us in the dark at any moment.

I smiled, ladylike in the extreme. "For now? Your master."

The plan was falling into place. But after Andrea and Wilkes had dispersed, there was something else I had to take care of.

"I'm sorry," Harriet told me as we walked back toward Miss Welsh's home. "Dalton Sass asked me to help him with the tea cakes and I set the bottle down."

"Never mind the obvious danger of leaving a bottle of arsenic lying around for anyone to take as they pleased," I grumbled, remembering to keep the point of judgment out of my tone. Otherwise I'd remind her too much of her mother and she might shut down.

"I knew he was up to something." Harriet wrung her hands together. "I just didn't know he'd try to *poison* you."

Yes, and poor Miss Welsh's mother had taken the brunt of Sass's attack. Well, she was the Royal Sussex County Hospital's problem now.

As we approached Miss Welsh's home, I watched as Bertie, Sass, and Davies got into the same carriage together and took off. This was an unholy union that would be difficult to break apart. Luckily, with Miss Welsh off to tend to her mother, my wife lessons were, for now, suspended. I'd regroup in Chatham and figure out my next move.

"Harriet, remember that Dalton is dangerous." I gripped her hand. "He's not the kind gentleman he pretends to be. Don't fall for any more of his tricks."

"What are you going to do, Sally?" Her bottom lip quivered.

"What I always do."

Find out what he knew about the Institution.

Then dismantle him.

But first, I needed to use Wilkes while I had him on the bait. Bambridge, my next target, was about to get the full brunt of my wrath.

Windsor Castle – 1856

"Relax, Sally. Yes, yes . . . that's a *good* girl."

He spoke to me as if I were a dog. A girl of thirteen, I absolutely could not relax, not with William Bambridge's slimy voice coaxing me in such an unsettling manner. His arrogance had only exploded since the last time I saw him. Back then, he was merely present while I was being gifted to Queen Victoria, courtesy of Captain Frederick Forbes. Now he was the official royal photographer to Queen Victoria. He'd already photographed many members of the royal family on their hunts. Even photographed a few of their pets. What was another one?

"Surely you can relax, girl?"

I couldn't. The dress the Queen's ladies had put me in was too tight. It didn't matter that its lace collar and silky sleeves would have been envied by any socialite in the country—it was too tight. I felt squeezed by them. The Queen had ordered the same ladies to do my hair. Of course, they had no idea what to do with its texture. The brush they used to comb Princess Alice's hair was a weapon of torture against my scalp. Tears leached from my eyes as they pulled it back into a clean sweep, parted in the middle with some fabric covering it on both sides to make it more palatable for the cameras. I could still feel the pain rocketing through my scalp as I sat here, desperate for this photo session to be over.

Sighing, Bambridge threw off the dark blanket used to cover his head as he peered through the box camera. He straightened up and glared at me as if I'd wounded him. As if *his* scalp felt raw and tender.

"Look around you, girl. The Queen herself has given you this private room to have your photo taken."

It was a royal room, despite how little it was, with all the best furniture royal money could buy. The sunlight would have burst through the arched windows to my right if not for the drawn, thick red velvet curtains. The marble floor was covered by an expensive Turkish carpet gifted to her by princes of the Ottoman Empire, or so I was told.

At my side was a modest table, upon which a medley of random white fabric was placed. For what, I didn't know. For the aesthetic, I supposed. It was Bambridge's idea. The whole concept of this photography session was his idea.

"I will not hide her Blackness, nor her natural features, as shocking as they may be," he'd told the Queen. "I want the public to see her body, to see how it contrasts so greatly against the delicateness instilled in her by polite British society. I want the public to see the true Sarah Forbes Bonetta, which Queen Victoria has excavated from the barbarity of her outside shell."

I'd been standing right there as he spoke. And here in this uncomfortable wooden chair, remembering his words, I clenched my teeth. This was a royal room indeed. But it was no different from the room I danced naked in as a child all those years ago, when Forbes had first presented me to his gallery of rogues. His spoils from his trip to the Dahomey Kingdom. How Bambridge had delighted in me that night as I debased myself for him and his villainous friends. Now there was no delight in his expression. He had a job to do, praise to gain from the Queen of England, and I was stopping him from gaining it.

"What's that?" Bambridge tilted his neck when he saw me tugging at my collar.

My hands paused. Oh no. I hadn't meant to tug at my neck. I'd specifically ordered myself not to before entering the room.

"N-Nothing," I stammered in my young voice, but Bambridge was already striding toward me. I tried to cover my neck and chest, but to no avail. He tugged my hands away, reached down my blouse, and found them.

My Egbado beads. I didn't know how in the world I'd managed to keep them all these years from the moment I was captured by King Ghezo, throughout the trip to the Atlantic, to Sierra Leone and back. After Miss Sass would beat me in the Institution, I'd pray to them for luck and support. Tiny, alternating red and white. They were my family charm. My tether to my old life, to the parents I'd lost and yearned for. To my mother, who passed them down to me. Who used to sing to me folktales under the swaying palm trees and the hot sun, with the red sand underneath our bare feet. Songs passed down from her mother and her mother before her. Songs I could no longer remember.

"They're making your collar look uneven." Bambridge held out his hand expectantly. "Take them off and give them to me."

"N-No," I whispered. My sleeves felt heavy. Or was it my body?

"What?"

"I want them to stay on." They were the only reason why I could still breathe.

His face contorted into a baffled expression. "Are you defying me, girl?" He didn't even sound upset. More amused. But even as a child, I could recognize the threat in his voice.

"Give them here," he said again. "Now!"

I found my voice. "No!"

We fought like that for some time, first with words, until Bambridge began digging underneath my blouse, as if just for the one moment he wished I was no longer the young, delicate woman of society he was trying to portray me as. What a joke. He never once saw me as such. The tussle between us became so violent, the table I was to rest my elbow on began rattling, the beautiful red tablecloth and basket of fabric sliding back and forth.

Finally, with an angry yell, he grabbed my Egbado beads and tugged them. The necklace broke apart, red and white beads falling all over the carpet.

I couldn't breathe.

"Come clean this up," Bambridge said to his assistants, who waited by the door. "Collect them and put them in the bin quickly. I want to finish this session by lunchtime, confound it."

They swept my beads into the trash. With it my mother. My father. My ancestors. The last physical connection I had to the life I led before they transformed me. They'd already emptied out the trash bin before the session had ended.

The photograph was to one day be part of London's Royal Collection Trust. But for now, Queen Victoria was given the photo as part of her private collection. She loved it. The way my elbow rested on the side table. The way I held my hands together, clasped ever so slightly.

Sally Forbes Bonetta, a native of Abeokuta. The caption underneath the picture.

Who was that person? Her three names confused me. Her empty eyes haunted me. I memorized them. I drew them over and over with quill and ink. My drawer in Chatham was filled with them, each rendition of "Sally Forbes Bonetta" hollower than the last.

The portrait had captured my shattered soul, a fractured self with nothing to tether to but the fear only I could see in my expression. The night I lost my mother's beads, I returned home and was overcome by panic so visceral, I felt like I might die. The Schoens didn't understand the fuss. They gave me some water and told me to sleep. I'd be better by morning, they told me.

It wasn't. I spent days in my room, paralyzed. Staring at the scratches in my wall as if they were alive and mocking me, my mind filled up with fog, my skin crawling with phantom pains, my heart periodically going into overdrive, as if I would die any second.

The panic never really went away.

NINETEEN

PORCHESTER TERRACE: A crown jewel of Bayswater, London. There were quite a few artists who held studios here. I walked inside the one William Bambridge had never meant for me to find. The room was small and painted blue, with some windows on the ceiling and some on the left side of the room with the curtains drawn. There were scratch marks on the light wood floor where Bambridge had shuffled his camera tripod here and there.

Charles Wilkes stood at the front of the room, the heels of his boots pressed back against the stage where Bambridge's subjects were to pose for him in front of a black wall. He grimaced when he saw me enter. Rui, on other hand, was delighted. Next to the inspector, he sat on the stage, his fingers interlocked. His right corner of his lips quirked up into a little smirk. They had both been waiting for me.

Red-and-black-patterned fabric covered the stage, giving the place the allure of luxury. But there was nothing luxurious about what Bambridge had been secretly doing in his own time.

Wilkes looked like he'd aged a decade during the last couple of days. I didn't know how he'd managed to find this place, nor how he'd broken in, but I suppose that was a detective's work. He'd done what I told him to do. How useful he was as a pawn. "They're in there."

He flicked his head back, gesturing toward the small closet next to him.

"Have you seen them?" I asked Rui. He was here for insurance.

The criminal prince gave me an intoxicating, mischievous grin. "You won't believe your eyes."

I stepped carefully toward the closet and opened the door. It was a darkroom. Yes, most photographers should have one of these in their studios. The workshop was tiny and claustrophobic, with photographic paper set upon a wooden table in the center of the room. I recognized some of the equipment on the bench lining the walls: a bath with chemicals. A daguerreotype apparatus. A thin iron tintype for portable photographs. I was more interested in small golden-framed photographs resting against the rightmost wall.

Oh . . . *goodness*.

Four photographs. Each more interesting than the last.

I checked them, lined them up, and drank them in. So Mrs. Mallet's intelligence was correct. "When did Bambridge have time to come to Windsor Castle to do all these?" Or perhaps the Queen had been spirited here in the middle of the night. If anyone could make it happen, she could—especially if she was desperate enough.

Judging by these photographs, she was certainly desperate for *something*.

"You know, if you keep the door opened, the photos might get ruined," said Rui, leaning against the door frame. He wasn't looking at me. He kept one eye on Inspector Wilkes, who came into my line of sight, his paling face screwed up in disgust as he stared at the "special" portraits on the floor.

"I don't know too much about photography, but I don't think the light would ruin these already-finished photographs. Like those." I walked back toward the center table. Thin paper photographs mounted on thick paper cards. These albumen prints were all the rage in photography; for some, they were more sought after than tintypes and daguerreotypes. It made sense that Bambridge would dabble in various photographic styles.

The only problem was, these weren't his photographs.

"Marcus Sparling's work is quite good." I picked up one photograph of an old man smoking a long pipe. "Fenton is an important member of the Photographic Society. Inspector Wilkes, when I told you to steal his assistant's work and plant them here, I didn't think you'd be able to do it so quickly. I'm impressed."

"Devil." Wilkes was shaking as he said it. Rui let the detective pass him and enter the darkroom; I didn't mind. I loved seeing a high Englishman brought low. It was the air I breathed. Let him come to me. "You really think your plan is going to work?"

I shrugged. "Now that all the pieces are in place, I don't see why not."

Bambridge and the Queen. The gossip. The stain on her image. I almost licked my lips in anticipation. With slow, cocky steps, I walked up to Wilkes until I was close enough to fix his bow tie. "You're not going to betray me at this crucial moment, are you?" And then I did fix his bow tie. "Not with everything you have to lose."

"Witch!"

Wilkes reached for my neck so quickly, I hadn't time to gasp. My breath caught in my throat, the blood rushing up to my head. The bloodlust in the inspector's snarl almost shook me. But his fingers didn't manage to reach my flesh. His fingers twitched, aching for their target. But Rui had caught his wrist before they could find it.

"You'll do as you're told, won't you?" he whispered in Wilkes's ear. That's when I saw the pistol Rui had hidden in his brown vest. With his other hand, he stuck the barrel against Wilkes's temple. "Like the young lady said, you have a lot to lose if you don't."

I exhaled, letting my body relax, but seeing Rui fight for me, protect me, moved me in a way that was hard to describe. "Thank you," I said, lowering my gaze to the floor.

When I looked up, Rui's dark eyes were twinkling. "For you? Anything."

My cheeks flushed. The sleeves of his white shirt were rolled up so the elegant shape of his muscles were just visible with the light streaming in from the studio. They flexed as Rui pressed the gun harder against Wilkes's head, making the man yelp in terror. I couldn't admit it to my partner in crime—just how deeply his ruthlessness had etched itself into the most tender parts of my flesh. All he had to do was show me one more act of aggression and I'd go feral.

I wanted to touch him. Seeing Rui take a man's life in his hands so mercilessly, here in this claustrophobic room cloaked in darkness, the reality of it nearly knocked me off my feet. I wanted to hold him. To kiss him. To feel his tongue upon mine. I wanted us to hold that gun together while we did it.

Returning to reality, I straightened my back and walked out of the darkroom with a haughty lift of my chin.

"Don't forget the time and place, Wilkes. And, if I may, a little advice?" I turned. Wilkes's back was still to me. Rui hadn't lowered the gun. The two men waited.

I smiled. "Don't be so stiff. Relax! We're going to have fun together, you and I."

At a gallery event no one would soon forget.

The carriage brought me home to the Schoens' home safely. Mama was horrified to hear what had happened, but ensured that she'd teach me whatever Miss Welsh couldn't while she was busy with her mother.

"Wow. Thanks, Mama," I said without an ounce of mirth as she hugged me tightly.

It was already past midnight, but I couldn't go to bed. The memories of the evening's exploits still buzzed in my flesh. I was in an excited state.

But I also didn't want to go to my room. If I did, I'd take out those pictures—the ones I'd drawn by hand. I'd stare at them until I became cross-eyed and could no longer recognize who the girls I'd drawn were supposed to be. Not that I could recognize them now.

I sat out on the front steps as night fell. The Queen of Spades, which I'd slipped out from underneath my bedroom pillow, was pinched between my fingers. I twisted and turned the card absently. The black queen seemed to vanish in the darkness.

The stars were clear here in Chatham. I could hardly ever see them in London with the filth of industry. Here, greenery enveloped me—I had to squint to see the next house over. In London, the slums were packed and the streets cluttered with feet, hooves, wheels, bodies, and every manner of item that could be sold. I always felt the contrast deeply. I always missed the fresh air when I was away from here. It didn't matter. Soon, I'd be taken away from England entirely. Brought back to Lagos as someone's backup bride.

I didn't hate Captain Davies by any measure, but like anyone who claimed power over me, I couldn't let him have his way either. When I was through with my revenge, I had to find a way to stop the wedding from proceeding. And right now, as I stared up at the moon, feeling the seconds of my freedom tick away, there was only one way I could think of accomplishing it.

I needed to flee. That was the only option. To disappear such that no one would ever find me on the face of this earth unless I wanted to

208

be found. And I had less than a month to figure out exactly how to do it.

"Disappear," I whispered, shaking my head. Would I really have to take such drastic measures? "Is there no other way for me to live?"

"Why not? You've made others disappear. I'm sure you're an expert at it by now."

My blood froze in my veins as I heard his voice. I held my breath, confused, afraid, and unable to stop my body from turning. He slid out from behind the corner of the Schoens' house. He stopped just short of the window on the front exposure and rested against the brick. He didn't approach me nearer than this.

Dalton Sass.

No. But that couldn't be right. I saw him leave with Bertie and Davies. . . .

The Queen of Spades slipped from my hand and onto the front steps. "You . . . followed . . . me home? You came to my *house*?"

He answered with a grin that made me jump to my feet.

Dalton Sass. He ran his hands through his floppy, curly brown hair and leaned over sideways, taking in the sight of me in my nightgown. It wasn't with lust or appreciation but fascination that he stared at me.

"You look so innocent," he said, rubbing his chin. "If only they all knew."

"Knew what?" I snapped. My body was poised and ready for a fight. If he made any sudden movements, I'd put my finely pointed nails to good use.

But Dalton only folded his arms over his chest. He was still wearing the same shirt and brown vest he wore at the garden party. He hadn't showered. He must not have had the time if he was following me around like the stalker he was.

I waited.

"If only they knew that you murdered my mother."

The cold wind nipped at my bare arms, fluttering my nightgown. I could feel the light fabric against my legs.

"According to you, she killed herself." I lifted my chin. "Your anger is a bit misplaced, isn't it?"

"You know, she always talked about you when I was little. After the fire, that is." Dalton kept his gaze on the moon, the light of which captured his long eyelashes. "How she was sure she saw you running from her office just before. She tried telling her superiors, of course, but nobody believed her. It was her cigar, after all. Everyone knew she was a smoker. It was one of her unsavory habits." He tilted his head to the side. "But I'm sure you knew that. I'm sure you knew their prejudice would guide their sense of justice."

"It's funny." I tugged at my sleeves nonchalantly. "During all the days she beat us at the Institution, she never once mentioned she had a son." And then, when I saw him seize up, I blinked in surprise. "Oh, didn't you know? What an abusive, evil witch she was?"

Dalton's hand instinctively flew to his left arm, sheathed in its jacket sleeve. He squeezed it curiously, but kept his eyes on me almost as if he hadn't yet realized what his body was doing.

"Whatever wrong my mother has done in her lifetime, you could never call her a witch without hypocrisy," he snarled. "Not you, the disgusting wench who drove her to her death."

He rubbed his arm for a moment before letting his fingers slide off his jacket. "Yes, I know all about you, Sarah Forbes Bonetta. Our beloved Queen's beloved goddaughter. My mother spoke about you constantly. How you challenged her every chance you got. How you thought yourself smarter, better. How you flaunted your intelligence with the pride of the devil."

210

I let out a laugh. "Is that what you're really angry about? About the fact that she seemed more inclined to talk about me, a lowly African student, than she did her own son?"

Sass boosted himself off the brick. "*Murderer.*"

"I murdered no one. Unless you have any proof that I did, I suggest you put your tail between your legs and get the hell out of my town." I squeezed my fists. "Oh, and you should know: in this society, the mad ramblings of a ruined woman, now sadly deceased, is not exactly what would count as hard evidence. Those aren't my rules. But take that as you will."

Sass's expression looked murderous. I quickly checked his hands to make sure he wasn't hiding any secret weapons. For a moment, I almost wished he did have one. I suddenly felt quite hungry for a good fight.

"I'll go to the prince."

"And he'll believe *you*, someone he just met, ranting about someone he doesn't even know and has no reason to care about?"

"He may. With the right evidence."

I remembered his standoff against Lord Ponsonby and felt the blood pumping through my fists. "I don't believe you have any. And truthfully? I don't believe the letter you used to frighten Ponsonby qualifies. After all, what care does that old man have for me?"

Dalton looked taken aback. He didn't know I'd seen him that day.

"No . . . the letter you showed him that day is dangerous to the Queen, not me." I raised my chin in defiance. "And Ponsonby wants to protect her—of course he does. That's his life work: protecting the Queen against evildoers like you who'd use such foul means to worm your way into the lives of her children."

Dalton's sneer made my flesh crawl. "So it seems we know quite a bit about each other. But don't think about getting to Ponsonby. With how I terrified the old man, I know he'll keep his mouth shut for as long as I need him to. Self-preservation is quite the motivator. Besides, with what's in my letter, the last person he'll talk to is *you*."

So the letter did have something to do with me after all. Was Dalton goading me into making the wrong move? I had to think and act carefully.

"So you'll use Prince Bertie as a piece on a chessboard." I made a show of shaking my head. "To think of such a thing. How incredibly callous."

"We've become quite good friends in such a short amount of time." And when Dalton's expression changed from contemptible to saccharine in a flash, I knew he was telling the truth. He had the skill of a conman. The confidence of a liar. Bertie was used to sycophants surrounding him. It wouldn't take much to slip onto his radar.

Then again, I wasn't just anybody either. I tapped my chin. "That is true," I conceded. "Perhaps he trusts you already. But then, you *did* just try to poison me. Poor Miss Welsh's mother drank the arsenic tea instead. The old bat may even be dead by now." I shrugged. "Should we go to Bertie with both our tales and see which one he believes? I think, then, it would be decided once and for all: Who's the better storyteller? And most importantly, which one of us has the stronger bond with the Prince of Wales?"

Sass's body was tense and poised for attack and I was just as poised to meet him. Good. Come get me. Whatever fear had arisen within me was long gone. Now all I could remember was Sass's cane. My fingernails dug into my palms as if each lash came fresh against my back, my arms, and sometimes my legs for the fun of it. And not just Sass. Bambridge. Bellamy. The Forbeses. Phipps. McCoskry. Dancing for them in the parlor. The HMS *Bonetta*. Ade being flung overboard. The beads being ripped from my neck by Bambridge's clammy hands. Every injustice piled up one on top of another until I was begging for this stupid boy to come after me with everything he had just so I had an excuse to rip him limb from limb.

He didn't. He relaxed his body. He sighed. And then he lowered his head with a smile.

"Sarah Forbes Bonetta. Goddaughter of Queen Victoria." His laughter was quiet, like the rippling waves of a river. "Well now. You've shown me your true face. I won't rest until everyone else has seen it too. I can't wait to take you apart."

I knew that look. The thirst for revenge. The ecstasy of having your enemy in your sights and imagining their total annihilation.

I gave him my own, ladylike smile. "Try your best."

Then I screamed at the top of my lungs, "Mama! Mama! Come quick! A thief! Help!"

Startled and cursing, Dalton backed away before running from the house into the night. By the time Mama burst through the front doors, he was too far away to identify. If I said it was Sass, would she believe me? For now, she held me close while I cried.

"Oh, Mama, I was so scared!" I sniffed. "I never imagined I'd see a thief here. I didn't get a good look at his face, but he must know of our connection to the royal palace!"

"Don't worry, Sally, my precious girl. I'll inform the palace. No thief is ever going to make his way here again."

I wiped my tearful face. "Thank you, Mama."

Perhaps I could have just told her it was Sass. But I had my own plans for him. He'd had the audacity to stalk me to my home, putting not only me but Mama Schoen in danger. That was unforgivable. No matter how many arguments Mama and I had had in the past, she was dear to me.

That was more unforgivable than trying to poison me. And I was already quite furious about that.

Whatever I did to Dalton Sass required the same kind of care and precision that I brought to the rest of my enemies.

He came to my bloody house. He was now on my list.

And if he wasn't careful, he'd follow his abusive monster of a mother to the grave.

TWENTY

"OH, SALLY, THANK you for inviting me to the gala!" Gowramma and I clinked our wineglasses inside the private gallery. The Victoria and Albert Museum was packed full of society's elite, and why shouldn't it be? This event had been advertised for months. A gala funded by the Photographic Society of London. A joint exhibit featuring the works of all of their most prominent artists. It would make a fine stage.

The greater the stage, the better the show.

Gowramma grabbed my free hand with hers and drew it up to her nose.

"Are you . . . okay?" I asked, eyebrows raised as she sniffed it.

"What lovely perfume." She sniffed again before letting me go and rubbing her chin. "Is that lilac?"

"Are you drunk?"

"I'm getting there!" She raised her glass and took me by the crook of my elbow. Not much got past Gowramma even when she was tipsy. I supposed I should have washed my hands a little more before coming to the event. Hopefully no one else would notice.

The late-afternoon sun streamed in from the second-story windows. A beautifully crafted mahogany banister curved in luxurious arches, separating the second floor from the open space below. Those on the walkway above could look down and see us below in this vast marble-floored room. Pinned to the walls were the photographs in this exhibit, framed in gold that sparkled from the light of the chandelier hanging down from the ceiling's round, white clay medallion. Wooden podiums were strewn about the spacious room, on which smaller photographs were placed behind glass placards that had been screwed into the structures.

All around me were photographs of Queen Victoria with her family in happier days, back when the Queen still had the desire to be seen out in public at events such as these. I could see Princess Mary Adelaide of Cambridge, a robust woman, and next to her the deceased Prince Albert. But the crowning pieces of the exhibit were covered by red velvet curtains. At the front-most wall in the center of the room, the billowy curtains attracted all eyes. Guests talked in low voices, everyone wondering what lay behind them.

I couldn't wait to show them.

Gowramma nudged me and pointed at a picture to my left. "Those were taken by Camille Silvy. A Frenchman, I believe."

"And part of the Royal Photographic Society." I could see other works of his here. A portrait of a French river. A couple of musicians on the street with their guitars next to grand black iron gates. Silvy was here, clinking drinks with Henry White, a landscape photographer.

I had to strain to find him—there were too many bodies amongst the crowd. Too many ruffled hoop skirts of every color and top hats of varying ridiculous sizes. But eventually I did see him: William Bambridge stood near the opposite wall. He threw his head back as he chatted with his mates, entirely unsuspecting of what was about to occur.

"I think I see *you* over there," I told Gowramma, pointing in Bambridge's direction, where a photographic portrait of her that had been taken when she was a child hung on the wall. I dragged her through the crowd until we reached it. Indeed, there she was in a white dress, mirthless, with her hands rigidly on her lap and one foot on a cushion, the other dangling behind it. Her figure, at least, popped against the simple black backdrop as she stared into the camera.

"God, I look miserable," she said, shaking her head and drinking her wine. "And look at my hair!"

In the portrait, the strands of her hair fell flat and limp on her head and were parted into two down the middle like all of us girls.

"Were you miserable?" I asked her, giving her a sidelong look while watching Bambridge, just a few steps away, out of the corner of my eye.

She thought about it for a moment. "I . . . I don't remember," she whispered. Whether she remembered or not, it seemed to genuinely bother her. "I *do* remember how *particular* my father was in how I behaved even before I came here."

"The Rajah?"

"He made sure I adopted the habits of the English. He was always so frantic about it. Why?" She paused, staring at the portrait of herself. "Why was he always so *frantic* about it?"

I watched her carefully, curiously, tighten up her jaw as William Bambridge finally noticed the two of us and couldn't resist.

"Sally Forbes Bonetta. What a pleasant surprise. And Princess Victoria Gowramma! Well, isn't this, as your people say, *kismet*?"

"That's an Arabic word, so no, we don't say that," Gowramma grumbled. I raised my eyebrows. I wasn't used to such defiance in her voice. It was sudden. New to me. But William Bambridge didn't hear her as he clapped us both on our shoulders and laughed.

Yes, for him, it must have been fate of some kind. Photographers worldwide had wanted a chance to capture the likeness of the "savage" wards adopted into the royal family. Such a curious phenomenon unique to Queen Victoria. How had they managed to turn these creatures of the so-called dark places of the world into perfect members of British society—integrated into the royal family, no less? It was a task William Bambridge has been praised for far and wide since the moment Queen Victoria had given him the go-ahead to terrorize me during his photographic shoot.

"Roger! Roger, come, look at this! Look at these two!"

I wondered how much Gowramma really remembered. Something sparked behind those vibrant brown eyes as Roger Fenton joined Bambridge. Our two childhood photographers stared at us as if we were animals in a zoo.

"Gowramma, it's been so long." His eyes were large. Or at least, they felt large. They felt as if they swallowed up his whole body as he drank in the sight of us wards. "How is your husband? Surely, you came with him?"

"Yes." Gowramma was oddly quiet, her gaze on the marble floor. "He's here somewhere."

As a married woman, it would have been almost unthinkable for her to come to an event such as this without him. To bring Gowramma here, I needed his permission. It wasn't part of any scheme. I only supposed she needed time away from home, away from the loose bowel movements of both her charges—baby and husband alike. And since at the moment Bertie wasn't throwing any secret illicit parties she could sneak off to . . .

"Who knew the Indian girl in this photograph would end up doing so well for herself, eh, Fenton?" said Bambridge. "And Sally. I remember the day I photographed you in the palace. You were so vibrant and modest. So good-natured and—"

"Malleable?" It was a word I know they all liked. I gave him a pleasant smile.

"Yes. And well-behaved." He nodded to Fenton, who nodded back, both of them not even bothering to hide the pride they took—not in us, mind you. In their work. "I know your likeness, captured by me, will endure for centuries."

So will my trauma. My smile grew languid as I remembered the Egbado beads ripping from my neck.

"*Well-behaved* truly is the word. It's wonderful how docile Gowramma was."

"Yes, yes! Such a surprise! I thought they'd be wild . . ."

They continued on like that. The way he and Fenton spoke to each other felt as if they were in a world all their own that excluded us in some deep, foundational way that felt wrong. We were here, but as subjects. As still as photographs hanging in the exhibit.

"They've both become true Victorian ladies, by my estimation." It wasn't Fenton who'd answered. The Prince of Wales had found us, splitting the crowds as he approached. Fenton and Bambridge bowed.

"Your Royal Majesty! You were able to make it!" Bambridge rubbed his hands together. I thought he'd lick his lips soon. "I'm honored. And your mother, the Queen? Will Her Royal Highness be making an appearance?"

Whatever effect their flattery had had on him disappeared in an instant at the mere mention of the Queen. Bertie, dressed all in black and white like proper Victorian gentleman, including his bow tie, took off his top hat and tucked it underneath his armpit.

"No, she will not." His gold-brown hair was slicked back with gel. I could see the lump in his throat fight its way down as he swallowed. "I'm here representing her. I'm to unveil the photographic piece of the night." He gestured to the red curtains on the front wall. "Shipped in from America. Robert Cornelius . . . or some such."

He probably didn't ask nor did he follow up to check the pieces one last time before the event began. How like Bertie to be so sloppy. He would come to regret it.

"Ah, yes. How unfortunate Her Majesty couldn't be here. The Queen hasn't really been the same since the Prince Consort's passing," Bambridge said.

He would certainly know. I stifled a snicker as my thoughts roamed to the darkroom of his studio.

Bambridge was one of those in elite society who knew how to feign sympathy so well it no longer fooled anyone. The attempt only left the target with a feeling of slight annoyance and the taste of hypocrisy. Bertie's lips began to curl into a snarl until he stopped himself.

Bertie had dealt with Bambridge for much of his life, and from the looks of his grimace, his experiences were nothing to cheer. He turned to Gowramma and me instead.

"Victorian ladies indeed," Bertie said, mirth creeping back into his voice. "You both look astounding." He perked up as his eyes lingered on me. "Especially you, Sally. Dare I say, you look a vision?"

I looked no more frivolous than anyone else here, though I had to admit, mustard-seed yellow was my color. It was the perfect contrast to my skin. I almost didn't mind that the heavy layered skirt swept the dust off the floors.

"Alas, not everyone in this city can meet the standards of civil society," Roger Fenton said. "My assistant, Mr. Sparling, has been the target of a theft."

I covered my mouth with the rest of them. Ever so surprised.

"Theft?" Bambridge's bushy eyebrows furrowed together. "Not Marcus!"

"Unfortunately." Fenton shook his head. "Some of his photographs have gone missing recently—and all before he could even show them to his clients. It's why he didn't come today."

"I'm sure he's beside himself with worry," I said, my gloved hand still covering my mouth. In these moments, it was probably more prudent for me to stay silent, but it was hard not to inject yourself into a scene of such comedy.

Fenton bristled with righteous indignation. "There are too many scoundrels infesting the city streets these days. They have no regard for morals and rationality."

He sounded like Henry Mayhew railing about the "nomadic races of England" as if they were like we "pagans" in need of proper religion. I wonder if tonight's surprise would be enough to challenge Fenton's prejudices. Probably not. But it would be of great fun to me nonetheless.

Bertie rolled his eyes, clearly bored of the conversation. "Fascinating. Anyways—" And he held out his hand to me. Gowramma gasped. "Would you accompany me somewhere, Sally?"

He must have seen my unimpressed expression, because he straightened up and looked at the other spectators with a blush on his cheeks. Bambridge and Fenton exchanged glances, thoroughly confused.

"Would you both come with me?" he corrected himself, offering his elbow to Gowramma. "There's something I think you both should see."

But his eyes were pleading with me. I sighed. What in the world did he want with me now? And in front of all these people? Gowramma's grin was a little devilish, a little knowing, as if she'd suddenly become aware of some secret but had decided to guard it as churlishly as a troll his gold. *Great.* I shook my head.

"Yes, Gowramma and I would be honored," I answered. After curtsying to Bambridge and Fenton, I took Bertie's other arm and followed him to another part of the gala, ignoring the onlookers and their whispers. Bertie didn't have to care about any implications. At least, he certainly didn't have the intelligence to care. Gowramma on his other arm softened the blow of the gossip, but I was still annoyed as we made our way through the crowd.

My irritation didn't stem from Bertie alone. For me this wasn't a social event. Each second that passed, I kept an eye out for Harriet, who was to have been here by now.

Bertie stopped when we came across a photographic portrait I knew all too well. My shoulders slumped. I turned away.

"There *you* are, Sally." With her arm linked with Bertie's, Gowramma leaned over.

Yes, there I was, rimmed in gold. Empty and lifeless. Some said it was the way photographs were taken. It was the style of the mid-1800s to look dead-eyed at the camera.

But no. Those dead eyes were as real, as honest as my own heart beating furiously against my rib cage. They were not the result of Bambridge's direction. They were the genuine item.

Gowramma looked down for a moment and touched her throat. "Strange," she said. "I'm not feeling so well."

Her face did suddenly have an ashen look to it. She touched her stomach. "Something I ate, perhaps."

Gowramma already confided in me that her sex life with her aging husband was by now nonexistent, so I knew she wasn't pregnant. If I were to hazard a guess, it was this gala. The sickness in her was the same nausea I felt from deep within my core.

Someone who has never had to worry about being *looked* at could never understand the disembodied experience of being the star of a show you never wished for . . . especially when that "stardom" came at the expense of your very self.

But this phenomenon was hard to put into words.

Gowramma didn't try. She cleared her throat. "I think I'll go see what my husband's up to," she said, pulling her arm out of Bertie's grip. "Sally, I think yours is around here somewhere. If I were you, I'd do the same." She winked at me before leaving Bertie and me to stare up at my likeness framed in gold.

Once she was gone, I pulled my arm out of his as well and wrapped both around my chest. Sarah Forbes Bonetta loomed over me like a vicious tyrant after my very life. I didn't want to be this close to his portrait. I took in a deep breath to calm my nerves.

"Husband," Bertie grumbled once she was out of earshot. He repeated the word as if he swore. "You don't need to find him, Sally. Last I saw he was in another room having quite the vibrant conversation with Camille Silvy."

I raised an eyebrow. "Silvy? The photographer. Why?"

"How should I know?"

The two of us fell silent. I hadn't even thought to find out if Captain Davies would be here. I was focused on other things. Now that he was, I hated that a part of me questioned if I had an obligation to see him. To speak to him.

I shook my head. No, those were the rules talking. That was Mama Schoen talking. I didn't owe anyone anything. There was only one man I wanted to see today, and until Harriet made her appearance and gave me the signal, I couldn't be sure if he would even show up.

"Mother's been good to you, you know," Bertie said, combing his fingers through his hair, ruining the careful coif. He gestured toward the picture. "Adopting you into our family. Giving you all these things. It was quite surprising to me when I first found out."

"As I remember, you treated me like you treated everyone else: with the carelessness and nigh disdain of an heir to the throne."

He clenched his jaw. "I did *not*."

"You dumped honey on my hair."

Bertie cowered beneath the weight of my glare. Oh, yes, Albert. I remembered.

"D-Did I?"

I stepped closer to him, lifting my chin so my aforementioned glare could bore into his skull. "You said it wasn't silky or sweet like yours."

Bertie coughed out a nervous chuckle and ruffled his own hair. "Nothing silky about this mess now, is there?"

A few women nearby tittered behind their fans. I rolled my eyes. He truly didn't get it.

"You forgive me, don't you, Sally?"

One more step toward him. I tilted my head with the sweetest of expressions. "No."

I brushed past his shoulder while striding down the wall of portraits. Harriet had to be around here somewhere.

Bertie followed. "Oh, come on, now. Sally!"

I wish he wouldn't. Being Queen Victoria's adopted African goddaughter made unwanted attention a frequent occurrence at these events. I didn't need Bertie drawing even more curiosity my way. But the prince, as usual, didn't have a clue. He grabbed my wrist rather roughly, letting go of me almost immediately when he realized he'd gotten a bit too heated.

"Isn't there anything you've come to like while being at the palace?"

I purposefully kept silent, thinking back to my experiences. The snow underneath my brown leather boots the first winter I spent at Balmoral Palace in Scotland. How some attendant explained to me the process of how water became snow, as if I didn't already know. Watching the snow melt in my cold little hands, and seeing Ade's face in the water that had pooled there. The striking fear of what might happen to me should I let my tears fall in front of them when I was supposed to be grateful.

Bertie sighed. "I don't blame you, I suppose. Not much to like about the royal life, is there? Even for me?"

I already knew of the royal life. *My* royal life, when I was princess of my clan. But bringing that up would only confuse the lout. "What are you going on about?" I muttered, shaking my head and continuing to the next pictures. And he followed me *still*.

"I'm sure you felt trapped the moment you came here. Am I right? Like the walls were closing in." He trailed me, close behind.

Yes. Though I doubted he could ever understand why.

"Nobody thought I was worthy of being an heir from the moment I started talking. Nothing I do is ever worthy. I'm not studious like Vicky. Not responsible enough for the throne. Not according to my father. And especially my mother . . ."

He trailed off and it took me a moment to realize he'd stopped behind me. When I turned, I saw he was staring at Camille Silvy's portrait of his father, Prince Albert. Prince Consort: a confident pose, a bend in the right knee, a suit fit for royalty. His figure was more portly than the miniature sculpture of Venus de Milo on the table next to him. The globe at his feet made him look worldly and intelligent. He'd hoped his son, his namesake, would have the same excitement for knowledge and innovation. What he got instead was the Party Prince and a number of complaints from his tutors and military officers.

"The last conversation I had with my father . . . ," Bertie began, and didn't finish. He didn't need to. We all knew his father had been lecturing him in the rain about his love for actresses and the scandals it could cause. He soon fell ill and died. The stress, his mother insisted. If only Bertie hadn't given him so much stress.

"I told my mother I'd be coming here in her stead. She wouldn't even look at me." Bertie tore his gaze from his father and turned to me. "Sally, it's not easy being here. If you feel that way, I understand. Even still—" He grabbed my wrist lightly with a tenderness unbecoming to him. "You need to appreciate the freedom you have."

I slowly frowned. "Freedom?"

"You can't possibly know how it feels to be in that mausoleum-like palace day after day knowing no one there takes you seriously. It's the worst of all feelings. And I have no one who understands me. No one I can commiserate with." He shook his head, his hair, now loose, fluttering back and forth. "It's hell," he whispered. "It's—"

My laughter cut off whatever stupid thing Bertie was going to say next. His face reddened as he reached out to calm me down—at least if I was to laugh I shouldn't be so loud. People were watching. But I couldn't help it. It was just the stupidest thing I'd ever heard.

"Sally—" He pouted, turning his back to the crowd, folding his arms. "Well, glad to know how you feel about my trauma."

"Oh, Bertie, you know I've never taken you seriously." I slapped him on the back like an old schoolmate. "But if you want people to take you seriously, perhaps you should take a closer look at the people around you and see how you can use that incredible power you wield quite by accident to actually help them. Like the slums your royal carriage passed by on your way to the grand museum named after your parents. The people who can barely find food to eat."

Bertie shifted uncomfortably on his feet, embarrassed, probably, that he couldn't refute what was obvious.

"Or the people around you who are more trapped than you could ever imagine." I tugged up my long yellow gloves, in danger of falling past my elbows. "Take a closer look at them once in a while too. You may gain another perspective on the life you lead."

Bertie studied me for some time. And when I began to move away from him, he grabbed my shoulder. "Do *you* feel trapped, Sally?" he asked suddenly, in a quiet voice. No one else could hear him. "By your marriage? By Captain Davies?"

Who was he to ask? What was he playing at? Sympathy? With a huff, I answered his question with deflection.

"Worry less about my company and more about yours. I hear you've been making friends with that boy from Freetown: Dalton Sass."

Bertie scratched the back of his head. "Oh, Sass? He's a good lad.

Wealthy. He's joined me at a club or two. Always good for a laugh."

Well, as long as you were good fun at a club or two, and could keep your mouth shut, you'd cleared Bertie's benchmark for friendship. I let out an impatient groan.

"What are you worried about there, Sally?"

Far too much. I started to protest, but just then Harriet appeared amidst the crowd. She didn't come near me. She wasn't supposed to. But when she winked, I knew, from her signal, that my special show was about to begin. Sass would have to wait. Any good host knew that an event wasn't an event until the entertainment arrived.

"Isn't it time for you to unveil Robert Cornelius's photographs?" I gestured toward the red velvet curtains.

With a heavy sigh, Bertie rubbed the back of his head. "Yes, I suppose so."

Before he left, I touched his shoulder and smiled. "And for the record," I told him, "about my predicament, whether I feel trapped or not, dear Bertie, Captain Davies is my betrothed. There's nothing I can do but obey my fate."

Bertie didn't look pleased at my response. Little did he know.

There was no such thing as fate.

"Ladies and gentlemen." As the prince spoke, everyone quieted down, lowered their drinks, and watched him. "Thank you for coming. It is now my honor to unveil the pièce de résistance of tonight's gala, generously donated by—" He paused. The guest next to him, with a nervous smile and a top hat that didn't entirely fit over his head, leaned over and whispered in the prince's ear. "The American Philosophical Society. Our good friends across the pond." He cut short his own awkward laughter by abruptly clearing his throat. "Feast your eyes."

He nodded to two gentlemen who took each side of the red curtains and pulled them apart. The curtains rolled along the silver rod, splitting like the Red Sea to unveil the four gold-framed portraits behind the prince.

Gasps. Somewhere in the room, a glass shattered, likely slipped from someone's hand.

In one photograph, Queen Victoria sat in a chair as normal as any other. What wasn't normal was the silhouette of Prince Albert, her husband, wrapped in a white veil, sitting at her feet as if to nudge himself against them.

"What . . . ?" Bertie stumbled back, his cheeks flaming and his mouth agape. "What is this?"

In another photograph, Queen Victoria was hunched over in an elaborate black dress, very obviously weeping. Though faint, everyone could see Prince Albert's specter smiling down at her in the background.

"How frightening!" one patron said with a tremor in his voice. "Aren't these supposed to be photographs?"

"If they're photographs then how can we see the late prince?" someone else asked. "Or is Prince Albert . . . is he a—"

"Spirit!" someone cried. "The Queen is communicating with spirits!"

The room burst into scandalized conversation.

"My mother is . . . ," Bertie whispered. "What the hell has she been doing?"

"I've heard of this." Gowramma sidled up to me, a glass of wine in hand. "Spirit photography. It's all the rage in America right now, especially among those desperate to feel connected with their dead loved ones. It's all trickery and technology. I'm sure they're using multiple exposures. Still, such a dreadfully morbid act to partake in."

I thought so too, when Mrs. Mallet confessed to me the Queen's extracurricular activities that day at the open café. Though the pictures looked far worse here under such good light than they had in Bambridge's darkroom.

Gowramma squinted "Is . . . Her Majesty lying in bed with her dead husband in that one?"

Sure enough, that was Queen Victoria with the corpse of her dead husband, not yet decayed. There were many in Britain who believed spirits walked among us. But many skeptics and religious types detested such un-Christian activities.

The excuse that these were taken before Prince Albert's death were out of the question given the dates on the photographs: January 1862, a month after he left this world. Some photographers seemed very keen on dating their art—and signing it.

"William Bambridge?" Bertie had yelled the man's name loud enough for people to hear.

Bambridge's skin was as ghostly pale as Prince Albert in the last photo, holding his mourning wife. As everyone's judging gaze crawled over him like spiders, he began to shake, his lips sputtering out half-baked explanations that never quite formed into full words. But a little humiliation wasn't all I had in store for my former photographer.

"Men! There he is. Arrest him immediately!"

The crowd of England's upper crust gasped and watched, utterly shocked as Scotland Yard, led by the newly promoted Chief Inspector Charles Wilkes, marched into the museum exhibition and surrounded William Bambridge.

The crowd split into two, gathering around the ends of the hall. Good. I had a clear view from the opposite end of the room.

Bambridge let out a shriek-like whine. "What? What are you—?"

Seeing William Bambridge's ears turn red was so wholly satisfying I had to press my hand against my mouth so laughter wouldn't escape my lips. Roger Fenton sidled away from him as quickly and discreetly as he could.

"What is the meaning of this?" Bambridge finally managed to spit out as two officers grabbed each of his arms—rather *roughly*. Good. *Good.*

"You're under arrest for theft. We found the stolen work of Marcus Sparling in your possession."

The crowd gasped.

"Stolen work?" I heard a woman say.

"So after photographing Her Majesty in such a state, he was going to sell the work of a fellow artist?" a man whispered to his friend.

The guests stared at the Queen's royal photographer and didn't know what to think.

"You must be mad!" Bambridge screamed, struggling with the Scotland Yard officers. "Why in the devil's name would you think I had something to do with that?"

"Don't try to deny it. We found the evidence in your portrait studio in Bayswater."

William Bambridge's whole face sank at the mention of the studio no one was supposed to know about. The studio where he created works meant for his eyes only. Illicit works that would shock the royal family if they, like I, had discovered the hideout, tracked it down, and broken in to take a look around.

"How do you know about that place?" he shouted before he could stop himself. Not the smartest words of a man trying to prove his innocence. The chatter and accusatory gossip began almost immediately. Bambridge didn't know what to think. With his eyes bulging, he looked from wealthy guest to wealthy guest, hoping for someone to come to his defense. But no one did. Roger Fenton deflated as he stared at his friend, soaking in the betrayal.

"You'll have your chance to argue your case in court. But with the evidence we've found, I have a hard time believing you'll be seeing the outside of a jail cell in some time. Take him away, lads."

Wilkes didn't look at me as his officers wrestled with Bambridge. He wasn't supposed to.

Like a good little soldier, Wilkes did as he was told.

Bambridge, however, would not. I'd never seen an old man struggle as hard as he did. "Are you mad? Me a thief? Don't you know who I am? I am the royal photographer for Queen Victoria!"

Oh, by now everyone knew. If the ghoulish spirit photographs weren't proof enough.

"You've got the wrong man, you fools!" Bambridge fought as if his life depended on it. At some point, he knocked one of the officers in the eye and backhanded one in the face. One of the officers grabbed him by the collar and, in the midst of the battle, yanked off his bow tie. It fell to the ground unceremoniously.

"Take him away!" Wilkes ordered again.

As the boots of the Scotland Yard stomped on Bambridge's forgotten bow tie, as the photographer was led out of the museum screaming and crying, his reputation in tatters, I thought of my Egbado beads. Because of him, they'd been long discarded. They were far more beautiful than his silly little black tie. It was the greater loss. Hopefully my ancestors felt at peace.

Bertie began ordering men to take the photographs of his mother down. On the opposite end of the room, Harriet threw me a satisfied look.

Captain Davies strode up to my side as the crowd dispersed into their gossip silos. "Are you okay, Sally?" He took my hands in his and squeezed them. His wide brown eyes shimmered with genuine concern. Caring and tender.

Gowramma scoffed. "Goodness. You're acting as if Scotland Yard came for *her*."

"She's to be my wife, Your Highness. During times like these, I'd like to make sure she's okay."

Davies still had the tendency to treat me as a child—the child fourteen years his junior who he met in Freetown when I was a schoolgirl and he was a man of twenty-six. I wondered how old his former wife, Matilda, was when they'd met. Were they close in age? Was she his senior, looking to find her love and marriage match in a young, handsome boy on his way to success and greatness? Did love overcome all of it? What did it mean that I was expected to?

Davies seemed a virtuous man. He wanted to do right by me and I could see it. But there was too much I couldn't overlook. My expected voicelessness. The Queen's hand in it all . . .

Gowramma swept her long dark brown hair over her shoulders. "Well, in any case, I think we've all got enough material for about a week's worth of conversation. Though I don't imagine I'll be attending any more events this week, not if they're all as tiring."

Liar. She would attend them all if they were this fun. I did my utmost to hold back a grin.

"I can't believe it," Davies whispered. "Bambridge, a criminal. And those disgusting pictures of the Queen. How mortifying!"

That was the point. The Queen was at home right now, perhaps communing with some spirits. But this news would reach her soon. If she did manage to speak to some spirits tonight, whether she channeled her ancestors or mine, they'd tell her that this was only the beginning.

Later that night, over on Porchester Terrace, inside William Bambridge's secret studio, I wondered who was prouder: me, or Rui.

Well, I had done most of the work, bribing Andrea Bradley, using her to blackmail Charles Wilkes and finally moving the inspector like a chess piece to knock Bambridge off the board. Queen Victoria's reputation was already on shaky ground since Prince Albert had passed. It would take a deeper dive now in the public once word spread she had commissioned postmortem photography—such a strange and controversial pastime.

As for Rui himself, he sat in the green chair next to the stage, his legs folded. His black hair was deliciously unkempt. He reached out to me and when I took his hands, I noticed they smelled of lilac, like mine.

"Tell me," I asked him, pulling up my skirt to sit on his lap, pleased when he let out the faintest moan. "Was it difficult, sneaking into the museum to bring in Bambridge's portraits of the Queen? Did your men help you?"

Rui fluffed up my dress so it covered his lap, straightening the ruffles around the edges. "Are you sure you want to know all the dirty details?" He seemed to reconsider. "Then again, if it's you, I don't think you'll mind anything too dirty." He flashed me a confident, lopsided grin as he brought my fingers to his lips and softly smelled the lilac from them.

The heat between our hips was electrifying. The excitement from danger and mischief. The euphoria of a life deservedly ruined. It was intoxicating. I slid up closer to him. As close as I could until there was barely space between our bodies.

"And what about that boy? Dalton Sass?" Rui placed his hands on my bare thighs. My body warmed and shivered as his hot touch slid up and down my soft flesh. "If what you told me is true, he'll be a problem."

"I've taken down others. I can take him down too."

"Are you sure?" Rui gave me a sidelong look. "He seems to want to kill you."

"Then I'll just have to kill him first."

Rui's grip on my legs hardened in a flash and a groan escaped from his mouth. I let out a gasp from the pain, and a gasp as they slipped up my thighs, a gasp that was captured by the criminal prince's lips before I could catch my breath.

Finally, a kiss. And it was a kiss worth waiting for, full of passion, lust, and every other immodest emotion Miss Welsh and Mama Schoen had warned me against as they prepared me for a loveless marriage.

"That's it, Sally," he said to me in a harsh whisper, releasing my bottom lip, letting the wetness settle there. "That's exactly how you should be: ruthless without regret. How intoxicating it is to see a princess fall."

Taking off my gloves and throwing them to the studio floor, I gripped his black vest, slid my hand through his open shirt so my hand could feel his chest, and returned the kiss just as hungrily. Crushing him against the chair, I felt invincible. I remembered the girl in the portrait and saw the blood return to her face and the life to her eyes.

With one swift movement, Rui seized my bottom and lowered me to the floor. I wrapped my legs around his waist as my back hit the wood and his weight fell upon me.

Just a little bit more, I told myself as I drowned in our kisses and ascended to heaven. Everything would work out. Everything I plan always works out.

The euphoric revelation carried me through the night, my lips on Rui's neck, his legs intertwined with mine.

If only I knew that night that Bambridge's stint in prison would be a short one. A few days later, I learned of the monster's release.

Dalton Sass had arranged it.

TWENTY-ONE

AFTER I RECEIVED Harriet's letter telling me the dreadful news, I fast sent word for her to meet me in London.

"Bambridge's release from Coldbath Fields Prison is the talk of the palace," Harriet told me after she stepped out of her carriage in Bethnal Green. "I checked myself. He's gone."

I didn't imagine he'd be there forever, but I'd hoped he'd do some hard labor on the prison's infamous penal treadmill, pumping water and grinding corn, before being shipped to Tasmania by a furious Queen Victoria. How annoying.

Still, that wasn't why I asked Harriet to meet me here.

How deeply had Dalton looked into the circumstances of Bambridge's fall from grace before deciding to bail him out? The question left a corrosive knot in my stomach. I thought of Wilkes and worried for his mistress Andrea.

I'd soon realize my worries weren't unfounded.

A gruff, heavyset landlord pushed me out of one of the low lodging houses on Old Nichol Street. I tripped and fell back, colliding with the stone street.

"Sally!" Harriet crouched down next to me, grabbing my arm. "Are you okay?"

"Oi!" The landlord cut her off. "Andrea Bradley moved out. She ain't here." As pain needled its way up my back, the landlord wiped the spittle off his mouth and snarled.

"Moved out?" Harriet narrowed her eyes. "I've been here to see her myself. Recently. How can she move out so fast?"

Now how, but why. That was the question. The landlord, however, wasn't interested.

"How should I know? Now get out of my sight. Your kind isn't welcome around here."

With one last venomous glare at me, he slammed the rotting wooden door in our faces.

Here in Bethnal Green, coster lads raced across rooftops. A flyer slipped from the hands of a street vendor and blew with the wind straight into my face. A column of advertisements for some common maladies, news of some theater performances—and, oh, look, the Anti-Slavery Society had taken out an ad for their event on August 1, the one the Queen had rejected.

The flyer must have mistaken me for an ashpit, where all the other trash went to be disposed of. I scrunched it my hands and threw it upon the ground and stomped on it.

Some in the crowded streets underneath the clothing lines snickered at the sight of me pulling myself to my feet and dusting off my dark blue dress. Others were too caught up in today's talk to notice me.

"I heard the Queen's into some filthy stuff," one man said on the other side of the street. He and few of his friends gathered around an upturned fish barrel to play the gambling game Three-Up. They threw three halfpennies into the air and waited for which would come up heads and which would come up tails. I wasn't sure precisely how the game is played. Only that when the coins rattled upon the barrel's surface, two of the men jeered and pumped their fists in the air.

"I heard she took a photograph with her dead husband the day they buried him," one man said, gathering up the coins.

"The prince probably got the old girl into all that spirit bollocks. That's what happens when you marry a German man. Should have married a good English bloke."

A carriage cut him off from my line of sight, and then, from the opposite end of the street, a man carrying a wheelbarrow of fruits did.

"Looks like word of the Queen's hobbies is spreading even out here," said Harriet. The horses slowed to a stop in front of us. "That's a good thing, isn't it?"

"Not with Andrea suddenly missing."

I strode across the cobbled street. The gambling men stared up at me, their mouths agape as if I were some kind of rare animal in a zoo.

"You going to perform for us, sweetie?" one said, rubbing some coins between his fingers.

I didn't have time for this. "Andrea Bradley," I demanded. "Where is she?"

As the men bristled in anger at my haughtiness, Harriet grabbed my arm and pulled me back. "What my servant meant to say was, we're looking for a young lady named Andrea Bradley."

I scoffed in disbelief. "Servant?"

But Harriet nudged me in the side. Her ladylike grin seemed to placate the men for now. "Might you know where we can find her?"

"Andrea's been gone a couple of days," said one. "Haven't seen her around. It's like she and that great big belly of hers disappeared."

Harriet thanked the men and pulled me away, down the cobbled street. I let her hail a carriage as I stewed in my thoughts. Nothing about this felt like the victory it should have. Bambridge released from jail. Now Andrea Bradley was suddenly missing. These were precision strikes.

As Harriet climbed into the empty carriage, I let out a yell, frightening a nearby potato seller who cowered in his stall. "*How* did this happen?"

"Sally! Calm down, for goodness' sake!"

Hearing Harriet of all people admonish me was a strong blow. As I climbed into the carriage, I gripped my blouse, right over my frantic heart, and inhaled. Still, the chaos of my thoughts raged on.

"I don't know how Dalton paid Bambridge's bail," said Harriet as the carriage driver took us out of Bethnal Green. "It was set so high. Besides, who would want to be seen helping someone who'd just been so thoroughly and publicly humiliated?"

Someone with nothing to lose. Sass didn't much care about his reputation in high society. He only seemed interested in slithering his way into Bertie's life. And why wouldn't he? Doing so gave him access to me.

"He did mention his mother left him an inheritance when he died," I said, folding my arms. "He is an unknown element in society. A cipher with funds to spend on whatever he wishes. That makes him dangerous."

Of course he was. Whatever was in the letter he showed Lord Ponsonby in Windsor Castle could harm the Queen somehow. That meant that he had access to information about her that not even I knew about. How did he gain this access? What other resources did he have that I didn't know about? I needed to find out all I could.

"Andrea suddenly disappearing doesn't feel like a coincidence," I said. Curiosities didn't just occur by accident. Someone was very carefully pulling the rug out from under me. I was not going to lose this game.

"Harriet." I turned to her and paused, looking her from the top of her brown head to the tips of her black boots. "You enjoyed calling me a servant back there, didn't you?"

Gasping in terror, Harriet clutched her white blouse and shook her head furiously. "What? N-No, I would never!"

Wouldn't she, though? Wouldn't any of them? Clucking my tongue, I put up a hand to silence her. "First things first: look into where Dalton

Sass lives and document anyone he might be associating with. I want to know every establishment he frequents. Every brothel, every bar, *every lavatory he urinates in.*"

Harriet's eyebrows flew up into her hairline. Rubbing her neck, she let out a little cough. "Well . . . if it's information you want, you might just have a chance to find it yourself straight from the horse's mouth. And trust me, horses will be involved." Harriet slipped a letter out of her pocket. "I was actually instructed by Bertie this morning to give this to you."

I took the letter from her, turning it around as if it were the first time I'd ever seen paper.

I raised an eyebrow. "An invitation?"

"He's hosting a stag hunt tomorrow."

Indeed, the letter was addressed to me, this time, written by Bertie himself. I could tell by the terrible penmanship:

> *Royal Estate, Surrey, England*
> *July 24 at eight in the morning*
> *Consider this a stronger apology.*

Either he had gotten over his mother's public disgrace rather quickly or he had something else in mind. I crumpled the letter in my hand. "You're right, Harriet. I wouldn't be surprised if Sass was invited too. If that's the case, I'll need a way to separate him from Bertie somehow and get my answers."

Or would I have to use his connection to Bertie to finesse the information out of him? Either way, I needed to know more about him. Information gathering was key to crushing your enemies, but it was like this Dalton Sass had appeared from thin air, created by the heavens for the sole purpose of driving me mad. I wouldn't let him get in my way.

As I plotted, Harriet tugged at the loose string peeling off the carriage's cushion beneath her. Her shy stuttering tried and failed to drag me out of my thoughts.

"S-Sally," she started, and stopped, biting her bottom lip. But I was only half listening. I'd need to find an appropriate hunting dress by tomorrow. I wondered if Harriet could get me something from the palace. I'm sure nobody would miss it.

"Sally!"

I rubbed the back of my neck. "What?"

"Is there something between you and Bertie?"

I gaped at her. Between Bambridge, Bertie, and Sass, I'd never felt so fatigued in my life, and now what was this nonsense?

"Something?" I repeated. "Meaning?"

Harriet's long brown braid tumbled over her shoulder as she whipped her head around to face the window. She didn't want to look at me.

"He was adamant I give the invitation to you. He really wants you to come to the hunt. He was following you around at the gala as well the other day."

I sighed, squeezing my neck muscles, wishing with every ounce of my being that I had the time to get a massage before going off to war against Sass tomorrow. I needed my limbs loosened. Though it'd been days, my body still buzzed with frustration from the way Rui and I left things off in Bambridge's secret studio—with Rui suddenly stopping his delicious assault on my flesh, leaving me alone in the room, heaving on the floor, furious. Just to tease me.

"Harriet," I explained with the sternness of a schoolteacher, "the Prince of Wales is a child. He thinks of no one but himself. Born with a false sense of superiority from his 'high' status but knowing that status is entirely unearned has given him an insatiable foundation of *inferiority* that requires him to seek validation from every source he can find."

"And you're one of those sources?"

I sighed. "I suppose I am. One of the unfortunate side effects of being 'part' of the royal family."

Harriet didn't look convinced. Even as I closed my eyes and breathed to calm my nerves, I could feel her gaze on me.

"He doesn't seem to like Captain Davies very much."

"He doesn't much appreciate any man smarter than him. Which, unfortunately, is quite a sizable number of people."

"Are you sure he doesn't—"

"Harriet." I placed my hand on her shoulder firmly, without slamming it down, though I wanted to. It was enough to make the girl go silent.

I wasn't a fool. I knew that Bertie's behavior had always been obnoxious around me, even more so now that my marriage was announced. Perhaps he was upset that one of his favorite toys was being taken from him. Who knew? Right now I had too much on my mind to care one whit.

"I'll need a hunting dress for tomorrow." I smoothened out my hair. "Harriet, make sure you find a way there too. You'll be my guest."

"Really?" Harriet said. "You want me there with you? Are you sure?"

"It may seem counterintuitive, but you can actually learn a lot about a man when he's busy killing things. But then I might be too busy killing things myself. A second set of eyes and ears will be important."

"Sally . . ." she started, and for the thousandth time trailed off. "You and I . . . we *are* friends, aren't we?"

I took her hand in both of mine. "We are, Harriet. Know that if you ever feel uncomfortable with any of this, you can let me know. I won't force you to do anything you don't want to. Just say the word. You can tell me anything, you know. I'd never use it against you."

Not unless I had to.

"I can tell you anything. . . ." Her skin reddened. With a slight blush, she nodded while the gentle rumbling of the carriage against the stony road carried us off into silence.

TWENTY-TWO

WHY BERTIE THOUGHT inviting me to come to his country house to kill some poor unsuspecting creature should count as any kind of apology was beyond me. Did he even know what he was apologizing for? The past decade of having to know him?

I yawned, adjusting the sashes of my black riding hat. Harriet had found me an elegant blue riding habit I could wear over my trousers. The skirt was silk and wouldn't drag me down while riding. I didn't have much practice on a horse—not as much as Harriet, who stood fiddling with the reticule dangling from her belt. But I wasn't here to impress anyone with my riding skill.

The sparse forest beyond the Surrey cottage was about to be trampled upon by the prince and his shooting party. And what a large party it was—larger than I was expecting.

"Sally! You came! I knew you couldn't resist me." Bertie, in a black velvet jacket and high red leather boots, wrangled his Thoroughbred by the leather bridle toward me.

I brushed a strand of hair out of my face. "Yes, I figured you'd need to kill something after the gala debacle."

Bertie stiffened. The smile he forced soon disappeared when he tugged his horse's bridle too suddenly and it struck his face with its nose.

Not far behind him his royal cottage was lightly shrouded in morning fog. The two-storied, gray-bricked home had smoke coming out of its chimneys. There were a few of them along the blue roof because the cottage was longer than it was tall, spreading itself along the acres of royal land.

As Bertie groaned and rubbed his cheek, Harriet slid out from behind me and curtsied to him, before shooting me a strange look and heading toward the crowd of attendants and hunters.

I wasn't looking at Bertie. I was looking at my betrothed behind him. In a shooting coat, long in the waist, Captain Davies patted his horse along the long white strip down its nose. I hadn't been sure whether he'd be here. It wasn't his presence that bothered me so much as the fact that he was currently in the middle of a robust conversation with William McCoskry.

"Who's that man?" I asked Bertie, and pointed at him as if I didn't know.

"Oh, him? That's William McCoskry, an old friend of my mother's. I met him when I was a child. He was a merchant then, but now he's been a governor in Africa for the last few years."

"And why is he here?" I hadn't anticipated he would be. Another surprise I didn't appreciate. McCoskry clapped Davies on the back as they jostled their horses together.

Bertie waved an attendant over to bring me my horse. "Didn't I tell you? He's a friend. I've been asking him about his work of late. When I told him I knew you, he was curious to see you in person." Bertie chuckled. "Quite the popular lady, aren't you?"

I was indeed. Dalton Sass rode in on his horse, clopping gently against the grass with none other than Charles Wilkes riding next to them, the two of them in matching red jackets.

And with matching, hateful grins.

I was surrounded by enemies.

"Ah, Miss Bonetta. It's been too long, too long indeed since the luncheon." McCoskry gave his horse's reins to his personal attendant and strode toward me, his arms spread open for a hug. Both Bertie and Captain Davies intercepted him before he could reach me.

"That's right." Davies, though shooting him a friendly smile, gripped his shoulder a little too tightly. "I hear you've known my wife-to-be since she was a child!"

"As did you all, apparently," I mumbled underneath my breath, catching Davies off guard. As he cleared his throat, McCoskry nodded.

"Oh yes, I was there when she was first presented to the Queen." His voice was loud and obnoxious, his Scottish accent as boisterous and prideful as the strangely shaped red beard colonizing his face. "An adorable little thing even then. And so entertaining. She danced for us just the night before. A performance from an African princess."

Only Captain Davies seemed to notice how violently my body stiffened. Without hesitating, he took my hand. He couldn't have known why I was squeezing my jaw at the sight of him. But perhaps part of him did understand. Perhaps he could feel the shame radiating off my skin as I stayed silent through his long, detailed, humiliating account.

McCoskry described everything but for the fact that I was terrified and naked. He saved me that indignity now in a way that he should have when I was a child, though it was probably more out of a sense of self-preservation that he skipped certain details. The dance he described was playful, joyful even. He spoke with the smile of a brazen louche remembering his "good old days" when he groped women and gambled in bars. And as he spoke, the desire for blood overcame me. But I wasn't the only one in this hunting party whose bloodlust could be felt.

"Are you okay, Sally?" Captain Davies had turned to me and whispered it so only I could hear. It took me by surprise. I couldn't answer.

"I didn't know Sally *danced*." Sass rode up to us, his horse greeting us with a quiet snort. "I'm sure she was adorable when she was a child. But we tend to become very different as we grow up, I find." He turned to his other half. "Don't you agree, Inspector?"

"Quite." Inspector Charles Wilkes avoided my eyes as he answered. He could barely grunt the words out, he was so furious with me. His white hands flushed red with the blood pumping through them. Both Dalton and Wilkes knew more about my true intentions than anyone here. What had Miss Sass's demon spawn told the inspector that gave him the go-ahead to bail Bambridge out of jail?

What was Wilkes willing to tell the party here and now?

"The weather isn't perfect," said Bertie, looking up at the cloudy sky. "But the companions more than make up for it. Looks like there'll be much to talk about on the hunt. Gather the hounds and the guns. It's always a good day for shooting something, I say."

Something told me we were all in agreement there.

Men went out with bang sticks, trying to draw out the stags while the hounds hungrily swiveled through the trees. They were lucky for their keen sense of smell because it was hard to see much between the shade of the evergreen leaves, the cloudy skies, and the light touch of fog. According to Bertie, it all made for a better challenge.

My challenge encroached me on all sides: the man who would be my next target, William McCoskry, riding out front next to Bertie. The man I blackmailed into destroying my former target, Inspector Wilkes. And beside him, the man who insisted on bringing chaos to my plans, Dalton Sass. Everyone had their shotguns out.

One fired. With terrible neighs, the spooked horses came to a flailing stop. To my left, Harriet trembled, her cheeks red with embarrassment.

"I'm sorry!" She bit her lip and avoided all eye contact. "I thought I saw something."

"It's all right, Harriet," said Dalton directly behind her. "I'm sure more than one of us here has an itchy trigger finger."

We exchanged steely glances as the party moved forward more carefully through the ancient woodland.

"It's a shame the Queen couldn't come out with us on this hunt," said McCoskry in front of me, and just the sound of his voice made my gun grip tremble. At least he wasn't wearing a kilt. It would have made the view far more awkward. "She's always been so fond of sport. But then I suppose after what happened at the museum . . ."

He trailed off.

"Precisely," Bertie said in a grave tone. "She's not at all pleased those . . . 'photographs' were revealed to the public. Have you seen the papers? The cartoons about it are terrible. Of course, Mother blames me."

I was sure Bertie got an earful. He was the royal representative in charge of the exhibit. The Queen would have blamed her disappointing son for her mortification.

"But," Bertie continued, "if you're interested in seeing her, you can always come by Windsor Castle tomorrow to catch the séance."

"Séance?" Captain Davies adjusted his top hat on his head. Luckily for him it hid his bald spot, or perhaps that was by design.

"Oh, Mother quickly arranged it and made sure all in her circle knew. She'll be trying to contact Father again with a different medium this time. Who knows, maybe we'll get to see a crystal ball. Only her closest friends have been invited—people Father knew to help jolt his spirit from the afterlife." He let out a sigh. "It's all so mad."

Bertie's bitterness was palpable. Harriet, fully aware of the intricate, morbid goings-on of the palace, shifted uncomfortably on her horse.

But was it really mad? Now that the Queen's macabre hobbies had been revealed, why would she lean more publicly into the spiritual? Something about her movements felt strange.

"I don't know about madness," Captain Davies said, "but we Yoruba believe that one's life doesn't end with physical death. Our ancestors live on, though we don't always see them. They can even be reborn into our families under the right circumstances." He glanced at me. "Isn't that right, Sally?"

It felt odd being able to talk about beliefs with one of my own kin. I wished so badly it felt more pleasant. Davies was right, of course. But my perspective had changed so drastically since childhood, conversations like these hurt me more than anything. I'd driven myself crazy thinking of my parents, thinking of Ade's fate in the next world—whether he was happy. Whether he was at peace. Whether he still would ever speak to me again after I let his life be taken by those murderers, the Forbeses. What he thought of me now, bearing their name . . . ?

I used to go to sleep in Freetown expecting to chat with my mother in my dreams, for it was only in my dreams that she could speak to me. And we did for a time. We'd cry together. She'd warn me of dangers to come.

Ade would speak to me in my dreams too. He'd tell me those words over and over again so that I would never forget: *Their "love" for you is conditional, Ina.*

Despite my enslavement to Britain's Queen of Hearts, I'd managed to maintain those connections before the beatings got worse and my mind broke as my body broke. Now thinking of traditional beliefs left me feeling frail and cold. Now when I shut my eyes at night and saw nothing in the darkness of my dreams, I wondered if I believed in anything anymore.

"Why, Captain Davies, I thought you were a Christian?" McCoskry looked back. "And educated by the best."

Davies straightened his shoulders, lifting his head in defiance. "One can believe many things at the same time. It's not so necessary to force one thought above the other."

"No one loves armed missionaries," I added in support as I sat uncomfortably upon my horse's black leather saddle. "Wasn't that said to be the first lesson of nature?"

Support was probably something Davies didn't expect. As Captain Davies shot me an approving smile, Bertie turned back. "Ah yes," he said with an obnoxious nod. "I've heard those words before: spoken by Plato, of course."

Captain Davies and I exchanged glances.

"Robespierre," Captain Davies corrected him. And while Harriet giggled and Bertie's ears burned, he added, "Though I can imagine why *you*, a royal, wouldn't be so fond of memorizing that particular man's works."

"Liberty, equality, fraternity, or death," Dalton shouted in an operatic voice. "The last, much the easiest to bestow, O Guillotine!"

Davies leaned over. "That one *wasn't* Robespierre, by the way."

As Bertie muttered something and slouched over, Davies gave me another conspiratorial grin, but I returned it only weakly. Was this something to be proud about? How thoroughly we'd had Europe's history and philosophies forced into us?

"I'm less worried about the dead than I am with the living these days," Inspector Wilkes said, and the sound of his voice forced me to refocus. There was nothing fun about this hunt no matter how easy it was to make short work of Bertie's ego.

"Yes, I heard about that whole business with William Bambridge," McCoskry said. "It's rather unbelievable. I thought he was an upright enough man."

"Well, it turns out that new evidence has been brought to light that might exonerate him."

My body chilled.

"Is that so?" McCoskry laughed. "What kind of evidence is that?"

"Very fascinating," Dalton answered for him. "It's why I paid Bambridge's bail. He's staying with me for a few days, lying low, you know, as he's under house arrest. So I hope you'd keep it to yourself for now until this whole mess is cleared up."

Without a word, I reacted as naturally as anyone would. As far as they were all concerned I was just as in the dark and scandalized as any gentlelady.

"You need to be careful with these things, Wilkes," said McCoskry. "As governor in Lagos, I witnessed all kinds of crimes from former slaves and slave owners."

Even participated in a few of them yourself. I tightened the grip around my gun, saying nothing. McCoskry wasn't the only one with a long memory. But it wasn't time for *that* just yet.

"It's sometimes hard to know who's innocent and who's guilty," the red-haired man continued.

"While other times it is as clear as cut glass." Wilkes's glare bored into the back of my skull.

The hounds suddenly went into a frenzy. Bertie put a hand up. "Enough chitchat. Let's go see what they've found."

We raced through the woods. But the stag wouldn't be caught, not so easily. It evaded the bullets Bertie and his party lobbed at it, using the fog as cover. Hollering, Bertie kicked his horse, beckoning us all to split up amidst the trees.

The smell of blood took me through a winding path to my right. Captain Davies rode off with McCoskry. I thought Harriet was following close enough behind until I entered a clearing, turned around, and found myself alone under the canopy of leaves.

"Harriet?" I called out, shuddering when a flock of birds took off from the rustling treetops. I pulled my shawl around my neck and called again, louder, "Harriet? Where in the world have you gone? Have I lost you?"

"You've lost something, I suspect. Your bloody marbles, you witch."

Inspector Wilkes. He rode into the clearing, one hand on the reins, the other on his gun, as Dalton followed close behind.

"Alone at last, Sally." Shadows from the leaves painted sinister shapes across the Freetown boy's face. "We have a lot to talk about."

TWENTY-THREE

NOBODY HAD MOVED a muscle since we dismounted our horses. Who would? We each had a weapon. I certainly wasn't afraid to use mine.

Dalton plunked the butt of his shotgun on the grass and leaned on the barrel. "You know, now that I look a little closer, you do look like the devil's *dew-beater*, doesn't she, Wilkes?"

"So what is this?" I jumped in before the inspector could pry open his foaming mouth. "Some grand team-up between an adulterer and an evil little clotpole?"

"The only evil one here is you!" Wilkes took a menacing step forward, his arms up, stopped only by Dalton. "That you, you . . . *negresse* had the audacity to bribe me into framing an innocent man—"

I snorted. "Please. Nobody's innocent."

"Quiet!" Wilkes's ears flamed red the more furious he became. "You manipulated me."

"Using your indiscretions against you," I added smoothly. "But as I've been told, Miss Andrea hasn't been found of late." I looked at Dalton. "Is that your doing?"

Leaning on his gun, Dalton crossed his legs with a cocky grin. That seemed confirmation enough. "You have your connections and I have mine. Miss Andrea's on a trip to Australia at the moment. Which means the leverage you have over the inspector has vanished down under with her."

I hope he at least put her on a proper ship with proper food. I scowled. "And when you told Wilkes his problem was gone, that's when his lips loosened." He ratted me out as soon as he could. Well, it wouldn't have been difficult to put two and two together with how Wilkes reacted at the sight of Andrea at Miss Welsh's tea party. All he would have to do was hunt her down.

"When Wilkes told me what you'd done to him, we bonded quite well. We're very similar, you see, since we both have reasons to despise you, Miss Bonetta."

I rolled my eyes and groaned. "Enough with the theatrics. What do you want?" I sounded nonchalant, but my heart was beating hard. My hand's grip on the gun grew ever tighter.

"I want you in handcuffs, you—" Wilkes's whole body swelled. He looked as if he wanted to jump me and tear out my hair. Again, Dalton stopped him.

"You can arrest me," I told him. "But then you'd have to reveal your part in this whole dirty affair. You're the pride of Scotland Yard and you were willing to frame a man just to keep your wife from finding out about your extracurricular activities." A devilish smile spread across my lips. "Speak a word about this to anyone, Inspector Wilkes, and there's no scenario in which you come out unscathed."

"You filthy—"

"Also I believe I left no evidence of my involvement with Bambridge." I shrugged. "In fact, by getting rid of Andrea, you got rid of the one person whose existence could provide concrete evidence of your blackmail. If the crime doesn't exist, then neither does the criminal—and how in the world can anyone punish a criminal who doesn't exist?"

It was Dalton who spoke next, as Wilkes seethed, stepping out in front of him, closing the distance between us just enough to threaten.

"Wilkes and I had this discussion. And we came up with a solution." He tilted his head, his mocking gaze challenging me. "We go to the Queen."

I shifted on my feet, swallowing the growing lump in my throat. "You're going to tell on me?" The irritation was clear in my voice. At least, I hoped it was.

"Why not?" Dalton shrugged. "Unlike the law, the Queen doesn't operate based on specifics like evidence, rationality, and logic. You're the Queen's ward. Imagine if the rumors of *your* extracurricular activities came out?"

He was right. Gossip knew no logic and needed no evidence. The Queen would not want any rumors to spread about her goddaughter. It would only reflect poorly on her and she didn't need that, not now of all times.

"So she'd keep it quiet," I snapped back. "She'd make sure the whole dreadful truth never saw the light of day. Which means, I suppose, we're both saved. You get to keep your job without anyone questioning your easily malleable morals and I keep my illusion of innocence."

"And how do you think Queen Victoria will keep the affair quiet?" Dalton said. "If Wilkes is fired suddenly, so soon after his promotion and the very public arrest of Bambridge, it'll only make people ask questions. The Queen won't like questions. But I do wonder: How well does Her Majesty like you?"

I gritted my teeth, my expression grim because I knew the scenario Dalton was painting before my eyes. The Queen, to keep things quiet, would let Wilkes carry on with his job. Whatever reprimand he received wouldn't ruin his standing—the blame would fall on me, the wayward, rebellious goddaughter who clearly didn't know her place and role in society. The fact that she was forcing my marriage to Davies was proof she already didn't trust me. If she knew what I was up to, if the threads began unraveling, what would she do to me? Would she move up my wedding? Banish me to Australia like so many criminals?

Would she get rid of me entirely?

I thought of Ade's glassy eyes as he sank beneath the ocean waves, and began to tremble. I couldn't stop it. I placed a hand on my left arm to tamp it down, but thinking of Ade's death sent a wave of panic through me. I was a good child. Brilliant, kind, and of fair temperament. That's what Captain Frederick Forbes had said about me to anyone who would listen. To the Queen. And what happened to the ones who didn't play their roles?

I hated Dalton because the question he'd asked was too easily answered. How well did the Queen like me? Nonsense. Her love for me was conditional.

"From the pained expression on your face, it's very clear you'd rather me not tell the Queen about what you've been up to."

I hadn't realized my face had changed at all. I'd practiced for so long to keep it unreadable. My hands balled into fists.

"Here's what you will do to make it up to poor Inspector Wilkes, who has suffered at your hand like so many innocents." Dalton picked up his gun and twirled it around. I gripped my own weapon, ready. "You will become Wilkes's puppet from now until he deigns to relieve you of your duties. Isn't that right, Inspector?"

As Dalton looked back at Wilkes, still flushed but somehow satisfied at the turn of events, he puffed out his chest. "I wish to enter politics. You, Miss Forbes, will insist upon the royal family's endorsement."

"Politics?" I laughed long and hard. "Despite your proclivity towards corruption, I'm afraid you have neither the intellect nor the grit to win a seat in your own broken home, let alone Parliament."

As Wilkes bared his teeth at me, Dalton took over the negotiations.

"You will do as he says or he will voluntarily reveal your treachery to the Queen. I believe Bertie says she's having a séance soon, is she not? What a perfect stage to air out one's demons."

Dalton exchanged a triumphant glance with Wilkes, but he wasn't fooling anyone. He could give a whit about what Wilkes wanted. This was about what he wanted. It was why he found Andrea and went to Wilkes. Why he paid Bambridge's bail.

Sass was using Wilkes. Now that he had Wilkes's complete trust, he could easily one day twist my servitude to the inspector in his own favor. If I refused to do as they pleased, they'd go to the Queen. My activities would be revealed. My freedom, maybe even my life, would vanish.

But something was bothering me about this arrangement. Something about Dalton's priorities in all this didn't quite make sense. . . .

"Well, that's settled then, isn't it?" Inspector Charles Wilkes clapped Dalton's shoulder before mounting his horse. "I'll see you at the Queen's séance, you little wench. I'm sure the prince won't mind giving me an invitation. You'd better be there too, to sing my praises. That's my first command. I have a political campaign to get ready."

He kicked his horse and left Dalton and me in the clearing. The fog was starting to lift, but only ever so slightly. The chill still prickled at the nape of my neck. Though it was Dalton's unhinged grin that made my hair stand on end.

"How does it feel to lose, Sally?" Dalton balanced his gun on the back of his neck as I slid closer to my horse. "To be beaten."

"But have I been beaten?"

Dalton's slow frown told me I had his attention. Good. I patted my horse's light brown hide gently as I continued to "think aloud."

"Revealing me to the Queen. Even without concrete evidence, using her fear of scandal and gossip to expose me. That should be enough for you. So why not just do it? Take Wilkes and demand an audience with Her Majesty right this moment. You could get revenge for your mother without having to waste another second. What's this 'be Wilkes's puppet' nonsense about?"

My hand paused on my horse's hide. "Unless." I gave him a sidelong look. "Wilkes won't let you. That selfish man wants to use me and he won't let you ruin it for him so quickly."

I could tell even with his mouth closed that wicked Miss Sass's wicked son was licking the top row of his teeth. Miss Sass used to do that too, right before she brought out her cane.

"You must know men like Wilkes. Pompous as they are ambitious. It won't be enough. He'll want to use me for other schemes and plots. There'll never be a point where he's had his fill. He'll never let you go to the Queen to tell on me. He'll never let you wield that secret, special letter in your possession, the one you used to frighten Ponsonby and sneak into Bertie's circle. If what's in that letter can truly threaten the Queen in any way, he won't let you use it, not while he still needs her favor. I'm sure you didn't think about that, now, did you?"

Tauntingly slow, I applauded him, the crisp clap of my hands echoing in the morning sky. "Oh well, we can't all be the type to think of everything. I'm sure eventually you'll find a way to twist this all to your favor. You've done well so far."

"Quiet," he hissed, taking the barrel of the gun by hand. "Don't you dare patronize me. When it comes to a battle of wits against me, witch, you can never win."

"Did your mother think that?"

Dalton went deathly still. I loved a direct hit. I rubbed my horse's ear as if it were a lover, listening to its little pleased snorts as Dalton glared daggers at me.

"I remember long ago when I was at the Institution. Miss Sass was

257

in her office writing a letter to her cousin, Julia Emily Sass. The new school's new superintendent. I was there as a punishment. I'd spoken out of turn and for that alone earned myself a beating, which was the norm for us students."

Dalton didn't seem to like hearing that. His gaze wavered to the ground, unfocused and quivering as if he didn't know where to direct his anger.

"In the corner of her office I had to stand holding stacks of books. Tomes that weighed more than I did. I stood there for maybe an hour. Maybe more. And Miss Sass, you know, she loved to talk to herself. Or maybe she was talking to me. She was certainly talking as she wrote her letter. She spoke about how much she hated children. How she'd never met a single one she didn't want to slap in the face. How vile and easily corruptible by the devil they were."

Dalton's hands were red. I could see them from here, twitching.

"And now I wonder—could she have also meant you?"

For the second time, Dalton's hand flew to his left arm instinctively, and I knew. Without fear I waltzed up to him. Startled, he lifted his gun.

"Stay back!" He pointed it at me. "I said, stay back, you witch!" he added again, because I wouldn't. But he wouldn't shoot either.

"Did she also mean you, her own child, when she talked about how much she hated children, how vile they were, how she'd never met a single one she didn't want to slap in the face?" I stepped closer and closer. "It's strange, Dalton, because she never once mentioned to us that she had a son. But wouldn't mothers be proud of their sons? Wouldn't they at least make reference to their existence once? It's just so strange. And yet, by your own admission, she talked about me to you all the time. It's all just so strange. . . ."

"S-Shut up!"

I stalked up to him until the tip of his gun pressed against my chest, and before he could react, I grabbed his left arm and pulled up his sleeve.

The gun dropped from his hands onto the ground. "Yes, I knew those marks. The marks of a cane, Sass's favorite weapon."

I shook my head. "You do all this for a woman who doesn't deserve it. Worse still—" I looked him straight in the eyes. "You do this for a woman who didn't love you. And how does that feel, Dalton? To know that even as much as your mother hated me, she seemed more concerned with me than she ever was with you?"

Dalton opened and closed his mouth but no words came out. He was shocked, stunned into silence.

"No matter what you do here to me, you will never earn her love. She wouldn't give it to you in life. Why now would she bother to give it to you in death?"

I turned, mounted my horse, and left Sass a quivering mess in the clearing. My aim was to catch up to Bertie's party. I could follow the sounds of hound and horse that grew louder as I rode through the woods. In the distance, men shouted and laughter and shots rang out into the air. I used that to gain my bearing.

And yet, as I grew closer to the sounds, something felt wrong. My skin was crawling. My flesh, deep inside me, chilled. As I stopped my horse by a large oak tree, an acute sense of danger told me to stay alert. To look behind me.

I did.

Dalton Sass was a few feet away from me, on his horse under a canopy of leaves, pointing his gun at my head.

He shot. My heart leaped up my throat as I jumped off my horse, just in time to see the bullet pierce the oak tree's bark. My elbow and hip hit the ground hard, and as the shock of pain rocketed through me, I rolled onto the grass, a plume of dirt billowing up around me. But Sass wasn't done. He aimed again, cocking his gun with lightning speed, his blood-shot eyes bulging. I dragged myself back, the branches on the ground tearing my dress and cutting my legs. My throat closed.

"Dalton!"

"Sass!"

With furious speed, Bertie, Harriet, and Captain Davies rode to the scene on their horses, the galloping of hooves rumbling the ground. Davies and Harriet jumped off their horses to lift me off my feet.

"Sally, are you okay?" Harriet brushed her hair out of her eyes to give me a once-over. "Oh, you poor thing!"

I gave her a strange look. Poor thing? She'd never referred to me in such patronizing terms before, but now she made a big show out of patting my head and checking for wounds while Davies held me around the waist.

Bertie dismounted, strode toward a suddenly terrified Dalton, and dragged my would-be murderer off his horse.

"What in the hell were you doing?" Bertie screamed, throwing off his riding hat. "You could have killed Sally! Are you mad?"

"I'm sorry, Your Grace." Dalton stumbled for an excuse. "It discharged by accident!"

I politely pushed both Davies and Harriet away from me. "No," I said as I dusted myself off. "I'm quite sure you tried to kill me."

Crows screeched above our heads in the chilly air. Dalton shot me a glare that made him look truly mad for one moment before he calmed himself down with deep breaths.

"And why would I do something foolish like that?" He stared at me before breaking out that fake, affable smile. "Come now, Sally, be serious. *Kill* you?" He laughed, rubbing the back of his head, just a silly old chap in front of his fast friend the prince. It sickened me. "Is there any *reason* I would have, Sally, to try to end your life?"

A warning. Exposing Dalton meant exposing my past. I didn't speak. Neither of us did.

Bertie let out a heavy sigh, looking around him. "The fog still is a bit . . . ," he tried, but something about the situation was a bit too strange to explain away. The look he gave Dalton held a hint of paranoia, but it was only a hint. He left Dalton to tend to me.

"Are you okay, Sally?"

But Davies pulled me closer to him. "My fiancée seems to be fine, Your Highness. Thank you for asking."

The awkward tension that resulted between them wasn't something I needed to deal with at the moment. Even Harriet seized up, her face somehow longer today, mirthless.

Dalton spoke out loud what I was already thinking. "I'm quite tired. I should probably make my leave. But I'll be seeing you all at the séance, I suspect."

The séance. Where I was to help Wilkes ill-conceived bid for political office or have my schemes exposed to the Queen.

Bertie rolled his eyes and folded his arms. "You don't have to go to that stupid thing."

"Oh, I will. To support you, my prince. Wilkes as well, if you'd grant him the honor. We've become close as of late."

Dalton stared at me as he spoke. I looked up at Davies, who was watching the two of us. With interest or suspicion, I wasn't quite sure.

"Do whatever you want." Bertie waved his hand dismissively. "The more the merrier."

He jumped on his steed and I began to plan my next move.

TWENTY-FOUR

THAT NIGHT, JAMES Ratcliff, the former policeman turned Rui's fight-club associate, met me in an alleyway near a brothel on Cable Street. It was a brothel Rui owned, but Rui was nowhere to be found. The dark of night obscured the scars on Ratcliff's bald head.

"So Rui sent you to meet me instead?" I said. I hadn't changed out of my riding habit. My nerves were still too agitated from what had happened earlier in the day. Rui and I were to meet here. It was in the letter I quickly wrote and handed to Harriet to send to one of Rui's men to give to him. Such a roundabout, tiresome form of communication wouldn't have been necessary if he'd just told me where he lived and slept at night. It was like he was everywhere and nowhere. Other times, that might have been alluring.

"He said he's got business. Disappointed?"

A little. But no matter. Ratcliffe's information on Wilkes had been helpful. He would surely be of use now. I stretched my shoulders as Ratcliff gave me a file. "If it makes you feel better, we've been looking for information on your little cretin for a few days now. Though I dare say I did my fair share of work there."

"As expected of a former officer." I took it from him, opening it to find slips of paper inside. On one page, clearly torn from a book, *Mary*

Sass was scribbled next to the title *mother*. Father unknown. I was looking at Dalton Sass's record of birth.

"There was no civil registration of this boy's birth," Ratcliff said. "But I found this in a dead preacher's record book left behind in St. Clement Danes. It was buried under the floorboards. Someone didn't want it found."

"October 24, 1839." It was hard to hide my frustration. "I don't see how knowing his birth date will be at all helpful."

"Read the next page."

I flipped to the next torn page as Ratcliff's eager grin egged me on. A journal entry. It was in the preacher's handwriting.

March 8, 1844

Mary Sass's boy, born in sin out of wedlock, has shown how easily the devil can slip into our midst. The boy called Dalton by the missionaries was found yesterday stabbing pigeons behind the church with a dining fork. Now he sets them on fire. He's been thoroughly disciplined by his mother, but the case has become too severe. I fear for the safety of the parishioners if we let Sass and her wayward son stay for another second. I'll recommend that she relocate somewhere far—another country where her son's violent behavior would not harm anyone of consequence nor reflect badly upon this church.

And the preacher signed his name.

Anyone of consequence. I thought of the girls in the Institution and bristled with anger. No wonder Sass never mentioned him. No wonder she homeschooled him. There was no telling what he would have done to us if he was allowed anywhere near the Institution, though knowing Miss Sass, she was more concerned for her own reputation than our safety. I wouldn't have been surprised if she never let him out of the house until the day she died.

"All that bunk about not remembering England." I scoffed in disbelief, shaking my head. "He was at least five years old when they left for Sierra Leone." I snapped the folder shut. "I must show this to Bertie. He's been getting in my way for far too long. It's time for Dalton Sass to be excised out of my life for good."

"He's a dangerous bloke to be around." Ratcliff folded his arms. "You have a plan?"

Better yet: I had a party to attend.

The next morning, Mrs. Schoen drew my bath in the largest bucket she had. The warm water soaked my skin, easing the pain in my shoulders and neck.

"I hope you haven't been too idle since Miss Welsh canceled her lessons." Mama washed and brushed my hair with a wide-toothed comb to prepare for tonight. "Remember, you're getting married soon, Sally. I'm not sure it's the time to be attending all these events."

Then why did her voice sound so chipper? She seemed plenty happy enough to see how deeply I was still accepted in these royal circles. She parted my hair in the middle, as was the style, and used the prettiest silver clips in her possession to pin it down.

"It's a séance, Mama, not a ball. There'll be a medium and everything. Doesn't that unnerve you? Especially after that business at the museum photography gala."

"Yes, that was . . . rather unfortunate, wasn't it?" Mama Schoen shuddered. "But the talk has changed. I hear more and more people might give this . . . spirit photography a chance. I mean, if the Queen is doing it."

I turned my head so quickly, the comb flew out of her hand. With an irritated grunt, Mama went after it.

"You're not serious," I said, accidentally kicking the bucket in shock and stubbing my toe. "I can't believe that people wouldn't be completely disgusted by Her Majesty."

"But if the Queen is throwing a séance after everything that happened at the museum, she clearly doesn't think of those photographs as a scandal." Mama bent down and picked up the comb. "In fact, she seems rather firm in her stance on spiritualism. I heard a few of the girls talking about it down the street—that they feel sorry for her."

I clenched my fists underwater. They feel sorry for her, did they? Yes, of course they would. I should have guessed that the Queen would retaliate for her humiliation by leaning into her spiritual activities, giving others permission to dabble without fear of reprisal. This was the same monarch who'd turned white dresses into a must at every wedding. I should have known she'd have something up her sleeve. I gritted my teeth.

"To be honest, I feel sorry for Her Majesty too," Mama said. "She hasn't been the same since Prince Albert died. Everyone knows that. She still refuses to make public appearances. Wears black every day. Some will find it morbid, while others will relate to her. Though if you ask me, it is all a bit morbid."

We were past morbid and into delusion as far as I was concerned, but I didn't dare say it as she dried me off and dressed me in an appropriately black dress trimmed with lace. We stood in front of the mirror in my room, stuffy because I refused to open the window.

"I suppose," Mama continued, "losing the love of one's life can make a woman do strange things."

"I think if it's the dead she's interested in, there are far more suitable candidates for her to contact than her husband."

Mama's hands paused atop my head while she was fidgeting with the black bow. "What do you mean by that?"

I clenched my teeth and turned away from my image in the mirror.

How many lives had been lost over the years in the name of the Queen of England? How much land taken and drugs trafficked? Children lost to war and empire and ego? Only for her to fuss about her husband. For a queen, her world was inescapably small.

"Then again, from what I've heard, the Queen seems to have found a companion of a different kind." I didn't know why Mama spoke in hushed tones. We were, as always, the only ones in the entire house. Still, I was intrigued.

"What do you mean?"

Mama covered her mouth coquettishly before making a point to look over her shoulders and leaning in. "There's a man at the palace. Rumors say he sticks to her side like grease on a pot. They may even travel to Balmoral together in a few weeks. Maybe sooner. You'll probably see him tonight. If Her Majesty is to be there, so will he."

I frowned. "Who?"

"John Brown. The Scotsman."

At the sound of his name, my thoughts turned to Rui. It was he who had wanted me to arrange for his arrival at the palace. Did Rui know how quickly he'd befriend the Queen? Did he anticipate their bond? Or was it a fluke? With Rui, I could never tell. And he wasn't around to tell *me*.

Just what was this Scot to the criminal prince of the East End?

The séance would tell me more.

It was all a macabre affair, and yet everyone came in their finest jewels, suits, and dresses in different dark colors: garnet, purple, one courageous green, and, of course, black. Lots of black: fur shawls, top hats, gloves, and canes. The violin was playing the moment I walked into the crimson drawing room where some of the Queen's closest friends—I counted at least thirty of them—milled about greeting each other, kissing hands as if they hadn't met for years despite the fact that I'd spotted some of them at the gala just a few days ago.

I glided past the women who watched me and gossiped behind their hands.

"The Queen's goddaughter did come."

"She really is so dark in person."

"From the darkest parts of Africa."

All this nonsense again. They always made sure the fuss they made was just loud enough for me to hear. They were bothered that I out-ladied them in all manner and behavior. I could tell. What they didn't know was that I was bothered by it too. Ignoring them, I slipped past the heavy red velvet curtains, only to be greeted by a familiar enemy.

"Sarah Forbes Bonetta." McCoskry hadn't gotten rid of that bad habit, throwing his arms open wide and expecting a hug from me. I lifted my hand instead and he, surprised for a moment, laughing the next, took it and kissed it. Thank goodness for my gloves. "I believe I saw your betrothed jousting with the prince close by the gin. Come."

He offered me his elbow, and if I didn't take it, I'd draw even more eyes. Touching it only slightly, I walked with him through the crowd. His red beard was still playing tricks on me with its strange shape. I couldn't look at it directly.

"How is your uncle George? His mother has told me he's ill with fever."

He was rotting in the asylum last time I checked and there he would stay. What I had in store for this fiend would be just as terrible.

I gave McCoskry a languid smile. "And what about you, Mr. McCoskry? It couldn't have been easy being the acting governor general of Lagos."

"Oh yes, you know the place well, don't you? Actually"—he leaned in—"you helped me get that particular job, Miss Forbes. Or Sally, shall I call you?" He didn't wait for an answer. "I was but a mere merchant before you. Of course, a successful one. But my connection to the Forbeses, the Queen and, Sally, to you, an African princess saved from slavery, gave me the boost I needed to gain the people's trust—the kind of trust that leads to a position."

My fingers twitched around his elbow. "I'm happy I could help," I said with no emotion in my voice. "I know you did your best for the Yoruba people."

"Indeed, I did." He rubbed his beard with his other hand. "The Liberated African Yard continues until today to employee freed slaves looking for labor."

"You also did your best for the slave owners. Making sure those that could keep their property did."

McCoskry stopped, his mouth paused in midair. It was then that I spotted Bertie and Davies by the gin just as the acting governor had guaranteed. When Bertie spotted me, his face flushed even redder, if it was possible. But he drunkenly waved us over to the white-draped table.

"Sally. I've been trying to tell your future husband that he's wrong about Lord Byron." Bertie grabbed my hand and pulled me out of McCoskry's grip toward him. "He wasn't a deviant. He was a poet. A genius."

"And a deviant who had a relationship with his own sister." Davies, far more reserved, rolled his glass of gin around in his hand. "Or, I suppose, his half sister."

"Half? Okay, then it wasn't that bad. Maybe she was lovely?"

I shuddered as McCoskry laughed at his joke. Well, I suppose inbreeding wouldn't be such a big deal to the British royal family.

"Regardless of his private life, he contributed much to the arts of his country. 'Ode to a Nightingale' was . . ."

And just as Bertie was about to kiss his fingers in appreciation, Captain Davies cleared his throat. "That was Keats, Your Highness."

Bertie inhaled a frustrated breath, glaring at Davies before tugging me to his side. Davies bristled but didn't make a move to stop him. He was a prince, after all. "Sally, I see you've been escorted to our conversation by one William McCoskry."

"He was just telling me about his work in Lagos." I smiled up at him. And how much horror he wrought to the slaves he purported to help. McCoskry scratched his jawline through his bushy red hair with an awkward expression.

Captain Davies spoke. "By chance, are you a member of the Anti-Slavery Society? They've got an event scheduled in a few days. Sadly I won't be able to attend—too many wedding preparations of my own to do."

As Captain Davies grinned at me, Bertie spoke up, suddenly slamming his glass of gin down on the table. "My father was a member. Or at least, he did work for them. Before I was ever born he gave an abolition speech at Exeter Hall. It was a smashing success."

He fell silent. The shadow of his father loomed ever larger.

"I recall hearing about it," said Davies, who did very well not to let his annoyance toward the prince show. The mask he wore was a heavy one. I should know. "Your mother couldn't give the address because of her position. But your father was very passionate about the subject. The society's putting on an event on the first of August. I heard they'd reached out to you to attend, Prince Albert, but you declined."

Bertie squirmed.

"That's too bad. I had wondered if you would follow in your father's footsteps." Captain Davies topped off his drink with the decanter and walked up to my side. I could feel Bertie's eyes watching us.

If Davies was trying to make Bertie insecure and jealous, that would only help me. I played along. "In the twenty years since your father gave his speech, slavery still hasn't been abolished everywhere," I said.

"The war they're fighting in America at this very moment." Captain Davies shook his head. "Every day that I breathe free air I'm reminded of the days I didn't." His gaze slid to me for just a moment and I suddenly thought of my family being slaughtered. Rusty machete blades against tender flesh. Clenching my teeth, I shut my eyes against the memories.

But Bertie, as drunk as he was insecure, shifted on his feet and gave only a noncommittal grunt in response. "I'm not my father," he whispered, before falling back into silence.

Over by the marble table displaying ceremonial plates stolen from Egypt was Harriet, with a small envelope under her arms and her mother, Mrs. Phipps.

"If you'll excuse me, gentlemen." I curtsied, excused myself, and began toward the two women.

I glided by guests who clinked drinks as they chatted next to the Balinese vases taller than I. Others were gossiping by the oil lamps, or by the painting of kings that hung on the walls and underneath the chandelier.

"The new medium Queen Victoria had found is an expert," I heard someone say very loudly so all could hear. "Not like those other conmen. This one is a true clairvoyant."

"Perhaps it's the Wizard Queen, Georgiana Eagle." I gave a start as Dalton Sass slipped into my view, a glass of wine in his hand. "Unless the mesmerist is overbooked? What do you think, Sally?"

And at his side: Inspector Wilkes. "I think young Miss Forbes has more to worry about than the psychic du jour."

Both men were dressed to kill—kill me, if I would hazard the guess.

"The Queen should be here at any moment." Wilkes took a sip of his own wine, gesturing to the entrance manned by royal guards. "When she does, I suspect you know what to do. Otherwise, Her Majesty will be in for a particularly intriguing story about her obedient Negro goddaughter by the day's end."

He didn't bother to hear my retort. He'd come only to give me his warning. Soon he was off joining his wife in hobnobbing with society's elite. But Dalton stayed.

"I don't know what you're so proud about," I said, watching him loosen his black bow tie. "Is it that the royal guards still let you in despite the fact that you tried to murder me yesterday?"

"Didn't you hear? That was an accident. The fog, the prince concluded." He gestured around him as if he'd conjure it up in the air as we spoke. "Besides, when I'm done with you, I suspect you'll be the one hauled away by the guards tonight."

I frowned as he downed his gin. "And what do you have planned for tonight, Sass?"

"Oh, me?" He wiped his lips and, with a little chuckle, leaned in. "Your complete and utter disassembling, you wench."

He whispered low so that only I could hear his threats. My body seized. He seemed slightly more off-kilter than usual since the hunt. I suspected my taunts had cut deeper than even I'd expected them to. After meeting with Ratcliff, I knew now precisely what he was capable of. But I wouldn't give him the pleasure of seeing me react. Even as my heart sped up in fear, I kept my breathing a quiet, rhythmic lull.

He straightened up, fingers combing his brown curls. "Well, enjoy the rest of the night, Miss Forbes. By the way, Bambridge says hello."

Curling my fingers until they dug into my palms, I let him leave. We would soon see who disassembled who. The corners of my lips quirked into a vicious grin before I replaced my mask and continued on.

The closer I got to Harriet and her mother, the better I could hear their conversation.

"How can you let that bloody girl who's been in the palace less than a year be promoted before you? Do I have to remind you of your lineage? Of all your father has done in this court?"

"No, Mother." Harriet shook her head. She looked terrified.

The feathers in Mrs. Phipps's French antique headpiece shook too as the woman bristled. "You are the daughter of Sir Charles Beaumont Phipps. The granddaughter of Henry Phipps, the first Earl of bloody Mulgrave. Being a courtier is in your *blood*. I made sure of that. And now I have to deal with the girl's mother bragging in earshot, mocking me with that horrible yellow grin of hers all because my own daughter is such a lazy, good-for-nothing fool."

"I'll try harder, I swear," Harriet said in a hush, looking around, hoping no one had heard her mother lambasting her. That's when she saw me approaching. Whatever terror her expression had shown turned immediately to embarrassment and then bitterness. With red cheeks, she turned away as I curtsied again.

"Hello, Mrs. Phipps," I greeted her.

"Oh, *you*." Mrs. Phipps couldn't even feign civility as she snarled. "See, Harriet? As much as I am loath to admit it, even this African girl is more capable than you. Look how she carries herself. And look at you *slouching*. How can you let yourself be outdone by even someone like her?"

"*Mother!*"

Mrs. Phipps seemed to only then realize that I was standing right next to her and could hear every word. But this wasn't anything new for the woman. That night too in the parlor, when I was a child, she insulted me to my face as if I wasn't there. As if I possessed no emotions.

It was why I wouldn't mind when the time came to treat her in the same way.

Mrs. Phipps refused to apologize. She only adjusted her shawl over her shoulders with a defiant "humph" and left to go greet one of her friends with her nose up in the air. Usually Harriet would profusely apologize on behalf of her mother the moment the woman was out of earshot. This time, she adjusted the dark violet lace covering her shoulders before becoming suddenly very preoccupied with the Egyptian plates.

"The envelope." I pointed at it underneath her arm. "You found what I asked?"

Harriet made sure no one was near. "Police reports going back decades. Confirming the juvenile criminal activity of one Dalton Sass."

I knew it. I knew that given what I'd learned about Dalton's past, there was a chance he'd committed other deviant acts—acts that may have been documented. Harriet passed the envelope to me and I took a peek at the slip inside. My eyebrows rose at what I read.

"So he went from stabbing pigeons to stabbing lads-men," I whispered.

"Excuse me, pigeons?" Harriet frowned, scandalized, and bumped into the table she backed into. The Egyptian plates rattled.

"That's why I spared you the dirty details. It's not a surprise that he'd graduate from animals to humans—and child thieves at that. It says here the parish tried to cover it up. I'm sure they covered up much of his activities before shipping their little problem off to Sierra Leone, but not everything in one's past can be so thoroughly erased."

I slipped the torn pages Ratcliff had procured for me out of my left glove and added them to the envelope. "Thank you, Harriet. This will help me get rid of that eyesore for good."

Harriet was usually happy to be privy to my schemes, playing the Blandy to my Cranstoun. This time her gaze remained on the back of her mother's dark red fitted bodice. Defeated. "Will you go to the prince, then?" she asked me. Fatigue echoed from deep within the cavern of her slender body.

"Don't worry, Harriet." I gave her elbow a supportive touch. "I'll handle things from here. You've done a wonderful job. Try to get some rest when you can."

In a flash, Harriet ripped her arm from my touch. "*Rest?* I don't need rest. I'm not a child, so don't speak to me like one."

A few guests began to stare, but none were more surprised than I. Even Harriet seemed to suddenly realize we'd become the center of others' attention. She curtsied quickly and scurried off. It was her mother, no doubt. That woman was going to destroy her own daughter. I felt sorry for her, of course. But I couldn't have Harriet breaking down before this was all over.

"Come with me."

I gasped, hearing Bertie's whisper in my ear from behind. He grabbed my wrist and pulled me away from the crowd, refusing to listen to my protests. Out of the drawing room and away from the congregation, we came to a stop underneath a winding golden staircase, draped in red carpet that stretched up both sides of the palace hall. The Grand Staircase. I could tell by the statue of George IV at the head. An opulent royal tribute to a man who illegally married a Catholic. A touch of rebellion Bertie probably identified with.

We didn't go up either staircase. Instead, Bertie hid me beneath the left crook, pushing me against the white plastered wall with drunken brazenness.

"What are you doing, you lout?" But when I pushed him away, it only seemed to excite him. He brushed both hands through his blond hair, by now a mess, and then pressed his hands against the wall on either side of my face.

"What am I doing? Do you really not know by now, Sally?"

His blue eyes were unfocused, dazed with alcohol, but they didn't waver. He leaned in. I covered his face with my hand and pushed him away.

"You're drunk," I said. "At a séance. Only you."

Bertie shook my hand off his face and let out a sigh. "The séance hasn't begun. Why? Because mother's with that John Brown, probably having a little séance of her own."

I glanced up the stairs, where the Queen could come down any minute with John Brown and her attendants. Then my expression turned sour thinking of the Queen "séancing" with that burly man before the true event began.

"He's a medium himself, you know. He's got this . . . this hold on her. He says he can communicate with Father. Can you believe that?" Bertie loosened his tie as if it were strangling him. "He's probably a conman. I don't know why you had me bring him here, Sally."

Rui. But what Rui was planning, I couldn't tell. I hadn't seen or heard from him in days.

As Bertie bristled in front of me, I missed Rui. His calm and charm. The memory of his kisses on the floor of Bambridge's secret studio had me flushing before I could stop myself.

Bertie had clearly mistaken my body cues for some kind of signal. Before I could stop him, he grabbed my cheeks and pulled me toward him. A kiss. A passionate one. He cradled my head with one hand, the small of my back with the other, crushing me against him.

I ripped my face away from him, taking in the deep breath he'd deprived me of. "Bertie!"

"Please, Sally, don't turn away my advances. This is . . . this is surprising for me too."

And he did look it—surprised at himself. But with his shoulders drooping and his chest heaving, he also looked strangely helpless. What nonsense. How many girls had Bertie gone through before he decided it was my "turn" for an illicit affair?

I reached into my bodice and pulled out the envelope I'd hidden there. "Dalton Sass," I said, snapping my fingers to get him to focus. "He's a criminal."

Bertie shook his languid head. "He's a what?"

"A criminal. You've let a criminal into your circle. These police reports dating back years prove it. If you don't want your mother to despise you any more than she does, I would get rid of him as soon as possible."

Bertie pulled the contents of the envelope out and read the first couple of pages. "Stabbing pigeons?" He squinted as if he'd read it wrong. "Laundering and extortion . . . Bloody hell . . ."

My fingers were itching to show him more; the boy read slowly, even when he was sober.

"You're the future King of England, Bertie. Do you really think leaving Dalton Sass alone is going to end up reflecting well on your choices of confidants? Besides—"

"I don't care."

I pulled back, blinking. "You don't—?"

"Care. I don't care." He shoved the papers back into the envelope, tucked it underneath his arm, and cupped my face. "I don't care about anything right now except you, Sally."

A mixture of fury and confusion building up inside me made me want to scream. "You cannot be serious. After what you've learned? After what I just told you?"

But Bertie wasn't listening.

"Captain Davies is pompous and overly proud of himself," Bertie said through gritted teeth as he looked down the corridor at the statue of his ancestor. "With a little bit of education he aims to embarrass me at every turn, all the while pretending to be a polite gentleman. He isn't right for you, Sally. You're a firebrand through and through. You'll be bored to tears with him."

My head was starting to throb. Did he really not care about Dalton?

Or perhaps, in his lucid state, he couldn't help but admit he cared more about romancing me than securing his reputation as a responsible heir.

This was madness. The prince's feelings were nothing but lust. It couldn't have been real.

It couldn't have been.

Bertie cared for no one but himself. I'd learned that when we were children. I could still feel the honey dripping down my forehead. The humiliation and rage I felt even then. This wasn't a man who could love anyone and he wasn't a man anyone should love, least of all me.

And even if he did love me . . .

I pressed a hand against my head, my thoughts swirling until a familiar chant emptied out the voices.

Their "love" for you is conditional, Ina.

I would never forget, Ade.

Standing up straight, I looked him in his eyes. "Captain Davies? I suspect I *would* be bored to tears with him," I agreed, because it was true. "However, can you tell me your anger towards Davies has nothing to do with his ability to embarrass you at every turn despite his race?"

Bertie looked taken aback, like they always did when you spoke what was meant to be unspoken. "N-Not at all. You have me all wrong, Sally!"

I didn't. Bertie wouldn't have been half as annoyed at Captain Davies's virtues and abilities if his skin were a different hue. Being in this country taught you that much.

Still, I needed Bertie on my side for now. It wouldn't be prudent to spurn him. So when he reached out to me again, lightly touching my cheek with his bare fingers, I didn't move away though I wanted to. And when he leaned in to kiss me, I let myself lean into it, taking his loosened bow tie and drawing him deeper into me.

"Sally," he whispered after we'd parted. "This may sound insane. . . ." He paused as if he believed it was. The words forming on his lips, wet from my mouth, must have sounded insane to him, the Crown Prince of England, as he played them again and again in his mind. And while he mulled over whether or not to speak them, I watched the envelope he'd tucked underneath his arm, my fingers itching to pull it out and show him the rest of the contents.

"Bertie," I said before he could speak. "I care about you."

Bertie's ears flushed red.

"And that's why I need you to look at those contents again. All of it." I pointed to the envelope. "Look and then tell me what kind of man you are."

Bertie fell into silence. The tension between us was so palpable, we almost didn't hear the sound of the double doors above the grand staircase opening. I ran out from underneath the stairs into the hall. Queen Victoria descended with her party of attendants and ladies-in-waiting, her sullen face covered in a long black veil. At her right, holding her hand firmly, was Rui's Scotsman: John Brown. He was burly, with his thick, hairy legs showing just above his knee socks and below his kilt. His jacket and dress shirt were buttoned tightly over his sturdy chest. He spared Bertie and me a glance before fixing the train of the Queen's black dress.

"The Queen is ready," he said. Lord Ponsonby, who trailed behind them, would have been the one to say it except now, with John Brown in the picture, he'd become utterly redundant as Queen Victoria's secretary.

The Queen put up her hand to silence him. "Not quite yet." Though a little woman, she was imposing whenever she crept up to her target as if they were her prey. Bertie flinched and squirmed back, but I stood my ground as the Queen sidled up to me.

"Sally." She looked me up and down. "So you came."

"I was invited."

"Yes. You do seem to like being where the action is these days, don't you?"

Her eyes slid to Bertie, who floundered on his own behind me.

"You were at the museum that day too, weren't you?" the Queen said.

"Yes, with Gowramma." I kept my voice pleasant. "Did she tell you?"

"No, a detective—Inspector Charles Wilkes—told Lord Ponsonby."

Silence. Everything fell away. We stared into each other's eyes, neither one of us wanting to give up our neutral expressions, as strategic as they were. The universe, at this moment, consisted only of two queens.

"That's all he told him, however." The Queen adjusted her veil. "But your acquaintances have become quite unexpected." Her blue eyes darkened. "I don't like unexpected, Sally."

My body didn't relax, not even when John Brown bent down until his lips were to the Queen's ear. "We've been given word the medium has arrived."

"Then," Queen Victoria said, her words a low mumble from behind her funeral veil, "let us go contact Albert."

TWENTY-FIVE

A CHILD. I did all I could to hold in my laughter, but in truth I didn't know whether or not this was a laughing affair. To all, here in the crimson drawing room, it was unthinkable—the Queen had been driven so into madness since her husband's death that she was now seeking spiritual clarity from a thirteen-year-old boy.

But here he was, being ushered to the circular table in a crimson drawing room by guards. Queen Victoria's invited and esteemed guest of honor: Robert James Lees. Even dressed in his little suit and tie, he was knobby-kneed and lanky, his light brown hair cut like any other schoolboy his age. Did his parents know he was here?

"I really can't even fathom this," Bertie muttered as he took his seat at the mahogany table. It only seated eight. The rest would have to watch from behind.

Someone dimmed the lights in the room. As John Brown sat Queen Victoria at the table and took his seat next to her, attendants brought candles and plunked them upon the surface in their silver candelabras. Once each candle was lit, they moved to leave.

"No, that is not all," the boy said, and I was shocked by the deep crevices hidden in his boyish tone. "Bring the bust."

Made of white clay, it was not your typical bust of Prince Albert. It had two faces, one looking north, the other south.

"Like Janus," Captain Davies whispered to me as he sat on my left at the table. "The two-faced Roman god of doorways."

The god of transitions standing between life and death. Bertie pulled out his chair roughly and plopped down next to me, throwing Davies a dirty look before leaning on the table. He stealthily placed the envelope into the inside pocket of his jacket. I suppose he cared more about his rivalry with Captain Davies than the supposed murderous nature of the man who nearly shot me the other day. Some great "love" he had for me.

"The Roman god of doorways, yes. Well, we *all* knew that," Bertie mumbled with a childish sneer. Both of his father's two heads looked as disappointed in him as his mother did.

As the candlelight flickered across her husband's faces, the Queen was mesmerized, her hollow eyes wide and sharp like a hawk's.

"Ladies. Gentlemen. You will remove your gloves," said Lees with the grim wisdom of an adult thrice his age. "And then you will join hands."

"He sounds just like the Prince Consort," someone whispered amongst the crowd and tried to take a seat, but she was cut off at the knees. Mrs. Phipps moved fast to grab seats for herself and her daughter, who sheepishly remained steadfast in her inability to look at me. Along with Bertie, Captain Davies, John Brown, the Queen, myself, and the medium, the table's central party was complete.

"What fun this all is, isn't it, Inspector Wilkes?" said Dalton behind me, and I instinctively hunched over. When had he snuck his way through the crowd?

"I'm more excited for what may transpire *after* the party." They were close enough that I could hear them amidst the crowd's chatter. By design. How foolish. I wouldn't be so easily intimidated.

"To commune with the spirits, you must have patience," said this little boy, Lees, who despite his little, lanky frame had taken complete control of the room. "You must suspend your disbelief. You must shake off the coils of every rule that tethers you to the known world."

"You must count backwards from ten and relieve yourself on cue," Bertie muttered. If only the room hadn't suddenly become so quiet. Everyone heard him.

"Bertie! How dare you! *Silence!*" Queen Victoria's shriek echoed off the high ceiling, shocking all in the room, especially her son, who sat up straight and stared back at his mother, terrified.

Awkward tension filled the silent room. In one moment, the prince crumpled where he sat and said nothing more.

The medium was undeterred. "Please, hold each other's hands," Lees said again.

Still bristling from the uncomfortable energy that lingered in the air, I took Captain Davies's hand, hesitating at his touch. He gave me an encouraging smile, which drooped into a frown when Bertie grabbed my other hand with a yank, still red with anger.

"You must understand that the spirit realm is not a place you can enter without the utmost serenity. Clear your minds. Imagine yourself swimming in the void of nothingness. Free yourselves from the material world. Breathe and enter a world where space and time hold no meaning."

But when I cleansed my mind of all thought, faces still remained. Dalton Sass and his mother. Bellamy, his neck twisted in a pile of his own booze. The two Captain Forbes wailing and screaming in the night of my treachery.

And Ade. I saw his face. I saw his sickly smile as we played together in a dingy cabin of the HMS *Bonetta*, both of us dressed in shabby old agbadas that the Forbeses draped us in despite the fact that they were too big and only worn by men. We played with shillings, not knowing what they were. We struck them with our fingers and watched as they rolled around the room, spun, and flopped to the floor. We ate the slime they called food because everything better went to the brothers and their crew. Who knew what was even in it. Rat? Did it contribute to Ade's poor health? Would he have been fitter if they'd given him nutrients? Would he have survived?

The more these questions arose in the deep recesses of my mind, the angrier I became. And as my anger began to bubble over, a deep groan erupted from Lees's mouth. The crowd gasped as my own beating heart leaped into my throat.

"Oooh . . . Alexandrina . . ." Lees breathed in deep, swaying from side to side.

Breathless, Queen Victoria jerked in her seat. "Albert?" John Brown's sturdy grip on her frail hand kept her seated. "Albert, is that you?"

"Alexandrina Victoria . . ."

The crowd didn't dare speak. They were all very impressed, but I couldn't say the same. He was clearly a conman taking advantage of the Queen's bereavement. My thoughts turned instead to Dalton, whose reflection in the mirror on the wall I could see, grinning at me. As my anger flared up once more, so too did the deep groan from Lee's mouth. I wasn't paying attention. I was thinking of Sass's cane marks on my back. Of my parents' decimated bodies. Of Ade's body in the Atlantic Ocean with so many of my kin. Of my loss of freedom. My loss of self. How it was all torn away from me.

"Sally?" Captain Davies whispered because he must have noticed I was shaking. I answered by squeezing his hand so tightly, it might have broken if it weren't for his military strength. But I wanted to break something. I wanted to break someone. Everyone.

"Alexandrina Victoria . . . Empress of a Broken World . . ."

It was then that Lees's body was taken over entirely. The crowd screamed as the boy swayed and bent in angles that couldn't have been possible for a human body. The boy gasped for air, as if he was drowning. He gripped his throat, clutching, scratching the bare pale skin, before falling flat upon the table, his cheek smashing against the wood.

Before anyone could move to help him, his head trembled upward, his unfocused eyes bloodied and dangerous, ready for battle. I didn't know what to think.

> *Empress of a Broken World,*
> *You summon the spirits but you do not know us,*
> *We speak for the dead,*
> *The trail of bodies your legacy has left behind. . . .*

His voice didn't sound like the Prince Consort's anymore. It sounded ancient, from the depths of the earth. Hollow and furious. Lees spoke with an accent very few in this room would have been able to understand if they weren't used to it. It was the accent I used to speak with.

The accent of my people.

> *Empress of the World You Broke,*
> *You seek your husband,*
> *It is our judgment you receive instead.*
> *How many have died at your hands?*
> *At the hands of your ancestors?*

And Lees began singing—it was a song I recognized. A song Davies knew. We both looked at each other, lips parted in quiet shock as we heard the little English boy sing a chant to Oshun, the river deity. He stopped. And after a time, he spoke again.

You pillage and kill, and then cry only for your own loss.
Do you think yourself mighty?
À ń pe gbẹ́nàgbẹ́nà ẹyẹ àkókó ń yọjú.
You are nothing. The Queen of Ruin.

He began singing the chant to Oshun once more. But soon, the boy's cackling broke through. It wasn't the laughter of an ignorant English boy. It was high, feminine, haughty, sensual and proud. The laughter of a queen mother. As if Oshun herself was challenging the second queen dressed in black.

"Goddess of Rivers . . . ," I whispered, and thought of Ade's drowned body. Tears began prickling my eyes.

Do not cry, child.

The voice wasn't feminine anymore. No . . . it wasn't one voice at all. I heard many jumbling together, old and young, bold and shy, each furious and dripping with honey sweetness. They spoke to me as if they'd brought me into this world themselves. I heard my mother's voice. My father's. I heard Ade's voice. Young, weak, but rebellious.

Do not cry, for your retribution is close at hand,
And the freedom you seek will be yours,
The evil will reap their punishments,
You go with our blessing,
And a little bit of luck . . .

I couldn't breathe. What was this? What was happening?

The weight of so many lives lost suddenly fell upon me at once, knocking the wind from my lungs. Lives crying out for justice. It was too much. My throat closed as I bit the inside of my mouth, trying and failing to calm myself.

"This is madness." Wilkes's terrified voice pierced through my thoughts. "Dalton, come with me. There's something we need to talk about."

"Wait," I called out, wanting to stop them, but Queen Victoria gave me a look so withering it chilled my very spirit.

"You will sit down and do as I say, child. You will *not* break the circle. *I* am Queen here."

My mouth went dry. Ah, so this was her true face—the one behind all the false platitudes and niceties. The face of my savior. But I couldn't move. As the Queen turned back to the young boy, her cruelty willed me to stay in place. It made my heart crash against my rib cage. In that moment, I did as I was told.

Ade was wrong. Her "love" for me wasn't conditional. She had no love for me at all.

Wilkes and Sass disappeared through the crowd, but the séance wasn't done. The Queen wouldn't let it be done.

"Albert. Albert! Let me speak to my husband! Please!"

"Your Majesty!" John Brown tried to keep the Queen still, but she wrenched her hand out of his grip and began shaking the poor boy, nearly breaking his neck. Brown managed to grab her around the stomach and pull her away, but the damage was done. The boy fell down once more upon the table. The bust of Prince Albert rattled with the candles.

"Albert! Speak to me!"

The Queen continued to shriek until finally Robert Lees, only thirteen years old, sat up straight and looked at her curiously. He tilted his head, his bright eyes empty.

"Gutes Weibchen?" Lees said in a perfect German accent.

His voice had changed again. It was that of a man in love. A husband lost. Queen Victoria hugged John Brown, whimpering, tears dripping down her cheeks.

"Albert! Albert, it's really you. . . ."

As the Queen sobbed John Brown reached into his jacket pocket and drew out a handkerchief. He lifted the Queen's veil like a bride on their wedding day, ready to wipe her chubby cheeks and her clear blue eyes. . . .

Several gunshots rang out into the air. The crowd parted with screams, clearing a straight line to the table. The man in a beige hooded robe couldn't be seen in the dark, not with only a few candles to light the room. All eyes were on his gun, aimed at John Brown and the Queen.

It cocked and shot. Brown tackled the Queen to the floor, the bullet missing them by a hair. As Captain Davies put out an arm to shield me from danger, Bertie jumped out of his seat and approached his mother.

"Mother? Mother, are you hurt?"

The Queen shrugged him off with an almost-superhuman viciousness. "Oh, stop it, you stupid boy. Where is my husband? Where is Albert?"

"Mother!"

Every guard in the vicinity must have entered the room, but in the darkness they bumbled and tripped over themselves. In the ensuing chaos, the hooded man escaped the room; none of the wealthy elite at the séance were courageous enough to follow. Mrs. Phipps shrieked at the top of her lungs. The other guests held on to her daughter for dear life as Harriet clutched her braided hair.

With Bertie's help, John Brown got the Queen back up on her feet.

"What in the blazes happened?" asked Brown to a screaming crowd. After checking for wounds, they helped her sit back down in her chair—or more forced her into it.

"Who's done this?" the Queen demanded. "Who broke the boy's concentration?"

I wasn't surprised she didn't care much about the assassination attempt. It wasn't her first and surely wouldn't be her last. A part of me was disappointed the shooter had missed. The bullet seemed closer to grazing John Brown's head instead. . . .

A girl's scream interrupted my thoughts. It had come from outside the drawing room.

"Murder!" the girl screamed. I recognized it—it was one of the Queen's courtiers. "Murder! He's been murdered!"

I wouldn't let Captain Davies tie me down to my chair. I leaped to my feet and pushed through the crowd. I arrived with the rest of them to find Inspector Wilkes shot dead on the floor. Blood was flowing from his head onto the pristine marble. The only thing bloodier was Dalton Sass, draped in the beige hooded robe, his hands holding the murder weapon.

Seeing Wilkes dead made my body feel as heavy as stone. I couldn't pry my eyes away, not from him, not from his wife running to him, crying over his dead body. I didn't know how to feel. The nerves underneath my skin gave a painful twinge as an electrical current shuddered up my spine. What was this? Guilt? But I hadn't killed him. It wasn't my fault. . . .

The crowd parted again for Bertie to step through, the click of his heels echoing across the ceiling.

"Sass . . ." Bertie looked as shocked as I felt. I knew the two had left the séance early. I assumed it was to plot their revenge upon me. They were working together, weren't they?

Finally snapping out of his stupor, Dalton dropped the gun. It clattered on the ground. "It wasn't me," he said hurriedly, sliding the robe off his body. "The hooded man shoved it in my hands. He threw the robe onto me. . . . It wasn't me!"

The strange thing is, I believed him, even if nobody else could in this situation. Dalton looked at the gun like he'd never seen it before. The look of terror on his face looked so completely alien to him. And he had no reason to kill Wilkes. No reason to stay here and wait to be caught.

But it didn't matter the reason. A situation had fallen into my lap. As my mind began to work, I shoved away the strange emotions welling up inside me. A plan materialized, and before I knew it, I was running to the prince's side.

"He's done it again! He's mad, I tell you, mad!" I clutched my chest as any civilized English lady would after being so thoroughly scandalized by wicked things too evil for her innocent eyes. Bertie held my shoulders. "It's just like when he tried to shoot me!"

"Yes . . ." Bertie looked at Dalton Sass, as if finally seeing him for the first time. "Dalton Sass is not what he seems."

Dalton glared at the two of us wide-eyed as John Brown brought the Queen to the entrance of the door, guarding her from danger.

Bertie pulled the envelope out from the inside of his jacket pocket. "He has a history of violence. Stabbing animals. Setting them on fire. Harming people from a young age. It's all in these reports I gathered."

Prince Bertie always had to play the hero even if it meant claiming deeds that weren't his own. Prince Bertie's machismo left me out of the narrative—except as an innocent victim, of course.

Furious, Dalton stood. "That's a lie!" Hardly convincing with so much of Wilkes's blood dripping from his hands.

"And I do remember the hunt. I thought it strange that he would shoot at you, Sally." His expression grew grim. "But I'm starting to think it wasn't such an accident after all, Sass."

"Sass . . . ," I heard the Queen mutter from the entrance, and while my blood chilled, I kept my focus where it needed to be—on the fumbling Dalton Sass, whose world was crumbling around him.

"I swear to heaven I didn't do this!" Dalton stretched out his hands, pleading with the guests. They backed away from him, terrified.

"I saw him leaving with Wilkes during the séance," said one woman, and others agreed.

"I've heard enough!" John Brown's authoritative growl held not a hint of fear. One wouldn't think he'd almost been killed moments before. "Guards! Arrest this man!"

As Dalton tried to fight against the guards' vise grip, Lord Ponsonby stared at us all from behind the doors, too scared to make his way to the murder scene. His reddening cheeks and wobbling body told me he had much to say about Dalton Sass. But telling everyone of his blackmail risked reminding everyone that he was the one who'd invited Dalton into the inner circle weeks ago with my luncheon. That was how Sass had blackmailed him into keeping quiet about the—

—the letter!

"Wait," I said quickly, "you must check his person! Make sure he doesn't have any more weapons that could harm Her Majesty!"

"Good thinking, Sally." Bertie nodded to the guards and they checked every nook and cranny of Dalton Sass's body, but they found nothing. No knives, no guns. No letters.

Damn it. He must have taken it somewhere else. If he really did have information that could endanger the Queen, I wanted to see it. To use it. To wield it. But that damn Freetown boy had hidden it. For insurance?

Dalton Sass screamed and whined as he dragged away, his legs stumbling upon the floor. Bertie went to tend to his mother. A pair of hands swiveled me around until I was staring at Captain Davies. I could barely feel his palms. My whole body was numb.

"The barbarity of these people," he said in a low voice. "I'm more convinced than ever that I need to take you away from this place. Sally? Are you okay, Sally?"

I opened my mouth by instinct to say yes. Why wouldn't I be okay? I'd finally gotten rid of the thorn in my side—two in one fell swoop. But

Mrs. Wilkes's cries as she followed the body of her husband out of the palace ricocheted against my skull. The truth is, I wasn't okay. I wasn't okay at all. I had won. So why didn't I feel it?

Why didn't I feel it?

TWENTY-SIX

THE ASSASSINATION ATTEMPT on the Queen had made it into the morning's newspapers, becoming the new talk of the country. I got one off a huckster in the market near my Chatham house. Even people here were gossiping about the murder suspect, Dalton Sass, and his maladaptive disposition that drove him to kill a beloved member of Scotland Yard.

"I heard Wilkes took the bullet for the Queen," said the shopkeep who sold the soaps Mama loved. It seemed in the mind of some who didn't care to read the details in the papers and learned news through street talk, Wilkes had died a hero. He would have liked that. Even if they knew the truth, nobody would think he'd gotten what he deserved. I wasn't sure I did either.

> *The evil will reap their punishments,*
> *You go with our blessing,*
> *And a little bit of luck . . .*

Luck. They'd given me luck. My gods. My ancestors. My people watching me from the realm of the dead. They gave me their blessing. They supported my retribution. My revolution!

So why did I keep hearing the cries of that woman throughout the night? Mrs. Wilkes. Even when I buried my head in my pillow, I couldn't seem to silence her. She haunted me still.

What about Bellamy's wife? said a nasty voice in my head. *Don't you think she wailed just as loudly? Don't act as if you have a conscience now.*

What I was doing wasn't wrong. If it was, Ade wouldn't have given me his blessing. He wouldn't have smiled and laughed along with Oshun, and my mother and father, and all the others whose names I didn't know.

Or was it them? Could it have been them? Could that English boy, Robert Lees, channel a cadre of spirits whose existence he likely didn't believe in or acknowledge?

Captain Davies didn't think so. I'd asked him outside the palace as I waited for a cab to pick me up and take me home.

"It was a trick," he said, shaking his head firmly.

"Are you kidding me?" I tugged his jacket sleeve, but even as he shrugged noncommittally, he avoided eye contact. Not at all convincing. "You heard what they said. You heard the adage. The song. Their voices—"

His fingers were trembling. "I believe what I can see," he snapped, though without any anger or energy. He looked winded, like the night's events had stolen his peace and he might collapse without it. "Channeling the gods . . . What nonsense. You're educated, Sally, like me. Don't let yourself be so easily fooled by parlor tricks. You're better than that."

"Oh yes," I'd retorted in a huff. "I'm so much better. Good enough at least to become your child bride."

The casual manner of my insult clearly had him rankled. "Sally!"

"What? That's what this is, isn't it? Complete with you scolding me like a father. You know, Edgar Allan Poe married his cousin when she was thirteen and he was twenty-seven. It makes you wonder. What is it with you men and your demand for younger and younger wives?"

"I'm not having this conversation again." Captain Davies waved over a nearby carriage. The horses trotted over. "We'll just end up going around in circles. You already know what I want. A wife. It's what every successful man my age wants and needs."

"And what about what I want?"

"What do you want, Sally?" Folding his arms, he looked over to Bertie, the Prince of Wales, tending to some guests still in shock as they rode off in their carriages.

It wasn't too hard to read what he was thinking. I grimaced, sickened at the thought. "You can't possibly believe—"

Captain Davies lowered his eyes. "I don't know what to believe."

"Well, you never asked my permission to marry me in the first place, so I find your display of jealousy and disappointment quite hypocritical."

"Figure out what you want, Sally, and then we'll go from there," he told me before leaving me by my carriage.

What did I want? As I lay on my bed now with my face in my pillow, his question had taken on a new meaning. I thought of Wilkes dead, his wife crying, bodies and more bodies to come. Screams of agony. Of grief. I thought of my ancestors and the weight of the crimes committed against me. And then I thought of my own soul. It had already been shattered to pieces since the moment they brought me to England. I thought with each victory I could stitch them back together somehow. Instead, a troubling, deep confusion had seeped inside the crevices and cracks. Blood and grief and rage. I no longer knew how to react to any of it.

What did I want?

"Sally! Sally!"

Mama called me from downstairs, but for the second day in a row, I couldn't lift myself out of bed. I'd been hearing too many voices in my head since the séance, friendly and unfamiliar, vicious and sweet, grieving and vengeful. I'd told Mama Schoen I'd fallen ill and not to bother me unless it was something of grave importance.

The arrival of the Prince of Wales was indeed of grave importance to Mrs. Schoen.

I couldn't even fathom what he was doing here, but the commotion downstairs intrigued me nonetheless. Mama sounded beside herself as she ushered him in. I could hear her making excuses for the state of the house as if we hadn't just cleaned it yesterday: "Oh my goodness, Your Highness, if I had known you would be visiting us, I would have brought out the finest dishes I have!"

"No, that's quite all right." Bertie sounded like the perfect gentleman. A farce. He'd probably laid up with an actress the night before to decompress after the séance. "Is Sally up there?"

"Yes . . ." Mrs. Schoen hesitated. "Yes, she's in her room, but—"

"Well, I'll just pop up to see her, then."

I could feel Mama's disapproval from here. A boy in my room? And while I had a fiancé no less? It was unheard of, but the Prince of Wales did as he pleased. Mama couldn't stop him.

Bertie wouldn't have come to my house unless it was an urgent matter. These days, there were plenty to choose from. But what did he need from me? I readied myself, sitting up in my bed just in time for Bertie's knocks against the door to get me to fight. "Come in."

Bertie blushed when he saw me in a thin white nightgown, but clearing his throat, he shut the door as if he hadn't just been staring like an oaf.

"Bertie, what on earth are you doing here?" I asked.

He seemed fascinated by my room. The simple drapes covering the windows, the iron candelabra, and unlit candles on the dresser drawer next to my bed. Oh yes, the bed. His eyes lingered on that too. It took every part of me not to roll my eyes.

He took a seat at my desk. "There's a matter of importance that I'd like to speak to you about," he said, trying to sound very official.

"Is it about Dalton Sass?" His howls of innocence haunted me in my dreams.

"No." Bertie sat in the chair backward, so he leaned against the slat, using the top rail to support his arms. "You won't have to worry about him. He's being investigated as we speak. Some of what we found in his house is quite gruesome. Let's just say he never got over his fetish for animal cruelty."

I shivered. It was a good thing he was out of my way for good. "Then everything is fine?"

"Well, yes . . ." Bertie rubbed his arms with a dour expression. "Except that my mother blames me for the whole affair. I was the one who let Sass mingle in our circle for so long."

I knew this was coming. Bertie wasn't difficult to figure out. With his relationship with his mother worse than ever because of his father's death, he needed some kind of maternal replacement. His unrelenting search for it at the bottom of a bottle of whiskey or between a woman's legs had obviously yielded very little so far. It was clear what he needed. One only had to give it to him to obtain his loyalty.

"It's not your fault." I sat on the edge of my bed. "Though it's true you do need to learn to keep better company."

"You should have heard her, Sally. My mother shrieking at me for the better part of an hour before refusing to even look at me . . ." He lowered his eyes to the ground. "And you tried to warn me. I didn't listen."

We remained silent for a time, letting his pain dictate the rhythm of the conversation.

"But that's why I'm here," Bertie said, lifting his head. "I'm ready to listen to you now."

I blinked, intrigued. "What do you mean?" What was this spoiled boy going on about?

"I've been thinking of something since the debacle at the museum. I just haven't told anyone yet." Bertie ran his fingers through his blond hair nervously. "As you know, there's an event happening this Friday at Exeter Hall. The Society for the Abolition of Slavery are to host a small congregation of important local policymakers to discuss the issue of slave trade still occurring in parts of the world from the Americas to Africa."

"Ah," I said. "Yes, I think Captain Davies mentioned it at the séance."

At the sound of my bethrothed's name, Bertie grimaced, but he continued on. "I know I initially refused when you requested I make a speech, but . . ." Bertie swallowed the lump in his throat. "All of the recent scandals have tarnished the Crown's image. My mother doesn't show it, but it's all getting to her. And she's getting to *me*."

Good. I hid the upward curve of my lips behind the back of my hand before donning my poker face once again. "So? What is it you want from me?"

Bertie straightened his back. "Perhaps I *should* try to be more like my father. It may finally stop my mother from endlessly chasing his ghost."

Not only that. A public event for an important cause would help lessen the impact of the prince's many public disgraces. So the gears in Bertie's brain did turn on occasion.

"I want you to tell me." He fiddled with his fingers. "If I were to tell them that I changed my mind . . . if I were to make a speech like my father did all those years ago . . . how would I go about it? Do I even have enough time to write one?"

This Friday. August 1. That was in four days. I rubbed my chin, deep in thought. But it wasn't for his sake.

There was one person on my list who hadn't yet gotten his share of my wrath. Even after the chaos Dalton Sass had wrought, William McCoskry was still prancing about like a peacock. He needed his feathers clipped and now, as Bertie waited for my response, the beginnings of a scheme began percolating. A simple plot—I had the resources. So did Rui. Exeter Hall could indeed be a grand stage for a downfall. But four days didn't give me enough time to work.

Not enough time . . .

How much time did I need to truly finish this macabre business of revenge once and for all? Across the room, Bertie looked lost. Panicked. I didn't care. I needed this to be finished.

What the hell. "You're the Prince of Wales," I said, walking up to him. "If anyone can make it happen, you can. And just imagine! If you make a speech, you can redeem your reputation. Think of what your mother will say."

"Think of what my mother will say if I fail."

"You won't fail. Maybe you can find someone to help you. A partner that can guide you through. A joint speech, if you will." I touched his arm gently. "And I know just the person: William McCoskry."

The Crown Prince scrunched his face in confusion. "McCoskry?"

"With his pedigree and experience, he'd be perfect."

Bertie rubbed his sweaty palms against his legs. "A joint speech . . . Yes, I think we could manage it. Of course, I'd make him do most of the talking."

"Of course."

"An incredible idea, Sally. Thank you!" Bertie clapped my shoulder a little too hard. I winced from the impact. "You'll be there too, I expect?"

"Of course I will. Believe in yourself, Your Majesty," I told him, my tone honeysuckle sweet. "If anyone can do this, you can."

I noticed that his hand stayed on my flesh a moment too long. He noticed too. Withdrawing it, he rubbed the back of his neck with a laugh.

"That's why you're famous for your smarts, Sally. You've always got the best ideas. And just in time too—McCoskry's on his way back to Africa in a couple of weeks."

Just in time. I gave him a docile smile. "Then this historic event will come not a minute too soon."

TWENTY-SEVEN

HARRIET WAS BECOMING increasingly erratic, between dealing with her mother, the magic and mayhem, and the murders. Not that she was the only one. Still, I made my way to Devil's Acre without her. If I was going to pull off this trap, I'd need Rui.

"Rui?" Inside the underground fight club, a bookie in a dirty blue newsboy cap took his eyes off the filthy, bloodied pit for just a moment to answer me. "I haven't seen him around here in a while. Seems he's been busy."

He spat out something yellow onto the ground as the crowd cheered and demanded blood. If Rui wasn't here fighting against men twice his size for a group of rowdy spectators, there was only one other place he could be. Though it was a gamble.

A *gamble*. I chuckled to myself bitterly as I ran back up the winding stairs and hailed a carriage the moment I was back out into the streets. I never gambled when it came my scheming. I'd previously treated my revenge with the deliberate care of a chef preparing a delicacy. Now, as I arrived at West India Dock Road, I simply hoped Rui could gather enough men to help me pull off my stunt by Friday. I couldn't let the opportunity pass. Dalton Sass was out of my way, but not without a heavy cost. And now my mind was a torrent of thoughts, images, and blood-curdling screams that made my heart rate feel as if it would never ease. I needed my takedown of McCoskry to be over with, and with as few bodies left behind as possible. Maybe then these accusatory howls would finally cease.

Taking in a deep breath, I entered the Strangers' Home for Asiatics, Africans and South Sea Islanders. The repatriation center for Black and Asian sailors always had their arms open, ready to embrace my kind. There was nowhere else I knew I could find Rui.

"Where is Rui?" I asked several people, but to no avail until a Sri Lankan man in the humble little atrium finally nodded and guided me up a rickety staircase to the second floor. This floor was filled with bedrooms. Each fit at least four beds, most of them occupied by tired sailors and others without a home, I imagined. The man stopped by a wooden door in the corner of the hallway. It was opened just enough to fit an arm through. That's why I could hear a pair of young men talking in hushed voices inside the room.

"Thank you," I said to the man, and after he left I leaned in and listened carefully to Rui's light laughter peppering the air.

"This isn't a laughing matter," said a deep but delicate voice I didn't recognize. "We can't keep him in a place like this. He needs medical care at a hospital."

"You mean your hospital in Edinburgh?" It was my first time hearing Rui sound so bratty, like a defiant child. "You really think they'll treat a fugitive with such care?"

"Keep your voice down!"

Fugitive? Without making a sound, I inched closer to the open crack in the door.

"And whose fault is it that he's a fugitive?" The other man spoke in a hushed, conspiratorial tone. "You broke him out of prison when I told you to wait for the law—"

"Wait for the law to what? You saw how quickly they convicted him. It was a Chinese man's word against a royal attendant. They saw him and saw a criminal."

"And you're doing such a good job of dissuading those prejudices with your choice of lifestyle."

I finally found my way to the opening and peeked inside the room. I couldn't see much. There was a bed in the room, but I could only see the rickety wooden nightstand to its left. Next to the leftmost wall, two men faced off against each other. One, Rui, his white shirt just barely tucked into his brown overalls. The other was a taller man with a long face I couldn't fully see. Between his brown britches, perfectly ironed vest, and carefully coiffed black hair, he was done up as if for a Sunday visit to church. When Rui's eyes instinctively slid to the door, I whipped around quickly.

"My choice of lifestyle is what's paying for his medical support here," Rui said.

"What little you can give him."

"And it'll pay his way back to our family in Guangdong—"

"If he even survives the trip."

"—*which is what he wants*." Rui paused, catching his breath because he'd said everything in one rushed sentence. "It's what our father wants. Don't you care about that anymore?"

Our father. He was talking to his brother. What was his name? Luk Ham. The doctor from Edinburgh . . .

"I heard you're being called 'Rui' here." Luk Ham laughed bitterly. "Is it fun for you, Wong Yeu Ham? Will playing criminal get the treatment and respect our father deserves after everything he's achieved in life?"

Wong Yeu Ham. Rui's true name. It sucked the air out of the room. Nobody spoke. Not even I could breathe, the tension was so thick.

302

"When we came to England," Rui continued, "Father made us speak English only. He said it would help us fit in if we sounded like them. And what did fitting in get him? Look at him." Rui flicked his head toward the bed. "He just barely survived apoplexy. If I'd left him in prison, waiting for the justice system to save him, he'd be dead by now. Bringing him to one of your 'proper' institutions will land him back in jail the minute they find out who he is. His achievements never mattered to them. Yours won't either."

The brothers were silent for a moment.

"That's enough," Luk Ham said with an irritated sigh. "This conversation isn't going anywhere. I'm staying in London for the time being. I'll come back once you've come to your senses. I expect a different answer when I do."

"My answer won't change," Rui told him.

"Then our father's death will be on your hands."

I slipped into the next room the moment I heard Luk Ham approaching. I just missed him—or rather, he just missed me, stalking down the staircase with angry steps. I kept the door open a crack so I can see his tall figure descending.

"Madam, is there something you need?" said a man behind me. I jumped a little and turned around. He stayed underneath the covers of his bed, his light brown skin and shaven head just barely seen over the white sheets. He was one of four sailors in the room I'd just barged into. Each looked at me with curiosity and confusion.

"Oh, no, nothing at all!" I said a little too loudly, entirely embarrassed.

"Except manners."

Rui pushed open the door and loomed over me. "Eavesdropping isn't very ladylike."

With a sheepish grin, I waved at him before dragging him downstairs.

"I'm only here because I have an idea to take down McCoskry," I said, still embarrassed, hoping my businesslike demeanor would offset it. "I just need your help."

We entered the dining hall filled with sailors eating their fill of what the missionaries could procure for them: game and bread and humble vegetables boiled and soft to eat. Even though there were two men on the other side of our long wooden table drinking their soup, I doubted anyone could overhear us in this noise. Sailors tended to be quite chatty.

"I need a handful of men belonging to my race who will accept a job for a stunningly immodest fee. And I need them by Friday."

"Well, you've come to the right place. There are quite a few here who'd be happy to help with whatever you need from them—as long as the price is, as you say, stunningly immodest." Rui's attention was elsewhere. He crossed his legs, looking around the dining hall, then up at the rafters in the ceiling. "Though you would know about immodesty, wouldn't you?"

His sarcasm was a sharp bite. I bristled. "I didn't mean to eavesdrop."

"And yet you did."

"I was looking for you." I leaned over, my hands on the table. "I didn't know I'd find your brother too."

I paused because Rui's own problems had only briefly distracted me from my own. Too many voices were arguing in my head. Voices whose arguments only further blurred the lines between right and wrong. That rage that had been burning in me for years was under attack by confusing emotions I couldn't deal with. All because of Wilkes's murder.

Charles Wilkes wasn't what I would call a good, kind man. He'd turned himself into an inconvenience in my pursuits. But I'd drawn him into this mess for my own benefit. And when I thought of Wilkes's wife wailing in tears, I wondered if it was really okay to dismiss him as an "inconvenience."

Wait. Wilkes . . .

I stared at Rui for a time, my heartbeat quickening as I considered letting the question at the tip of my tongue slip from my lips. But now that Rui was in front of me, I couldn't resist.

"Did you kill him?" I'd asked it so matter-of-factly, it took Rui by surprise. Across the table, Rui watched me with a neutral expression. "The robed man that interrupted the séance. Was that you?"

Rui didn't answer.

Checking to make sure the rowdy sailors were too busy playing Shove-Halfpenny to notice us, I leaned in and lowered my voice. "You have no reason to assassinate the Queen, as far as I know. But you were the one who told me to bring John Brown to court."

"You want me to help you take down McCoskry on Friday?"

Rui's voice was surprisingly cold. Unnerved, I sat back in my seat. "Yes."

"How badly do you want it?"

I bit my lip. In the face of Rui's chillingly ambiguous expression, I couldn't help but be honest. "I need this done, Rui," I whispered. "I want this done fast."

"Then stop asking unnecessary questions—especially those that have nothing to do with your goal. Remember, little princess, all I'm doing for you isn't for free. It's a contract between you and me. Do as I please and I'll do as you please."

Nothing to do with my goal. I already knew Rui was a murderer. *I* was a murderer. Whatever the truth was, there was no high ground I had to stand on.

Rui reached across the table and grabbed my wrist in a flash, so quickly my cutting gasp almost sounded like a yell. "Don't relent now. You're so close, Sally."

I studied him, his slender face and high, sharp cheekbones. The passion in his eyes that normally ignited so much passion in me.

I slipped my hand out of his grip. "You said no more unnecessary questions," I said. "But here's one more: Why 'Rui'? Does it hold some significance to you?"

Rui sat back and considered my question. "Rui . . ." As he crossed his legs, an almost-whimsical expression appeared on his handsome face. "I don't know. It was the name of a man who used to live here. I figured it was as good as any. You and I both know how quickly names can change for people like us."

People like us. Yes, he was right. Sometimes my own names frightened me because each felt meant for someone else. Rui . . . Wong Yeu Ham . . . he must have felt the same way.

I couldn't stop myself from pressing on. "Why are you helping me?" I asked him, risking drawing his ire. "Does it have to do with your father?"

Rui looked down at the table. For a moment, I didn't think he'd answer. "When we cross borders into this country, we are sold many promises," he began. "The promise of a good, fair life, in exchange for good, fair work. That if we follow the rules, the rules will work for us. Has this been your experience, Sally?"

I didn't answer. Years' worth of trauma must have curdled my expression because Rui nodded as if I'd spoken a single word.

"Neither has it been mine. I wonder if we're kindred spirits, Sally."

He looked almost hopeful. How lonely had he been all these years fighting battles on his own while his father was in prison and his brother was judging him from afar.

306

"Your brother thinks differently." I pulled my wrist from his grip and clasped my fingers together. "He believes in this world."

"And what do you believe in, Sally?" Rui stood from his seat. "Find that answer, and then come to me."

Confucius had said something about revenge, overly quoted in moralistic circles. I always hated it. Here, in Strangers' Home, I was left alone wondering how many graves I had left to dig.

TWENTY-EIGHT

THE FIRST OF August came quickly. I stood outside Exeter Hall in the sweltering heat amongst the crowds of England's adoring public waiting for the Prince of Wales's carriage to arrive. I adjusted the purple bonnet with flowers pinned on the brim. At least it was wide enough to block out the unforgiving sun, but it was hard to see above so many heads.

"There! I see it coming!" Gowramma tugged my sleeve and pointed down the road. Ever since I told her about the event, leaving out the more exciting details of course, Gowramma had insisted on coming. "Fun things always seem to happen around you, Sally," she'd told me with a coquettish wink. Now that she was here, she was rather useful as a lookout.

The royal carriage rumbled down the street, pulled by white horses, the gold lining twinkling underneath the morning sun. Officers kept the crowd under control, but they still tried to rush the prince anyway as he stepped out in his bright red military regalia.

"Your Majesty!" they screamed as he soaked in the adoration from his subjects. Obsessed royal watchers. Unlike others in the country, they didn't care a whit about any scandal as long as they could glimpse their favorite family every once in a while. Bertie probably appreciated the flattery.

He wasn't alone, as I knew he wouldn't be. William McCoskry got out of the carriage and followed behind, waving pompously to a crowd of people who hadn't a clue who he was. The crowd parted as Bertie and McCoskry strode through the white Corinthian columns to the front doors of Exeter Hall.

Bertie grinned at me from ear to ear before giving Gowramma and me a gentlemanly bow. "Shall we?" Bertie offered me his arm.

"How scandalous!" Gowramma said what others would have been thinking if they saw me walk into a public meeting arm in arm with the prince.

Reddening, Bertie retracted his arm and straightened out his jacket. "She is my god-sister," he mumbled.

"Exactly." Gowramma wouldn't let him get away with such a flagrant display of affection. That, I appreciated, given the prince's socalled affections were like scattering pollen in an ever-changing wind. Besides, there was work to be done.

"Let's go," I said, gesturing toward the door.

Bertie, his ears still as red as McCoskry's misshapen beard, entered the hall.

Exeter Hall, broad and vast, was the home of many important and intriguing gatherings. Men and women of importance in society often met to discuss pressing social issues. Regardless of the organizations they belonged to, they purported to have one goal: the advancement and betterment of humanity. Of course, the abolition of slavery was one of them. They were all here, a crowd of thousands, packed into the first floor of the Great Hall. We were taken up to the platform on the east end, separated from the rest of the hall by a curved railing. Behind us were rows of seats where the most influential guests were already seated. The most prominent members of the Anti-Slavery Society nodded in approval as the prince greeted the chairman.

"There must be at least three thousand people here," Gowramma whispered to me as we took our seats. "Maybe more."

"I've never known Exeter Hall to take more than four thousand at the most, but this certainly is challenging that perception." I watched McCoskry take his seat next to Bertie's.

I thought of William McCoskry licking his lips and rubbing his red beard the night I entertained them like a caged clown in Mrs. Phipps's drawing room. He licked his lips now. He looked as pompous, as entirely lacking in empathy, as the day I was presented to Queen Victoria. The memory of his laughter made my hair stand on end.

Mr. Bellamy. Mr. Bambridge. Uncle George. McCoskry. Phipps . . .

It was startling how none of them had changed since my childhood. Instead, they'd only gotten worse, more brazen in their arrogance. They all needed to be brought low.

"The meeting is in session," said the chairman, who wore a long jacket with a forked tail almost dragging upon the floor. "We are delighted to present Albert Edward, Prince of Wales, who has agreed to hold a speech about the need to support the abolition of slavery wherever its vines have spread across the world."

Sweat drops were building beneath Bertie's hairline as he stood up and greeted the crowd. He looked to me for help, his eyes wide in silent panic.

And yet he was usually so confident when in the presence of booze and cabaret dancers. I urged him on with a polite, endearing smile.

Wiping his forehead, he sucked in a breath and began his speech. "Almost two years ago," Bertie began, his voice struggling a bit before finding its volume over the hushed crowd, "I was invited by British North America so that I could—well, a-as they wrote in a letter to my mother— witness the progress and prosperity of this distant part of our dominions." He paused, clearly trying to remember his speech. "When I went across the pond, well, it was certainly an arduous journey, you know. I didn't know what to expect."

An audience member coughed. I resisted the urge to make a bet with Gowramma as to whether or not Bertie would pull himself together.

Bertie cleared his throat. "It was an arduous journey," he repeated, "but upon arriving to Upper Canada, I saw the majesty of British civility. Even in the furthest-flung places of the world, I could feel the people's loyalty and their love for the throne. This love, loyalty, and indeed prosperity is what the British Crown has given them."

Which people? I wondered. Certainly not the Indigenous nations, whose populations were decimated by disease and treachery?

What had my mother always told me back in Africa? The hand of the giver is always at the top. I'm not sure she meant it like this. But now all I could see were the lies of the Crown's civilization project parroted from its inheritor's mouth faithfully and without question. I stifled a sigh. This was going to be a long speech.

Indeed, Bertie droned on, talking about the natural wonders he saw, Niagara Falls, something about a man tumbling down in a barrel. I could see certain members of the society behind me squirming impatiently, wondering, as I did, when he'd get to the point.

"And when I came to America, I was met by the most kind president—or former president, James Buchanan, with whom I stayed three days at the White House."

Most kind. I wondered if Dred Scott would agree. It was Buchanan who supported the continuation of slavery, after all.

"While I was there, I met a number of interesting fellows. Among them, it is my discussions with Ralph Waldo Emerson that have remained with me. It is his work, his writings that I recalled as I prepared this speech for you today. And his resounding call—a reminder to us all: civilization depends on *morality*."

He let the last line boom through the hall. It was a crowd-pleaser. Applause erupted, with many of the guests nodding in agreement. Bertie waited for the applause to die down before he proceeded.

"And what, can I say, is at all civil or moral about slavery? They call it an institution. I call it a *destitution*."

"Ooh, good line," Gowramma leaned over and whispered in my ear as the crowd applauded again. Yes, Bertie seemed very proud of himself as the crowd nodded eagerly. It was a good line. A familiar line . . .

"Imagine!" Bertie shouted, for the applause had given him a second wind. "The stealing of men and setting them to work. How many years has it lasted? How many years has it yielded cotton and sugar? All honest men strive to earn their bread by their industry. Slavery insults the faithful workman at his daily toil—"

"For such calamity no solution but servile war, and the Africanization of the country that permits it."

I finished Bertie's sentence under my breath. We spoke the same sentence, word for word, because I now knew where Bertie had stolen his words from: Emerson's article for the American magazine *The Atlantic*, published only a few months ago in April. Bertie must have been counting on most people in Britain having no access to it. Oh, what criminalities royal privilege enabled.

I sighed and shook my head. Bertie was never very good at doing his homework properly, but I didn't imagine he'd stoop so low as to pilfer the words of a man whose abolitionist sentiments didn't seem to exclude actual racism. It was the Africanization of America that enabled its insistence on slavery? An interesting hypothesis. He also called us "brutes" and "savage tribes" in the same essay. It was an ill-kept secret by now that most professed abolitionists didn't actually like us very much.

Still Bertie continued. "The British Empire abolished slavery decades ago. But what of other nations? If there be a country where knowledge cannot be diffused without perils of mob-law and statue-law, where speech is not free, where liberty is attacked, where the position of the white woman is injuriously affected by the outlawry of the black woman—"

"The outlawry of the what?" Gowramma muttered, aghast as I reeled in my seat, glaring at him with full disdain.

"—that country is not civil, but barbarous, and no advantages of soil, climate, or coast can resist these mischiefs!"

The crowd gave a standing ovation. For the Prince of Wales or Ralph Waldo Emerson, I didn't know and, it seemed, neither did they. It didn't matter either way: both men were ridiculous. But we were just getting to the good part. Bertie gestured toward McCoskry, who impatiently jostled in his seat, ready.

"If there's anyone here who knows the evils of slavery firsthand, it is this gentleman beside me. Serving as the acting governor of Lagos in West Africa, he saw slavery in a colony that was meant to have ended it by British decree. There, in his dealings with slaves, free and bound alike, he learned the true meaning of liberty and civility. Please join me in welcoming Sir William McCoskry."

The crowd went on clapping even as they sat in their seats. McCoskry straightened out his jacket and greeted Prince Bertie with firm hand-shakes, smiling for the cameramen who took their shot from the edges of the hall for the upcoming newspapers. McCoskry probably thought this would be one of his crowning moments. And if Rui didn't come through with his end of the bargain, it would be. Even if I angered him at Strang-ers' Home, surely he wouldn't let my opportunity for revenge slip away from me.

I watched the entrance on pins and needles.

"Yes, it is true, my fellow Britons. I, William McCoskry, who began my work as a humble merchant in Lagos, soon found myself becoming acting consul, and then acting governor of the Lagos Colony."

With one eye on Exeter Hall's entrance, I used a gloved hand to cover my snarl. I was right. He hadn't changed. Still aggrandizing himself. Still lying, as if he hadn't used my homeland as his own personal playground. And the people here drank it all up, such self-serving fools.

"In Lagos," McCoskry continued, "I gave protection to runaway slaves and dealt with the issues of domestic slavery that continued across the colony. Slavery is not limited to America, as bloody as their current war may be. Its evils continue throughout the world. And though I have returned to being a private merchant, I will continue my good work on the African continent. I will not stop until the evil of slavery has been stamped out on this earth."

The crowd was too busy cheering to notice the troop of seven Africans who had just burst into Exeter Hall. All of them dressed in working-class britches, shirts, and dresses, because in England, this was all most could afford with what few work opportunities they had. Not all were lucky enough to be adopted by a Queen. That's why the money offered to them had to be, as I promised Rui, "stunningly immodest."

I let out a relieved sigh and watched the play.

"William McCoskry!" cried one man, his graying beard almost as long as McCoskry's. He walked with a limp as the line of Africans pushed their way to the front of the hall just below where Bertie and McCoskry were standing. "You speak of stamping out the evil of slavery. Then why, during *our* trials in Lagos, did you rule in favor of our slave owners when we came to you for help? Why fight so hard for their rights and not ours?"

McCoskry squinted in confusion, looking around, baffled. He wouldn't remember them. They were sailors from Strangers' Home.

They had never been under his jurisdiction. Rui had chosen well—these men were great actors.

Even if they were former slaves under McCoskry's rule, he wouldn't have recognized them individually. That was how little he cared. The blood drained from his face.

"You never cared. You sent me back to my slave master, who beat me!" cried a man, his natural hair a halo over his head. "You laughed at me!"

"I heard it with my own ears," said another, a young man with long, slender limbs. "That when I fled slavery you compensated my owner with money. Where was my compensation?"

Their anger felt real. As real as mine. Maybe it was the money they were paid. But it couldn't have just been that. There was a deep pain we all shared here, all of us Africans forced to survive in the land of the ones who'd so irresponsibly twisted our homes as if our land, our kingdoms, our cultures, were nothing more than their playground. That anger was real. It was real for all of us, whether we realized it or not.

"William?" Shocked and barely able to move his face, Bertie stiffly turned to McCoskry, looking for answers. McCoskry could give none. His smile had turned into the picture of terror, pasted on his face. Both men were frozen.

A second man, who looked around Davies's age, beat his chest with his palm, his glittering eyes burning with the pain of his past. "It was you who, during my trial, said that slave owners had the right to keep their property. Was I property to you, McCoskry?"

The crowd was whispering, gossiping until the sounds of disapproval lifted into the air.

"McCoskry is a liar!" said one amongst the crowd. "He doesn't support abolition at all!"

315

"He kept the Africans enslaved!"

"What is he doing here? How could the prince invite him? Is he mad?"

"This is a disaster," said one member of the Anti-Slavery Society behind me with a deep groan, his head in his hands.

A disaster. Just as I'd intended.

The sailors began shouting at once, in unison with the scandalized abolitionists and the confused, angered crowd who began pushing each other to get to McCoskry. Gowramma and I stayed in our seats for our own safety, but I was sure my friend was just as curious as I was to see how the messy event would unfold.

It unfolded exactly how I thought it would. With a riot. Men and women didn't wait for McCoskry's excuses. They charged the podium, determined to run them out of the hall—perhaps even out of town. As the chairman shouted for order, pushing off those upon him, Bertie and McCoskry escaping their humiliation through the back exit.

McCoskry would never be able to show his face in England again. Every detail of this farce of an event would be recorded and sold in tomorrow morning's newspapers. And the Queen? The Queen's reputation would take another hit. Her son wasn't up to the task after all. His father's royal ghost would be spinning in his grave if he wasn't so busy posing for postmortem pictures with his obsessed wife.

I wanted to hug that little girl dancing for fear of her life in the drawing room. Dancing for those self-serving ghouls. It felt, for a moment, as if Ade was hugging her. Hugging me. Telling me to rest. But I couldn't rest. Not until my revenge was complete.

"I told you fun things always happen around you, Sally," Gowramma said, fluffing her dress over her knees and fanning herself.

TWENTY-NINE

I WAS SUMMONED by Queen Victoria to Windsor Castle that evening. Her officers had almost quite literally hauled me out of Gowramma's drawing room, where we'd been laughing about the fiasco with a bottle of champagne.

"Do come by and visit me and Edith sometime again soon, Sally," she said with a wave, holding her baby in her arms outside her mansion while some court officials shoved me into the carriage. She really did live for chaos. I suppose it was always easier being a spectator.

I stared at my defiant reflection in the carriage window. I couldn't give McCoskry's real victims the justice they deserved, but through these proxies, I believed in my heart that I'd given them an opportunity to speak their truths and expose an immoral swindler. That this just happened to coincide with my own personal quest for justice was simply the icing on the cake.

Justice? Or vengeance? Are they the same?

Wilkes's wife began screaming again. When I closed my eyes, I could see the bullet hole in her husband's head.

I didn't stop shivering until I'd entered the palace. I was led to one of the Queen's dressing room. There, the Queen's courtiers were moving clothing, blankets, and other paraphernalia out of the room, casting me mousy, secretive little glances as they passed by me and scurried through the door.

Queen Victoria sat in a blue chair lined in gold at a desk covered in flowing white silk. She was looking at herself in the mirror. I wonder if she saw her younger self—the bright blue-eyed teen girl who'd fallen madly in love with her husband. Or if she saw herself as she was now, dour and dressed in black. The love seat, couch, and chaises were also draped in black sheets. The grand mirror at the end of the room was turned around. The drapes for the windows had been shut. And so every day would be.

Lord Ponsonby and John Brown stood in front of the extravagant oak drawer between the two windows. I could see the candles flickering behind them on the wood. Each man glared at me with suspicion. But it was the Queen who I was watching. She didn't speak to me for as long as I stood there waiting. She was glaring at herself.

"Sally," she finally said, unmoving, her back to me. I could see her reflection in the little mirror on her desk. Her sunken eyes. "How is Mrs. Schoen?"

Taken aback, I bowed my head almost by instinct. "Well, Your Majesty."

"I see." The Queen paused. "I will be going to Balmoral Castle in Scotland tomorrow. Before then, I wish to ask you some questions."

I shut out Mrs. Wilkes's screams and prepared myself. "Yes, Your Majesty." I curtsied.

"I'm sure you've heard what happened at Exeter Hall the other day. That disaster. It's all over the papers." The Queen sucked in a long breath through her nose as if trying to calm herself. "William McCoskry is bound to leave England as soon as he can arrange it."

So I'd sent him fleeing across the Atlantic with his tail between his legs. Good. After this fiasco, the Anti-Slavery Society would surely open up an investigation on his so-called governorship. He wouldn't be able to hide in Lagos either. He was finished.

"Were you there at Exeter Hall the moment it happened?"

I pursed my lips. I couldn't exactly lie. People had seen me being ushered in by the prince himself.

"Yes." I kept my face solemn. "Bertie's speech, at least, was wonderful."

"He didn't tell me he was making it. I know he's been trying to prove himself since his father passed. But why in the world would he ask McCoskry to aid him?"

Lord Ponsonby and John Brown watched me from the oak drawer. Only the latter actually seemed intimidating with his height and burly brawn. And the intensity of his gaze—like a rabid dog bred only to protect its master.

"I'm sure Bertie believed McCoskry would be of some help."

"Mistakenly so," said the Queen.

I nodded. "Yes, unfortunately."

Silence. The Queen clucked her tongue and placed one hand upon the other.

"Then again, I know my son. He's not one to think deeply about stratagem. I'm not even confident he wrote his own speech."

Well, in a way, she was right about that. The Queen squeezed her hands.

"Tell me the truth: Was it your idea that Bertie would bring William McCoskry to his address at Exeter Hall?"

I stayed perfectly still. There was no evidence that I did. Bertie didn't discuss his speech with her.

"No, Your Majesty."

"No?" The Queen's tone was graveyard quiet. "But earlier today, Mrs. Schoen told me it was."

My heart stopped. "P-Pardon?"

"While you were at Lady Gowramma and Colonel John Campell's residence, I had a few men visit your mother in Chatham. She let Bertie into your home. She heard your conversation."

I bit the inside of my cheek to tamp down my anger, but it didn't work. How dare this banshee wield Mama against me? Mama wouldn't have known the implications and she certainly wouldn't refuse the request of a court official for "innocent" information.

My chest rose and fell as I calmed myself.

I lowered my head in a show of pure shame. "I'm sorry, Your Majesty. You're right. I did suggest it to Bertie. I just wanted his speech to go well. I thought it such a good opportunity for him to show his worth in public."

Lord Ponsonby stepped forward, hands clenched. "That is not for you to decide," he started, but Brown gripped his shoulder and kept him in place. This was Queen Victoria's investigation.

"You must have known that although we publicly support abolition, given the prince's position, any mishap would cause public scrutiny."

The key to feigning innocence for me was imagining a deer in the forest, sprinkled with dew. I'd seen one once while exploring the woods and while I wasn't very impressed, I thought it a good reference. I tried to channel one.

"He is the Prince of Wales. I never once doubted his ability," I said.

"Then you haven't been paying much attention to Bertie, have you?"

John Brown cleared his throat while Ponsonby shifted uncomfortably on his feet. What a rare display of maternal affection from Her Majesty.

"My son has been acting strangely around you. I've been receiving reports. Mrs. Schoen herself confirmed that he visited your house. But this strangeness . . . I saw it myself the night I tried to contact my dear Albert."

I was shocked she had paid attention to me at all during the séance, or could see me through that thick black veil she wore. Perhaps the sight of her son holding my hand so desperately bothered her.

I planned some kind of excuse on my lips, but it didn't have a chance to form. I jumped, startled, as Bertie burst through the dressing room doors. Attendants flailed behind him, trying to stop him and failing miserably.

"What is the meaning of this, Mother? Why have you summoned Sally here?"

"Prince Albert!" This time Ponsonby rushed forward without Brown's burly grip to stop him. "This has nothing to do with you. Please return to your room—"

Bertie shoved him off. "This has everything to do with me." He turned to his mother, his hands balled into fists. "I was the one who bungled the speech at Exeter Hall. I was the one who created the humiliation and yet you summon Sally here. Why? To blame her for your son's foolishness."

"What can be blamed for my son's foolishness, I wonder?" The Queen stood up, vicious despite her diminutive stature. She clearly intimidated her son, who took a sudden step back. "It can't be our genetics because otherwise you would have gotten my sense and your father's intelligence and propensity for study. It couldn't be your tutors, for they did all they could in trying to wrangle out your disobedience so that you could learn history and arithmetic. It surely isn't the military officers and the professors who complained about your wayward ways. So what is it, Bertie? What has caused your absolute and complete *foolishness*?"

She banged the table with her hand, rattling the mirror. John Brown rushed to her side, gripping her other hand, but the woman was shaking, actually shaking in front of us.

"If not for that foolishness, my husband would be alive, I'm sure of it. Oh, you horrible boy." The Queen looked away from him, crumpling over the desk.

And Bertie. Bertie, who must have heard this a thousand times, in different words, stared at the floral-patterned carpeted floor, gripping his brown trousers as if he might tear them off.

"You needn't worry about Father anymore, Mother," he whispered. "You've clearly already found his replacement."

The Queen whipped around, mouth agape as if he'd committed blasphemy. But it was hard to deny anything with John Brown wrapped around her right in front of him.

Bertie took a forbidding step forward, the sight of the two of them incensing him more by the second. "You're going to Balmoral soon, aren't you? A nice little romantic getaway, I suspect."

"Your Highness!" Ponsonby waggled about helplessly and rather uselessly; by this point there was no one in the room willing to even acknowledge his existence.

"Are you going to give him my inheritance when all is said and done? He'd certainly make a better king than I, don't you think, Mama?"

"You terrible, terrible son!" The Queen broke free from Brown's grip and stepped forward, stomping her feet on the ground like the petulant child she was when she became the ruler of the empire, or so some whisper.

Bertie turned his gaze to me. He soaked me in, absorbing everything from the feather bonnet on my head to my high-heeled boots. "Well," he said, grinning at his mother. "We all need our support in the wake of

Father's death. Alice just got married. Vicky has her husband. You have your support." He strode toward me and grabbed my wrist. "And I have mine."

He pulled me into a kiss, long and deep, his hands pressed against the small of my back while he crushed my head against his. It was an aggressive kiss, one meant to prove something. I could hear everyone in the room gasping, and somewhere in the room, the legs of a chair screeched against the carpet. I peeked out of the corner of my eye: it was Ponsonby. The man looked as if all his hair would trickle off his scalp and land in a pile on the floor all at once.

But it was Queen Victoria's reaction that ignited me. Her expression of utter disdain and disgust. But I was her precious goddaughter and she my good-hearted, altruistic mother who believed in the equality of peoples. The Queen of the Whites who brought an African slave into her royal family out of the goodness of her heart. She didn't seem upset when Bertie dumped honey on my hair. She didn't stir when her own attendants and courtiers mocked me loudly whenever they saw us together. But now, now she seemed very interested. Scandalized.

I wanted to punish her. I felt, indeed, that she deserved to be punished.

I returned Bertie's kiss so passionately even he was taken aback, but that didn't relieve his tongue, which found the crevices of my mouth and flicked my lips.

"This is absolute madness!" John Brown growled. And he was a big man. When he growled, the whole castle could hear it.

Bertie didn't care. He grabbed me by the waist and pulled me to him. "What's madness is that I've been putting up with my mother's nonsense for so long and for no reason nor gain."

He was a brat. A brazen prince who only saw himself and his own well-being in his mind's eye. In that way, I suspected, he was just like his mother. Perhaps utter and complete self-absorption was what it meant to be the heir to the throne of England. But what Bertie didn't know, as he was using me, was that I was also using him. Seeing Queen Victoria's expression twist and turn and make shapes I never thought possible made my heart tremble with glee. I hadn't felt so alive in so many years. It took everything I had to hide my triumphant grin.

The room was silent. The grandfather clock in the corner of the room ticked as time ominously seemed to slow to a halt.

The Queen parted her lips. "Tell him, Sally. What you did to Captain Frederick Forbes."

My arms fell to my sides. I couldn't feel them.

"What? You mean the man who brought Sally here, don't you?" Bertie looked down at me and shook me a little. "What's she blabbering about, Sally?"

The Queen said nothing more. She knew. Somehow she knew that Forbes didn't die of an illness. His medicine had been replaced by poison by a frightened and furious little princess. He'd saved her from ritual sacrificial in Africa only to sacrifice her soul to a different god. He'd killed her friend.

I didn't confirm or deny anything. I gave her a noncommittal frown with a hint of confusion, looking up at Bertie, because there was no proof. As long as there was no proof, what did it matter? Bertie would never believe her. That she would know her goddaughter was a murderer only to ignore it for years, likely for the sake of her own reputation.

The Queen's gamble was nothing but an empty threat. I snuggled closer to Bertie.

And yet.

The hisses of those I'd gotten killed in this war was pandemonium battering my skull.

But Ade. My ancestors. My gods. I could hear them cheering me on.

I could see my younger self dancing in Mrs. Phipps's drawing room, crying on the inside.

They started this.

I placed my head on Bertie's shoulder, my face a perfect mask while the storm raged within me. It felt like the air had been sucked out of the room. Like nobody could breathe unless they were given permission by some higher being. I didn't want them to breathe.

If we were to all die, then let us die together.

I wouldn't feel guilty. I had no reason to.

They started this.

Because, from the start, their "love" for me was conditional.

The door opened behind me. Lord Ponsonby, John Brown, the attendants. The Queen. Their gazes tore away from Bertie and me and toward the entrance.

My throat closed. Queen Victoria was shrieking.

Time slowed. My nerves tingled as if they'd been set on fire. Bertie and I turned to find Dalton Sass shutting the door behind him with his gun pointed at me. My heart stopped.

"What in the blazes!"

"Protect the Queen!"

I don't know which man said what. All I heard was Dalton calling my name.

"Sally . . . dear Sally . . ."

Dalton? My mind was playing tricks on me. What stood in front of me must have been some kind of specter. It's what my mind had tricked me into believing until he began to taunt me.

"Do you know why my mother hated you so?" He bared his teeth, his eyes unfocused. He was wearing dingy clothes that hadn't been washed, his face bruised, perhaps roughed up by the police officers who were supposed to have him under lock and key. "I suspect for the same reason the Queen's love for you is nothing but a façade. You were nothing but a project from the beginning, Sally, and had you shown your true face from the beginning, the Queen would have had you disappear like so many others."

Behind John Brown's protective figure the Queen stiffened. I saw her out of the corner of my eye. She whispered something in his ear. And he nodded.

"My mother knew it. She knew the truth about you children. And she wasn't the only one." He looked over at Ponsonby and grinned. "Oh dear, look who's grown back his confidence. Lord Ponsonby, don't stand there as if you aren't anything other than a sorry sack of excrement. Last we spoke, you were terrified as any that the truth would come out."

As Ponsonby's knees knocked, I gathered my courage. "What truth? What are you talking about? Or is this just more of the rantings of a madman?"

Dalton batted his jacket pocket by his hip. "You would love to know the truth, wouldn't you? But the Queen would just die if you knew. About you wayward children. You 'Wards of the Empire'—"

I'd been so captured by Dalton's ramblings, his sudden appearance, that I hadn't notice John Brown bring out a revolver.

If I had been but a moment quicker. But nothing was faster than John Brown's trigger finger. The shot rang out, rattling my bones, the noise slicing through my skull. And it took me a moment to realize.

John Brown shot Dalton Sass in the head.

I screamed, stumbling backward. Bertie backed up until he was flat against the luxuriously papered wall. Ponsonby fell to his knees. The only ones who didn't move a muscle, who remained perfectly still and in control of themselves, were the Queen and her John Brown.

I stared at the pool of blood seeping out from Dalton Sass's skull, staining the carpet. I stared at it for so long, I couldn't remember whose blood it was. Was it Bellamy's? Wilkes's? There was just so much. Endless, like a rippling river. My head felt light while my body felt heavy. How strange. I couldn't feel my arms.

I crumpled to the floor.

"Take him away this instant," said the Queen. "And tell no one of this. I don't want the press knowing anything about this."

Dalton wouldn't have been the first person to sneak into a British palace. Years ago, a lad, Boy Jones, snuck into Buckingham Palace despite its security. He had done it so many times he became a folk hero. But that wasn't what Dalton was trying to achieve. He was here to kill me. And not just physically.

I stared at him as Ponsonby and John Brown lifted his body. Wards of the Empire . . .

"Wait a minute," I said as they began to take his body away, because I spied something in his jacket pocket. I took my chance and ran toward him, hugging his body as if grieving. "He was our friend. Oh, what a terrible tragedy!" I cried as my fingers snagged the slip of paper from his pocket.

"Sally, you poor girl, don't do this to yourself," said Bertie, rushing to my side. "You'll faint, poor thing."

He didn't notice me slipping the bloody paper into the top of my glove.

When Dalton beat his hip, it wasn't just for theatrics. This was the true weapon he'd come here to wield.

The letter. The Queen hadn't seen me pocket it. But it was clear from the words Dalton had uttered and her wild eyes and heavy breath that Lord Ponsonby was right to be wary of it.

"He was a madman. And perhaps if my mother wasn't so busy with her John Brown and her séances, we'd have better security around here."

He shot his mother a glower and grabbed my shoulder. "Come on, Sally. This is all too much. I'll take you home."

He began to push me toward the door when Queen Victoria cleared her throat. "Mr. Brown! Separate them," the Queen ordered.

John Brown did as he was told, grabbing both of Bertie's arms and hauling the cursing boy away from me.

"Sally," she called after me as I stood paralyzed by the door. "I don't know what all of this nonsense is about, but it's clear you are at the center of it. You are to marry Captain Davies as *soon* as I return from Scotland. Then you will be taken back to your home in West Africa, where I suspect you'll spend the rest of your days. Until that time comes you will behave. You will not spend your last two weeks in Britain making trouble. I forbid it. And I will ensure it. Be the obedient, malleable little girl I first met all those years ago."

Malleable. I pressed my lips together. "That's not really a life," I whispered.

"But at least you'll live."

Bertie wasn't smart enough to hear the direct threat. Both of us seemed to have left our masks behind in this civilized, murderous struggle. I gave Queen Victoria one final curtsy before leaving the bloody dressing room with her son.

PART THREE

CONDITIONAL LOVE

We came home, found Albert still there, waiting for Forbes and a little negro girl who he had brought back from the king of Dahomey. Her parents, and all of her relatives having been sacrificed. Captain Forbes saved her life by asking for her as a present. She is sharp & intelligent and speaks English. She was dressed as any other girl and when her bonnet was taken off, her little black wooly head and big earrings gave her the true negro type.

—*Queen Victoria, 1850*

THIRTY

DALTON'S LAST WORDS before being gunned down by John Brown: *Wards of the Empire*. It was not a program, per se, but a promise. A set of rules designed to keep the Queen of England from falling prey to her own fetishes.

By the time I arrived at Strangers' Home, Dalton Sass's blood was long dry on the slip of paper I'd stolen from his corpse. I hadn't washed it off my dress. With bloodshot eyes, I began screaming at the missionaries to bring me Rui. They locked me in a stone-cold room near the kitchen where they kept the meat in slabs on wood tables and potatoes in sacks on the floor. They were frightened for the safety of the sailors, but they needn't have been.

"Sally!" It was in the dead of night that Rui unlocked the door and barreled inside. "Sally!" He took in the sight of the blood on my dress and hands. A mixture of concern and intrigue danced upon his twitching lips. He rushed up to me and bent down. "What happened? Who did this to you?"

I stared at him without blinking. "The Queen of England," I whispered, and gave him the letter I'd stolen from Dalton Sass. His trump card to stay in Bertie's circle.

I told Harriet once: letters were material evidence that could be used against you. They revealed your darkest secrets. This letter seemed to be from a journal. I remembered the yellow tint of Sass's papers. The width and length of the size. She'd used her journal as a weapon against me multiple times, after all, slapping me with it across the face when I didn't answer her quickly enough. This was a page from her journal. One Dalton must have pocketed before darkening the shores of England.

Rui read it.

January 1, 1855

Even in the New Year those children are still as miserable as I left them, whining about seeing their parents for those who still had them. And worst of all, yet again, was the girl, Sarah Forbes Bonetta. I see nothing but Satan in that girl's beady black eyes. Pride and a pompous regality that doesn't fit her.

Today she asked me where I was born and then proceeded to talk about how she was a princess of the Egbado Clan. Royalty in her own right.

Something about her reminded me of the workhouse and I lost my senses. Worst still: she didn't cry when I slapped her in the face. It may seem cruel, but I wanted her to cry. And when she didn't, I felt the distinct weight of my own failures crushing me.

Did she think she better than me because she was now Queen Victoria's goddaughter? Did she not know that she easily could have been one of the children left behind?

Rui stopped reading and raised an eyebrow. "Children left behind?"

Pulling my knees up to my chin, I grunted. "Keep reading."

With a sigh, Rui obliged.

One of the Queen's courtiers let the secret slip in a letter to me last year. Lady Lena Login, whose husband was put in charge of rearing the Black Prince of Perthshire, the defeated Punjabi Maharaja, Duleep Singh. The Queen seemed to love finding new toys across the globe. She adored the gifts her captains gave her when they deposed of kings and conquered nations. She adored them more when they were children.

But only the good ones. The Queen couldn't be seen adopting a child who turned out to be a disobedient savage. There was another child who should have been presented to the Queen along with Duleep. He didn't arrive to England.

Duleep had passed the test to become one of the Queen's wards: the Wards of the Empire, as she liked the call them. The Good Children. Exotic and easily displayed. Those were the children that were to be brought to her. All others were to be discarded.

I wonder what that pompous little girl Sally would say if she knew? For every chosen child, there's a child thrown away.

If only the Queen had known what a monster it was that she'd taken as her royal pet.

"It would have made my life so much easier," I finished, because by now I'd memorized the journal entry.

Silence stretched between us as Rui lowered the blood-soaked letter. "Sally . . . what is this?"

"Confirmation," I said, standing up. "That Ade's death wasn't just an act of cruelty perpetrated by the Forbes brothers. That his death was the result of an informally institutionalized policy that came directly from the Queen herself. And that as a consequence of this policy that organized the Queen's toys in a neat little row for her, Ade wasn't the only one who died."

Rui stared at the letter again, reading it over. I clenched my teeth. This was what Dalton meant by the Wards of the Empire. And he was shot dead before he could breathe another word. The second he mentioned it, Queen Victoria whispered something to her dog, John Brown, and that was the end of Sass's wayward son. It couldn't have been a coincidence.

"I want to publish this in a newspaper. The *Illustrated London News*, perhaps, in exchange for a full exposé on how I got rid of their former editor, Mr. Bellamy."

"Sally," Rui started, but I wasn't listening. I'd begun pacing in this tiny stone room.

"Or I could blackmail George Reynolds. I already did my research on the editor of the *Reynolds Weekly Newspaper*. He'll pay me back for the gift of scandal I gave him at the beginning of last month."

"Sally!"

Rui gripped my arm and pulled me toward him. That was my cue to suck in a deep breath, but it hardly calmed me down.

"How do you know Dalton didn't write this himself?"

"I was her student. I know Miss Sass's handwriting as surely as I know my own. It's the genuine item."

Genuine. Which meant that Miss Sass truly did write these things. And why would she write them unless they were true?

Wards of the Empire. Was that what the Queen considered us? Me? Duleep? Gowramma? And others, no doubt, in the future? Children from all corners of the world who fascinated Queen Victoria as her bottom grew fat on taxes and stolen resources from her colonies. As she paid mediums for silly séances and ate seven-course meals without ever leaving the comfort of her many estates paid for by my people's blood.

Rui gripped my cheeks softly, drawing me back to reality. "Sally," he said with the sternness of a man used to the world of crime. "This is a journal entry. It's not proof. Even if you recognize this woman's handwriting, there's no definitive proof that others can point to as it being written by her. And even if it was, how do they know it wasn't just her mad ramblings? As far as the public is concerned, it can easily be dismissed as fiction."

"Then what do you suppose I do?" I gripped his hands, but didn't pull them away from my face. Angry tears brimmed in my eyes. I felt detached from my own body. Like my spirit and mind had been conjured by a madman or written in a children's tale. But they didn't exist. I didn't exist. Or rather, our existence didn't matter. Not mine. Not Ade's.

My body contracted, rigid in this room filled with slabs of meat. Because that's all we were to her. Slabs of meat. A corpse sinking to the bottom of the Atlantic Ocean. Oh, Ade. I'd never felt so stripped of my humanity.

It was insane. That the Queen would allow for the culling of children as if we were cattle, all for her own image's sake. But was it really out of the realm of possibility for her to do? There was an enslaved African man in America who once started a revolution that could have freed his people. Nat Turner. And in response to his bid for freedom, what did the slavers do? Execute him and use his skin to make a coin purse. Not satisfied with that, they boiled his flesh into grease to be consumed as medicine.

The world created by Queen Victoria and her ancestors allowed for monstrosities such as this. Cannibalism was only an atrocity when we were imagined to be the cannibals. Were a few discarded children really out of the realm of possibility for the Queen of an Empire of Ruin? No. Not when I'd seen it with my own eyes.

How many others? How many others died like Ade? I couldn't stop myself. The tears slipped down my cheeks one by one.

Rui brushed them with the back of his hand. "Sally, we need

something more concrete. Something written to the Queen—or better yet, by the Queen's hand."

"The Queen is going to Balmoral tomorrow with John Brown and her attendants."

At the sound of the man's name, Rui's touch suddenly was not so gentle. He withdrew it, clenching his fingers.

"Have your friend search the palace in the meantime. I'll do what I can."

"I don't understand." I wiped the remaining tears in my eyes, shaking my head. "What did we ever do . . . ?"

All of us children. Ade and Gowramma and Duleep. I'm sure there would be more taken from their lands, cut off from their communities. What kind of special property did we have that made us so ripe for collecting like jewels of an ancient tribe?

Rui gripped my shoulders and forced me to look at him. He leaned in close, so close I could smell the faint spice on his breath. And he smiled.

"Well, dear Sally," he said. "That's what revenge is for."

After my last standoff with the Queen, I found it in the best interest of my sanity to stay clear of the palace. Even with the Queen off to Balmoral with Ponsonby, John Brown, and her attendants, I couldn't bring myself to return. Harriet stayed behind. She was to join them with Mrs. Phipps in a few days.

"Harriet," I told her, meeting her at a café on Change Alley. "I need you to search the Queen's correspondences for anything concerning me, Victoria, Gowramma, and other, shall we say, exotic wards."

"That'll take a long time. . . ." She clasped her glass of water, her eyebrows raised.

"You have a few days before meeting the Queen's party in Scotland, correct?" I thought for a moment. "Start with old correspondences

Queen Victoria had with Captain Frederick Forbes and his brother George. James Stuart Fraser as well." The man who brought Gowramma to England after disposing of the Coorg ruler. "John Login as well." He cared for Duleep Singh after he was overthrown by the British after the second Anglo-Sikh war. "Especially the letters dated in the late forties and fifties. That might narrow things down."

Harriet huffed, exasperated. "You ask so much of me," she muttered. "And what is this for? This doesn't seem to have anything to do with your revenge."

"This has everything to do with my revenge."

I didn't know I'd yelled it, not until I realized I was on my feet. People were staring. I had to calm down. Who knew how the passersby would interpret this, with me, a furious Black woman, frightening a young English lady who looked as if she wouldn't hurt a fly. These were the ridiculous hoops I'd had to jump through since being dragged across the Atlantic against my will.

With a sigh, I sat back down, not at all surprised to see Harriet grimace, scandalized and disturbed. "I'm sorry," I said, and tried very hard to mean it, but some gentlemen were still staring at me from across the street. Chatting and staring. Like they all did in Britain. At me. The fate I was resigned to because of their queen. Anger bubbled up inside me again and I wanted to lash out at something. I couldn't hide it, not even if Harriet sat back in her white chair across from me to create distance between us.

"I'm sorry," I said again roughly. "But I need your help. I can't go back to the castle, not now." I straightened up in my chair. "Besides, you wanted to be a part of this. When I came to you, you said you'd do anything your mother wouldn't approve of."

"I know. I *know*." Her shoulders slumped. I watched my once-faithful henchman deflate before my eyes.

"Please just . . . just do this for me. Okay?" I leaned over, closing the distance between us. "It's so incredibly important. I'm so close to finding the truth. . . ."

Taking her hand, I gave it a warm squeeze. But, to my surprise, she pulled it away.

"Fine. But I want you to promise me something."

"Oh?" I placed both my hands on my lap. "And what's that?"

"Tell me the gossip around the castle isn't true," she said quietly, unable to meet my eyes. "You're not actually . . . with Prince Bertie, are you?"

I frowned, watching the girl stew quietly in her seat. "What? Harriet—"

That's when she looked at me. She was serious. About Bertie? It couldn't be. Harriet had never shown any romantic inclination toward him before.

"I've heard some strange rumors, Sally," she continued. "That the prince is thinking of calling off his engagement to be with you."

My shoulders rose to my ears but I did my best to keep silent. The night Dalton Sass was killed, Bertie had kissed me in front of so many attendants, it would have been impossible to keep it under wraps.

"Don't worry about him. Trust me when I say that boy is incapable of love. And as for me, I don't have romantic feelings one way or another for anyone. Not even my own husband-to-be."

I smirked as I thought of Captain Davies. He was right about the barbarity of the Crown. I wonder what he'd do if he knew just how right he was. Would it stop him from demanding his bride? Or would it make him even more determined to whisk me away from this evil land?

No matter how hard we tried to assimilate, we would never be truly wanted. He must have known that.

Rui did. I thought of him, my heart beating ever faster. And I'd just told Harriet I didn't have romantic feelings for anyone. But what's one more lie?

"Harriet, why would something so silly matter to you in the first place?" I asked her as she breathed a sigh of relief.

She scrunched up her nose and turned away. "It's not silly. I agree with you on many things, Sally. I've enjoyed wreaking havoc on my mother's friends. But there are some rules—" She paused and swallowed carefully. "Not all of this is 'silly,' you know. Not to me."

Perhaps she did love him. Well, if that was the case, then she could have at it once I was finished with him. When he was king, he was sure to have more mistresses than issues with his poor future wife. She could be one of them, if she so chose.

"It's ridiculous, Harriet. Just forget such things." I dismissed it all with a wave of my hand. "You know how he is. He'll be onto some cabaret dancer or an opera singer after he's done with his little infatuation."

"That even the Prince of England himself would be infatuated with you in the first place."

I blinked, not quite sure what I'd heard. "Excuse me?"

Harriet stood. "Never mind. I'll look. I'll scour the palace. Then I'm taking a break from all this."

My fingers twitched. "Of course!" I took my teacup and sipped. "Absolutely. I won't ask anything of you again, I promise. You've been wonderful, Harriet. A real friend in all this."

"Friend." Harriet rolled the word over her tongue and fell silent. I watched her carefully and studied everything. Every twitch of her nose. Every direction her gaze turned in order to avoid me.

"Goodbye, Sally," she said.

"Until next time, friend." I said it again, as if to remind her. She did not respond.

I watched Harriet's back as she walked away. When I was first taken

341

to England, I steadfastly refused to make any true friends. A friend was too troublesome a thing. Loneliness made brooding far easier. Even during my time at Freetown, I found it difficult to relate to any of the other children. Innocent as they were, they felt wholly separate from me, like they were from another earth where children could learn to forgive and adapt even in the face of the harshest realities. Love is conditional. Ade had taught me this and I'd kept this lesson in my heart.

I remembered his lesson now. And as I did, my heart curiously sank into the depths.

Loneliness was easy. But it was unbearable.

Perhaps I didn't have the right to expect anything out of Harriet.

But it was unbearable nonetheless. It followed me home, that loneliness. It embraced me in the middle of the night as I slouched on the front steps of my house in Chatham. Not even when Mama wrapped a shawl over my shoulders and sat next to me did it lose its grip.

"The stars are beautiful tonight," Mama said, looking up at the night sky. "You know, I got a visit from Lord Ponsonby the other day. I wonder if they're worried about your upcoming marriage? I told them they needn't be. You're a good girl, Sally."

I didn't confront her about leaking information about me to the Queen. What would be the point? She hadn't done it to hurt me. How could she? She didn't understand the grave context of my situation with the Queen. She didn't know what I knew. How happy she was to be friend to the Queen of England.

"You'll be happy, Sally, once you're married." She rubbed the back of my neck outside this empty house that hadn't seen her evangelizing husband for the past few weeks. "You'll see."

The roses we had planted just the other day were already starting to wilt despite Mama's daily care. I buried my face in my hands, still shivering in the cold.

♠ ♠ ♠

The next few days that passed, I felt the sword of Damocles dangling over my head, lowering inch by murderous inch. Under the pretense of checking on Mrs. Forbes after Uncle George's regrettable fate, I searched through boxes of letters in every room in the Forbes estate. The Wards of the Empire were never once mentioned. There was nothing to even suggest that the Queen had given her horrid instructions on what kind of children she sought or what fate she'd condemned them to should they not meet her high expectations. The only letters that referenced me were that of Captain Frederick Forbes gushing over my intelligence.

For her age, supposed to be eight years, she is a perfect genius; she now speaks English well, and has a great talent for music. She has won the affections, with but few exceptions, of all those who have known her, by her docile and amiable conduct, which nothing can exceed.

I'd read these words before. In the context of what I now knew, I shivered more deeply than I thought I ever could.

Ade was right about their love. He died never knowing how truly right he was.

Still, this wasn't enough to accuse the Queen. I needed something more concrete.

By Monday, Harriet had found nothing, as I expected. Which was why I'd already put Bertie on the task of searching through the Queen's correspondence as well, just in case Harriet's newfound apathy caused her to miss something important. But he didn't find anything either. The Queen was very "clean" about things. Of course she was. She wasn't one to get her hands dirty, not unless she slipped up by mistake.

But everyone made mistakes. Even a Queen.

Monday night I made good on my unspoken promise to see

Gowramma and Edith again. As I played with the child in Gowramma's extravagantly furnished parlor, I readied myself for any questions the girl had. And she had them.

"What did the Queen want from you the other time?" she asked me while brushing her hair with her fingers, staring into a hand mirror.

I lifted the pudgy little baby up high in the air, terrified she might throw up on me. Wasn't that what these things did? "She thought I was at fault for Bertie's failure of a speech on Friday."

"Well, weren't you?"

I nearly dropped Edith. Instead, I placed her safely onto my lap and stared at Gowramma.

"What?" she said, lowering her mirror. "You think I'm stupid? All the chaos around you lately so carefully planned. Your uncle being committed, Bambridge and McCoskry's disgrace all in a few short weeks. If I didn't know any better, I'd say you were behind it all."

Sucking in a breath, I gave her a sidelong look. Gowramma was already pouring herself a glass of chardonnay. "And what if I told you I did have something to do with these things?"

Gowramma laughed so loudly it shocked poor Edith. As the baby began to cry her mother picked up her wineglass. "Then I say keep going. Serves them all right, the dolts."

I bounced Edith on my knee because I couldn't figure else how else to stop her from crying. But as Gowramma gulped down her chardonnay, I quietly remembered the hollow look in her eyes in the gala as she stared at the photographic portrait of herself. How she'd walked, afterward, as if she'd slightly lost her balance. I remembered this and took a chance.

"Have you ever heard of the term *Ward of the Empire* before? Perhaps in relation to your adoption by the Queen? And perhaps . . ." I considered it. "Perhaps in any conversations you might have had with Duleep Singh? You two were betrothed at one point, weren't you?"

Gowramma put her glass down and blinked. "Ward . . ." She stayed quiet for a long time. It was the first time I'd seen her look so serious. She rubbed her lips with a finger and stared at the framed photograph of herself and her elderly husband.

"When I was seventeen," Gowramma began, "a woman named Lady Login did indeed try to force my marriage to Duleep. I refused, of course. What fool would let herself be married to a man of someone else's choosing, especially some out-of-touch old crone?"

She stopped and gritted her teeth sheepishly, covering her mouth as I shifted bitterly on her Persian love seat.

"Anyways," she continued, "I set up a meeting with Duleep myself to speak to him about the whole affair. We were in agreement—neither of us wanted to marry each other. But he did say something quite interesting."

"What?" I said, holding Edith close to my chest, patting her on the back while she sucked back her tears. "What did he say to you?"

"He told me that Queen Victoria would love to play matchmaker between her favorite *wards*. Surely we wouldn't be the last either. But knowing what it meant to be a ward, he was steadfastly against it. He called it his defiance. He didn't want the Queen to have her way. . . ."

Duleep . . . did he know about this whole evil affair? I was holding Edith a little too tightly. When she began to squirm in my grip, I handed her to her mother, who regrettably had to put down her alcohol.

"When I asked him to explain himself, he only said that he'd written the Queen so many letters about it from Mulgrave Castle. But he never had the courage to send them."

Mulgrave Castle: an ancient castle built centuries ago near Whitby in North Yorkshire. Duleep had indeed lived there for a time.

Gowramma leaned in next to me with a conspiratorial grin. "He's still renting the castle. We're good friends, you know. I think he's in Scotland visiting his mother. A letter from me, and I'm sure he'd give us the keys." She winked. "Wanna go?"

"You're rather keen to." I tilted my head. "Make no mistake. This isn't a vacation."

She shrugged. "It is to me. Goodness knows I need to get out of the house."

I watched her pat her child on the head curiously.

"What do you think of all this? You don't care? About any of it?"

"You mean I'm not crippled by my hatred for the English? Why? Despite a few indignities I've had to suffer, I have everything I need here." She brought her daughter up to her face and nuzzled their noses together.

"And it is worth the indignities?"

Gowramma didn't answer. Not everyone was ready to unpack this horrid institution. For some, it was easier not to. But wherever she was, Gowramma enjoyed a good mess. That alone was beneficial to me.

Since it brought me one step closer to the Queen's ruin.

THIRTY-ONE

I SENT A letter to Bertie writing only that I wished to placate the Queen about our relationship and clear up any confusion that Bertie himself may hold. We were to meet at Marlborough House, near St. James's Palace. It would soon be his main residence with Alexandra of Denmark, but for now, he was free to use it as he pleased. And he did. He'd thrown many parties in his home away from home. Brought many an actress and dancing girl. Now I was to be next.

I'd been in this drawing room before, the night I met and danced with Dalton Sass, though I had no clue what horrors he would bring into my life. I had not, however, been on this love seat. Usually this was reserved for Bertie's girls. And because that was the role I was to play, I sat down and waited for him to arrive.

The moment he blew through the door, he plunked himself onto the velvet seat and kissed me. I let him. No, I matched his hunger. It was everything he wanted.

"I knew you liked me better than him," Bertie said, coming up for air from kissing my neck, his shirt discarded on the carpeted floor.

"Who?" I lay back on the red love seat, my dress remaining steadfastly on because I wasn't nearly as interested in this romantic rendezvous as he was.

"Captain Davies."

The moment he tried to climb upon me, I pushed him away from me and sat up on the couch. Everything in me told me I should be feeling guilty. That I should be ashamed of myself, betraying a good man who was to be my husband. That was the Institution's instruction, no doubt. The lies they told girls to accept their terrible fates, at the core of which was the lie that they had no control over their fate. I knew I was programmed to feel this guilt. That I chose nothing about this marriage, but I felt it anyway.

"Captain Davies is not a bad man. He's intelligent and wise."

And perhaps still heartbroken over the loss of his first love. He was my kin. But sometimes that wasn't enough. He needed to know: he wasn't owed my love or trust because of kinship alone.

"He's too old for you." Bertie stood up, annoyed, snatching his shirt off the floor.

He wasn't wrong. Still, I didn't want to hear that from an ignorant, foolish, childish, self-absorbed . . .

I sucked in my breath. Stick to the plan. "Forget about all that." I gave him a smile. "I have a proposition for you. How about we take a little romantic trip? Secret, away from everyone. Mulgrave Castle. Singh gave me the go-ahead."

Bertie mulled it over. My wedding was fast approaching. I only had a few days to expose Queen Victoria for the monster she truly was. I didn't have time for him to "mull it over."

But soon, he broke into a lecherous grin. "All right." He leaned over and lifted my chin. "I'd be delighted to. If it would make my mother furious, I'd be down for anything."

That's what it came down to. He had his reasons. But I had mine.

We were off to Mulgrave Castle the very next morning. It was a long journey by carriage. And when we finally arrived, I looked upon the great estate with awe. This Mulgrave Castle, the one Duleep had leased, was a country house constructed on the same grounds by the order of James II's illegitimate daughter. A duchess, apparently. I couldn't keep track of these entangled, circular royal family trees.

The fog hanging over the white three-story mansion was more unforgiving than it was the day of the hunt. A shame for Bertie, because with the green slopes and thick woods it was the perfect place for shooting.

"We'll have to find other ways to occupy our time," Bertie said, giving me a kiss on the cheek before helping me out of the carriage.

The mansion did feel reminiscent of the days of the Normans with its white watchtowers straight out of the medieval era. It made the rest of the house—a normal, bricked country estate with stretched, tiered windows—feel somehow out of time. What mattered was not style but pedigree. And pedigree was exactly why Harriet had decided to join Bertie and me on our "romantic" excursion. Her carriage stopped just behind ours on the three-forked cobbled road leading up to the front staircase. She stepped out with her shawl in the cold, her head lifted high.

"I'm still not sure why she had to come with us," Bertie said without an inch of self-restraint as he patted our carriage horse. The driver had run to bring our bags.

"This is my ancestral family home," Harriet shot back because she'd heard Bertie. Of course she'd heard. Bertie wasn't trying to be discreet and couldn't be if he tried. "Your *friend* Duleep is only leasing it. This mansion has been in my family since the beginning of the eighteenth century. That's over a hundred and fifty—"

"Yes, yes, your family lineage is quite impressive; I'm sure you're very proud. Your mother certainly is." Bertie waved her off and ascended the steps to the front door.

Harriet was glaring at me when Gowramma stepped out of her

carriage. By the time the latter had paid the drivers, Harriet was already striding past me through the arched wooden entrance. The door slammed shut.

Gowramma and I stared through the windows.

"She seems angry at you, you know," Gowramma whispered to me as we tried to peer through the same window.

I sighed. "She does indeed."

"She was supposed to go to Balmoral. It's like she came here as a challenge—to you."

"Very obviously."

"Do you know why?"

I thought back to her mother humiliating her during the séance. Her frustration ran deep. It was more multifaceted than that of a daughter being crippled under the weight of her lineage and her overbearing parents. But that, perhaps, was the seed from which everything else sprouted. At any rate, I would get to the bottom of her malice later. Now it was time to investigate.

"Bertie will probably try to keep me occupied, so do as much searching as you can on your own when you have time by yourself," I told her.

"How exciting!" Gowramma scrunched up her nose before entering the castle.

The castle was unlocked without Duleep's permission. Nobody knew that but me and the men awkwardly stuffed into servant tuxedos in the foyer. Six in all, the three stood waiting for us under the bright, twinkling chandeliers, their black heels clicking on the wooden floors as they got to work taking our belongings up the winding stairs to our rooms.

They didn't move like servants. They certainly didn't look like them, with their clothes, gloves, and top hats covering their scars. They didn't speak like servants either.

"Take your bag, ma'am," whispered one in a heavy Cockney accent. He lifted his head and tipped up his hat just enough for me to see the scar engraved over his left eye: the crossing, curved lines of Rui's "chi" symbol. I smirked. So thorough, that boy.

"I'd love to search the mansion," Gowramma said, spinning around where she stood, her eyes up at the stone ceiling as if she were in a fairy tale. "The place looks marvelous."

"As long as you don't go near the kitchen, ma'am," the "servant" said. "There's a bit of a rat problem, but we're taking care of it, though."

Gowramma's spinning came to a stop. She scrunched her nose in disgust. "How crude. Well, as long as I don't taste rat in the food, I suppose I'll be all right."

"Will you be staying long, then?" the scarred man asked.

"No," I told him. "I'll get what I came for soon enough. Until then, I trust you'll make sure nobody disturbs us here."

"No unwanted visitors. We guarantee it." Rui's man winked and disappeared with our bags. How Rui had snuck his men inside Mulgrave Castle—how he even knew about my trip to Mulgrave Castle—I had no idea. But it somehow comforted me to know I had their backup.

"And what is it that you came for?" Harriet placed her hands on her hips at the open entrance of the parlor room opposite the mahogany stairs. "And why would you choose my family's home to do it?"

Harriet let out a little frightened gasp as Bertie hooked his arm around her neck playfully.

"You're not going to be like this the whole trip, are you? Because then otherwise, you're welcome to . . . how shall I say this . . . piss off to Balmoral, where our mothers are surely waiting. I'm sure my mother in particular would appreciate you waiting on her hand and foot when Mr. Brown isn't around."

Harriet's cheeks flushed as Bertie clapped her on the shoulder and began exploring the mansion. With downturned eyes, she pressed her lips together.

"This is *my* family home," she whispered before running up the stairs.

I watched her go. I hated that I felt disappointed. I'd only ever considered Harriet as an ally. How foolish of me to believe she'd remain that way.

Her mother was a terrible wretch and she was under enormous pressure. Perhaps that's all this little tantrum was. I hoped so. There were so few people I could count on in this war.

Whatever the case was, I had to reach out to her fast.

Before she ruined everything—including our friendship—to the point of no return.

The chance came at dinner. I wasn't aware that Rui's men could cook. That was them, I gathered, inside the kitchen. I could see no ordinary servants around. But if Rui had the time and resources to spare a few of his men and send them here, he should have sent the ones with talent in cuisine. They brought out into the grand dining room an interesting assortment of overcooked chicken, soup with chunks of something in it, and slightly stale bread.

"I thought Duleep would have paid for better chefs than this," Bertie muttered as the plates came down underneath his nose upon the white tablecloth.

"We do have profiteroles for dessert, sir," said one man with a burn mark on his cheek, hastily but not perfectly covered with women's makeup. "And plenty of wine."

"Then we're set!" Gowramma clapped her hands together and immediately ordered a bottle to be brought with a plate of treats.

All the while, Harriet poked at her chicken. We ate mostly in silence, listening to Bertie prattle on about his mother. He and Gowramma were enough entertainment for the evening.

Bertie set down his wineglass and stretched his arms. "I'd better drink all I can get here. I'm sure my mother will expect me in Balmoral soon enough. The sight of her with that Scot makes me want to—" And he gave a very gentlemanly reenactment of tossing one's guts all over the floor. Gowramma giggled at the sight of my eyes rolling to the back of my head.

Bertie then turned to me and caressed my cheek with the back of his finger. "We need to make the best of this moment, Sally. It won't be long before the two of us are tied to our 'significant others.' Might as well have a little fun before then."

"Adultery and affairs." Harriet folded her arms over her white blouse, one of the nicest she had. Usually Harriet didn't much care about her clothes. Her mother dressed her for events, though she would never admit it to anyone. "You seem quite blatant about it."

Bertie rested his arm across the back of my chair. "And what do you mean by that?"

Harriet struggled with her words. "You're just so . . . strange. Adultery is nothing to flaunt, especially with—" She paused and quickly looked at me before downing more of her wine.

"Especially with what?" I leaned over, my elbows on the table. Terrible manners, which I made a point to throw away in front of her. On the other side of the table, Harriet trembled a little when I closed the distance between us. "What exactly has been bothering you, Harriet?"

I knew Harriet would crumble when put on the spot. Gowramma

watched too as the girl's fingers twitched upon her wineglass.

"Mother always talks so highly of you, Sally. But it's not what you think. It's not because she likes you, you know."

I tilted my head. "I'm quite aware of that."

My serenity bothered Harriet even more. She straightened up. "It's because everyone always talks about how ladylike and genius you are."

"And for some time you've been among them." I shrugged and sat back in my seat. "In fact, you've been one of my biggest flatterers over the years."

"Yes, but!—" Harriet's face flushed. She opened and closed her mouth several times, but only unfinished sounds managed to slip out. "How can you be here cheating on your husband with the Prince of Wales?"

Bertie shrugged too. "They're not married yet."

"It's all so!—" Harriet shook her head. "It's all so . . ."

Harriet fell silent.

"I've got it!" Gowramma raised her glass and pointed it accusatorily at Harriet. "I've figured it out. You're in love with Sally, aren't you? Admit it!"

"What?" Harriet's expression contorted into fury.

"Gowramma," I said with a stern note of finality, and immediately the woman backed down. She'd caught the sight of my unimpressed frown. If it was true that Harriet had any kind of romantic interest in me, to expose her in front of a crowd was cruel. But I knew that wasn't the case. It was hard to admit, because Harriet had been such a helpful part of my journey of revenge, my journey toward some kind of solace. But deep down, I'd long known what the problem was. . . . I'd known this would happen.

"Sarah Forbes Bonetta is so brilliant, so formidable, so genius and beautiful that even I can't resist her charms. Is that what you're saying?" Harriet stood out of her chair, gripping her blue silk skirt. "But of course," she smirked, "why wouldn't I fall for her? Even the prince has."

I never saw jealousy as an immoral trait, not the way they taught me in the Institution. According to Miss Sass, the missionaries and their teaching, women especially were made less desirable the moment they displayed anything other than piety and innocence. Jealousy was seen as an aberration. To me, it wasn't. It was a normal emotion like all else. But there were some issues that complicated the matter, turning it into something truly ugly.

"So you're in love with . . . Bertie?" Gowramma frowned, perplexed and a bit disgusted.

Bertie glared at her. "It's not that unbelievable."

"I'm not!" Harriet slammed her hands against the table. "Of course not. Ugh."

Bertie seethed in his chair. "It really is not *that* unbelievable," he muttered, taking a gulp of wine.

"I'm not," Harriet repeated again, "but good God, Bertie, how can you fall in love with a Negro girl?"

And there it was. In her confession I heard Harriet's mother telling Harriet she was a blight on the family name—a fact made more shameful because of how she seemed outmatched in every way by the Queen's adopted African goddaughter, someone who by her account was more beast than woman. Harriet admired me to a point. But that admiration, that awe was always haunted by disbelief and confusion. At some point, between her society's teachings and her mother's hatred, that admiration was always going to tip into envy and bitterness.

"Okay, this has gotten very awkward, very quickly." Bertie stood from his chair. "Sally, come join me in my bedchambers when you're done with . . . this." He waved his hand dismissively, patted me on the back, and walked out of the room, taking a bottle of wine and a half-eaten profiterole with him.

It was only the three of us left in the dining hall. I said nothing. I only looked at her. Not hurt. Not disappointed. Well, perhaps a little. Not surprised. At all.

But golden-framed portraits of the Phipps family were staring down at Harriet. Her parents. Her ancestors. Each stern face hung on the mahogany walls. Lady Catherine Sedley, Countess of Dorchester, with her plain face and curly brown hair, seemed the most ashamed of her descendant. "Even someone as unremarkable as I was able to attract a King of England. Yet you're left in the shadow of a former slave writing letters of her brilliance," she seemed to say. Harriet dropped down into her chair, defeated.

"I told you." Gowramma pointed at Harriet with her wineglass before taking a sip. "They really can't stand us unless we're at their feet. When the pressure's on, the truth comes out."

"And what will you do now?" I asked Harriet, my tone neutral, my body relaxed as I lay back in my chair. "Where does this leave us?"

Harriet stared at the white tablecloth—its brilliant gold embroidery around the edges. "I don't know," she answered finally.

"Will you betray me?"

Harriet's head snapped up. "No, I—!" She swallowed her words, looking between Gowramma and me, then at the portraits on the walls. She lowered her head. "I've always been such a failure. To everyone. None of this should surprise you."

"But I am surprised, Harriet," I whispered. "For I thought we were, at least, friends."

Tears prickled Harriet's eyes. "I'll take my leave," she whispered, and left the table. "Have a carriage prepared for me immediately," she shouted at the doorman as she marched out of the dining hall. Off to Balmoral, then. Would she betray me to the Queen? Or would she keep her mouth shut?

Either way, I had to be prepared.

"Sorry about all that," said Gowramma, taking another sip of wine.

"Me too."

And I meant it.

THIRTY-TWO

IT WAS IN the dead of night when Gowramma beckoned me into the basement wine cellar. There she'd found a small box of letters tucked behind a shelf of merlot. I kicked away the piles of hay and searched through each one with her.

It was Gowramma who found the letter.

The Queen's letter.

October 22, 1855

Your accusations wound me deeply, Duleep. And it is not one that should be made by such a young boy of 17. I've invited you into my royal home. I let you play with my children in Osborne. Oh, how Bertie loved playing with you. How he lit up with mirth while photographing you in your regalia. Oh, how much fun it was to draw your likeness with my own hands—a sketch, you told me, you loved.

It is my understanding that you are staying in Perthshire. Remember that it is because of me that you've been given your annual pension—more than most men and women in Britain will ever see in their lives—so to speak so ill of me is as distressing as it is shocking.

Do not speak of the past. I've spoken many words to my captains as they search the far-flung regions of the world for treasures to bring back to me. What Sir John Login told you was only half the story. The "Wards of the Empire." I say these words because a line must be drawn. There are children who possess the potential to lead the empire into a new stage of enlightenment. On the other hand, there are those who would only validate the closed-minded fools in the world who believed that the Indian and the African and the Native can only remain savages. Look at yourself. Since you've converted to Christianity your world has expanded. You've toured the European continent. You've become a member of societies and organizations of the most upright nature. You are an example of Britain's civilizing mission. Proof of my and Albert's grand cause during such a time when the evil tentacles of slavery still runs amok, choking out our civilization's future.

And what would have happened if that boy Aarush would have arrived in England with you? If he would have been presented to me in court alongside you? With his reportedly boorish ways and uncivil manners, he would have only proven those right who insist that the savage is but a brute that cannot change. That the Black cannot be assimilated. At such a delicate moment, such a mistake cannot be made. The East India Company has been given its orders to find the proper children. Those that are discarded are but a sacrifice for the future.

Your presence in Europe, your fame among my people, stands as a beacon of hope for all of your kind around the world. Your existence is the path towards civilization. And I support you wholeheartedly as much as I love you. Never forget that.

The continuance of your pension is also dependent upon your enduring obedience to the British Government. Please do not forget that either.

I write this letter in person as your Queen and friend because I trust in your loyalty. Nothing written here needs ever be spoken to anyone else. You are, as always, my precious Duleep.

Victoria

"It's the genuine item," Gowramma said. "It's signed by the Queen. . . . It has her seal."

Because she truly believed in it. In her power. In Duleep's fear. In her propaganda. In his obedience. Without a word, I took the letter from Gowramma, and folded and tucked it into my dress.

"I never knew . . . I never thought . . ." Gowramma was, for the first time since I'd known her, without words. Silence hung in the air before she could speak again. "My father had capitulated to the British. As a child, to me, it had always seemed so . . . *un*-coerced. But what if I was wrong?" She pressed her trembling hand against her chest. "What if my father knew this fear too? What if he understood just how horrible it is?"

I closed the box, stood from the pile of hay, brushed my knees, and began to leave.

"This doesn't change anything," Gowramma whispered. "I'm here now. I have Edith to think about. I can't make a fuss. If I do . . ."

I heard echoes of Ade's fear in her weak admission: *I'm scared*, he'd told me. Because he knew. He'd warned me before. Their love was conditional.

It was clear, from her fidgeting, and the droop of her expression, that the revelations had left her disturbed. How did one find the words to respond to such cruelty?

Gowramma shook her head. "I want Edith," she whispered suddenly. She wrapped her arms around herself. "Sally, I'm going home. Tonight."

"You do what you need to," I told her.

She recoiled. My words had stung her, but she didn't respond.

As for what she needed—that was something she had to find out for herself. Only deep searching within her soul would tell her the answer. I gave her the firmest hug I could manage. I clung to her almost as if I'd lose her if I'd let her go.

"Just don't lose yourself in all this," Gowramma said before scurrying out of the cellar.

I stood alone with rage in my heart. The kind of rage that made one want to laugh and cry all at once. I laughed first. The hair on my arms stood on end as my cackling echoed off the walls. My body shook as I thought of how frightened Ade must have been, up against two adults carrying him like a log of wood. How sharply cold the water of the Atlantic would have been that night or any night. How I would never see him again.

"It isn't right," I whispered.

I crumpled to the ground and cried.

Island of Gorée – 1850

I didn't know why Captain Forbes had us stop here. I'd heard such terrible things about this island listening to the men on the ship. All the people who'd been brought here in chains over the many long, torturous centuries. The human feces built up in the horrid slave quarters while their traders from Europe dined in mansions. So much misery. It made me want to cry thinking about it. Why did we stop here? We were on our way to England, weren't we?

"They won't even let us off the ship," Ade said as he lay on the flea-ridden blanket that had been placed on the floor for both of us to sleep. "Or out of this room. I heard the crew say we were near Senegal. There must be something they want here."

The candle on the floor had long gone out and there was no one to help us light it again. We were alone in the dark.

We spent most of the days at sea in this tiny room on the HMS *Bonetta*. We were only let out for lessons—sometimes the Forbeses would let us stretch our legs, but we weren't to run on deck and bother the crew.

During our lessons, I would dazzle them by reading parts of English books. I read a page from a new book called *Jane Eyre* and it made Frederick Forbes applaud and clap his brother's shoulders. It was just one dense paragraph. Frederick had pointed it out to me and, though slowly, I formed the words perfectly with my little full lips. I read it exactly as it was written:

"It is far better to endure patiently a smart which nobody feels but yourself, than to commit a hasty action whose evil consequences will extend to all connected with you—and besides, the Bible bids us return good for evil."

"You see," Frederick had said once I was finished. "Look how smoothly she read the words. She'd be perfect for Her Majesty, wouldn't she, George?"

Uncle George laughed and nodded, and they patted each other on the back for a job well done. They'd found a very good girl. A "great girl" indeed, like Helen Burns, who took her "smarts" with the grace and piety expected of a proper woman-in-training.

But Ade. Ade wasn't so good at English. When he was given the same paragraph to read, he stumbled and quit before the second clause. He sneered at the language as if it were his enemy and he looked at me and said in ours, "What is this rubbish? It sounds so stupid."

I wasn't sure if Frederick Forbes could understand what he'd said, but the sneer he gave Ade made him look like a demon that day. I saw the blood drain from Ade's face right that moment, leaving a dull, ashy color. It was the color I saw now that he was lying on his blanket, curled up in the fetal position, his little head balanced upon his arms.

"I'm scared, Ina," he told me, dragging his knees closer to his chest.

"I overheard that man George say something terrible about me. That I could never 'make a good name for myself' in England. What do you think he meant?"

"I'm sure they just want us to live good lives in this new land." I sat next to him, my arms wrapped around my dry, scratchy knees. "Since we have no one now but each other, we have to work together to make sure we live well once we arrive."

"But will we arrive?"

My large eyes widened in confusion as I looked back at the boy. He was shaking. I hadn't noticed it until now, but my friend Ade was trembling on the blanket beside me.

"My father came to me in a dream, Ina," Ade whispered. "He was in a wooden boat about to leave the shore. I'd seen this dream many times after he was killed in the raid. Every time, before leaving across the ocean, he'd stretch his hand out to me and I'd say, 'No, Father, not yet.' He'd nod and leave without me." Ade erupted in a series of coughs. This wasn't anything out of the ordinary. He was a sickly boy. Had been even before we were taken by the Forbeses. "Every time he'd leave without me and I'd watch him sail off into the white skies. But not this time. This time, when he stretched out his hand to me . . . I took it. And I went with him."

My tiny body seized up in fear. I knew what it could mean, but I didn't want to admit it. Our parents, grandparents, our family and ancestors, even our enemies. Living or not, they often made guest appearances in our dreams, so it wasn't odd to see them. But one had to be very careful about the messages from the dead. One had to be very careful what you did when near those who'd already crossed over into the realm of spirits.

I felt suddenly cold. "Ade . . . ," I said, my bottom lip curling. The sheet I wore as a dress to cover myself scratched against my skin. I grabbed the fabric around my chest, bending over. "Why did you take his hand?"

He didn't answer. A heavy sense of foreboding weighed over us children. The silence of the ship pierced through my very spirit.

"I'm scared, Ina," he whispered again, suddenly in the dark. "I'm scared. I don't want to die."

But he did. Days, maybe weeks after we'd left the island, he went to see his father. Yes. That's what I told myself to cope in the days following his death, when my mind was broken and my eyes sore from crying. I told myself that sweet lie until I let the terrible truth dawn on me.

He was murdered.

Ade was a reminder of what it meant to be cruelly cast into the shadows. And the people in this country would never know him. To the Crown and its henchmen, his was a life without meaning. A lump of flesh that had breathed for only a moment. And few would never question why so many of my people had met the same fate.

No more did the screams of Mrs. Wilkes bother me. In fact, I laughed at her. My cackling echoed off the walls, my heartbeat raging in my chest as I ascended the steps with unearthly, ethereal grace. With the letter in my dress, I wandered like a ghost into Bertie's chambers. The Prince of Wales was downing another bottle of wine, stopping only when he saw me enter. I closed the door behind me without a word.

His reaction to the sight of me in silk was immediate—the tightening of his pants. I let the letter drop from my hands onto the floor as he wiped his mouth and struggled to strip himself. I didn't let him get too far before I climbed upon the bed, pushed him onto his back, and straddled him.

My touch was light at first. A caress up and down his Adam's apple, his stubble prickling my fingers. But as the rage and despair of memories

364

began to boil over, my fingers clenched, my grip stronger until his windpipe was at the mercy of it.

And then I began to strangle him.

Death couldn't be undone. Ade knew this. That's why he was so scared. And he never had a chance. Her child shouldn't have a chance either.

"Sally—" Bertie coughed. "Sally, what are you—?"

I shushed him and continued to squeeze, tears building in the corners of my eyes, Ade's death replaying again and again as if I were frozen in time, watching a cruel play. Bertie's hand gripped my wrists. Still, I didn't let go.

They'd broken the world, these monarchs of a ruined nation. I would end their line here.

Bertie's hands found my hips and dug into my skin. The tickle made me start just enough for him to free himself from my grip. For one confusing moment, terror paralyzed me. I'd just tried to murder the heir to the throne.

I'd failed.

My heart raced in my chest. Surely this was it. I'd be executed.

But then Prince Bertie was laughing. I watched him, baffled, my mind spinning, unable to form a coherent thought. He wasn't angry with me. Of course he wasn't. The bottle of booze on the table next to the bed was empty.

He flipped me over onto the bed and kissed me ravenously. I tried to resist, but his herculean grip kept me in place. He was too drunk to notice my grimace. Too cruel to care.

"Is that the sort of thing you like, Sally?" he asked with a lecherous grin. "Good. Good. I've done all kinds of naughty things too. I can teach you a few other tricks in the trade of pleasure."

He was slurring his words. And when I felt his tongue on my cheek, my body quivered in disgust. I wanted to knee him in the groin, but a terrifying thought paralyzed me: If I fought back, would he realize my hands squeezing his neck wasn't foreplay but attempted murder?

"What shall we start with?" He grinned, his eyes unfocused. "How about—"

A swift metal bang crackled through the air. I gasped for air as Bertie slid off me, his body bouncing off the white sheets.

I sat up, my fingers twitching. Bertie was unconscious. Rui stood over him at the side of the bed with a frying pan.

"R-Rui . . . !" I squirmed as slid off the bed, tears sliding down my cheeks as I ran to his side and hugged him.

"He must have liked my food a little too much." With one arm around my waist and another hand wrapped around the frying pan he'd used to cook our dinner, Rui looked down at the sleeping prince. "Hurry and strip his clothes."

I frowned up at him. "What?"

"Do it, quickly. Toss them around the floor. When he wakes up, he'll have a bump on his head to be sure, but he'll chalk it up to a rather kinky night."

Rui handled his britches. The tears fell freely as I took off his shirt. It was all I could stand to do before turning around and wiping my face dry.

I gathered up the letter I'd left on the floor. Someone had to be made to pay.

Even if I'd managed to kill the prince, it wouldn't be enough. His mother, his wicked mother, needed to suffer. But even that wouldn't fix this broken world.

Could anything?

With a soothing, gentle hand, Rui led me out of the prince's room. Harriet had left. Gowramma had retired to her room. Rui and I walked across Mulgrave Castle to an empty room where no one would disturb us.

"When my men learned you'd be coming here, I figured I should get here first to make sure everything went smoothly with the prince," Rui said, shutting the door behind us. "Who knew my instincts would be quite so astute?"

With his arms folded, he walked to the mauve-papered wall next to the window. The white drapes were closed. The candle flickering upon the desk illuminated the hardcovers of first editions stashed in the nearby bookcase.

Books.

I remembered one in particular as Rui leaned against the wall.

"If people were always kind and obedient to those who are cruel and unjust, the wicked people would have it all their own way." I sat on the green velvet sitting chair next to the cupboard cabinet. *"They would never feel afraid, and so they would never alter, but grow worse and worse."*

"*Jane Eyre*."

"So you've read it too?"

"I've read a few works by the Brontës. I wouldn't say any of it was impressive enough to memorize, but I'm sure you have your reasons."

I did have a reason: lack of choice, a constant in my miserable life. I turned the letter in my hands again and again.

"None of it is fair, Rui." I shook my head. "This world is so wicked."

"I learned that long ago." With delicate fingers, he nudged open the left drape. Starlight streamed through the window. "And when I learned that, I made a decision. If this world was wicked, then I'd get what I wanted out of it. So?" He dropped his hand, letting the drape flutter shut. "What do you want, Sally?"

I thought of Mama Schoen, completely oblivious to my suffering. Harriet, who finally showed her true face. I thought of Ade, whose bones must have been at the bottom of the ocean by now. I shuddered.

"I don't want to be alone," I whispered, shaking my head.

"That, you aren't."

Rui approached me step by gentle step, unhurried. And when he reached me, he took me by the hand, lifted me out of my seat, and wrapped his arms around me. There, he let me cry.

I didn't only cry for Ade. I cried for all the lost children—and all the children who would soon be lost because despite my play at revenge, I had no power of my own.

I lifted my chin just enough for Rui to catch my lips with his. It was a somber kiss. A tender one. So unlike our embrace in Bambridge's secret studio. It was the kiss of another lost child who understood.

But it wasn't enough for Rui. He pulled me away, taking in the sight of me.

"Are you finished, Sally?" he asked. "Is this how your tale of revenge ends?"

His question caught me by surprise. My fingers curled against his shoulder, the fabric of his white shirt caught in my nails. Over. Was it really over?

I turned and stared at my own reflection in the mirror tucked away in the corner of the room. My red eyes. Face puffy from crying. Was this how it would all end?

My blood began to boil as I thought of Queen Victoria enjoying herself at Balmoral. My fingers dug into Rui's flesh.

No. I'd said it before. Somebody had to be made to pay.

I'd said it before and I meant it.

Rui seemed to notice the change in me. "I told you, didn't I? If this world is wicked, then you simply have to get what you want out of it." He hungrily drank in the sight of me. "So what is it that you want, Sally?" The corner of his lips twitched into a deliciously malicious grin. "What have you decided?"

I stopped picturing Ade's corpse. I pictured him instead, standing by the window, a little wicked smile playing on his face.

My mind finally cleared. I pressed my hands against his chest. Rubbing my cheek against his, I let my lips touch his ears as I whispered another line from that silly book. *"When we are struck at without a reason, we should strike back again very hard—so hard as to teach the person who struck us never to do it again."*

I breathed, in and out, trying to catch my breath as if I'd run here. But I had been running. My whole life I'd been running from their foolish rules of morality, their hypocrisy. The cruel lessons they taught me to keep me bound and obedient.

I would never be obedient again. To anyone.

I would take what I wanted.

I grabbed Rui by the back of his hair and yanked his head so he could feel the pain. And then I leaned in and whispered, "Let's make them pay."

Rui grabbed me by the behind and carried me over to the bed. We fell deep into the soft red blankets. His hands wasted no time. Lifting me up by the small of my back, he kissed my neck from one ear to the next. His tongue found my chest, and then I felt his hands hot between my legs. I groaned as my sensitive flesh burned from the friction of his relentless touch.

"We will, Sally," he promised as he began to take off my dress. "We will make them all pay."

THIRTY-THREE

BERTIE WOKE UP naked. That, along with his nasty hangover, had convinced him that something wonderful must have happened last night. I let him believe what he wanted.

"Go ahead, dear." Standing outside the mansion in the cold morning, I kissed him on the cheek. The carriage had just rolled up to the stairs. "You have things to take care of in London. I'll stay here for a day more."

"You like this place, do you?" Bertie gave me a wink. "Or perhaps what you really like are the memories it now holds for you?"

He leaned in to kiss my lips, grunting in disappointment when I turned my head to the side just in time.

"Go ahead, Bertie. Gowramma will keep me company."

What he didn't know was that Gowramma had left last night.

"Don't lose yourself in all this." Gowramma's final words to me before she fled Mulgrave Castle.

I wouldn't lose myself. I'd done some soul searching of my own. I knew what I wanted. What I needed.

Once Gowramma and Bertie had gone, Rui and I had Mulgrave Castle to ourselves.

We lay in the bed, half-asleep and immobile, our bodies entangled in each other, prey to the chill in the room. I didn't let Rui leave. I wrapped my arms around his back and laid my head against the pillow. He nuzzled his nose in the crook of my neck, about to sleep.

"It was John Brown, wasn't it?" I whispered to him before dreams could take him. "He's the one behind your father's predicament."

Rui let out a surprised huff, hot against my neck. Not exactly what he was expecting to hear after a morning like this, but I needed to know. I figured by now the deal we'd struck in Strangers' Home no longer held. We were . . . closer now. With a little smile, he rolled over onto his back. He stayed there for a moment, still catching his breath, his eyes closed.

"He had accompanied the Queen's husband on some secret excursion through Whitechapel. In disguise, of course. Royals like to do that from time to time. A man attacked him at a pub and escaped. My father would never enter a pub. But he passed by one that night. He was in the wrong place at the wrong time. John Brown wrongfully accused him. Well, I guess he couldn't tell him and the attacker apart."

Rui opened his eyes, staring at the white ceiling. "My father was jailed for nothing."

"I suppose that's why you took your chance to kill John Brown at the séance."

Rui paused. He was choosing his words carefully, I could tell. "I didn't manage it," he whispered. "But I did manage to get rid of your problems."

"Wilkes and Sass."

He shrugged his shoulders. "Two birds. One stone."

"Except it was Queen Victoria who had Dalton Sass in the end."

Rui sat up and looked down on me, baffled, I suppose, by my pleasant, serene expression. "You're not angry with me?"

"Why should I be?" I scratched my head through my thick hair, now not so tidy. "You did get rid of my problems in one fell swoop. I thank you."

Next, Rui narrowed his eyes, studying me. "You're not conflicted."

"Not anymore." I turned and looked at Queen Victoria's letter, which I'd left on the brown ottoman next to the door. "Not anymore. No more guilt. No more apologies. I will not apologize when no one has ever apologized to me."

Rui lowered his head with a satisfied grin. "I think we finally understand each other, Sally."

"I think we do." I sat up and gave him a kiss, one he returned happily. But when he held my shoulders and gently pushed me away from him, I caught the hint of warning in his eyes.

"If you understand me, then you understand this: nothing matters to me more than punishing those responsible for my father's pain." He leaned in and, after kissing my ear, whispered, "I hope you understand that, Sally. I expect your full cooperation."

A warning. A threat perhaps. I didn't know. The very idea of either lit a fire inside me. My passion went beyond the pleasures of the flesh. What I'd always wanted—what I'd always needed—would soon come to fruition.

Ade and I were almost there. . . .

It was a busy few days in London after I left Mulgrave. First, I surprised George Reynolds, editor of the *Reynolds Weekly Newspaper*, at a gentlemen's club in the West End. He came there every Thursday night. I pulled him into a private room away from the cigar smoke and shoved the Queen's letter in his hands.

"I have your mistresses on standby, complete with birth records of your illegitimate children," I said, pressing him against the door as he read the Queen's letter in horror. I took it from him before he could tear it or tamper with it in any way, giving him the copy I'd perfectly created in its place. "I expect this letter to be published by the end of the week. Don't delay."

When I returned home, Mama Schoen was waiting for me.

She stood on the doorstep and held a letter stamped with the royal seal. My lips pursed as I took in the sight of her worried eyes.

"A royal attendant delivered this to me earlier today," she said all in one breath, her hands shaking. "The Queen requires your presence in Balmoral immediately. Captain Davies has already gone. Isn't this wonderful?"

I took the letter, but didn't read it. It didn't matter. If the Queen wanted to see me I wouldn't have much of a choice once the carriages arrived. But that was all well and good.

I crumpled the letter in my hand. Mrs. Schoen covered her gasp in shock as I dropped it callously to the ground.

"Sally." Mama gripped my wrists so tightly I thought they'd break. "What in the world . . . what's gotten into you?"

It was a question better suited to the Queen.

Balmoral Castle would be the perfect stage for my final act—and the Queen's demise.

That night I had a strange dream.

A dream long forgotten by day's break.

I was standing on the shores of my motherland.

Grains of sand rubbed between my brown toes.

Ade sat in a boat about to leave the shore.

A wave of crystal-white waters crashed against my bare legs.

Ina . . . , he said, and reached out his hand to me. . . .

THIRTY-FOUR

THE TRIP TO Balmoral was lonely and dismal. The Queen had asked for me alone. That was good. At least I could keep Mrs. Schoen out of harm's way. What I aimed for in Scotland . . . what I had prepared myself for. It was a gamble that could end in my death.

I arrived in Balmoral by nighttime. August 9. Five days until my wedding. I wondered if it would be a similarly somber occasion. The horses trotted on the grounds, taking me through the stone gates of Balmoral Castle with tall lit torches stuck in the ground to light my driver's path. I'd been here only once before, when I was little. The bagpipes had been playing just as they always did whenever the Queen arrived to Balmoral with her party, the shrieking melodies spinning up to the granite Gothic turrets. I'd found it all fascinatingly strange back then. Now no such lightness existed within me.

The attendants were startled when I walked up the stone steps in a silk dress as bright gold as a warbler about to take flight. If I was to be reprimanded by the Queen, I should be reprimanded in style. Especially because I was determined to make sure this was to be her undoing, not mine. My white gloves stretched up my arms, which were hidden by my glittering silver cape and its bell sleeves. Though a cold Highland breeze rustled the fabric, the Queen's letter to Duleep Singh remained safely nestled within my inside pocket.

The maids in white aprons and bonnets did not bow as I walked through the heavy wooden door, down the long carpet.

"To the ballroom, ma'am," one of the maids said. "Your presence has been announced and your company awaits."

Company? The standing candles at the burgundy walls lit my path as the attendant showed me the way. I'd expected many horrors awaiting me. The Queen's accusations. Harriet's betrayal. A host of Scotland Yard officers ready to arrest me. What I didn't expect was the jaunty melody peppering the air growing louder as I approached the ballroom. The violins were playing furiously and guests clapped in time with the folk music. By the time I stepped onto the ballroom's red marble tiles, I saw the Queen's intimate party decked out in their dresses and jackets, clapping and swinging each other around while Scottish musicians danced on the small stage above.

Queen Victoria saw me first from the middle of the ballroom. Beaming at me in her black gown, she bade me forward.

"Captain Davies," she said, more jubilant than I'd seen her in years. "Your bride has arrived! Congratulations on your wedding day!"

My heart jumped up into my throat. "Wh-What?" I spat, my head spinning.

The guests cheered as Captain Davies, dressed in a black jacket, his bow tie crushed with a Scottish red-and-green sash, took me by the hand and began jumping around to the music like the rest. My feet stumbled beneath me, but Davies kept me upright, beaming from ear to ear as the Queen beckoned him to take John Brown's hand. Davies took it while the Queen grabbed mine, and with Harriet and Mrs. Phipps, our group danced the Highland jig in a circle while alcohol and cheers flowed through the ballroom.

My feet performed the dance by pure memorization. But my mind hadn't caught up yet. Wedding day? What did the Queen say? The dancing kept me off balance. I couldn't grasp the situation while my head spun and my stomach churned.

That old *witch*. My hands shook with rage, but neither the Queen nor Davies would let me go.

Harriet stared at the ground, every once in a while giving me sheepish looks that I didn't return. Her mother was too drunk to notice the state of her daughter, though she passed the look off with the grace of an elite courtier who'd been to enough parties that she knew by instinct how to hide her inebriation. Captain Davies tried to catch my attention. He squeezed my hand once or twice, hoping I'd look up at him and smile, but I never did. The last squeeze was one of frustration.

The Queen's gaze slithered toward me a second before she let go of John Brown's hand and took mine away from my husband-to-be. She didn't blink, didn't tear her eyes away. Only laughed and grinned with the brightness of a thousand suns as we spun around in the middle of the room before the intimate cadre of guests. We were the center of the attention, she and I. I wondered if she could feel my intense, burning hatred for her through the heat of my gloves and dripping off my stretched lips.

She didn't take her eyes off me until the music came to its end.

"Welcome, Sally," she said, loud enough for all to hear. "Welcome to your nuptial ceremony."

All applauded and cheered. The Queen's grin stretched from ear to ear.

"But my wedding is still several days away," I said, equally as loud. But mine wasn't the voice these guests cared about. Not even on my supposed wedding day.

"Oh, Sally, I thought it would be a delightful surprise, and Captain Davies agreed to it. Though it is unfortunate that not all of your relations could join us today—"

Like Mama. I suppose bringing her up to Balmoral never crossed the Queen's mind. This was how Queen Victoria thought of her little pawn.

"Still, the priest is ready to bless your union."

There the gray-haired priest was, sitting in the corner in his black robes. He passed his drink off to a gentleman sitting next to him as his silver cross dangled around his neck. A makeshift wedding indeed.

Queen Victoria outstretched her arms. "Tonight, my friends, we celebrate the marriage of Sarah Forbes Bonetta, my goddaughter, whose wedding tonight will no doubt be the talk of the British Empire."

My fingers clenched as the crowd applauded. She was indeed the Queen of Propaganda. I was part of her project, after all. To everyone in this crowd, it seemed a success. I was an African princess turned slave, saved by the Queen of the Whites, as Frederick Forbes had called her. And I would soon ride off in a horse and carriage with my prince similarly saved and assimilated.

Would they believe the gruesome truth behind it all? Or would they turn their heads and shut their ears as they always did?

"Captain Davies, you have our congratulations," said the Queen.

"Yes, and thank you for inviting us." Davies bowed. "Your Majesty, I wonder if I could steal my fiancée for just a moment. There's a matter of grave importance about which I wish to speak with her."

The Queen glanced between the two of us. "Well, I don't see why not. Remember, you will join us in the drawing room promptly at nine. Then the service will commence."

That was in a little over ten minutes.

"Of course, Your Majesty."

I didn't protest as Captain Davies led me by the hand out of the ballroom. As we crossed the threshold, I looked over the shoulder to find the Queen still watching me.

♠ ♠ ♠

The upper servants' quarters reminded me of the dour dining room in the Freetown Institution. Dull and destitute. At least here, a painting or two of Scottish landscapes hung on gray walls. They hung next to open cabinets of a fine dining set of white plate and teapots. The long, dark wood table wasn't set. The candles upon them, however, were lit enough that I could see my fiancé's frustrated grimace. I stared at the flickering flames while he paced up and down the room.

I didn't wait for him to speak. This time, I spoke first.

"I'm calling off our wedding."

He stopped. So he was the type to lick his lips when he was truly upset. I didn't realize it before because he'd kept himself together well enough and for long enough. But this time, he couldn't let this insult go. He grabbed the chair and crumpled over.

"Why, Sally?" He shook his head. "Why would you do this to me?"

"My name is Ina," I told him, standing on the other side of the table. "Omoba Ina. In all these days you've known me you've never once asked me what my true name was."

The flames cast shadows across our faces.

He paused. And I waited.

"I know the name that you need in order to survive."

"Is that what you're doing, Captain Davies? Surviving?"

He turned his back to me. "My parents were slaves. We were liberated by the British. Everything I've done since our freedom, everything I've done since their death, has been to honor my mother and my father."

The wetness in his deep brown eyes wailed out for his losses. And because I knew loss, knew it so viscerally, so spiritually, I recognized the look well.

"For them I became a schoolteacher. For them I joined the British navy. I joined the ranks of the men who freed us. For them I bought my own ships and became titan of trade and farming. And now, for them, I must continue my path, no, my duty, to represent the cultivation of my society. Our society. Our marriage will stand as a testament to the industrialization and civilization of our people. It will be studied and celebrated for years to come."

"At what cost?" I sat down at the servants' table and realized it was a fitting place for us, a fitting place for this sorrowful conversation, for we were only here as servants to the Crown.

"I told you that the model marriage you seek comes at the expense of my freedom. But look at you. Are you free?"

I patted my cape where Queen Victoria's letter rested. "Once upon a time I had a friend named Ade. When I was eight years old, he was supposed to come with me to London to be presented to the Queen as a gift. But he was sickly. He was, as they said, of ill temperament. And so, the navy men who freed me from slavery murdered him. The British officers who were celebrated for their service to abolition, I'm sure much like the ones who freed your family, threw my sickly friend overboard like so many of our kin."

Captain Davies's eyes grew wide in horror. The tears wetting them dripped off his lashes.

"They deserve nothing from us," I told him, holding my right palm over the flames, feeling its heat. "They deserve no praise for freeing us from the very conditions they set in place to begin with. They deserve no reward for dressing us in their clothes and parading us for their own benefit. I will not be beholden to them anymore. To anyone." I looked at him. "I was born free. I must be free."

Davies stayed silent for a moment that dragged on as the bracket clock ticked on a table in the corner of the room. Then, quietly, he pulled out a chair and sat down.

"Do I seem to you, Sally, like your captors or like the British?" he asked without lifting his head to meet my gaze.

"Not at all." And it was true. "But those with power tend to abuse it. Why should your needs supersede mine?"

"This is not just about the British, Sally," Davies said, leaning across the table. "You know how our people are. I tried to be free with a love of my choosing."

I nodded. "Matilda," I whispered. The woman from Havana who had captured his heart.

"I tried and failed. But I grow older. There are expectations of me. I've accomplished so much in my life. I've worked hard to make not only my parents but my people—our people—proud. But without a marriage, without children to call my own, my accomplishments will come to nothing. I'll be seen as a failure."

The pressures of tradition bore down on us both. Even if my ancestors supported my bid for revenge, I knew deep in my heart that there was another side to the coin. Especially for me, as a woman, to go childless and without a husband was considered an aberration too many. But I'd accept their judgment. I welcomed their chiding.

"This is my life," I told him. "And I need to live it free."

The clock ticked, filling our silence.

"What will you do, Captain James Davies?"

Captain Davies curled his fingers upon the dark wooden table, swallowing the lump in his throat, breathing heavily as my words seemed to echo throughout the quarters.

The clock dinged. It was nine o'clock. The Queen awaited. The truth.

"We go to the Queen. When in her presence, listen to all that has to be said," I told him. "And consider my words carefully. You owe them nothing."

I got up and left the room.

THIRTY-FIVE

THEY ALL SAT waiting for me in the vast drawing room: the Queen. Her son, the Prince of Wales, who'd just arrived, looking particularly miserable. Her servant John Brown, who grew more faithful by the day; her secretary Ponsonby; her ladies Harriet and Mrs. Phipps and a handful of other attendants. They sat spread across the room, the cheerful mood from the ballroom festivities dashed. The other guests who'd danced with us had already left. This was a more intimate gathering—one of the Queen's inner circle.

Here, secrets would be shared.

I wondered when Bertie had received his summons to Balmoral. I hadn't seen him since Mulgrave, hadn't bothered to contact him. Now stiff, with his lips curled in indignation, Bertie sat on the ornate chaise on the wall farthest from me, next to the fireplace with its marble mantels and its black slate hearth. Mrs. Phipps and Harriet were attached at the hip on the leather love seat, much to the latter's chagrin. Harriet kept her eyes on the white ceiling medallion, her fingers intertwined on her lap.

The Queen stood in front of the row of windows lining the walls—the centermost of five. With the curtains drawn I could see the Highland woods under the moonlight. The stars streamed into the room, casting light upon John Brown, who stood next to the bust of the Queen's husband, black as her robes.

No one spoke as I passed a fretful Ponsonby and walked through the doors.

It was the Queen who was to always speak first. A rule that endlessly bothered me. But this time, I was curious as to what she was going to say.

"Before I summon the priest to commence your wedding, there are a few loose ends to tie up," the Queen said, her hands behind her back as she gazed out the window. "Bring it out, Harriet."

"Go on." Mrs. Phipps nudged her in the ribs, drawing a pained yelp from her daughter's mouth. She narrowed her eyes, biting her lip, and for a moment, it looked as if she might defy her mother and the Queen. But then the most malevolent glare from Mrs. Phipps had her jumping to her feet. She reached inside her jacket pocket and threw it upon the carpeted floor.

The Queen of Spades. Its plain black and white didn't seem to suit the carpets colorful spread of primary colors.

"It has not gone unnoticed that you and Sally have been gallivanting around England," Queen Victoria said. "Now tell me the truth. Is Sally the cause of recent misfortunes?"

Harriet buried her head in her hand.

I waited.

"It's true," she whined, her voice muffled by her palms as my spectators gasped. "She was behind everything. She destroyed them all: Mr. Bellamy, the former editor of the *London Illustrated News*. William Bambridge, the royal photographer. William McCoskry and even the Forbeses . . ." She sniffed, brushing her fingers through her hair, and I could tell from her wide, bloodshot eyes that she was truly distressed. That didn't make the betrayal sting any less.

"The Forbeses," the Queen repeated. "Fine men, who brought you here from the jungles of Africa out of the goodness of their hearts."

"Oh, did they?" My laughter shocked all in the room. The Queen glared at me, her small body rigid. "And as for Harriet, I wonder how willing she'll be to tell you *her* role in these supposed 'crimes'?"

"Quiet, you evil little wench!" Mrs. Phipps spat as Harriet whimpered and cried on the couch next to her. "Harriet had the wits to catch on to your little schemes in time before you could ruin any more lives!"

Such praise would have drawn a cry of joy from Harriet's lips if they weren't based on lies. As Harriet hid behind her hands, Bertie let out a mocking laugh.

"You're all mad." He sat up. "Sally wouldn't do those things, you know that. You know that and yet even still, you try to frame her all because I expressed my affections."

"Affections!" Mrs. Phipps, thoroughly scandalized, made a face and covered her mouth. "Affections for this vicious little African girl?"

"You try to frame her all because I defied you, Mother!"

"Quiet!" Queen Victoria whipped around, the white train on her black bonnet twisting behind her. "Do not presume that you know better than your queen."

Bertie hushed up, but he still boiled where he sat.

"The girl is guilty of heinous acts," said John Brown, only infuriating Bertie further.

"And what is your queen guilty of?" I took a defiant step forward. "What heinous acts has she committed? Shall we ask her?"

The Scotsman gaped at me as I spoke, his disbelief clear as he whipped his head from one side of the room to the other, his little braided ponytail flailing with him.

"What did she whisper to you, Brown, before you took out your revolver and shot Dalton Sass in the head?"

Mrs. Phipps and Harriet gasped. Surely it couldn't be true, Harriet's face begged me. But the Queen and her servant returned my steely glare without remorse. While Ponsonby shifted guiltily on his feet, Bertie turned to his mother.

"What did you whisper, Mother? Before Brown killed Sass?"

"She gave the order to kill," I answered for him. "And her manservant obliged. All because no one was to know about how you curated and controlled the children you called Wards of the Empire."

Queen Victoria's clear blue eyes widened, but my hands had already found the letter in my cape. "October 22, 1855. In a letter to her precious Duleep Singh, she wrote her confession: *Do not speak of the past. I've spoken many words to my captains as they search the far-flung regions of the world for treasures to bring back to me. What Sir John Login told you was only half the story. The 'Wards of the Empire.'*"

"Stop it!" The Queen clenched her frail fists, looking to John Brown for some kind of help, but Brown looked back at her, paralyzed in his confusion.

"*I say these words*," I continued, my heart beating fast because the time had finally come. My hands were wet and shaking, but the words slipped from my lips without fail. "*I say these words because a line must be drawn. There are children who possess the potential to lead the empire into a new stage of enlightenment. On the other hand, there are those who would only validate the closed-minded fools in the world who believed that the Indian and the African and the Native can only remain savages.*"

Bertie stood, appalled. "The letter has the Queen's royal seal. Mama? What is this?"

Gritting her teeth, the Queen turned back toward the window, placing a hand upon the square pane. "So my Duleep has betrayed me. . . ."

"I searched for the letter and took it myself. Do not hurt him like you hurt Aarush." My lips trembled. "Like you *killed* Ade."

"What?" Bertie yelled while Mrs. Phipps gripped her daughter's arm.

John Brown's growl could have frightened a bear. It certainly frightened me though I stood my ground valiantly. "You dare accuse the Queen of such horrid things—"

"She has revealed her true nature herself." I waved the letter. The rest I recited from memory. *"And what would have happened if that boy Aarush would have arrived in England with you? If he would have been presented to me in court alongside you? With his reportedly boorish ways and uncivil manners, he would have only proven those right who insist that the savage is but a brute that cannot change. That the Black cannot be assimilated. At such a delicate moment, such a mistake cannot be made. The East India Company has been given its orders to find the proper children. Those that are discarded are but a sacrifice for the future."*

"Enough," said the Queen over her shoulder, her voice strained. "That's enough, Sally."

My throat hurt. I felt like I could barely breathe and yet I was gulping in air greedily as if I'd run here. I have been running toward this moment. All my life. Running toward this very scene, knowing it could be the end of me.

The Queen faced me, her black mourning dress fanned out across the carpet. She placed one hand upon the other, proper and regal. The Queen of Ruin.

"Some children are not fit to be in your position, Sally. And what matters more? The lives of those children? Or the immortal life of my empire?"

I nearly crushed the letter in my hand as my body began to quake, the blood rushing from my head to my limbs. All of me was ready to batter this murderer who stood unapologetically in front of me. "And so she confesses," I whispered. "And so she confesses."

"Confesses to *what*?" Mrs. Phipps stood. "It's you who should be confessing, you witch. My daughter has told you everything!"

"I haven't." Whimpering, Harriet rubbed her long brown braid over her shoulder. "I . . . I haven't told you everything, Your Majesty."

Harriet and I looked upon each other, our eyes locked for what felt like an eternity. Her mother gripped her sleeve and she tore it away, first sliding to the edge of the love seat. Then, with what ounce of courage she had left, standing, and stepping toward where she'd thrown the Queen of Spades. She stared at the Black Queen, her shoulders slumped, before she lifted her head and faced the White Queen.

"Everything I told you that Sally did. She could not have done it without me. I aided her in everything."

Mrs. Phipps blinked. "Wh-What?" She turned to Bertie, then to Ponsonby. "What did you say, Harriet?"

"I betrayed the Crown willingly. And I did it for Sally, whose intelligence and courage, I freely admit, far exceed mine. I am nothing next to her."

"Why?" Queen Victoria demanded, her voice cold as the blue in her eyes.

Harriet answered, "Because I hate you, Mother." She said it without flinching, looking directly into her mother's eyes. Mrs. Phipps grasped the pearls around her neck. "I hate you so much I can barely see straight."

Harriet began crying again. Mrs. Phipps gasped and slid further into the love seat, her hands sliding against the fabric. "This isn't—this isn't—" And she turned to the Queen. "Don't listen to her, Your Majesty. We, the Phipps family, are forever your faithful servants."

"And yet I would gladly betray the Queen if it meant I could see you suffer, Mother."

Harriet's words drew a wail of tragedy from Mrs. Phipps's lips. It wasn't what I had planned. But it was a fitting enough punishment of the woman I'd long wanted to see suffer. Like her daughter, Mrs. Phipps began to cry into her hands.

"I'm ruined," she bawled. "My family name is tarnished!"

"What in the bloody hell is going on here?" Bertie whispered to himself in disbelief before striding across the room to me. I let him snatch the letter from my grip and he read it out loud to its completion. I took it back from him after he stumbled back and fell upon the floor.

"What am I to do?" Bertie said, his legs spread out over the floor. "Who am I to believe?"

"Even if both tales are true, Albert, your choice is clear." Queen Victoria lifted her chin and glared down at her son, lifeless on the ground. "I am your mother. And I am the Queen of England. What Her Majesty says is the law of this world."

"And I am Omoba Ina: Princess of the Egbado." I felt all the weight of my ancestors behind me as I declared it. My chest swelled, whatever fear that was in me dead and gone. I lifted my chin to match her arrogance. "And I will make you suffer for what you've done to me."

The windows burst. Everyone screamed and covered their faces. John Brown lunged for the Queen, but he was thwarted by the impact of a body crashing into him. Hastily packing the letter away into my cape, I lowered my other hand from my face to see Rui with his gun pointed at Brown's skull.

"We will make you all pay," he said before pulling the trigger.

THIRTY-SIX

THE GUN JAMMED. The chance stroke of Rui's bad luck saved John Brown's life. In the confusion, Brown tackled Rui to the ground, knocking the gun from Rui's hand. Shrieks from the onlookers split the air as the two began to wrestle upon the carpet, rolling around on the ground, beating each other's skulls with blows that made bones crack.

I froze. I didn't expect Rui here. Had he followed me? My thoughts were whirling as Mrs. Phipps and Harriet screamed on the other side of the room. Some attendants had already escaped in the commotion.

"Protect the Queen!" Ponsonby shouted, but nobody moved to save her. Harriet and Mrs. Phipps ran to the corner of the room, nestling by the grandfather clock away from the mayhem. Bertie let out cowardly whines as he scurried backward, dragging himself across the floor until his back hit the cabinet.

Rui managed to flip the burly Highlander onto his back and punched him repeatedly in the face until he spat out blood. Ponsonby chanced it. He ran toward the Queen, grabbing her hand and leading her out of the drawing room while Brown lifted Rui and threw him down upon the coffee table. The wood smashed.

"This is madness!" Mrs. Phipps cried while Harriet covered her ears and screeched.

And in the chaos of this madness, the Queen was getting away. I wouldn't allow it. Quickly, I grabbed a piece of the shattered wood, its sharp point transforming it into a stake, and followed her out of the room.

I won't let you get away, you witch. I gritted my teeth as I ran through the corridors of Balmoral. *I can't.*

It didn't matter if Ade forgave me or not. I would never forgive myself.

"Stop!" I screamed as I entered the foyer. As Ponsonby and the maids ushered the Queen toward the door, I lunged for them. Ponsonby tackled me first, but the man was a coward. He wasn't any match for someone whose rage had been forged in the flames of sorrow and violence.

Bending down, I dodged his arms as he tried to grab me and elbowed him in the gut.

Bile flew out of his mouth as he shuddered and heaved. The maids let go of the Queen to scream as I punched him in the face and kneed him in the groin. One more punch and he was out cold. The maids forgot about their queen entirely. They ran out the door, saving themselves. But in her haste, one knocked over the tall candelabra next to the wall. The fire caught the carpet and began flickering.

"No," I said as the Queen tried to slip through the door. "Stay right where you are."

"Sally! You're mad!" the Queen cried as she cowered in the corner of the foyer.

"But Your Majesty, madness is your family trait." I shrugged. "A product of generations of inbreeding, is it not?"

"Sally!"

"Go back to the drawing room," I ordered. And when she didn't move, I dragged her by her ridiculous billowing black sleeve and dragged her back to where Rui and John Brown were fighting to the death.

My nerves were shot, my hands trembling, but my breaths shallow as I marched Her Majesty back into the room, the point of my blade against her back.

"You have so much to pay for," I said through gritted teeth, tears stinging my eyes. "So much loss. So much pain."

"I would change it if I could," said the Queen. The rubbing skin around her neck jiggled as she panted in fear. "I would have your little friend live again."

"Ade. His name was Ade." I ripped off her bonnet and threw it to the ground. "And my name is Ina. Say it!"

I poked the back of her spine, drawing a yelp from her lips. Rui hit John Brown with a swift uppercut, but the Queen's servant wasn't so easily defeated. He tackled Rui to the ground, biting his arm. Rui let out a pained gasp, but my focus wouldn't be deterred, for the Queen hadn't yet spoken. She hadn't yet done as I'd told her to.

"I am not Sarah Forbes Bonetta. I am not named after my captors and their murder ship. I am not a gift, a pet for you. And you are no queen but the Queen of Ruin. Say it. Say my name!"

The Queen remained silent. Her pride as a monarch was absolute. She would rather die than give in to me.

"This letter will be published in the papers," I said. "I've already set everything in motion. Your ruin is upon you, you old crone."

Queen Victoria turned and looked at me over her shoulder, her expression filled with the malice I knew she always had inside her.

"The British royal family will not be ruined," she said. "Not today. Not by you."

"What's going on?" Captain Davies barreled into the room, covering his face from a flying piece of wood knocked out of Brown's hand. "What are you doing? We need to go! There's fire! The castle's on fire!"

It was that one moment of distraction, that one moment I turned to Davies behind me, that Bertie needed. Leaping off the ground, he pulled his mother away from me and threw me to the ground. The stake flew from my hands.

"Sally, stop this! You've gone mad!" He fell on top of me, pinning me to the ground as I struggled to reach for my stake. "No matter what she's done, she's still the Queen of England."

"No matter what she's done," I repeated in disbelief. He'd heard everything. Her crimes. Her sick fetish that led to murder. He'd heard *everything*. "Is this your answer, Albert?"

"Sally!" Rui screamed, and turned toward me. That's when John Brown dove for his gun.

"No!" I screamed as an injured Brown aimed and shot.

Rui gasped out in pain as the bullet pierced his side.

"Rui!" I scrambled to push Bertie off me but the prince's weight was too heavy. He held me in place, cursing and begging.

The look Rui and I gave each other may have lasted for a split second and it could have lasted a millennium. It would never be possible to remember it clearly. But in that moment, I saw Rui choose. I saw him look at me, restrained by the Prince of Wales, captured as a prisoner of a war I didn't start. I saw him see me in danger, bound for the gallows.

I thought love would send him charging toward me, unafraid of the dangers that lay between us.

I saw him choose himself.

Brown aimed his gun at Rui again, but even with a bullet in him, Rui was too fast. He jumped out of the broken windows and disappeared into the woods.

"You were right, Ade," I whispered as I stopped struggling. "Their love for me is conditional."

391

The Queen fell to the floor. "Have her confined immediately," she ordered all in one breath. Needless to say, the wedding would be postponed.

I lay upon the ground, a rueful chuckle upon my lips. The game was over.

THIRTY-SEVEN

Brighton, England – August 14, 1862

BY SECRET ROYAL decree, the newspapers did not print the letter that would indict the Queen for her part in Ade's death. They were too preoccupied with the spectacle of Sarah Forbes Bonetta's wedding to Captain James Davies. They surrounded St. Nicholas Church—outside and inside—chatting to each other as they soaked in the sight of strangest wedding, by their estimation, they'd ever seen.

"Do you see them?" one journalist said to another. "Four bridesmaids of dark color and four fair bridesmaids. African and English bridesmaids in similar attire. What pleasing confusion . . ."

"Yes, yes." Oh, I recognized that journalist from the *Islington Gazette.* "White ladies with African gentlemen, and African ladies with white gentlemen . . ."

"Personally," said a man with a mustache, "I see a distinct absence of that abruptness in the features often seen in the females of the African race, which gives the air of ferocity. Look at her. Her eyes are expressive and tender, beaming with intelligence. Ladylike in the extreme. . . ."

"I hope you now know," hissed Uncle George in my ear as he led me down the aisle of St. Nicholas Church in my opulent white wedding dress, "what it feels like to be confined against your will."

Perhaps he meant my marriage. Or perhaps he meant the days I spent in a Scottish prison. It was all done very quietly so as to not embarrass the Queen, and very quickly so as to not delay my wedding any further. For three days, I sat in the cold cell with my back against the brick, staring at the little rat scurrying past my feet and into a corner of the wall. For three days I thought of my journey. Every step, every decision that brought me to that dank hole.

And I regretted nothing.

I told the Queen this as she peered at me through the iron bars of my cell. I told her with a smile on my face and a song in my heart.

"Your feelings towards me are irrelevant, Sally. You will become Captain Davies's wife. You will go with him to your homeland and be a dutiful mother. You will be remembered as my brilliant, loving god-daughter." She straightened her back. "And the empire's reputation will remain."

"We'll see about that, you old hag."

Uncle George walked me down the aisle to Captain Davies, who waited for me by the altar. No one else but him saw the look I gave George before I left myself—a look that could strike down a god. He let out a terrified yelp, stumbled back, and fell onto his backside.

His mother rushed to his side. "George! George, what are you doing?" he said as the man trembled on the ground, gazing up at me with fear. As he should.

"Maybe we released you from the hospital to soon," I said. The groomsmen and bridesmaids whispered and gasped. Mrs. Forbes sniveled in dismay, grabbed her son, and dragged him to the back end of the church.

"Are you ready, Sally?" Captain Davies asked me while the bishop who had just arrived from Sierra Leone began officiating the ceremony.

I beamed at him. "Indeed, James. The future rests on the horizon. It's time to begin."

Everyone had to make a choice. We exchanged knowing glances and clasped hands in this blooming, ornate white chapel, the sunlight beaming through the arched windows, before a congregation of eager celebrants.

Bertie was not among them. He sent me his regards: a bouquet of fresh flowers and a card. One of Princess Alice's bridesmaids, Lady Susan Vane-Tempest, had delivered it and gave me her congratulations. I quickly threw it onto the side of the street. I suppose my assault on his mother, for all her crimes, was too far. But I knew as well as he did it wasn't his mother he was protecting. It was his own inheritance, the promise of his reign and power, which he wouldn't give up even if it meant his death. I was sure he'd find others ways to rebel against his mother in the coming days and weeks. This, no doubt, would be in women other than his fiancée. Like the incompetent and spineless coward he was, Bertie would surely bury his face in their necks when the reality of his own became too much to bear.

Harriet wasn't here either. Her family heritage alone ensured her lifelong job at the Queen's side, but nobody would ever forget her treachery and cowardice. Certainly not her mother, who, I heard, spent her days weeping and drinking alone.

"Do you, Captain Forbes, take Sarah Forbes Bonetta to be your lawfully—" The bishop stopped and cleared his throat.

The captain and I looked over at Mama Schoen, who was crying loudly on the front pew. Gowramma was next to her with a handkerchief, trying to calm her down. I shook my head with a laugh. How delighted she was to see how much money the Queen had spent on the wedding. How proud of her own hand in this historical event. She too would be remembered as the caretaker of the Queen's dutiful adopted African daughter.

History. I did wonder how history would record these events. What would they include and what would they leave out all for the sake of the Queen, the Crown, and the empire's reputation? Sarah Forbes Bonetta's likeness as a bride would be forever captured in Camille Silvy's photographs. Silvy, who had struck up a friendship with Captain Davies during the art gala, had me stand in the center of his neoclassical backdrop in my wedding gown, looking at his lens over my right shoulder. Against another backdrop he took the happy couple. The Greek columns of my solo shot were replaced by African palm trees as I was made to sit down holding a book with Davies in his tuxedo standing beside his wife, the proud groom.

He was proud today indeed. For he'd finally found an answer to the question I'd asked him that day in Balmoral Castle.

What will you do, Captain James Davies?

"I now pronounce you man and wife!"

The congregation cheered. The journalists jotted down their notes. The Queen didn't attend my wedding. She was still in mourning and thus opposed to public gatherings where possible. But she sent me her regards.

I sent my regards as well, in my own way. As Captain Davies and I signed our marriage certificate for the church's records, beneath Davies's name I signed my name. My true name: Ina Sarah Forbes Bonetta.

Captain Davies and I walked out of the church arm in arm as people threw rice over our heads. Just before entering our fairy-tale-like white carriage, a man bumped into me. He hadn't been invited to the wedding. I knew that the moment I caught a flash of the X mark over his left eye.

"I'm sorry, miss," he said, slipping a paper into my hand.

Captain Davies sneered at the man's rudeness and lifted me into the carriage. And when the door closed, we spoke in hushed tones.

"The preparations are complete, I suspect?" I slipped on a pair of black gloves, sighing with relief that the wedding was finally over.

"Everything's done just as I promised." Davies moved to squeeze my hand, but, thinking better of it, nodded his head instead. "It was an honor to meet you, Ina."

I unfolded the paper in my hand.

Meet me at tonight at the docks of Blackwater Basin.
Promptly at midnight. We have much to discuss. —R

If there was anything I truly regretted, it was my misconception of loneliness. There was nothing wrong with being alone. As exhilarating as romance was, it had blinded me from the truth—from the fallacy of finding companionship in someone who I thought was "similar to me." I was Omoba Ina. There was no one like me. No one who deserved me.

What little flutter of disappointment I felt remembering Rui's betrayal died when I tore the paper in my hands. Each long, unforgiving rip sent a flutter of pleasure through me.

Love is conditional, Rui. I threw pieces out the window. *Men.* I spat.

"An honor indeed," I said. "I'll remember that, Captain Davies."

The true honor came later that night. It was the honor I gave myself as I stood at the docks in front of a ship. Smaller than that of a trader's, its sails billowed in the cold wind that rippled through my hair. The Queen had prepared it for me and my husband. It was to take us back to Africa, where we belonged. Captain Davies's bribes had changed the plan.

I lifted up my chin, soaking in the cold night, breathing in the air. Then I boarded the ship.

"Are you ready, Miss Bonetta?" asked the ship's captain as he walked up to me, wrapping his long gray frock coat around himself.

I nodded under the stars. "It's been a long time coming."

Nobody in England would ever find out that this was the night

Omoba Ina disappeared, her ship carrying her and her alone to destinations unknown to anyone but herself.

The feeling of some kind of accomplishment I allowed myself as I fought for and won my freedom. A small compensation, perhaps. Something I could relish in place of the British Crown's ruin. But even that would come one day. Everything in its own time.

Yes. Queen Victoria would eventually learn that a lady's lust for revenge cannot so easily die.

The woman known as Sarah Forbes Bonetta had married her prince, Captain Davies, and disappeared from England. But Captain Davies would return to Lagos alone. He'd find his wife, I was sure. They'd keep things quiet. What he did from now on was his problem to bear. He'd made his decision. And he'd done it, finally understanding the meaning of freedom.

As for my freedom . . .

Aboard the ship, I smelled the sea air, closed my eyes.

"Now," I said as the ship sailed under the moonlight, "I wonder where I'll travel to first."

ACKNOWLEDGMENTS

Writing this book was a wild ride because it forced me to delve deep into buried histories and challenged me to play with the past. I first want to thank my agent, Natalie Lakosil, and my editor, Elizabeth Agyemang, for believing in this project and helping to shape it into what it is now. Thank you to everyone at Harper for bringing this book to fruition.

I was able to write this book with the support of my colleagues in the English Department of Lakehead University and because of wonderful libraries and archives that helped me learn more about Omoba Ina's life.

My family and faith have kept me on the path of writing and they will always be my guiding light even during the trickiest of times.

Finally, I want to thank Ina. As much as there is written about her life, there are also curious absences revealing that no matter how hard we try to assimilate and be "good children" of imperialism, our stories will never truly shine the way they should. I hope this book makes people curious to learn more about this formidable woman who lived a very intriguing life.

BIBLIOGRAPHY

Letter written by Captain Forbes. Forbes, Frederick E. *Dahomey and the Dahomans*. Longman, Brown, Green,and Longmans, 1851, https://doi.org/10.5479/sil.257101.39088000286781

Letter written by Sarah Forbes Bonetta. "Sarah Forbes Bonetta, Queen Victoria's African Protégée." English Heritage, www.english-heritage.org.uk/visit/places/osborne/history-and-stories/sarah-forbes-bonetta/. Accessed 06 Feb. 2024.

The Letters of Queen Victoria: A Selection from Her Majesty's Correspondence between the Years 1837 and 1861. Volume 1, 1837–1843. Produced by Paul Murray, Lesley Halamek and the Online Distributed Proofreading Team at http://www.pgdp.net

Brontë, Charlotte. *Jane Eyre*. Thomas Y. Crowell and Company, 1890.

Crowther, Samuel. *Journal of an Expedition up the Niger and Tshadda Rivers: Undertaken by Macgregor Laird, Esq. in Connection with the British Government, in 1854.* Cambridge: Cambridge University Press, 2010. Print. Cambridge Library Collection—Religion.

Islington Gazette. "Interesting Marriage at Brighton." August 23, 1862.

"American Civilization." Ralph Waldo Emerson. *The Atlantic*. 1862.